Goodbye, Henrietta Street

Lin Treadgold

First published in 2013 by Safkhet Soul, London, United Kingdom
Safkhet Soul is an imprint of Safkhet Publishing
www.safkhetpublishing.com

1 3 5 7 9 10 8 6 4 2

Permission granted to publish *Love Poems from Scilly—Richard.*
In memory of poet Anne Lewis-Smith who died 11 May 2011.

ISBN 978-1-908208-14-9

A CIP catalogue record for this book is available from
the British Library.

Printed and bound by Lightning Source International
Typeset in 11 pt Crimson and Worstveld Sling Extra with Adobe InDesign

Find out more about Lin on http://itslinhere.wordpress.com/
and meet her on Facebook at
https://www.facebook.com/lin.treadgold?fref=ts

Lin Treadgold	*author*
Chris Treadgold	*cover scenes photographer*
William Banks Sutton	*copy editor*
Kim Maya Sutton	*managing editor, cover model photographer, map artist*
Walter Richardson	*proofreader*
Sally Neuhaus	*cover designer*
Bianca Ahrkico Meyer	*cover model*
Mary Bongiovi	*editor*

The colophon of Safkhet is a representation of the ancient Egyptian goddess of
wisdom and knowledge, who is credited with inventing writing.
Safkhet Publishing is named after her because the founders met in Egypt.

To the people of the Isles of Scilly

Special thanks to Will and Maggie Wagstaff, Peter and Penny Rogers, Julie Love, Dave Love and Liz Grenfell at the Isles of Scilly Wildlife Trust, Linda Thomas and all the volunteers at Radio Scilly, my pen friend Lydia Birch, my dear friend Huberta Hollauf in memory of Franz and the late Anne Lewis-Smith. Thank you for your support to The Isles of Scilly Steamship Company, the Isles of Scilly Tourist Information, The Mermaid Inn (St Mary's), Juliet's Garden (St Mary's), Fraggle Rock Café (Bryher), Old Town Café (Old Town), Taylors of Harrogate Ltd (Yorkshire), Duke of York Inn (Whitby). I cannot forget to mention the support of all my writing friends in the UK, my editor Kathryn Robinson at Cornerstones, and my writing coach Jacqui Lofthouse. My thanks also go to my readers, the members of the Romantic Novelists' Association, and my virtual friends at www.mywriterscircle.com. Also thanks to Kim, Will and Mary at Safkhet Publishing for all their patience and help in making dreams come true.

Thanks to all who contributed to the publication of this book by pre-ordering a copy:

Tam Steele Daly, Kathryn Driscoll, Andrea Hollauf , Dr. Gabriele Hollauf, Huberta Hollauf , Samantha Lakour, Arthur Luiten, David C Nott, Dr. Claudia Waldhauser, Joanne Walter.

About the Author

Lin Treadgold was born in Yorkshire and attended private education. She is a qualified driving instructor, and owned her own driving school for twenty-five years. After travelling the world and visiting over thirty countries, she retired in 2001 to folllow her husband's work and live in the Netherlands. She has always wanted to write a novel; moving to Holland gave her the opportunity to fulfill a dream.

This time tomorrow you will be going,
Luggage in hand down the narrow stone quay,
Fishermen say the wind will be blowing
West, when you go on the tumbled grey sea.
This time tomorrow you will be leaving
Waving your hand as you clamber aboard
Telling us there, and we half believing
That you will be back, our friendship restored.
We shall be standing and watching your boat
Dip in the waves as she takes you away,
Straining our eyes as the grey of your coat
Blurs in the distance to uniform grey.

And I, I shall say as I turn away
The tears on my face are only salt spray.

CHAPTER ONE

Penzance, early June 1986

What was she doing, going away without him? A day ago, she had left Rob at Darlington station and now she wondered why.

'Luggage for St Mary's in this container. Please stand in the queue.' A young man wearing a navy-blue boiler suit directed passengers toward the ship's gangway.

Pippa waited in line, staring into the clear emerald water. Mirrored swirls reflected the ship's hull and as she took in a breath of salt air, she wondered if her plan to lead a more positive life would work. She sighed; in her thirty years, she had never been on holiday alone. Rob should be with her. Despite their mutual pain, she knew they could have done so much more together.

The ship's whistle, deep and throaty, resonated across the quay and into town; it was time to leave Penzance. The salty tang of the bacon sandwich from breakfast lingered on her lips. *I hope I'm not going to be seasick.*

'Lovely day—great sailing weather,' a passenger remarked.

Pippa sighed. 'Yeah, I'm just glad to get here. The journey was longer than I thought.'

The familiar odour of fish and the lobster pots stacked on the quay in neat rows reminded her of home. At last, the islands were within reach. Just a few more hours and she would be there. She hadn't felt so energised since before … *No, for goodness sake, don't think about it.*

A member of the crew, wearing merchant navy black and gold epaulettes, clipped her ticket. 'You're not on the day trip then?' he grinned.

'No, three weeks.' Pippa hoped to start moving forward in the queue.

'Lucky you,' a woman remarked behind her. 'I hope you'll find enough to do; it's a small place, you know.'

'Sure I will; I came here five years ago.' She'd done her homework, read all the leaflets and brochures about life on St

The Isles of Scilly

Mary's. The photos of the narrow streets and busy harbour snapped on the last trip never left her thoughts.

After looking around, she found a seat on the upper deck and a place for her heavy rucksack. Had she really done the right thing to come here? In a fit of temper, Rob had called her a stupid bitch. Did he really hate her that much? She wasn't going through all this by herself. Couldn't he see that? She had to take this journey, if only to relieve her sorrow. As she had stepped on the train, she wondered if their goodbyes might be the parting of a long relationship. He'd only given her a peck on the cheek.

A bang on the ship's hull made her lean across the rail to look. She watched as the crew withdrew the gangway. Moments later, she heard someone on the radio say, 'Let go aft,' and it wasn't long before the gap between the quay and the ship widened and they left Penzance at a leisurely roll.

Pippa closed her eyes against the sun and for a brief moment it was like the old days, before life had flung her into a darkened room. This very same seat was where she, Rob, and Daniel had squashed up against each other. She looked out to sea in a moment of regret and sighed again. *If only ... oh, don't!*

The breeze from the previous night had lost its strength and the pungent salt air lifted her senses as the ocean rocked in glassy curves along the coast. There had been no point in unpacking last night and the stay at the youth hostel had afforded little privacy. As soon as she arrived at the holiday cottage, she would change her clothes. She put on her sunglasses, then pushed the loose ends of her auburn hair into a ponytail.

The ship sailed past Newlyn and Mousehole with the Minack Theatre nestling in the distant cliffs above Porthcurno. Land's End seemed to shrink to a grey line on the horizon as the ship rolled like the gentle rocking of a baby.

Next to Pippa sat a family with two children. The boy looked a bit pale and asked, 'Are we nearly there yet, Dad?'

'Not long now, son. In about an hour, we'll see the islands.'

Pippa gazed at the child, his sweet young face smiling at his older sister. Wishing to not meet anyone's eyes, Pippa turned away. Without warning, the boy ran to the side of the ship and threw up. *Poor kid. I know how that feels.* In her pocket, she found a packet of tissues, which she handed to the mother.

'Thanks, he's not usually this bad,' said the woman. 'William, come here darling, the nice lady has given us a hanky for you.'

It seemed almost every parent had named their son either William or Harry in the last few years. Pippa moved away; there were too many memories.

Leaning on the rail and gazing out to sea, she recalled the conversation with her GP back home in Whitby. She'd told him she was going to the islands for a break, he seemed the only person to understand how she felt.

'You know, Mrs. Lambton,' he'd said, 'you ought to contact the local Wildlife Trust and meet like-minded people. It'll probably do you some good. If you go to Scaling Dam, there's a bird hide along the shore. I often go up there to relax at the weekends.'

'I'm not interested in all that stuff,' Rob had responded when Pippa had told him. He'd laughed when she'd bought a new weatherproof jacket from the sports shop in town. The sale price seemed reasonable; it was something to keep her warm. But Rob, thinking his comments amusing, remarked, 'Where's your deerstalker? Bloody hell, Pippa, you'll be buying a rifle next.' She'd felt impatient at his silliness, but held her tongue … *Why does every word have to be planned in advance, in case it's wrong or provoking?*

Rob had become more difficult and withdrawn, even though he'd applied to do a counselling course for his job. He thought it might help to sort him out, but instead it made him worse. It seemed he was always testing her and if their marriage was to survive, she had to get away from him for a while. His threat of divorce … *Enough is enough.*

His overpowering negativity caused her to want to disappear for a while, do something different. One afternoon, she'd taken a walk to the park and up through the cemetery. She'd sat in contemplation when a stranger said to her, 'Maybe one day, you'll find direction around the corner, where it's been waiting to meet you.' She remembered his words. *Ha! Yes, perhaps going away was what he meant.*

Puffins and guillemots rafted on the sea, immaculate in their black and white plumage. A puffin flew across the bow of the ship. She used to think they were much larger. In recent years, everything seemed larger than life: the agony, the sorrow, and the guilt. *Splash!* A couple of bottle-nosed dolphins surfaced in the ship's wake and with sudden enthusiasm, everyone stood on deck, dolphin spotting.

'Look, there's one, Dad! Get the camera quick!'

Pippa smiled. *He'll be lucky.* Daniel had spotted basking sharks during their previous visit. 'Mummy, look at the big whale,' he'd said. He had learned so much about the wildlife through the local young birders club. 'Aw, Dad, won't you come as well?' They always left home feeling a little sad and Pippa had to make excuses for Rob's lack of enthusiasm.

What if she died, too, joining her son? It might solve a problem. No, she must try not to be so silly—but there had been days when she could have hidden away in a corner with some pills and a strong sense to take the lot. How she missed her parents too, both now only faint memories.

She was about to cry but stopped herself. It was no good crying. What was the point?

The ship continued to roll and the boy, William, now looked quite ill. 'How's he doing?' asked Pippa.

The mother smiled. 'He'll be okay once we get to the other side.'

Pippa sighed and turned to look out to sea again. The dolphins were gone.

She stared toward the horizon and her thoughts changed to her best friends, Joan and Terry. They had always supported each other since childhood. And where was Rob when she needed him or *did* she need him? Lately, he seemed confused about himself. She craved his love and affection, but somewhere a great hole had opened up and nothing was left to bridge the gap. She had been a nobody going nowhere, until today. *Why am I here?* Perhaps there was another reason besides healing her wounds. Pippa had questions, many questions, and the answers were always the same.

Scanning the far horizon, her eyes searched for St. Martin's, Tresco, Bryher and St. Agnes—firing thoughts about her arrival at Gilstone House, which she had rented on St. Mary's. She planned to sit on the beach, palm trees waving in the summer breeze. Oh yes, this trip would be a soul-searching experience, for sure.

As she focused her binoculars, the blue-grey of the islands appeared on the horizon. *Ah, there's St. Martin's.* It seemed something strange had willed her to come here.

Swallowing hard, she shuddered with a yearning for her return to Scilly, as if an old friend on the other side was awaiting her, longing to hug her, kiss her and say, 'I'm so … *so* glad you're back. I missed you. You're going to be all right; I'll take care of you now.' *If only it were real.* This vivid imagination, this indulgence provided a sensation of belonging and hope: a bag of happiness waiting to be unwrapped, an overwhelming need for love. Just a little respite would be enough.

She leaned over the rail, looking down at the azure sea and the ship cutting through the swell. A gull flew overhead. Her doctor had been right, she needed the break; surely Rob must have realised, he was supposed to know about these things. *He's a nurse, for god's sake. Why doesn't he understand?*

The greyness of the horizon turned to green as she recognised the shapes of rocks. A helicopter hammered across the sky, about to land at the airport. It went down, down, down to disappear over the hill.

The ship rolled across Crow Sound toward The Road, a blue lagoon where the sea once flooded the palm of an imaginary hand, leaving fingers of land protruding above the waves. Pippa gazed into the depths of the water as the ship slowed and the crew prepared to dock. Fronds of kelp and bladderwrack swayed in the tides; ripples in the white sand revealed a playground for crab and lobster.

As the ferry entered the harbour, the drumming of the ship's engines quietened, then stopped. The gulls' calls made her really feel at home, as if she'd belonged here all her life.

The harbourmaster's voice echoing from the quay made her turn around. With a look of mock impatience, he gestured to the crew as if using sign language to the deaf. The first officer came out from the bridge to see who was making the commotion.

'Hey, you lot! You're like a pack of amateur sailors on a weekend cruise. Get that bladdy ship further down the quay.' He used his thumb in a backward gesture and rolled his eyes. Looking at the upper decks, he shouted, 'You might realise, folks, you've arrived on St Mary's. Welcome to Scilly, everyone.'

The passengers wore expressions of amusement and Pippa heard laughter behind her. It reminded her of the atmosphere from her last visit, the working relationship between shore-side and ship-side. She had seen the well-practised routine before. They were great people: a community in which goal setting was all about the challenges of living in a remote location where everything had to be imported. Her imagination had been captured from the moment she first came here with Rob and Daniel. They'd taken a holiday in Cornwall and decided to explore the Isles of Scilly. The islands had become her dream, and would remain so.

'Are you sure you want this 'ere? There're too many people wandering around. 'arry mate, get this area roped off before we unload, please.'

With the noise of tourists and dockers on the quay, Pippa pulled herself back to reality.

Holidaymakers strolled between the lorries and forklift trucks as the shore-crew tied the ropes. Within minutes, the ship's crane extracted cargo from the hold. Luggage containers were winched first, then a car, scuba-diving gear and a host of non-descript, numbered boxes. The forklift driver shouted to his colleagues on the quay, 'Stick them over there!'

Pippa spotted the lorry delivering luggage to hotels and holiday cottages. She had seen it all before. Fascinated, she watched the way every piece of cargo was dumped on the quay in what seemed to be organised confusion. *Is it going to be okay? Will I be able to cope with all this—the memories?* She loved how the granite harbour glinted in the sun, and the many coloured boats anchored in the bay nodded on their moorings. Day trippers returned from the outer islands, binoculars around their necks and rucksacks slung over their shoulders.

Soon, the salt air tasted of summer holidays and the happiness Pippa craved. She puffed out her cheeks as she lifted her heavy bag to her shoulder. *Heck, how much stuff did I pack?* It was only a ten-minute walk to the cottage, but she changed her mind about walking as she spotted a taxi and poked her head through the passenger window.

'Gilstone House, please.'

'Have you come far?' asked the driver as he opened the door.

'I've travelled down from Whitby in Yorkshire.'

'You got the same things up there, 'aven't you?' He wrinkled his brow and chuckled as he steered away from the cobbles on the quay and turned the corner by *The Mermaid* pub.

'I've come for some peace and quiet and maybe to do a spot of birdwatching, although I'm not very good at it. I don't know my seagulls from my terns, but I'd like to learn. Anyway, I think you've got better birds down here and the sea is bluer.'

The taxi driver smiled. 'The Birdman is away this month, but I'm sure you'll find someone from the Environmental Trust. They got an office way up there.' He pointed up the hill.

As they drove along Hugh Street, Pippa's memories were all too clear. She wondered how she would be able to ignore the images. She recalled Daniel walking by the shops with a small backpack on his shoulders. The place where they'd bought ice creams and the toyshop on the corner with the buckets and spades outside. The little old bus in which she'd toured the island caught her eye. They still had it, parked and empty. She could see herself coming down the steps.

Visitors and locals cycled along the street, and outside their cottages, people sat in the sun with eyes half closed. Two minibuses stood near the red phone box in the centre of town and she had a vision of Rob, *yes, Rob again ...* with Daniel on his knee, licking their ice creams in the park. *Why have I done this?*

Saying goodbye to Rob was hardly a favourable experience. He could at least have given her a proper kiss as he wouldn't see her for three weeks. What would all this mean, being here alone?

If only she could live without blame or forever seeking Rob's approval. *What if things had been different?* There had to be a degree of acceptance, a lessening of despair. Leaving her home on Henrietta Street for a while might make things easier: a time for reflection, a chance to consider what to do next. Joan and Terry, once neighbours, had moved away to the edge of town, perhaps it was her time to move on as well.

The driver stopped near the museum. 'Here's my card in case you need to call me again. Have a nice holiday.' Pippa paid him and he handed her the rucksack from the boot.

A piece of paper tacked onto the green wooden door caught her eye.

Pippa stepped inside the old stone-clad house. She felt like Alice peering down the rabbit hole, needing time to adjust from the sunlight as she explored the living room. From the scent of lavender polish, it was obvious Janice had tidied up only a few hours before. The cottage was bright and clean, with 1970s-style furniture, basic but pleasant. The description in the advert had been accurate: *'in the centre of town and easy access for the boats'.* The house seemed large for one person, but she liked the space and was pleased Janice managed to provide her with a cancellation at a modest price.

For the next hour, she looked around the old place and noted the hot water switch for the immersion heater. The groceries she had pre-ordered were in a cardboard box on top of the fridge. She stepped into the conservatory where a door led to a small back yard. A vase of flowers stood on the table to welcome her. *Just like home. Better even—home wasn't all that homely these days.*

She explored the bedrooms. In the corner of the double room stood a tallboy dresser with mothball-perfumed drawers and there was a clock radio on the bedside table.

She heard a knock and the front door opened as she returned down the stairs.

''elloo, Mrs Lambton … Sorry I wasn't 'ere when you came. As you can see, we don't usually lock our doors on the island; the crime rate is very low. They can't easily escape from St Mary's,' she jested. 'Still, 'ere's the key. We 'ave a lot of people milling around the place when the ferry comes in. So maybe it's best to lock up.' She placed the key on the dining table.

'Ah, you must be Janice! Great to meet you; thanks for fitting me in.'

'That's fine, my dear, a pleasure to 'ave you.'

'This is my second time on Scilly,' explained Pippa. 'The first one was a day trip about five years ago, but I've come to explore this time. By the way, call me Pippa.'

It seemed as if Janice was dying to ask why Pippa was alone, but good manners restrained her. Instead, she merely pointed to the instructions on the cork notice board for the smooth running of the cottage.

'I 'ope you'll be comfortable. If you need anything, ask. Electricity is on the meter; you'll need some new ten pence pieces. We don't mind if you want to use candles, as long as you're careful. My place is the last 'ouse near the pharmacy on the 'arbour, called *First and Last Outpost.*'

Pippa smiled; she liked the name of Janice's house, and of course, these islands were the last English outpost before the USA, so it made sense. She also liked Janice and her Cornish accent and wished she could stay longer. 'Did you get my cheque?' she asked.

'Er, I think so, er … yes, I did,' nodded Janice.

Her business methods seemed very lax; Pippa thought she might have been keener. On the phone from home, she had insisted on sending a cheque to Janice for the deposit and had asked about the cancellation policy. 'I'm not that bothered. 'There's always someone to fill the space in the summer.' Pippa smiled—life on Scilly seemed so carefree, although she realised Janice was now in a hurry, as she kept moving toward the door.

'Have a nice 'oliday, dear, and let me know if there is anything I can get you. Bye.'

Pippa watched through the lounge window as Janice hurried towards town. She sighed. With Janice gone and no one to share the house, she felt both relief and abandonment.

Despite this and everything she'd had to endure, she looked forward to settling in. She placed her shorts, jeans, and T-shirts into the old tallboy dresser. Perhaps if she took a walk after lunch, she could explore the town. With a desperate need to enjoy her holiday, she would try hard to stay calm and feel the sense of freedom she had longed for. Without Rob, perhaps the break would be more relaxing. No, she didn't mean it that way. The guilt of leaving Rob behind seemed too much. *If only Joan, Terry, and Rob could see me now.* It was astonishing to think that they had all been together for this long as best friends—how much longer could they live like this? Was the tension between them just her imagination? But, now that she was here, it was as if something marvellous was about to happen.

CHAPTER TWO

Rob yawned; all he wanted was his own bed. He squeezed his eyelids together. *Bloody night shifts*!

The light flashed on the answerphone; he listened to Pippa's message. 'Hi Rob, I'm in Penzance. Sorry I missed you. Bye.' Like everything else these days, the message was short and sharp. Living without her for three weeks had to be a test of his feelings. Suppose he didn't want to live with her anymore? He would need to move, but the house wasn't his to sell. She ought to have signed over to joint names after her father died—but never did.

He'd often told his patients, 'If what you are doing isn't working, you should change it'—a phrase he'd learned in his training. God, how he'd tried to make those changes, but his nursing career took up most of his time and this shift work … *Oh yes, all too fine for Pippa to go swanning off by herself, but I've got a life too.*

'Daniel is all around us; I can't stand it,' he'd told Pippa.

'Well that's only natural Rob. What do you expect? He was *our* son—remember?' Her tearful tone made Rob loathe himself for being so cold. *What was I supposed to say?*

'We have to move on. It's so frustrating. It's your choice.'

'Are you threatening me again?' *More tears!* She'd cried too many times for him to understand, even when he learned in the counselling course he ought to be empathic to her needs. He never wanted to appear mean and resentful but sometimes he couldn't help himself. The course wasn't making things easier, even though he might have learned something to help himself. It seemed that between them hung a time of dreadful change.

'You're provoking me, Pippa. I don't need this. Sometimes my life is better when you're *not* here.' Why did he say those things? It just came out that way. *If only we could find mutual ground again and stop playing mind games.*

'I didn't mean that.'

'Yes, you did, Rob, I get the message.' She'd stormed out the back door into the yard for a breath of fresh air, and he'd followed her.

'I think we ought to go for divorce. This isn't working, is it?

'Rob, for Christ's sake, leave me alone. I can't take much more of your up-and-down personality. It's like I'm married to two people at the same time. I have more arguments with you in a week than I ever had my entire life with my dad. All I need is understanding and love, not wham-bam-thank-you-Ma'am and "let's jump into bed and get this over before you go to work" kind of thing. Where's the love in our lives? I can't do this anymore. I have to find some "me time" to think this over.'

He had to stop thinking about this. Rob caught a glimpse of the end of Breakfast TV and finished his sandwich as he pressed the remote buttons, channel hopping. He was hoping to see the news about the FIFA World Cup, but he'd missed it. *Damn!* He closed his mouth after a huge yawn. The cold egg and bacon sandwich tasted like cardboard. His mind churned on, despite feeling tired and numb. *Now—what was I going to do?*

The last thing he wanted was Joan phoning him, but she usually only offered help. A support to the whole family, she seemed to understand, but he didn't need the phone calls—not today. If the phone rang, he wouldn't answer it, particularly if it were Joan. Well, he might be persuaded—after all, she had been most helpful in recent days.

Unable to find anything interesting to watch, he switched off the TV and made his way upstairs. Alone at last, he could try to get his mind around the days ahead. Driving Pippa for the early train had sapped all his energy. He shook his head in sheer frustration and weariness.

After passing the bathroom, he paused as sunlight peeked through the cracks in Daniel's door. The nameplate had been pulled off; all he could see was the outline of an empty space where the sticker used to be. *Why has she taken the sign off the door? Surely not … ?* He turned the knob and went in. *Oh my god, what has she done? When? Why didn't she tell me she had taken 'the shrine' away?*

The bed was now in a different place, made with a fresh duvet cover and no sign that Daniel ever existed. He glanced at the teddy on the windowsill. *Where's the rest of Dan's toys?* He opened the old oak wardrobe and discovered an overloaded black bin liner. A piece of Lego protruded from the bag.

He looked in the drawers. 'Oh my god, Dan's clothes are all gone.' He sat on the bed in what seemed like a different room and as he did so, a dreadful ache cramped his chest. For the first time since Daniel died, he allowed himself to let go of his grief and anger. *How could she?* His father always told him to stand up and be a man, but now he cried like a baby, the back of his hands salty-wet from wiping away the tears. He rolled on his side and lay on the bed where his son had slept. *Why? Why?* He found himself hating Pippa. *Why had she done this without saying a word? I never thought ... I wanted to be there as well, take things slowly with dignity, not sling Daniel's possessions into plastic bags and stuff them in the wardrobe! What was she thinking? God, she can be so insensitive.* Then he remembered he'd asked her to do it. *Even so ...*

He lay back on the bed staring at the ceiling and imagined himself as his own patient in one of his counselling sessions, but someone else, an imaginary middle-aged woman in a grey suit, was asking the questions.

What do you feel right now? *Betrayal.*

What does betrayal mean to you? *My parents, my lost life, my son, my wife.*

What are your feelings right now? *I'm angry.*

Tell me about your anger, Rob. *Pippa has gone away when she should be supporting me.*

Do you love her? *I don't know.*

How do you feel about her? *I don't KNOW!*

He must stop punishing himself.

Rob made his way to the bathroom, sniffing. He pulled down several sheets of toilet paper and dabbed away his tears, his mind working on lost time. *How am I supposed to feel?* He'd never cried in front of Pippa. Why should he start feeling this way today, and why did counselling never work when you tried it on yourself? He felt too beaten up and spat out to be bothered. Sometimes he had been two people. *Pippa was right.* The caring Rob, patients praising him and the Rob at home, with no sense of who he was anymore, and a wife who wanted to be somewhere else.

He looked in the mirror, stroking his hair. He ought to go and have it cut; his last visit had been two months ago. Maybe this time, he would ask the hairdresser to cut it shorter; he might grow a beard and re-invent himself. Perhaps he ought to change his way of living.

He knew he'd lost weight; while other guys had put on a few pounds since their marriage, he looked more like a stick. Maybe he should be grateful he wasn't fat. If he stopped smoking, he would bulk up. He tried to pull himself together and muster some enthusiasm. Later on, he had to go to work, but at the moment, sleep was a priority.

In the bedroom, he sat on the white sheets of the unmade bed and sniffed. *Bloody hell, how could she do that?* He took a deep breath and squinted at the clock through his tear-filled eyes. *What time is it?* Maybe he could snatch a few hours until Pippa called him and he could study for an hour before going to the pub. At least he had the evening off—it was darts night and with the free food there, he wouldn't have to cook tonight. He raised his hands to his face in frustration. Once he got his head down, he promised himself, he would be calmer.

He pulled back the covers, puffed up the feather pillows. Pippa hadn't made the bed; she hardly ever did. When one of them got out, the other got in. He took off his shoes and socks, undressed down to his boxers and listened to the ticking clock. He lay with the curtains closed and the sound of tourists and locals walking outside on the pavement. Living in a holiday town, people always looked through their windows from the street. If only he could shut everything away in an instant, but his mind refused to stop.

He lay thinking about his life in the sixties and seventies, and how he'd never tried to find his real parents. Yes, one day he would go looking for them, but not yet. Sally and Ralph Lambton had taken good care of him. He didn't wish to hurt them, but he knew something in his life wasn't quite right, almost as if a part of him had been turned off. He'd never felt more discarded than the day they told him he was adopted and they'd retire to live on the Costa del Sol. *And if that's not bad enough, now Pippa's gone too.*

Half an hour passed and he couldn't sleep, his mind rippling with recollections of his childhood and the sadness. The clock's tick-a-tock, tock-a-tick became intrusive like tinnitus. He thought he saw Daniel standing at the end of the bed. 'Daddy, I want a drink. Daddy, I'm cold, can I come into bed with you and Mummy?' He shut his eyes in case it was real.

On the dressing table stood a photo of Pippa. He had seen the picture taken at her eighteenth birthday party so many times, but today, he perceived her as a grieving mother, and the girl shining out from the photo was no longer the smiling woman he had married. *Oh boy, how I chased after her that day. Oh yes, of course ... Joan was going out with Terry by then.*

He used to imagine himself with two girlfriends, lying in bed with one on either side of him. He smiled to himself. *Hell, how self-assured I must have been those days. Pippa always seemed to be out of reach. God! She was a big tease, for sure.* He knew her laughter often hid the sad loss of her father eight months before.

'I've had to be brave over the years, losing both parents makes you feel like an orphan,' Little did he realise her words would come back to haunt him.

'I'm thinking of going into nursing,' he'd told Pippa.

'Great idea! They always need nursing staff and it's a good career.'

He'd heeded her advice and taken his training.

Perhaps the lure of her independence brought them together—or was it something else? *Did I really love her? It all felt so safe.* He recalled lying in bed on top of her, panting and moaning in pleasure. He'd become worried in case she got pregnant and he thought about Terry giving out condoms he'd nicked from a broken vending machine. He heard all kinds of rumours that they weren't reliable and was relieved when it was Pippa's time of the month two weeks later. The sex was as good as he imagined. He thought he was in heaven. *If only things were like that now. Was it all about sex, rock and roll, and bragging to the guys down at the pub?* Oh yes, he'd been proud of her all right. But love was only a word, it's what you did with it ... *I was never in love, I know that now. Only when Daniel was born, everything clicked into place.*

'Perhaps one day you might discover more about your parents.'

'To be honest Pippa, I'm not that interested. My real mother abandoned me, why should I want to know her now?' *Maybe I ought to find out who she is.*

But things had changed. *Everything turned bloody sour!* Pippa didn't want any more children—or sex. She thought she might get pregnant again and history could repeat itself.

She had complained he wasn't being romantic enough. 'A quick fix after work,' she'd called it. He'd only wanted to be supportive and sympathetic, but somehow he always ended up hating her.

His hand rested against his groin. *Right now, a good shag would be the answer.* He had to break this barrier between them. *I need to be stronger, make her realise I'm suffering, too. No more excuses not to do it.* All he could muster was a 'do-it-yourself' job when she wasn't around to listen. At least he hoped she wasn't listening.

I don't want to be like this anymore. There were days when he felt cheated. *Why did my real mother give up on me?* Maybe the time had come to go looking for her. Lately it had been impossible. Now that Pippa had gone away for three weeks to gather her thoughts, he also had more freedom to think about his future. There was one thing his counselling course couldn't tell him: who the hell is the real Rob Lambton?

Through the half-open bedroom window, the intermittent odour of smoked herring drifted from the kipper smokehouse. Whitby kippers were his favourite and the town had so much entertainment. Why would Pippa want to go to Scilly? Rob's own experience of the islands was not so different from being at home. They had a harbour and boats and fishermen. Scilly felt like a busman's holiday. He'd often told Pippa, 'Give me a mountain in the Lake District any day.'

Now that Joan and Terry had moved away, what else might change? *They've got young Jordan to think of, I suppose.* Rob's thoughts turned to Terry. Why hadn't he been back from the oil rigs in ages? *I wonder if he's left Joan without telling her, stringing her along with one story after another. Why the hell doesn't he come home?* Rob never dared to ask Joan in case he upset her.

It was the phone call, the one all parents dread, the one he would never forget. He thought about the tragedy too many times and he wished he could stop doing it. Another dog was out of the question. She had been the cause of his son's death, running out into the road like that! Why did Dan run after her? Pippa should have held tighter on to his hand. He'd been over this too many times.

He slipped a cigarette out of the packet on the bedside table and put it to his lips. His thumb flicked over the lighter and he hesitated a moment before inhaling. His mind still on Pippa, he blew relaxed smoke rings and watched himself in the mirror as a series of perfect O's chased each other. He kept promising Pippa that each cigarette would be his last. Would it be this one? He didn't think so. Now was not the time to give it up, not yet. He thought if he put the radio on, he might fall asleep. Stubbing out his cigarette into a half-full ashtray, he turned over and then turned back again. A few moments later, he lay on his back and sighed. Sleep refused to come; his whole body wanted it, but the visions wouldn't stop.

He reached over to the radio and pressed the switch. At least he'd smoked this ciggy without Pippa nagging him for smoking in bed. He knew he ought to practise what he preached, especially with all those campaign posters at work. He would fall asleep listening to Radio 4, and the voice of Brian Redhead on the 'Today' programme might help him drift away. It usually did.

CHAPTER THREE

Pippa headed into Hugh Town as the aroma of fresh-baked bread wafted across the street from the bakery. She made her way toward 'First and Last Outpost' at a steady pace. A flush of exotic flowers lined the path in front of Janice's cottage. The sway of the old granite wall provided a refuge for pennywort and mesembryanthemum. Spikes of tall agapanthus with trumpet-shaped blue flowers stood tall through the foliage.

As she continued toward the harbour, she noted the souvenirs for sale outside the old-fashioned shop windows. Brightly coloured tea towels with designs of puffins and seals hung on string, pegged as if on a washing line.

Pippa very quickly became aware of how she once walked this spot with Daniel and Rob. Wearing his red Start-Right sandals, Dan complained about having to walk so far; his legs were tired. She thought she could hear him talking to her. 'Mummy, my legs hurt, carry me.' Rob picked him up on that very spot and lifted him onto his shoulders.

She told herself not to crumble on the first day of her holiday, think of other things and keep busy. *You can do this.* Joan often warned her not to keep punishing herself with her grief.

She made her way down to the quay where notice boards provided information like shopping lists. The day had moved on; the next day's boat trips were already advertised.

The *Scillonian* was tied to the pier like an old dog waiting for its master. Tourists strolled along the harbour and Pippa walked almost shoulder to shoulder to meld with the crowd. Perhaps making enquiries for the birdwatching tours would be a start? She picked out snatches of conversation and listened as the atmosphere rang with voices.

'Don, what time you taking *Lily of Laguna* out tomorrow?'

'Mick, is your puffin cruise booked now?'

'And normally he has fish for breakfast.'

She smiled to herself. It was like Whitby; only the accent was different.

The name 'Don' was one she recalled from her last visit. *Oh yes, I remember him.* His infectious laughter and humour made her smile. She wanted to go over to him and say 'Hi, remember me?' *What a daft idea.*

Tourists wore the usual summer clothes: shorts, shirts, and sandals. Others donned weatherproof clothing for the deeper water out at sea. Pippa watched as day trippers mingled together, each going on a mission of pure leisure. A breeze blew across the stone pier and the anglers reeled in their tackle; the tide was falling fast. She followed them along the quay, with their rods in one hand and a small catch of fish in the other.

With the bustle of life in the harbour, she reckoned she might be lonely if she didn't push herself forward and join in. From her life in Whitby, she knew the ways of local people too well. You had to introduce yourself and be part of the scene. Despite being here for the relaxation, it was important to belong and be part of the scenery.

The morning trip returned from St. Martin's and moored alongside another boat. Passengers disembarked by walking across both vessels onto the granite steps. A well-tanned man with blonde hair caught her eye. She saw him packing up his telescope and making conversation with the skipper. He had his back to Pippa before turning to one of the passengers and assisting her in climbing the harbour steps.

'Bye, and thanks,' said the woman.

'Hope you enjoyed the trip.' The man continued to help the other passengers. He had a slight foreign accent; perhaps he was Dutch or German? Pippa found it hard to tell, as his English was excellent and he pronounced some of his words like a Cornishman.

'Many thanks. Mind how you go, Mrs Dewhurst. Don will take you back to St. Martin's at four o'clock. Oh, hello Sam, didn't realise you were on the boat today, how's your Mum? Take it easy, madam, step on this one first and then you're on dry land. Hang on to the rail, the steps are wet, be careful now. Well done … bye.'

Ten minutes later, Pippa gazed into the empty boat. 'Excuse me,' she called. 'Can you tell me if you are doing any more trips today?' She felt her awkwardness might show and wondered if her question was stupid.

The man removed his sunglasses, looked up at her and smiled. He climbed the steps so he could hear her and she saw how tall he was, and attractive, with eyes the colour of the sea. In a film star kind of way, his striking looks seemed to spell mystery and intrigue. She looked away from him, hoping she wasn't being a nuisance.

'I'm sorry, but the *Lily of Laguna* isn't going out again until tomorrow. You could try the other boatmen. We have a couple of repairs to do.' He paused for a moment. 'Erm … if you want to come with us, you can book for tomorrow if you like.' He smiled at her again.

Pippa brought her hand up to shade her eyes. The sun's reflection on the water dazzled her. 'Thanks very much, I'd love to.'

'Was there anything in particular you wanted to see?'

'I'd like to learn more about the islands, and maybe do a spot of birdwatching.' She touched the binoculars around her neck. 'I've just started and I'm not very good at it yet.'

'Well … I do the birdwatching tours, and most of my visitors are learning like you. My colleague, Martin, The Birdman, he's away now on tour in West Africa, but I'm here if you want to book a trip tomorrow, yes?'

She hesitated, then nodded. 'Oh of course, I heard about The Birdman, and yes, that would be excellent.'

'I'm doing a guided walk tomorrow and so far, we have seven bookings; I expect more later. We're going to St. Martin's. How about the morning trip?' He smiled straight at her, as if willing her to say yes.

'Yes, I'll get a ticket,' she said, realising her own enthusiasm. *God—what am I doing?* She found herself saying yes for the first time in ages.

He began to walk away from her. 'Come on then,' he beckoned, 'I'll help you. I'll see if Andy is in the kiosk and try to get you one of my special tickets.'

Unsure of herself, Pippa followed him a short distance along the old granite quay. He stopped and turned around to face her. 'It's a great place this, you know. We have a lot of history in these islands.'

'Mmh, I bet. So exactly who is this Birdman?'

'Oh well, we've always had a Birdman around the place since the late 1700s. His job was to collect puffins for food, an important source of meat in times of famine. These days, it's a title handed down through the generations. Of course now, nature conservation is the key issue.'

Again, he smiled at Pippa; his blue eyes seemed to read her thoughts. 'Anyway,' he added, 'I'm here doing these tours until my colleague returns in a few weeks' time. He's the expert; my usual role is to manage the nature reserve.'

This is what she needed. Someone with whom she could converse on her daily strolls down the quay.

He turned toward the boatman on duty in the kiosk. 'Just one ticket for tomorrow for the nice lady with the *Lily* please, Andy.'

'Two pounds to you, ma luv,' said Andy, giving Pippa the change from a five pound note. 'You're lucky to catch me here at this time, I only opened up for that big cruiser we had this afternoon. Just finishing up for a cuppa tea.'

Pippa thanked him and turned to her guide. 'So I suppose you're the expert now, then?' She hoped her question wasn't too impertinent. 'I'd like to find out more about it as a hobby. I'm here for three weeks, so what do you suggest I do?'

She heard Andy chuckle at the word 'expert'. He grinned.

'I suppose I am, really, if you put it like that. I think I had better introduce myself. Sven Jørgensen. I originally came from Norway, but I live here now.'

She took his hand; his grip felt genuine and welcoming. *Norway, eh? Gosh, he's so suntanned. He must spend hours on these boats every day.*

'I'm Pippa Lambton, I live in the north-east of England. How long have you been living in Scilly?'

'Oh, it must be, erm … almost six years now. I work for the new Scilly Environmental Trust and generally make a nuisance of myself. I'm actually an ornithologist. If you are interested in birds, then I'm your man!'

Pippa giggled to herself. His long blonde hair and suntan made her wonder whose man he really was. How silly, she hadn't realised he was the main tour guide for the islands. She was only trying to cheer herself up. He must have thought she was some dizzy woman on holiday trying to make out she was a proper birdwatcher. Still, he seemed helpful, which was something she needed right now.

'Listen, erm,' He scratched the side of his nose. 'There's a slide show tomorrow night in the church hall—perhaps you can come? You will learn a lot about the history of the islands and the birdlife. Bring your family and friends.'

Pippa replied immediately. 'Okay, sounds like a great idea. Although I don't have anyone I can bring; I'm here on my own, but I will be there. Promise.'

'Oh I see, well,' he hesitated for a moment.

Before he could finish his sentence, Pippa remarked. 'I'm just taking a break from life, the universe and everything. You know how it is, just a spot of respite.'

'Respite?' echoed Sven.

'Oh yeah, well, that's another story for another time, eh?' Annoyed with herself for hinting she had a problem, she moved on. 'I've been to Scilly before, on a day trip. I enjoyed the atmosphere here so much, I've come back for a longer stay.'

She didn't know why she mentioned this. She so much wanted to feel less pain in her daily life, but referring to her tragedy during her holiday might spoil things. She often couldn't help herself, a habit she would have to curb. If only she could stop being in eternal grief! Would it always be this way? The short answer was: yes.

'Give me a second. Are you walking back into town?' asked Sven.

Pippa nodded. 'Yep.'

'Let's go back to the boat. Just got to pick up a few things, and then I'll walk up that way with you.'

Pippa followed him as he carried on with the conversation.

'I'm pleased you came; it's a great place to learn.' He looked down at Don in the boat. 'Mate, pass me my bins and 'scope, can you?'

Don obeyed, giving Pippa a sideways glance. 'Watch 'im, young lady, he has an eye for all the young girls.'

'Thanks, Don.' Sven grinned and ignored the comment.

Pippa chuckled at his apparent shyness. She liked the way he spoke, his Norwegian accent, his politeness, and his gentle way of talking to her. He had well-cared-for teeth beneath a kind smile. He would be a useful person to get to know for all the information she needed about the wildlife tours.

Having changed from his boots to a pair of open-toe sandals, Sven tied the laces together, and slung the boots over his shoulder. He wore cut-off denim jeans, revealing long suntanned legs with hairs that had bleached in the sun. His white T-shirt seemed to accentuate his tan. He struggled to organise himself, a shoulder strap here and another one there, boots dangling and no sign of a bag to carry it all.

'See ya, Don. I'll be back down here later, as usual.' He flipped his hand in a gesture of farewell and continued walking with Pippa. They paused for a moment with their backs against the granite wall as a lorry loaded with suitcases turned the corner.

'I remember Don from my day trip a few years ago. He was telling me about Tresco and the gardens,' recalled Pippa. 'Yeah, he seems to be a good laugh. Nice guy.'

'Ah yes, you said you'd been here before. Where are you staying?' asked Sven.

She was glad he didn't ask her about the last trip. 'I've rented a place near the museum; Gilstone, d'ya know it?'

'Ya, sure, the old place is owned by Janice Stowes now. It used to belong to her mother before she got Alzheimer's and went into care. Janice is a very nice lady, although she can be a bit disorganised at times, but she has to visit her mother every day, so it's understandable, I suppose. Her husband co-owns a boat on Bryher. So, you're by yourself then, eh?'

Pippa had never been to the island of Bryher; it was on her agenda.

'Well, yes.' She gave a half smile, desperate to move the conversation elsewhere. 'I suppose I'd better find something to do this afternoon.'

Sven turned to her. 'Look, er … I could murder a cold drink right now. Would you like to walk up to Porthcressa with me? The restaurant is open and I could tell you more about this place, like which birds are here at this time of year. Perhaps I can help you decide how you want to spend your … what did you say, your "respite"?'

'Oh, that would be lovely. Much appreciated.' Pippa smiled. 'You look overloaded! Here, let me carry the boots.'

'Yeah right, you noticed the clutter. I'm like the Loaded Camel up at Porth Hellick—that's a rock formation, you'll see it soon on your travels around the island. Yesterday, I lost my rucksack overboard in the wind; the sea got a bit rough. The bag sank to the bottom before we could pull it out. I had some lead weights for fishing; no wonder it went down so quickly'

'Pass them here, then.' Pippa held out her hand like a mother. 'Good job your bins weren't inside, eh?'

She saw the word *Zeiss* on his binoculars and realised the famous brand.

'Oh no, I never keep them in my bag; all part of being a good birder. You never know when you might need them.'

Pippa loved his politeness and the way he said 'yeuw' instead of 'you'. Sven stopped outside the Porthcressa Restaurant and dropped his heavy gear on the lobby floor. 'I'll leave it and pick it up when we've had coffee.'

'Can you trust dumping your stuff there?'

'Oh, yes we never worry too much on St Mary's. This is an island.' Sven led the way through the empty tables and outside on to the veranda. He drew out a chair for her.

Aw … how kind. Rob had never done that all their married life. *Small gestures like this can make all the difference.*

The view from where she sat absorbed her thoughts; her mind taken with the shimmering sea and wonderful scenery. 'Wow, this is lovely,' she said, staring out beyond the bay.

Sven sat opposite her. 'I know— this is one of my favourite views too. I see it every day from my bedroom window. Don and I often come up here when he's not on the boat; it's a great place to relax and have a beer.'

The waitress came toward the table with her pad and pencil. 'What can I get you, Sven?'

He passed the menu to Pippa. 'My usual beer, Christine, please.'

Pippa scanned the list at the choice of iced cakes.

'I'll have a coffee, please, and oh … yes, a lemon gateau, thanks.' She looked up and smiled at the waitress.

'Good choice, but try the Black Forest one next time you come,' recommended Sven.

'You must have loads of friends here, don't you?' asked Pippa.

'Yeah, sure. My colleague Martin, you know, The Birdman I told you about? He's the big boss around here. Makes all the decisions when he's back in town. I just deputise for him now. It's the first time I've been in charge. I may not be here much longer when my contract runs out. I have to wait until he gets back. He lives with his wife just over the hill.' Sven pointed behind him toward The Garrison. 'It's not like on the mainland; here, everyone knows who you are, and sometimes things can be rather intrusive. You must have friends back home as well?'

'Yes, two very good friends and lots of the usual acquaintances.'

Pippa sat, resting her chin on clasped hands, hanging on to his every word. He seemed like a very interesting man. She reckoned she couldn't have found anyone better to help her.

'We have some great birds around at the moment,' he said. 'You'll find the common birds don't have any fear of people. The thrushes will come right up to you and feed from your hand.' He carried on listing the birds. 'Peregrine, roseate tern, puffins, guillemots, razorbills, the usual stuff.'

Pippa's mind began to wander; some of the names she didn't know, but she felt she could listen to his accent all day. His English was good, very good. She was thrilled about having already received an invitation for refreshments in her first few hours on the island. She jolted herself back to the conversation. Sven knew his birds for sure.

'… and you can do the shearwater trip if you like. You should see life here in October when all the "Twitchers" arrive. The place gets busy again. Oh yes, never a dull moment, I can tell you.' Sven laughed.

Pippa wondered why people would travel hundreds of miles, chasing after rare birds. Surely, they weren't real birdwatchers?

The coffee and cake arrived and Christine lifted the glass of beer from her tray and placed it on the table. She smiled at Sven and moved on to clear the other glasses.

'Where did you say you lived?' asked Sven.

'Whitby on the Yorkshire coast. I live close to the harbour. Pippa searched for the small photo album in her rucksack. 'Here, I have photos.' She pointed to her house. 'That's where I live. It's a very old street with views of the harbour from my kitchen window. I was born in the town; I suppose that's why I have this affinity with Scilly. It's just so much nicer on the islands. I adore the life here and the blue sea. Although, of course, Whitby is larger. It also has a lot of ancient history. Did you know it's famous for the Dracula stories?' Pippa seemed to enjoy the verbal tour of her town.

'Oh, I didn't know that. Spooky, eh?' Sven leaned on the table and mirrored her clasped hands, listening about her life in Whitby. After a moment, he sat back in his chair and picked up his beer, sipping from the top of the glass. He wiped his lips on the back of his index finger. 'So … what birds do you see in that part of the world?'

Pippa felt the usual dread of questions, having hoped he wasn't going to ask her about birds; she would have to tell him she didn't know. An involuntary movement of her hand caused her to drop a spoon on the floor and both she and Sven bent to pick it up. There wasn't any nicotine on his fingers like Rob's. How she hated cigarettes. They had put her father in hospital, the very same place where Rob worked. How could he not realise smoking was bad for you?

'Thanks, sorry,' she said, slightly embarrassed as Sven handed her the spoon. 'Ah yes, birds, the same as here I think, but not so many. We get a few … is it, erm … gannets?'

He smiled at her, ignoring the incident. 'So what got you into birding then?'

'Well, my father used to work on the Balmoral estate in Scotland before he married my mother, and then in later years, he was always interested in the wildlife on the Yorkshire Moors. He was a volunteer grouse beater. So I knew the names of a few birds before …,' she almost mentioned Daniel and stopped herself. '… my dad passed away some years ago. I miss him a lot.'

Sven empathised and drew in closer to hear what she was saying above the noise of the mewing gulls. 'I'd like to go up there sometime.'

'I live very close to the Abbey steps in the famous old Henrietta Street. Did you know there are one hundred and ninety-nine steps to the top? My friend always gets it wrong. You can see the jawbone of a whale representing an archway on the cliffs in Whitby. I think it was presented to the town's folk by the people of Norway,' she hinted.

'Sounds like a great place if they are friends of my country.'

Pippa felt the warmth of his smile, and was glad she had told him. She listened as he explained his father was Swedish and had married his Norwegian mother. They lived in Trondheim, his birthplace. 'I'm hoping they will come next year and visit me since they've never been here,' he said. 'The travel takes three flights and that makes it a very expensive holiday. My mother is a bit interfering sometimes, you know, like mothers can be.'

Pippa lowered her gaze as Sven continued his conversation.

'I've got no idea how she would cope in my little cottage, as they have a big house, but I suppose she means well. I don't have any brothers or sisters.'

Pippa looked up; she was an only child, too. 'Is your father also into nature?'

'No, my dad was an engineer; it was my grandfather who used to go seal hunting, but he changed his thoughts over the years.

He showed me a lot about wildlife, just as your father did for you, I suppose. Have you done a lot of travel then, Pippa?'

It was the first time he had used her name and it made her feel she belonged here.

'No, not really, well … normal living stuff. I spent most of my days in my dad's house in Whitby. My mother died when I was twelve.' She hid her sadness behind a smile and Sven seemed to understand.

'Sounds like an interesting place.' He glanced at her left hand resting on the table. She wore a wedding ring. Better not ask an obvious question; it was none of his business.

'I'm glad I met you. It's not every day I am able to take a lunch break like this, so thanks for the company. When you take your trip tomorrow on the *Lily,* I'll show you some really good birds.'

'That would be lovely,' replied Pippa. 'I am looking forward to it.'

'Sorry, but I have to go. Our secretary at the office, Margaret, has some work for me. Lovely lady, but she retires soon. Then I'm going home for a rest. I only live over the way. It's that white house up there.' He pointed. 'It's called Beachside Cottage, a little further up the bay. I'm pretty lucky really, the old house belongs to the Trust. I don't pay any rent.'

'Mm … that's a nice name for a house. Sounds like a great place to relax, eh?'

He smiled down at her as he stood tall beside the table and she wondered if there would be another invitation for the future: more boat trips, and perhaps another coffee?

'The refreshments are on me,' he said, reaching for his wallet in his shorts' pocket.

Pippa watched him as he stood and couldn't help feeling star struck by his presence. 'Thanks Sven, that's kind of you. My turn next time, eh?' she offered. 'And thanks for the chat, I really enjoyed it.'

'Bye, Pippa. See you at the boat tomorrow.'

He left the table and her eyes followed his path as he walked into the distance, overloaded with equipment and shoes. *Well, what an interesting and nice guy.* Left alone to enjoy her lemon gateau and the view of the bay from the restaurant, she looked around her. Most of the people here looked brown and weathered; summer had brought out the best in everyone. They all looked so healthy and Pippa wanted to feel that way, too.

As she lingered at the round wooden table, once again she looked out on the bay, listening to the screaming terns along the water's edge. A gull came to perch on the sea wall. It had its eye on the lemon gateau, and a battle of wills between Pippa and the gull ensued. Finally, Christine came out with the sweeping brush and chased the bird away.

Children paddled along the shore. Daniel had sat by the rocks with Rob, playing with his new bucket and spade. They had looked so happy making a sand castle, pressing limpet shells into the sand for the windows, some driftwood for a roof, and a bit of seaweed as a flag on the top. Pippa looked in the other direction in case she cried. As a matter of habit, she checked her watch. It always seemed to take her mind off the negativity so often invading her thoughts.

As the town fell quiet, a few late afternoon shoppers crossed the street. Day trippers were about to leave with the *Scillonian*. Pippa took in a deep breath of sea air. She felt a moment of bliss pass over her; perhaps these moments would last longer. She hoped they would.

The pale shingle and granite rocks along the shore tempted her to walk down to the receding tide. Alone with her thoughts, a good feeling kicked in as she looked toward the house Sven had indicated. There were many small cottages in the distance at the end of the beach, all painted white and facing out to sea. She looked through her binoculars and thought how lucky he was, having palm trees and wonderful flowers outside his front door.

She sat a while longer, enjoying the sounds of the birds before removing her sandals to walk barefoot to the cold clear ocean. The large grains of sand hurt her feet. The sea looked tempting with the sun glinting on its surface, and gentle ripples crept back and forth along the shore. She splashed her feet in the water and made a sharp retreat—it was very cold. She tiptoed across the sinking sand, leaving footprints behind her. The sea lapped over them, and soon they were gone.

With her back against a granite rock, she closed her eyes to listen to the sounds of Scilly. The lapping waves on the shore and the call of the terns, 'kree-ah, kree-ah', made her smile.

She opened her eyes and watched a gannet plunge into the sea beyond the bay. She almost heard the splash. The sounds made her want to stay until sundown, but she had agreed to call Rob on the phone.

She slipped on her sandals. Plodding over the sand, she made her way to the red phone box at the town park and then remembered Rob might not be at home for another hour.

On arrival at Gilstone, Pippa headed for the shower. It felt good to rinse the shampoo from her hair. She thought how much she enjoyed her conversation with Sven. He seemed very caring and obviously enjoying his life. Did he have a wife and kids? What exactly had brought him to these islands? He must have been here on her last visit, but the time had been too short to notice. Now she was here again. Perhaps this was her destiny after all, the three weeks would be perfect.

Stepping from the shower, she dried herself, then dressed, and made a sandwich. In the garden, she opened a can of cola and a packet of chocolate biscuits, and allowed her hair to dry in the sun. She combed it straight, and then shook her head from side to side to loosen the strands. She thought of how brave she had been to come here alone. Sparrows flew down looking for food. A thrush fluttered in and she held out her hand so it could take a crumb from her fingers. Sven had been right—they had no fear of humans.

The call to Rob could wait a little longer. Now … what should she do during her holiday? She needed more self-control for a start. Perhaps she should get involved with lots of outdoor activities to stop her sadness. Best of all, if Sven was around, she could go on his trips to the different islands and learn a lot more about the wildlife—perfect. Anything to stop this misery and pain.

No wonder she'd got increasingly depressed last year. All she wanted was for Rob to tell her he loved her—and when had he last done that? Ten years ago? Three little words—that was all, and he hadn't said them once. She always had to ask him; he just wouldn't say 'I love you' voluntarily. He would always answer, 'I don't have to tell you that, you should know.' He would never change—she had tried. Perhaps divorce really was the answer. He was right; they had grown up together, but it was different being married to him. Her father had warned her, 'You never really know someone until you live with them.'

She didn't know why but the negative feelings had crept back again and she scolded herself. *Day One—Exercise positive thinking. That's what Joan keeps telling me.* As soon as her hair dried, Pippa wandered back to the phone box, taking her time. She didn't want to call him; it would be the same old conversation.

Walking around the perimeter of the park, she noticed the blue spikes of agapanthus standing tall over the wall and couldn't help thinking how wonderful it would be to live here. Sven was really lucky; he'd made a great choice in his life. Inside the red phone box, she took out the coins from her purse and then dialled the number.

'Hello, Rob?' she shouted. A roaring motorbike drowned out the conversation as the rider sped away down the narrow street. 'Can you hear me okay? I'm fine, doing a bit of exploring. I met some nice people and had coffee with someone who does birdwatching and wildlife tours. Are you okay? Nice weather at home?'

Rob didn't get a chance to answer when the 'pips' sounded and Pippa put more money into the slot, which seemed to eat up the coins like a gaming machine.

'I'm washing up,' he said. She heard the faint clinking of pots. 'Hang on, got to dry my hands.'

Pippa pictured him with a hunched shoulder, the phone to his left ear and a tea towel in his hand. She also 'saw' his reluctant face; washing up was something he hated.

The motorbike returned down the street, and she had to listen hard with her finger in her right ear.

'You didn't tell me about the room,' scolded Rob.

'What room—oh, you mean Dan's room? Yes, sorry Rob, I was so busy packing and with you being at work I didn't manage to tell you. Sorry.'

'Pippa, how could you do that? How could you not tell me that you totally stripped the room?'

'Well, you asked me to change it lots of times, and you never go in there,' said Pippa, wishing not to be reminded.

'I thought we might have done it together.' Rob sighed.

'Sorry, Rob. These days, communicating with you is so difficult. I always seem to do something else wrong, and you're never around when I need you.' She recalled the number of times she felt like she was walking on eggshells, and then doing things behind his back just to keep the peace.

'Well, you surprise me, Pippa. Don't you think *I* might want to be involved in this? It was very thoughtless of you.'

'As I said, that's exactly what I wanted, to show you I could do it myself. I'm sorry, Rob, I didn't mean to be thoughtless, honestly I didn't, it's just my mind these days isn't clear. Don't you understand how I felt when I tidied up that room? I know I should have shared the task with you, but you weren't there. I was going away and I thought you might have been pleased, or even proud of me for doing it.'

Rob answered, but her head was now full of Daniel and she wasn't really listening.

She didn't want to tell Rob she had broken Daniel's name-plate on the bedroom door; he might have complained at her again. As she'd tried to remove it, she'd heard a heart-breaking *crack* and sucked in her breath. 'Oh no, I didn't mean to do that,' she had wailed, holding the two halves in her hand. 'Not this too.' She wished she hadn't bothered.

'Okay, sorry Rob.' It seemed she was always saying sorry to him, always apologising. It felt like he blamed her for a lot of the bad things that had happened in their lives. She had felt guilty enough when Daniel had let go of her hand—not that she remembered much about it.

'Okay, enough said, I suppose,' said Rob. 'I want you to think while you're away, you know … what we talked about … ?'

Her mind seemed all over the place. 'Pity I missed you yesterday, I did try to phone you,' she butted in, trying to smooth things over.

Pip, pip, pip, pip, pip. The pips stopped and she hurried through the last few words in case she got cut off mid-conversation. 'Oh, I have to go, the money is about to run out. It's all I've got in change for this call. Gosh, you don't get much time, do you?'

'Okay, take care then,' replied Rob and as suddenly as he was there, he was gone.

'Bye.' The farewell was just in time, followed by a long final tone.

She might as well have been talking to the furniture. A tear came to her eye. She hadn't found the conversation warm and encouraging. Having a heated discussion on the phone about their dead son's room wasn't what she had expected. *Is this how it feels to be divorced—disconnected—five hundred miles apart?* The tear dropped onto her T-shirt. *I never wanted to consider divorce, it was his idea. Damn him, why does he have to be like that?*

After dinner, Pippa walked down to the harbour. The local pub, *The Mermaid*, looked tempting but she became anxious as she stepped inside. She didn't like going into pubs alone, but felt drawn to the friendly sounds coming from within. This was Scilly—you could do anything out of the ordinary here, and mainland rules didn't always apply. Anyway, going into pubs on your own wasn't illegal, so what did she have to worry about? Nothing. It was all about having a good time and making the most of the island life.

The pub was frequented by the pilot gig teams. The oars hanging from the walls with photos of races past and present were an obvious sign. The gigs were handed down through generations and she read the famous names forever cheered on by the tourists: Bonnet, Golden Eagle, Czar, Men-a-Vaur and more.

She squeezed between locals standing at the bar and heard singing from the room below. It was a song she knew well from the folk club at home. The sounds of local folk singers serenading their sea shanties tempted her to go down the steps to the next room. She poked her head through the door

'For we're going to cross the water,
Heave away, me jolly boys, we're all bound away.'

Pippa ordered rum and cola and sat at a table on her own with a view of the harbour, but it wasn't long before conversations sucked her into the friendly atmosphere.

'Don't sit there on yer own, girl, come and join us,' said a voice from the next table. Before she could answer, the man was introducing his friends. The glasses huddled together on the tables showed the fun had been going on for some time. 'It's

Harris' birthday—he's seventy today,' the man called above the noise.

He introduced himself. 'I'm Charlie James. This is Mark, Sue and Lydia…' they each nodded. '…and Jan and Lisa from Holland.' Charlie pointed to a bearded man at the bar who held up his beer glass, and they acknowledged each other. Pippa assumed this was Harris.

'Sorry, I didn't catch your name,' she said, turning to the group.

'Lisa van Diemen.' The woman held out her hand to Pippa as a welcome. 'Dit is my husband, Jan.'

Pippa smiled, although she thought Jan seemed frail as he held out a skinny hand. She wondered if Charlie had gathered all the waifs and strays on the island and put them together on one table. She sat down next to Lydia who appeared to be about the same age as her. The group rallied and encouraged her to sing along with the sea shanties. She remembered the songs from the local folk club back home.

Charlie James looked about fifty years of age, tall and slim. Pippa realised he was rather worse for wear from all the beer he was drinking. She was unsure about him and got the impression he needed to be in the limelight to show he was in control.

'Ignore Charlie,' whispered Lydia when the singing finished. 'He can be a bit of an idiot when he's had a few pints. He works with Sven Jørgensen, 'The Viking'—you know, the guy who runs the bird tours? Charlie's a volunteer with the Environmental Trust.'

Pippa smiled at Sven's nickname.

'Where do you live?' asked Lydia.

'I'm from Whitby, up north.'

'Oh right, I have an uncle near there. He lives close to Scarborough where he's got a farm. We used to go for holidays when we were kids.' Lydia gave a reminiscent smile.

The music started again and everyone joined in the chorus. Pippa found herself laughing, something she hadn't done in a very long time.

As the music played on, she sensed an atmosphere of belonging. It was certainly like Whitby, but much more enchanting, with its sandy beaches and palm trees blowing in the Atlantic breeze. *If Rob hadn't been so stubborn, he might have enjoyed this.* But no, under the circumstances … They both needed a chance to think about their future.

Looking out the window, she watched the melting sun between the two hills on the island of Samson and became aware of Sven on the quay with Don. Her eyes followed his every move as he stood, hands gesturing, passing the time with his friend. He waved at one of the boatmen as they headed out into the bay. Pippa stared, mouthing the words of the song.

'Come on, girl, sing up,' said Charlie, encouraging her to join in.

Lisa said 'I know some of these songs; they are wonderful. We really like de English folk music.' Pippa turned to her, smiled and joined in the singing again. '*Way haul away... we'll haul away Joe.*' By the time she looked again, Sven was gone.

'I have to dash now,' announced Lydia as she glanced at the time. 'I'm catching a boat back to Tresco. Don Trewin promised me a ride back before it gets too dark.' She stood up. 'Nice to meet you; hope to see you around town. Bye.'

The partying continued, but the night had beaten the day. Pippa needed to visit the ladies' room and met Lisa coming out of the adjacent cubicle.

'Are you going up Hugh Street?' asked Lisa. 'We could walk up together. I was meaning to ask, are you on your own here? Do you always spend de holidays by yourzelf?'

'Yes, I'm on my own, but it's a long story. Much too long to tell you all the way up Hugh Street. Anyway there's a lot to do here. I'll be fine.' Pippa smiled, trying not to say any more and Lisa seemed to understand. Smiling your way out of sadness could make it easier to cope. She mustn't get like Rob, always inside himself, never practising what he preached. Pippa walked on with Jan and Lisa by her side through the dimly-lit street as people left the pubs along the way. Lisa told her she lived near Utrecht and that her husband Jan was here for a rest after a serious operation to treat his cancer.

'It's the perfect place, don't you think?' Pippa asked her. 'I do hope Jan feels he can enjoy his holiday, despite his illness.'

Jan replied,'I wis I didn't have to go home next week, it's been wonderfol.'

Pippa slowed her pace, bidding farewell to Jan and Lisa. She switched on the light in the porch and closed the door.

Janice had told her Hugh Town was one of the safest places in the world. Everyone looked out for everyone else. By habit, Pippa locked the door from the inside. This house must have many happy memories, she thought. She walked across the echoing stone floor and filled a glass with water, then made her way upstairs to bed. What would tomorrow bring? She looked forward to seeing Sven again; it was important to get to know people. Anonymity was pleasant for a while, but not every day.

Lying awake, she had good feelings about everything and despite her memories of Rob and Daniel walking down Hugh Street, the whole place was even more charming than she'd found on her last visit. She looked forward to meeting interesting people, discovering more about the nature of Scilly and island life. It was an excellent opportunity to be the person she loved to be, independent and happy. The drink played its part in allowing her to drift away into the night.

CHAPTER FOUR

Joan Marshall's coffee was getting cold. She had been chatting on the phone to her mother for the last half hour. As she sat on the kitchen stool, she twisted her short mouse-brown hair around her fingers.

'Yes Mam, I'll ask him, but it's difficult; he's on the North Sea. He can't get into much trouble out there.'

'It's important, Joan. Jordan needs his father; you got to be straight with him, love. He can't be away all this time, surely?'

'Well he is, and him being away doesn't bother me all that much.' Joan knew she'd told a white lie. 'I mean, it's a job and he earns good money. Anyway, I never see you and Dad now you're in Devon. No big deal these days.' She thought about what she'd just said. It didn't really make sense but at least she knew what she meant. 'Plus Carole baby-sits for me, and Rob is repairing Terry's old Matchless bike. Pippa's gone away for three weeks, so now I'm relaxing.'

She peeked around the door into the lounge. Her two-year-old son, Jordan, sat watching a TV programme and singing along to 'Postman Pat'. He seemed happy to stare at the screen. Joan smiled as she watched him mouthing the words in his own way. Her mother was still talking on the other end of the phone and Joan hadn't really listened to a word she'd said.

'Mam, I got to go now, and please don't worry. Bye Mam.'

'Okay Joan, take care love, I'll call you soon and don't forget what I said. Dad sends his love. Bye.'

Joan raised her coffee cup and took a sip; it was lukewarm now. A pile of washing lay on the floor ready to go into the machine. If only Terry were here. The tap in the bathroom needed a new washer and the front door weatherboard kept sticking: the usual domestic irritations where a man's strength proved an asset to his wife. Only Rob had been there to help her with the odd emergency. Pippa asked him a few days before she left if he could help fix the showerhead in the bathroom. He was good like that, and Joan felt grateful for their friendship. *When is Terry coming home? Is this how it's always going to be?*

She hadn't realised when he got the job that having her husband away was going to mean months without him rather than weeks. Most oil rig workers were only away for about two or three weeks at a time. *But three months?* Something inside her felt wrong. Did he not want her anymore? She'd tried so hard to please him. Was this an excuse not to come home? She must stop thinking like that, but the last time he'd phoned was over a week ago. She missed him more than ever. Joan understood he was earning more money now, but even so, she wanted desperately for him to come back to her, to see Jordan and be a father again.

Now they were living on the edge of Whitby town, their lives had changed in the social sphere. She wasn't sure which was best, having the money or having Terry back. She felt lucky to have him and to be able to buy the things she could never afford when she lived on Henrietta Street. Thank goodness Pippa was still her friend. She'd kept asking when Terry would be home. Joan couldn't tell her exactly when. Why was Terry evading the issue with every phone call? She must think of a way to ask him so it wouldn't sound as if she didn't trust him. *Oh yes, and I mustn't forget to phone Rob. Maybe have a word with him about the bike before Tel gets back. How pointless having a motorbike that isn't being used.*

Rob and Pippa had always been in her life and when Daniel suffered his fatal accident, Joan had felt it like the loss of her own child. She'd looked after Daniel as a baby, to help Pippa attain her teaching qualifications. At the hospital she'd kept a constant vigil over her friend, waiting for her to recover consciousness on the day Daniel died. *After all this sadness, no wonder she needed a break.* Joan couldn't see herself without Jordan, sharing the same agony and pain suffered by Rob and Pippa.

She pulled herself out of her thoughts, wondering where life was going to take her next. She ought to phone Rob and ask about Pippa's trip to Cornwall.

She dialled Rob's number. 'Hi Rob, it's me. I thought I'd give you a ring. Did Pippa arrive okay?'

'Yes, there weren't any problems. Trouble is, I'm not sure if this holiday is going to make a difference.'

'Aw, Rob, don't say that. You'll have to be patient, love.'

'Don't you think I've been patient for long enough, Joan? It's my job to be patient. I'm in nursing, for God's sake, it's what I do; I look after depressed people! Sorry, Joan love, I didn't mean for that to sound so harsh, I'm worn out, that's all.'

Joan frowned and was glad Rob couldn't see her. She didn't relish change either. 'Yeah, I know. These things take a long time. You were both so young to lose someone in that way. I understand your grief; I was there too, remember? You know, you ought to try and understand, considering your job and all that. You really should talk with Pippa when she gets back.' She knew she was scolding him but she also knew Rob wouldn't take it the wrong way. She heard Rob sigh and changed the subject.

'Have you eaten? Can I do any shopping for you?'

'No, not really. I got food in the freezer and I opened a can of beans for breakfast and made some toast and a bacon sandwich. Will that do?'

Joan smiled. She'd imagined him on the other end of the phone looking annoyed at having to fend for himself for a change, but it seemed he was coping fine. 'What on earth are you both going to do with the rest of your lives, Rob? I mean, it's all so tragic.'

'I don't know.' Rob sighed. 'I ought to give us a chance to start again. I mean, we can't carry on like this—you know, the way things have gone.'

Joan was about to make a suggestion about marriage counselling; she hated to see her best friends falling apart. The four of them had been good mates for as long as she could remember. To lose Pippa and Rob right now would cause her much sorrow. Rob always seemed like such a great guy; things might have been fine except for the tragedy they had suffered. Rob spoke, interrupting her thoughts.

'Well, honestly, the house is a shrine to Daniel and we do nothing but argue. We either have to move house or move on without each other.'

'Oh, come on, Rob, don't be like that.' She hesitated for a moment. 'But you do love her, don't you?' She picked up her pen and began doodling a heart on a pad, waiting for him to say something.

'I don't know anything anymore. Look, I must go. I've got all kinds of things to sort out, but I need my sleep first, I'm absolutely knackered.'

Joan sensed his agitation. She wanted to talk about Terry, but Rob's mind seemed to be somewhere else.

'Okay, Rob, sorry to bother you when you're tired. But think about what I said, won't you? Don't do anything rash. See you soon, love, 'bye.' Reluctant to close the conversation, she sighed. He'd had a bad time and, like Terry, he could be evasive. Perhaps it was a man thing. For a moment, she felt helpless. Watching her best friends' marriage falling apart was like seeing another tragedy unfold while not being able to do a darned thing about it. Would Rob ever get back on track with Pippa? A two-year counselling course might have helped him understand his patients, but it certainly wasn't helping him in his personal life. He just seemed the 'wrong type' to be studying that kind of thing. She knew he was a good nurse, but a psychologist—no! She smiled to herself. Rob was fine, just a bit muddled and who could blame him? Over the last few years, his and Pippa's luck had run out.

Now she came to think about it, Pippa mentioned things weren't right when they'd met in town for coffee. She'd told Joan that Rob depressed her, that he was never there for her. Joan felt sorry for both of them, knowing that Rob must work for their lives to carry on. He'd tried to help Pippa through the stress and grief using his professional knowledge, but it was different with family members—almost impossible. They were all in this together. *Where are we all going in this life?* All she wanted was for Terry to come home, and for Rob and Pippa to settle down again.

The calendar on the wall made her to look back at the last time Terry was home. Thumbing through the months, she found his birthday and, coincidentally, the anniversary of when Dan passed away. She and Terry had gone out to the pub to celebrate, when a mate of Rob's gave them the dreadful news. Only later did they learn that the situation was far worse than they'd expected.

Only weeks before it had happened, they'd all spent Christmas together at Rob and Pippa's place. It had been fun, with the five of them taking a trip to the steam railway on the 'Santa Special' and scoffing mince pies on the train. Terry and Rob played football with Daniel after New Year. A few weeks later, Dan was gone. It had left a void in all their lives until Jordan was born.

Now Joan began to think about their future. *How will life be when we are all forty-five? Will we still have each other?* Somehow, she didn't think so. It was her birthday soon and being thirty-one wasn't something she relished.

She felt a tear in her eye. 'Come home, Terry, I miss you,' she whispered. 'I can't do this on my own anymore.'

By now, Pippa would be on Scilly. What was it about the islands that were so special to her? Was she running away from all the turmoil?

Joan remembered when Pippa used to plait her auburn hair; it was so long she could almost sit on it. And the nights when they all went to the church youth club to listen to records and play darts; the girls showing off as they did in those days. Pippa had been such a fun-loving person. An Irish mate of Rob's at the pub once described her as having 'great choild-bearin' hips'. Was it supposed to be a compliment? Joan was never quite sure. Pippa seemed a lot more attractive in the last few months, almost as if her grief made her stronger, even more determined. But there were the bad days as well, days when she didn't want to leave the house. Before Daniel, they'd all been good mates. Joan knew Terry from school, and everyone said how well-suited they were.

Joan rallied. She had to trust Terry; he was working away from home, nothing more. He was her husband and she'd always supported him in every way, but when he was home, something was off—different. For one thing, their sex life deteriorated since Jordan was born. Perhaps Terry had a complaint, some difficulty with 'getting it up'? She'd thought he'd be extra keen after all that time away. When he first came back, she'd made sure Jordan could stay at her sister's house. She'd bought new perfume, set the scene. Terry had fallen asleep in front of the TV. She'd wanted to tell Pippa she was disturbed by his behaviour but knowing Pippa, she would have said it was normal, laughed, and probably told Joan not to worry.

Joan knew precisely when she must have conceived with Jordan. She pretended it was fun; in truth, the whole affair seemed unexpected and quick, although Terry said he'd enjoyed being with her. She would have to speak with him and get him to find some help. She exhaled deeply. Next time he called home, she would have to be stronger with him.

Jordan was still watching his favourite TV programme. There was enough time to put in the last of the washing before 'Postman Pat' finished and she would take the youngster to the bathroom for a scrub.

CHAPTER FIVE

Terry Marshall arrived in Aberdeen after a helicopter ride over the North Sea. He yawned; how he hated mornings. The headache he'd woken up with still hung over him. With his boarding pass in his shirt pocket, he waited. Some narked Scots woman had served a foul-tasting cup of coffee and complained when he'd given her a twenty-pound note.

Sitting beneath the loudspeaker, the airport announcement startled him. *'Ladies and Gentlemen, due to a technical fault, flight 226 to Teesside will be delayed by thirty minutes. We apologise for the inconvenience.'*

Terry checked his watch. How much longer would he have to sit here? Recently he'd come to accept the way of things in his life: things that, if he couldn't change them, must be endured.

One hour after the first announcement, Terry boarded the plane and took his seat next to a woman reading *Anna Karenina*. He closed his eyes and didn't speak to anyone except for a curt 'no thanks' to the air stewardess who served the usual coffee and chocolate-chip cookie.

Upon arrival at Teesside airport, a hire car awaited him. He ran through the rain; by the time he put the key in the lock, his shirt was soaked.

After driving through the industrial dismay of Middlesbrough, he stopped at a pub for lunch. He put some money in the pub call box to tell his mother what time to expect him and waited.

His parents only ever answered the phone with 'Hello'.

'Hi, Dad, it's me.'

'Hello, I thought it might be you, how are you? It's your Dad.'

Terry smiled. His father always had the knack of stating the obvious. 'I can tell.' He smiled, knowing his father's hearing was not very good. 'I'm fine, Dad.'

'Where are you, son?'

'In Saltburn. I'll be back in less than an hour. Is Mam there?'

'No, she's with Carole,' replied his father. 'They've gone round to a jumble sale thing. Jordan's been sick for a couple of days.'

'Is he awright?' Terry knew he should have phoned Joan earlier, but he needed time to think. He had put off calling her.

'Well … yes, I suppose he is. I was with them yesterday for a short visit.'

'Dad, you didn't say anything to her, did you?'

'What about?'

'You know what I mean, Dad!'

'Listen, son, don't you think it's time you two had a talk?'

Terry wasn't listening. He knew he had to pluck up the courage to tell Joan what he'd done to her. All the bleak facts in his life began to scream at him like the unrelenting nightmares he'd had as a child. He'd wanted to tell her, but each time he'd phoned, he couldn't do it. He'd never admitted his shortcomings, not even to himself. When Daniel died, it became impossible to explain; they had all been so involved in Rob and Pippa's grief. *Always too much going on.*

'I'll talk to her later, but I'll see you around three o'clock, Dad. Okay? Bye.'

After leaving the pub, he crossed the road to the car, drove down 'The Bank', a local beauty spot overlooking the sea, and made his way along the coast toward Staithes and Runswick Bay.

He would go to his parents' first; they were closer than home.

How he would approach the subject, he had no idea. Each day, he had felt as if he was sinking into a void. He couldn't possibly tell his mother. Should he first come out with his confession to Joan or should he build up a story? He had no experience with these things. His chest felt tight when he thought about it. He'd pretended he was fine. Perhaps he was mentally ill. Was it possible to be out of your mind and not realise it? He couldn't hold back with her anymore; it wasn't working—couldn't work.

He was almost in Whitby; as he drove along the sea front at Sandsend and up the hill toward the golf club, he switched the windscreen wipers to intermittent wipe.

The road was nearly dry as he turned the corner into Endeavour Crescent and saw his mother working in the garden. As he stopped the car, she stood and came to meet him, her arms held out.

'Terry, pet, how are you? Did you have a good journey?'

She embraced him and he loved her for it. Hugging his mother felt good, especially after being away for so long. He knew how much she cared, and right now, he needed her. 'Yeah, Ma, I'm fine.'

His father came into the hall. 'Ah, you made it, son! Well done, great to see you.' He patted Terry on the back as he used to when he'd been a good boy in school.

Terry smiled and almost cursed to himself; nothing much had changed.

'Let me make you a cuppa tea, love,' said his mother, fussing over him as usual.

'Thanks ma.'

'I'll have one too, Phyllis love.'

Terry poked his head through the lounge door. The furniture stood in the same place as it had been for the last twenty years, and he sensed his mother's home cooking as he sat down on the sofa.

He waited for his father to say something. There was a silence between them, neither wanting to be the first to speak.

Terry looked around the room. 'Nice to be back but ...' He leaned forward, lowering his voice to a whisper. 'Before you ask, yes, I am going to talk with Joan. You haven't said anything to Mam, have you?'

'Course not, but for God's sake, son, stop telling me about it. It's Joan you have to tell.'

'I will, Dad, but it isn't something you can just blurt out, is it? I have to work out what to say to her.'

'Terry!' His father looked him straight in the eyes and wagged a finger at him in an old-fashioned way. 'Just tell her! For God's sake, you're being unfair to Jordan as well. There's nothing to stop you from continuing your life as a family, is there?'

'I don't know, Dad. I can't exactly see her being pleased about it—hush, here's Mam.' He sat up straight, pretending everything was fine.

Phyllis entered the lounge with a tea tray, bearing her best Royal Albert cups and plates. Dark chocolate gleamed on the neatly arranged biscuits. It was a time for celebration; her son was back. She seemed to notice that the conversation between Terry and his father had stopped abruptly. 'Talking about me again, eh?' she said mockingly.

Terry realised he would never be able to explain things to her. He watched his mother pour the tea. *She must never know.*

After a while, his father excused himself to finish the model aeroplane for Jordan. Terry had the feeling his father had left the room with some impatience—or was it a good excuse to leave? He wasn't sure.

Phyllis sat with a cup on her lap. She asked the usual questions. 'How was the journey? How was work?' She settled back in her chair and the 'questions' Terry had been dreading began to pour out.

'Why has it taken you so long to come home this time? Little Jordan has been waiting for his daddy. He used to talk about you a lot until the last few weeks or so. Joan keeps a picture of you on the table so he can see you. Children his age can easily begin to forget who you are. What's going on? Why didn't you go home first?'

Terry felt cornered and the only thing he could do was lie. 'It's work, Ma. Joan understands, honest. Anyway, I'm going round there soon, but I thought I'd call in here first since it's en-route.' He was glad he could steer the conversation elsewhere. *Not now, Ma, leave it.*

'You look rather tired, pet. Why don't you go and have a nap first? I just remembered, Joan's gone to the nursery-school fête this afternoon, so you have some time before she gets back. I think she's going into town with Carole, afterwards.'

Terry's relief showed. The gap gave him the time he needed. 'Yeah, good idea, I'm knackered.'

'Do you want me to phone Joan for you later, tell her you've arrived?'

'No! I mean, no, don't do that, erm … I want to surprise her.'

'Oh, okay, I'm sure she'll be thrilled.'

Terry didn't want to hear those words; he knew 'thrilled' was the last thing Joan would be. How would he begin to explain his extended absence?

He went upstairs and lay on his old childhood bed. Despite his tiredness, it took him a further hour to fall asleep.

By the time his mother woke him, it was almost five o'clock. 'Are you going to see Joan, Terry? I didn't want to disturb you; I know what a long journey you had today.'

'Oh er, yes … erm … what time is it?' For a moment, he was back on the rig with the North Sea swell knocking underneath. He checked his watch. 'Bloody hell, I'd better go home.'

'Good lad,' said Phyllis as she went back downstairs. It seemed she'd forgotten how much of an adult he was these days.

He made his way to the bathroom to splash cold water on his eyes, and dried his face before going to the phone in the hall.

Oh, God, this is it. Remember what Frank told me on the rig. 'Approach it step by step, tell her how much you care about her and how it was at the time, then tell her how it is now. No lies.' No, he wouldn't say anything now with his mother lurking around, he would go home—but first, he wanted to be sure Joan was there.

He picked up the receiver and dialled, then put it down again. He sat for a few minutes longer before he tried for a second time. He listened to the *burr burr* of the ring tone but Joan didn't answer. *Where could she be at this time?*

Perhaps he should phone Rob, go to the pub with him until she got back. He was sure Pippa wouldn't mind. And Rob was a nurse; he would understand. Approach the subject in small steps, perhaps get Rob's help to explain it all. After all, he was learning about counselling. His best friend would be the perfect confidence booster. Right now, what he needed was a conversation with his mate. He would try phoning Joan again in an hour and started planning his opening words.

CHAPTER SIX

An ambulance stood on the side of the road in Hugh Town; multitudes of faceless people called her name.

'It's your fault the dog's in so much pain!' Pippa shouted.

Rob, or someone whose face she couldn't quite see, lay dead on the pavement at her feet. The ambulance crew placed an oxygen mask over her face, stifling her breathing. They were taking the animal to the beach to be buried at sea and it was still alive. Pippa shouted, 'Give me the dog, she's not dead!' She called out into the room and, with ghastly clarity, woke herself up from the nightmare. Fighting for breath, shocked, she gagged at the non-existent oxygen mask, unable to focus. So the nightmares were back! Cursing to herself, she stretched her eyelids with her fingers. *Where am I? What day is it?—Ah yes, Saturday.* The window was open; she dragged herself out of bed and gazed into the yard below. Perhaps one day there would be lovely dreams, but as long as there was still trauma in her head, the nightmares would never go away. She'd forgotten how to dream; her inner self screamed as she squeezed her eyelids together. *It must have been the alcohol.* She had a headache and reached into the drawer for the paracetamol.

With a need to get in a better mood for the trip to St. Martin's, Pippa took a shower and washed her nightmare down the drain. She had to hurry not to be late. The water streamed over her face and she closed her eyes to avoid the shampoo's stinging effects. The reassuring warm spray cascaded down her back. She turned off the tap.

Within minutes, she dried her hair, put cream on her face, and rushed around the room to find suitable clothes. The new shorts and strappy top she had bought in Whitby seemed a good choice. The folding backpack Janice had left for the visitors hung on a peg; she grabbed it to carry a bottle of orange juice and a light raincoat. Remembering what Sven had told her yesterday about the binoculars, she placed them around her neck, rather than in the bag.

On the way down to the harbour, everyone seemed to be walking in the same direction. She picked up her pace; the boat was due to leave in ten minutes. With her hair still damp and her swinging binoculars, she hoped she didn't look as bad as she felt, and that the small pimple on her face had faded.

Sven was already at the boat helping passengers to board. Pippa watched him for a moment. He was always smiling. She saw how relaxed he seemed, joking with everyone as they stepped across the boats, reminding them to take it easy.

Pippa stepped down to the boat and Sven greeted her as he helped her on board. 'Hi there,' he said warmly, taking her hand. 'Steady now, don't fall in, will you?'

Pippa grinned and found a seat at the front as Sven picked up the microphone in the wheelhouse and tapped it to ensure it worked.

'Good morning everyone. Welcome on board the *Lily of Laguna*. My name is Sven and I hope you all brought your seasick pills; I don't want a mess in Don's boat *again* this week.' He chuckled. 'If anyone is sick, I get the sack!'

Pippa smiled; he was quite a character for sure.

'How many people have we got this morning?' Sven counted the heads moving from the back of the boat towards the front, and, catching Pippa's eye, 'fifty-four, fifty-five, fifty-six … Glad you could make it,' he said to her above the noise of the diesel engine. Turning to the passengers, he continued, 'fifty-seven, fifty-eight, fifty-nine …' He looked at Don and put up his thumb; the boat was full. They were ready to leave.

He picked up the microphone again. 'Now today, folks, we are going to St. Martin's. It's a very beautiful island and those of you who have the wildlife tour tickets, please wait for me when we get there. We will land at Lower Town because of the tide. Later, we'll gather at the other side of the island at Higher Town Quay for the return journey. I will guide you through the birdlife and the footpaths, and tell you a little of the history of St. Martin's, so enjoy yourselves. It's a lovely day and the weather forecast is excellent. Thanks, everyone.' He put the microphone back on the hook and Don reversed from the pier.

Pippa looked up and smiled as Sven stood beside her. She felt her sense of belonging to the islands again, just as she'd felt earlier on the ship. Why did she feel that way?

'Did you sleep well at Janice's?' Sven asked.

'Not too bad—I had a bit of a nightmare. I think it may have been the rum. I was persuaded to join a party at the pub last night—which isn't like me. I don't usually drink much, let alone go into pubs on my own.'

'You weren't at Harris' birthday party, were you?' Sven raised his eyebrows and smiled.

'Well, I think I was. Some guy called Charlie James invited me.'

Sven laughed. 'Trust Charlie, he has an eye for the ladies. He's one of our volunteers; he takes charge of the nature reserve team when I'm not around. So, are you all right? I'm not going to get the sack, am I?'

'God, no!' Pippa made a face of revulsion and Sven laughed again.

A moment of shyness made her turn outboard and put her hand into the water. She gazed at the fronds of bronze kelp swaying on the surface and closed her eyes for a moment in the bright sunlight. As the boat left the harbour, she listened to the sound of the water lapping against its side and the gentle chugging of the engine.

The boat sailed into Crow Sound, and Sven glanced at Pippa, catching her eye. 'I'm sure I can help you learn a lot today. You know, you remind me of when I started to learn about birds. I used to watch the geese outside of my grandmother's home near Trondheim. She realised I was interested and bought me my first field guide.'

Pippa smiled. His personality and good looks seemed to shine in the morning sun, and she loved his accent.

'I learned most of the Latin names by the time I was sixteen and then went on to study at university. You see, you have to start at the very beginning and not feel awkward about it. Just go for it and become your own expert.'

'Yes, you're right, I guess, but I don't think I'll ever be an expert.'

Sven paused for a moment, looking back at Don in the wheelhouse. 'Well, this could be your lucky day,' he said with a grin. 'Anyway, I'm expecting my colleague back soon, and then I can get on with my real job, managing the nature reserve and the bird records for Scilly. I enjoy doing the tours, but I also enjoy going into the schools and doing some hands-on work on the reserve. It's more my kind of thing, I suppose.'

Pippa nodded; she knew what he meant. Her time teaching at nursery school had provided her with the job satisfaction she needed when Daniel was growing up. She'd taken a two-year course including training with special-needs children for her childcare qualification. She had loved it and hoped one day she might have the confidence to go back to work.

As the boat crossed to St. Martin's, Pippa looked up at Sven from her seat, and the two of them exchanged the occasional glance and smile. There was something very worldly and experienced about him; with his binoculars around his neck and his keen eye scanning the ocean for birds, he seemed to lead in everything he did.

'Puffins on your left, everyone, razorbill.' He pointed ahead. 'Look, there's a shag.' But the bird had disappeared under the water before he could finish speaking.

The passengers held up their binoculars, looking as if they were at a tennis match where everyone watched the ball, heads turning in the same direction. Pippa thought most of the people on the boat must be experienced 'birders' as they carried such expensive optical gear. Her 'bins' were old and needed careful adjustment. She didn't feel comfortable, but Sven encouraged her. He seemed kind and helpful—something she needed right now. She listened to him all the way; he seemed very knowledgeable and fascinating.

She took delight in everything around her and wondered how it might have been if she hadn't met Joan, Terry and Rob. What if her life had turned right instead of left? What if she'd met someone like Sven? *Bloody hell!* Such a fantasy would get her into trouble one day, she was sure. Too late, she had chosen this path and it had been a disaster. *Stop it.* She pushed her mind back to reality—they weren't too far from landing on St. Martin's.

A seal popped its dog-like head out of the water, looking quite endearing. 'Grey seal on the right!' Sven announced.

Heads turned and Pippa joined in. The seal was closer now and she saw the black speckles on its skin and its dark, loving eyes, nostrils pulsating with each breath as it kept disappearing under the water and re-appearing in a different place.

'Great, eh?' Sven remarked. 'They're so friendly when we go diving. How anyone can hurt them, I'll never understand. Sometimes I have to give them a gentle tap on the nose to stop them from being too close—they do tend to nip if I don't watch out. There's one … she adores me,' he chuckled. 'I call her Sasha. She seems to know me underwater, but when I approach her on land, she won't come near me.'

Pippa smiled to herself. *Gosh, he's a diver as well—is there anything this guy can't do?* She realised how much she had to learn and hoped she had enough time to fit it all into her schedule. She sucked in her breath sharply. *Oh heck, I forgot my suntan lotion, how stupid of me.* At least her headache had subsided, thank goodness. Since Daniel, she had developed a habit of forgetting things.

Sometimes, it had been impossible to change her thoughts about her son, always feeling she had to show how much she had loved him. If she stayed as she was, she would never recover and it scared her. She was too young to … *Stop thinking about it!*

Sven interrupted her thoughts. 'I'm glad you decided to come. I have loads to show you. The boat is fine now; it just needed a little engine overhaul. It was nothing serious, but we have to make sure.' He squinted as the boat changed direction into the sun. His blonde hair had turned wavy in the salt air. 'It isn't easy to get spare parts; we have to order them and sometimes it can be days, even weeks, so we have to compromise now and again, find alternatives.' He turned to Don in the wheelhouse. 'Okay, mate?'

Don nodded, the noise of the engine drowning his words.

Pippa reached in her pocket and found her green hair band. Sven watched her tie back her hair, sun rays highlighting her auburn strands. 'Ya,' he said, 'it can be windy once we get out of the lee of St Mary's.' He lifted up his binoculars to watch a shag on a rock in the distance. Don steered with one hand on the wheel, spray flew across the bow and some of the passengers held on to their hats.

The smell of diesel reached Pippa's nose and she turned her face to fresher air.

The boat, now in the lee of St. Martin's, rocked gently toward the island and the Eastern Isles. With the blue sky, lapping waves, and a very helpful guide, what more could she want?

Arriving at the quay, Sven threw a rope out to someone waiting on the edge of the pier. He tied up the boat and the passengers disembarked. Sven counted fifteen in his group of birders. They walked up the path and stopped on the higher ground. He explained the archaeology and the rise in sea levels. 'If you all come along to the slide show tomorrow night, I'll be able to show you more.'

As Pippa stepped from the boat, there was less wind. She loosened her hair again as they walked up the main path toward Higher Town.

'The sea air can make you burn very quickly,' Sven told her, 'so be careful, especially with your fair skin. Have you got sun cream?'

'Actually, I forgot it, I came out in a hurry this morning,' Pippa replied, annoyed with herself for leaving it behind on the kitchen table.

Sven opened his rucksack and pulled out a bottle of factor 30 sun cream.

'Oh, thanks very much, I should have thought about it.'

He opened the lid and tipped up the bottle. The cream spilled onto her fingers and she smoothed it over her face and arms. She was already turning red from sitting in the boat.

'Here, let me put some cream on the back of your neck—and you'll need it on your shoulders as well. You missed that bit there, do you mind?' He pointed to the spot.

Pippa turned to face him and their eyes met. 'I bet you offer this service to all the ladies,' she teased.

He laughed along with her. 'Oh! I wish. I always carry lots of sun cream with me. There's usually someone who needs it—best to be safe than sorry, and I have to take care as well.' He was already tipping out the cream onto his palm. He put the lid on the bottle holding it between his teeth, and screwing the bottle to the top. He gestured a circular movement with his index finger.

'Turn around,' he said. 'I'll do it for you.'

She could hardly refuse. She knew they would have to catch up with the rest of the group quite soon. Sven had offered to meet them at the top of the path.

'Thank you for being so considerate!'

With his fingers tips, he massaged the cream into her nape. If the circumstances had been right, she would have let out a satisfying 'Ahh', but opted to remain quiet and tried to keep her lips together to avoid a giggle. *My God, what would Rob say?*

'Ok … done! That should help a lot.' Sven gently patted her shoulder.

'Thanks Sven, that's kind of you,' she said politely, not daring to say anything else. She picked up her rucksack and walked on to catch up with the group.

'Hang on, wait for me,' Sven called as he wiped the cream from his fingers. He quickened his step along the narrow concrete path. 'You know … where I come from, in Norway, you have to wear lots of cream, otherwise your whole face and lips crack in the sun. I have a friend back home who was eating his breakfast and his own blood at the same time—delightful, eh?'

Pippa grimaced. 'Ergh! I don't intend to get *that* sunburned. I'll be careful, I promise.'

They walked on up the track, side by side, taking in the sea views with the warm breeze now blowing gently from the southwest. Pippa sensed Sven's eagerness to continue with the guided tour as they joined the group. Some people were already sitting on a large rock at the top of the hill, looking through their binoculars.

'Sorry about that, folks. Pippa here needed sun cream. Does anyone else want some?'

'Yes please, Sven, thanks. I forgot mine too, do you mind?' A woman wearing a blue top and denim shorts came forward. Sven handed her the bottle. This time Sven didn't offer to help and Pippa felt quite privileged. No one had paid her that kind of attention in a very long time; it was an odd feeling. She remembered the people on Scilly were very open and friendly. She accepted Sven's attention as natural; perhaps his Norwegian ways were a lot more approachable than she was used to. He was just a happy-go-lucky kind of guy, living the good life. *Lucky him.*

Sven walked silently for a while, lost in his own thoughts. He felt curious about Pippa; she had ignited his imagination. He admitted to himself he liked her, but she was just another tourist on holiday, here today—gone tomorrow. What chance did he have? Soon, she would leave. What was the point in pursuing a relationship under the circumstances? Anyway, she was married—but still, there was something odd about her situation. Perhaps it wouldn't be too imposing to try to find out. He realised he had become just as nosey as some of the residents of Scilly. Living on an island was great for many reasons, but not for long-term romance. Two-week partnerships were not on his agenda. He wanted something stronger and more meaningful. He would be thirty-something soon and without a girlfriend, people might think he was shy or even gay … *that's stupid but …* He hadn't fancied anyone since Astrid back home in Norway. Oh yes, there had been plenty of opportunities, but it seemed they were all after his good looks. He hated that. He wanted a girlfriend who could get to know the real Sven, instead of him being the so-called 'icon of the islands'. He had talked constantly about birds during that coffee break; maybe he should have asked more questions about her instead. There seemed to be sadness in her expression and she was so eager to learn. He would ask her, but not at this moment—he was working. Spending too much time with one person wasn't professional.

He stopped along the path and turned to his birders.

'The main industry of this island is fishing for lobster and crabs, but it's the fine beaches that attract visitors and birdlife.'

'Is this Tormentil?' a woman asked, pointing to a small yellow flower.

'Yes, well done, and the little pink flower over there is sea mallow. Most of you will have seen it all over the islands. It's well known that you could put all the inhabitants of Scilly on those beaches and still have room to spare. If you wanted to take off all your clothes on some of the islands, no one would see you.' The group laughed and he continued. 'Except … the residents of St Mary's … they all get out their binoculars every afternoon!' He had wanted to say those words for quite some time, especially considering his next-door neighbour, Nanette Bell. She had her nose pressed to the window every time he left the house.

'As we look out on to Chapel Down, we can see the Daymark, a navigation aid to shipping, erected in 1683 by Thomas Ekins, first steward of the Godolphin family to live on the islands.' He turned around and pointed toward the higher ground. 'If you would like to look through your binoculars, everyone, I can see a male stonechat sitting over there on the fence.' He erected his telescope and encouraged the group to look through it one by one. Pippa was amazed; she had never seen a stonechat before. Its black head and orange-pink breast were striking and very clear through the professional equipment.

'You know, folks,' said Sven, 'these islands are so fragile, everything we do here has to be carefully monitored, far more so than on the mainland. In the summer, we have to conserve water and if we get bad weather in the winter, we lose some of the less hardy plants to the wind and rain. We often have to lay down a few more rules and regulations to ensure the islands remain protected. Should there be a disaster like the Torrey Canyon, which almost ruined everything, it would take dozens of years to repair the damage. Life on these islands is not the same as living on the mainland. Scilly is a very fragile place to live; we are constantly made aware of it.'

Sven suggested that Pippa make a bird list during her stay on the islands. 'You never know, one day you can look back on your list and see if these birds are still nesting and visiting us here. If they aren't, we might be in trouble. These islands are unique; there's probably nothing quite like them. There is such a rich treasure of archaeology and wildlife here. We have to spend every moment conserving nature. We depend on our visitors to help us and this is one of the reasons I do the tours.'

'I'll buy a notebook in town later,' Pippa said with enthusiasm.

'Now everyone,' said Sven, 'look through here.'

He focussed the telescope and each birder took a turn.

'Ah, yes, it's a linnet. Great, eh?' said a man in the group.

'They're so pink on the breast, aren't they?' Sven agreed. 'You can usually tell linnets by their undulating flight and they have a variety of calls—listen!'

He paused to let everyone hear the 'djit djit' of the linnet.

'The song is almost like "linnet linnet". Okay, now let's move on down the shoreline. Oh look, folks, a rock pipit as well.'

Looking toward the shore, Pippa spied shags floating by, heads turned to the sky, making them look like haughty passengers on a raft.

Sven watched her. Helping her in her quest to become a birdwatcher was somewhat satisfying. He remembered when he was learning about birds and how inadequate he'd felt compared to the local experts in the bird club back in Norway. He knew how Pippa must feel.

Having spent the whole morning with his group, Sven stopped for lunch at the café in Higher Town. 'May I join you? he asked Pippa, thinking she looked distant sitting on her own. Perhaps now was his chance to talk with her.

'Yes, fine,' she nodded with a smile.

He set his plate on the table, then took a bite of a cheese and pickle sandwich. Pippa waited for him to finish munching, anticipating his next sentence.

'So, you said you're from Whitby, eh? I've never been, but from what you told me yesterday, it sounds beautiful.' He wanted to ask her what her connection with the islands was. What was she doing here alone on holiday? Instead, he said, 'When we get back, I've got to set up the slide show. Would you like to come early and help? I mean, if you're on holiday, I don't want you to be working, of course—but I thought, seeing as you're by yourself, you might like to come and be part of the scene.' He felt that this was maybe an imposition, but he sensed her sadness and he was anxious not to lose sight of her. After all, he was only being curious.

'I would love to help! Thanks for including me. It's not often I get the chance these days to be involved in something like this.'

It was as if Sven knew her well. She wanted to get in with the right kind of people: the real birdwatchers and the ornithologists. She would show Rob that birdwatching wasn't just for old men in wax jackets and woolly hats. Here she could learn more, and show him what Sven had taught her. It might also make Rob see she was trying harder to regain her confidence.

By the time Pippa got back to St Mary's, she already had a bird list of twenty species. It had been thrilling and a great morning for birdwatching. Above all, she liked the scarlet pimpernel and sea holly, and the different kinds of bees. For sure she would never see bees as one species any more.

When they arrived at St Mary's, she was the last to leave the boat. 'Here,' said Sven. 'Give me your hand, Pippa, and I'll help you across.'

It wasn't necessary; she was in control, but she took his hand anyway, in case by some misfortune she slipped and felt stupid. As the boat rocked and with his hands full, Sven muttered through clenched teeth with a pen in his mouth. Pippa laughed. He was obviously used to multi-tasking. 'Thanks, Sven, it's been great,' she said as she stood on the damp granite steps.

Taking the pen from his lips, he wrote the time of the slideshow on the back of her hand. 'In case you forget,' he said.

'Oh, I won't forget,' said Pippa as she walked up the steps. 'See you later then. Bye!'

It was as if her heavy heart lifted her back to normality—that chilled-out feeling. Sven was right; you could be sitting on a beach having cast off all your cares, getting to experience a treasured freedom. When was the last time she had felt this way?

Walking into Hugh Town, she thought about the morning on St. Martin's. It felt great that Sven had wanted to know her and that he offered his support. She smiled to herself; she had *almost* flirted with him and hoped he hadn't taken it the wrong way. *But it was just a bit of harmless fun. He's cute and he cares.* If only Rob was like that. He was all or nothing, and what had happened to caring? He was just as wrapped up inside of himself as she had been. Sven seemed, well … so different. Perhaps when she got home, Rob might have missed her and things would change. That was her reason for coming away, wasn't it? She only wanted to be strong … that was all.

It was mid-afternoon, and after a cup of tea at the bakery, she decided to walk to Star Castle and take a stroll around The Garrison. The last time she was there, she discovered a wonderful viewpoint and wanted to go back and see it again. Halfway up the hill, she saw Jan and Lisa sitting on a bench. With each step closer to the couple, Pippa noticed how Jan's bones seemed to float under his skin. It was sad to see him this way; in the sun she could see he was obviously very ill. Whatever Lisa must be feeling, she felt with her. *How brave to come all this way.*

'Good afternoon, you two. Enjoying the sun?'

Lisa smiled. 'Hello Pippa, nice to see you again.'

She stopped for a few minutes to tell them about her trip.

Jan raised a smile. 'Ja, you should make the most of the day while you can.'

'I know, it's beautiful, isn't it?' Pippa glanced at Lisa. Perhaps they should all make the most of what they had, she thought.

'You're right, we should enjoy every moment.' Pippa was about to say, 'as if it were your last,' but realised the last part of her comment wasn't appropriate and felt silly for a moment. Instead, she said, 'Have a great time; I'll see you both later.'

As she bid them farewell, she appreciated her luck at not having experienced such physical suffering as Jan. Her mental torture had often caused her to think she should end her life. Thinking about Sven, his job as a wildlife tour guide and the people of the islands, made her realise how worthwhile it was to carry on living. No wonder Jan had come here to recuperate; he might not be around for many more months. At least she wasn't ill; it was the 'forever grief'. Just a few days without it would help.

She found the seat where she had once sat with Daniel. A warm breeze blew across The Garrison, and she rested her back against a plaque of remembrance to someone "who loved these islands". It was comforting to think that years earlier, they had also sat here. Over her shoulder, she looked up at the stark greyness of Star Castle and the flag flying on the top. *There must be many 'ghosts' on The Garrison, with all that history.*

The breathtaking view provided solace, with most of the islands spread out like fingers into the Atlantic Ocean. The blueness of the lagoon shimmered in the sun, and the shapes of the rocks and the small coloured boats made this the perfect spot to sit. The smell of camomile drifted across the path bringing more memories. The last time she sat here was when Daniel had gone to play football with Rob; she'd brought her pencils and was sketching the view. She'd almost forgotten how to do all that. It would be good to try again.

Two yachts sailed in opposite directions: one to St Agnes and the other into St Mary's. Pippa sighed. *Are Rob and I like that, always pulling away from each other?* Behind her, two young men pounded the path as they jogged along; she felt their footfalls through the seat, and their voices became louder; she heard every word.

'Well, yes, because I thought I'd studied big-time and didn't think I'd done too badly.'

'Mm, you know what? I think…'

Their voices faded, the breeze blowing the conversation away.

Pippa sat alone. The overwhelming view, the vivid colours of the ocean and her grief caused her to cry. The grass grew tall over the seat and she felt hidden by the wildflowers. She sucked in her breath with a sob, hoping not to make a fool of herself, but hey! It wasn't silly to feel this way. The scent of the camomile and fennel produced a conflict between euphoria and sadness. The stunning view all but stopped her breath.

Something made her turn around: she saw a figure coming up the path, a child with blonde hair and a small football under his arm. The image of the child came closer. 'Oh my God, no … Dan!' she whispered. He was smiling back at her. She put her hands against her chest. *He looks just like Dan!*

The child kept moving toward her; he was waving and a tear dropped down her face as she thought she saw her son smiling back at her. It couldn't be.

Her eyes turned toward the ocean, the colours and the light. Was it really her imagination? Was Dan trying to tell her something? She dared not look again.

Further down the path, the child's mother appeared, breathless from running after him. Pippa turned again and watched as the woman caught up with the boy and took his hand. 'Keep hold of his hand,' she whispered to herself. *'Keep hold.'* Mother and son walked back the way they'd come and were soon out of sight. Pippa allowed her tears to flow without guilt. Her grief spilled beyond the distant islands, into the Atlantic Ocean. She sobbed her heart into the sea and never wanted to leave this place. Now that Dan was gone, it seemed futile to go home, knowing she had lost her way with Rob. What should she do? She wished she could stay here forever, but being realistic, she knew she'd have to go home at the end of the holiday. Henrietta Street had been her life, she couldn't just leave it all behind.

She would never find herself through guilty eyes; moving on was the only option. She paused in her thought, took out a handkerchief and blew her nose; someone was coming up the path again.

It had been her mission to find a way to survive. Her sobbing stopped and very quickly something transformed her fragile state of mind; it was like a balloon bursting, struck by a pin. *Bang!* The moment was over as quickly as it arrived. The balloon deflated. She took a deep breath and began to feel something had changed. The tears stopped and, like the blown seeds of a distant dandelion, it felt as if all her cares had floated away. She would return to this spot again soon; it was also to be *her* special place to sit as it had been for the person who donated the seat. She understood their passion.

With tears on her face, she stood to walk down the hill. Like the day when she changed the room at home, today she felt proud of herself for getting this far. Rob shouldn't have scolded her; all she wanted was a nice conversation with him on the phone, a kind word here and there. Today Sven had been there to listen to her. He was good and honest, and she gave herself a mental pat on the back for her progress, thankful for his support. At home, no one seemed to understand about conserving nature. These days, life was taken too much for granted. Perhaps the next time she went to the bank, she would put a contribution in the Environmental Trust collection box. Here you had to protect your lifestyle; especially when it stood hand in hand with nature.

Back home, nobody wanted to listen to a birdwatching woman. Only her doctor had taken her seriously. When she got home, maybe she would go and see him again, and ask if he knew of a local club she could join. It was his hobby too. These were all good and positive ideas, and she made up her mind that she would take things one day at a time.

Upon reaching the town, Pippa put on her sunglasses and hoped no one would notice her swollen eyes. It had been a beautiful, yet overwhelming day and there was still more to come.

CHAPTER SEVEN

The phone rang. Rob picked it up.

'Hi, Rob, it's me—Terry.'

'Oh, hi, Tel. Where the heck are you?' Rob wanted to ask another obvious question, but refrained. Perhaps he should wait and give Terry a chance to explain.

'At mam and dad's.'

'Oh, I see, you're in Whitby, eh?'

'Fancy a drink?' Terry asked. 'I phoned Joan, but she's not at home.'

'Yes, I know,' Rob said. 'She's round at Carole's, I think. She phoned up earlier asking my advice about Jordan's cough.' *Shouldn't he know where she is and not me?*

'Oh, okay. I only got home this afternoon. Can we talk?'

'As long as it's nothing too heavy. I've been dealing with patients and their problems all day and I'm on my own here.'

'Why? Where's Pippa?'

Rob explained how she had gone to Cornwall.

'Cornwall? Bloody hell! What's she doing there?'

'To use her words, she's gone for some "respite". If you like, I'll meet you at the Duke of York for a drink, within the hour.'

'Okay, see ya then.' Rob replaced the receiver.

Rob looked up from his beer as Terry walked into the pub. He noticed his friend had grown a moustache and seemed a bit weather-beaten since he had seen him last.

'Hi, Tel, mate. Great to see you. What can I get you?' He patted Terry on the back.

'Pint of Theakstons, thanks.'

They stood together at the bar for a moment before finding their usual seat near the window overlooking the harbour. It was as if Terry had never been away. Rob told him more about Pippa's sudden decision to go to the Isles of Scilly, and her departure a few days before by train.

'Really?' Terry said. 'I know how much she loved it down there, but I didn't think she would go without *you*.'

'It's a long story … anyway, I fixed the brakes on that old Matchless of yours and I managed to find a guy who deals in headlights. Don't leave it in the damp, Tel. I put a cover on it for you last week.'

'Yeah, thanks.'

Rob was still recovering from his discovery that the 'shrine' was gone and he didn't want to talk about Terry's problems. 'Didn't Joan want to come down here for a drink?' he asked.

'No, er … I'll pop round home after this,' Terry said. 'I only got back this afternoon and I was so tired. I slept at mam and dad's for a couple of hours.'

Rob couldn't believe he hadn't been to see Joan yet. He discovered he didn't know what to say to Terry; it had been too long. Turning up like that, he hadn't had time to prepare his man-chat. He felt awkward and thought Terry felt it too.

'I wanted to ask you something, Rob.' Terry fiddled with his glass, turning it in his hands. 'How has she been doing without me?'

'What d'ye mean "without you"? It sounds a bit final, doesn't it, Tel?'

'I know what you're thinking,' Terry said. 'It hasn't been easy for me either, you know.'

'So what's wrong? Why haven't you been home these last months? I didn't think working on a rig took you away that long?'

Terry sat holding his beer. Slow supping appeared to give him time to think about his answer. 'There's something wrong with me,' he said, looking awkward, 'and I thought you being a nurse, you might understand. I've been getting some advice from someone at work.'

'You ill, Tel?' Rob said.

'I don't know. I got these strange thoughts.'

'What kind of strange thoughts?' Rob began his counselling, thinking he meant schizophrenia.

'Look, this isn't the place to discuss it, can we go round to your house after this, Rob, seeing Pippa isn't there? Would you mind?'

'Sure, if that's what you want, but remember I'm a nurse and not a doctor.'

Rob supped the last of his beer and put the glass on the bar. They walked along the narrow street away from the bustle of tourists and as they reached the house, Rob opened the front door.

'Sit down, Tel.' Rob pulled up a chair and faced Terry. 'I'll make us a drink in a minute. So mate, what's up? You look tired.'

'Well, it's like this, see. I can't… you know, do it… Well, I can, but not with Joan.'

'You mean you're impotent?' Rob tried not to counsel his friend.

'Nooo, not that.' Terry seemed to find it hard to say the words, as if he needed Rob to say them for him.

'Then what?' Rob looked baffled. He had been trained to remain calm and allow his patient to do the talking.

Terry looked down at his feet, then his hands, and then the button on his jacket and still, he didn't speak. There was more silence. He breathed heavily and sighed while staring out the window.

Rob waited a few more seconds and was about to say something when Terry blurted out 'I'm not the man you think I am.'

'What do you mean, Tel? Are you trying to tell me you think you're—you're … homosexual?' asked Rob, thinking he didn't possibly have it right.

Terry looked shocked that Rob had come straight to the point. 'Well, yes … erm, oh God, this is so hard.'

Rob's stomach felt as if it was sinking. He'd dealt with this before with his patients but Terry … He tried not to show his feelings. How was he going to deal with this smack in the mouth? *Mustn't judge, stay professional—shit, what do I say?* '

'Are you sure?'

'I got this mate on the rigs, Frank, well, we kind of … did stuff, if you know what I mean.'

'Bloody hell, Tel, how long has this been going on?' Rob found it hard to stay calm. Joan didn't deserve this.

Turning back to Rob, Terry began to tell his story. He kept taking a deep breath with every sentence, almost sobbing.

'I hadn't realised, you see … even when Joan and I got married. I thought I had just gone off her, you know, stopped fancying her.'

There was more silence. Rob waited but all he could hear was Terry's tired breathing. 'You could be bisexual, you know?'

'No, I don't think so. I've been through all this with Frank. I had to go away on the rigs to sort myself out; it was an opportunity to think about what I'd done. I married Joan because it was the right thing to do, since there was a kind of pressure from you guys and we had Jordan to think of too.'

'I see,' said Rob. 'I hope you're not blaming Pippa and me?'

'No, no, of course not. You and Pippa got married, had Daniel, it seemed right—and then, later, Jordan came along. Sad to say, it was the one time I enjoyed sex with Joan and the outcome was our son. Since then it's been very half-hearted. I haven't exactly been a good husband; I know that. I don't regret having Jordan, he's a great kid, but he's always been Joan's son and somehow he always goes to her and not me. I've never felt like a father to him.'

'Well, I hope that it goes without saying you don't regret it, but kids can do that. Sometimes you are the best dad in the world, and other times you can't get through to them. Anyway go on ...'

Terry sighed. 'When little Dan was involved in that dreadful accident, it was all too much. There was no opportunity to talk about it to anyone. About three months ago, Frank was there for me, and it was a huge relief in my life. My dad knows, but you know how it is with my dad, his brother, you know the story ... but Mam would never understand, she's still in denial about Uncle Ronnie. She probably thinks it's a hereditary disease or something. Confessing to her would kill her. I can't do it. She's so old-fashioned; I know she would never understand. Even now in the eighties, you'd think we could talk more about these things, but it's not like that— she still lives in the past and she's a homophobe for sure. It comes from her upbringing. Frank told me *his* mother was exactly the same.'

'God, Terry, how will you tell her? And for goodness sake, you have Jordan. You have to be bloody sure about this.'

'I am sure, honest I am, I've never been this sure in my whole life,' said Terry. 'I've spent all these months wondering *how* to tell her. I thought you might help me through it. I tried to do the right thing but when you guys got married, I ignored my feelings and went with the flow of things.'

As shocked as Rob felt, he tried not to show it, guarding his emotions. He found it hard to be in counselling mode, especially with Terry. All he could do was be empathic to his friend's revelation. There was no point in using his skills on his best friend by attempting to use 'those kind of questions'. But what about Joan? How would she take all this?

'Look, mate, try phoning Joan from here. She'll be back now—see if she'll talk to you, at least,' Rob said. 'She's so innocent sometimes; she has no idea and I'm sure she's in denial about you being away for so long. Anyway, I suppose it will be a huge relief not having to live a life of secrets anymore. Believe me, I *know* how that must feel.' He tightened his lips with more than sadness in his heart; his adoptive mother had left it too long

He glanced at Terry; there was perspiration dripping down the side of his face. Rob handed him a box of tissues.

'Go on, Tel, do it,' Rob urged. 'Call her.' He saw the red light flashing on the answer phone and reminded himself to check his messages as soon as Terry had made the call. He wanted to explain his situation with Pippa, but now it wasn't going to happen.

Terry didn't say much about Jordan. He was a cute kid. Rob wondered how this might affect him in school. Would he be teased? He would need a father figure. Surely Terry couldn't just disappear with the love of his life, this Frank. He had to think of his son. Rob pushed the phone into Terry's hand and went into the kitchen while Terry dialled the number. He cupped his chin in his hands over the work surface, then ran his fingers through his hair. *Today's been a fuckin' awful day and it's not over yet. Bloody hell, Terry—gay! It must have taken some courage to tell me. God, poor Joan.* He switched on the kettle and prepared two cups of coffee. He sat on the kitchen chair, listening and waiting to see if Joan would answer the phone.

'Hi, Joan it's me.' Terry waited, holding his breath for a few seconds while she replied. There was a brief silence.

CHAPTER EIGHT

On arrival at the church hall, Pippa found the door locked. Unsure if she'd made a mistake, she waited for a few minutes. She checked her hand to look for the faint inky number seven, which she had attempted to wash off in the shower.

Moments later, a green van arrived, with Sven as the driver.

'Sorry I'm a bit late. I had to take a boat to Bryher, only got back forty-five minutes ago. I had to dash home, get changed and come down here with the projector.'

Pippa smiled at him. Not only was he very attractive with his tanned skin, blonde hair and—oh yes, those shorts, but he sure made her feel good. *The perfect tonic for a sad mind*, she thought. 'Here, let me help you with all those things, you always seem to have so much stuff with you,' she offered.

Sven paused to get the key from his pocket.

'Can you open that door for me, Pippa? Do you mind?' He handed her the key.

She took it from him; the metal fob felt warm. She held the door open as he brought in the boxes of slides and the projector stand.

'Are you okay? Too much sun, I think,' he said, gazing on her burning cheeks.

'Well, maybe a bit, although I'm looking forward to the slide show! I'll be fine.'

She held out her hand, offering to carry another box of slides and some leaflets. The grief she had experienced on The Garrison would not spill into the evening. She would like to have told him, but it was wrong, very wrong, and she feared she might chase him away. He might think she was whining—and why would he care? She scolded herself with a look of despair.

Sven's eyes scanned the room as he turned the wing nuts on the projector stand. He caught a glimpse of Pippa talking to someone who had arrived early. She was putting the leaflets on the table. His gut feeling was to feel sorry for her. What was it about Pippa? Sadness, yes, that was it! Her holiday just didn't add up; why *was* she here alone?

Their eyes met as she came toward him and he opted to say something to avoid embarrassment. 'I could help you improve your bird identification skills.'

Pippa smiled at him. 'Great, thanks a lot.' *Wow! Now there's an offer.*

She could still feel the tightness in her chest. Right now, she needed something to distract her. The slide show would be interesting and might take her mind off her time on The Garrison.

Sven plugged in the projector and tested the slides before the rest of the audience arrived.

'I bought a notebook this afternoon,' said Pippa. 'Thanks for the idea.'

Sven put up a thumb in approval. 'Great!'

Within half an hour, the hall had filled with people. Sven was prompt in starting; he raised the microphone and the chatter died down.

'Good evening, ladies and gentleman, welcome to the slide show. I look forward to taking you on a grand tour of the Isles of Scilly. There is a lot more to these islands than flowers, puffins and seals, so sit back and enjoy the view.'

He projected a map of the islands on the screen. 'First, I would like to show you the reason why Scilly is a group of islands. It wasn't always like this.'

Pippa listened with interest.

'The area known as Crow Sound and The Road where some of you were on the boat with me today, was once a place where you could walk on dry land. With the rising sea levels, it formed a lagoon.' Sven pointed to the screen. 'You will literally be up to your waist in the sea.' He showed a picture of a group of walkers wading across Crow Sound. 'At a very low tide, you can walk from St. Mary's to Tresco, but you have to play safe and get some proper advice, otherwise it can be very dangerous.'

Pippa thought she would certainly not be doing that. Absorbed in all he said, she watched him gesturing, having a joke with the audience. He laughed, then she laughed, and once again she drew on his every word in over an hour of entertainment.

There were magical names like Wingletang Ledges, Porth Hellick Down, and a tiny island rock named Daisy, which sounded like something out of a children's book.

'On the granite rocks, the ships HMS Firebrand and Association were wrecked in 1707,' Sven finished his talk.

Sven answered each and every one of the audience's questions, often with amusing anecdotes about life on St Mary's.

Pippa sat, hands clasped on her knee, listening, watching his every move, impressed by all that he knew.

As he came to the end of his talk, he smiled at his audience.

'Thank you very much, ladies and gentlemen; I hope you enjoyed the show. Drive safely along the "motorway" when you go home tonight.'

Everyone laughed, knowing that the narrow roads on St Mary's were hardly designed for major traffic, then clapped.

They stood up and began to leave the hall. Some of them waited in an orderly line to talk to Sven. He shook hands with a few of them and Pippa wondered what she should do next.

She saw Jan and Lisa leaving and waved to them. By the look on their faces, they had also enjoyed themselves.

'We hope to see you down at Porthcressa soon, Pippa, don't forget!' Lisa called out as she held onto Jan's arm.

'Yes—will do, I'll make a point of it.' She watched as they walked through the exit. *Poor chap, he looks so ill.*

Instead of hanging around looking lost, she packed up some of the gear, thinking she was helping Sven.

As the hall emptied, he came across the floor and spoke to her. 'I saw you laughing. Did you enjoy the evening?'

'I loved it all,' Pippa enthused. 'You're so knowledgeable; I find it amazing. Your presentation was great. I wish I could do that.' She recalled her days teaching at the school in front of an audience, and could hardly believe she used to have the confidence to give a presentation to parents.

Sven smiled warmly at her. 'Practice, I suppose. No, I do it because it's my life, but we all have to start somewhere. Maybe this is your chance as well. Thanks for helping out, by the way. I was worried that it'd be a bit of an imposition asking you like that, but I thought as you're on your own, it might just bring you into the way of things here.' Pippa gave him a grateful smile.

Sven passed Pippa the box of slides.

'Maybe you can put these in the van for me, is that okay? After this, I'd like to invite you back to Beachside Cottage for a coffee for being such a good help.'

Pippa felt herself go stiff and hesitated. 'Maybe another time, Sven, but thank you.' *What would Rob say?*

Sven wasn't used to refusal.

'Are you sure? Erm … I would like to, it's not often I get the chance to help a novice birdwatcher. It would mean a lot to me, and I don't bite,' he chuckled.

'Okay, I'll come round. Maybe I can learn more about island life with the locals,' she said with some secret delight.

'I'll walk you back afterwards. You'll be okay here, and it's very safe,' he assured her.

Again, Pippa had roused Sven's curiosity; he liked her enthusiasm to learn and her shy personality. He didn't want to frighten her away, but if she was only here for three weeks, he wanted to know her better. He was going through one of his 'doing-this-all-by-myself' weeks. He wished Martin would return soon, and Andrea hadn't been to see him in a fortnight; she had left the islands to be with Martin in Bristol. Sven missed her visits and the cakes that she would bring him. How he wished he had an 'Andrea' of his own. He enjoyed going to their house at the weekends for her special fondue evenings and her delicious chocolate cheesecakes.

Pippa wondered about Sven. His easy happiness made her feel so relaxed. She wanted to be part of it for the duration of her holiday, but most certainly didn't wish to give the wrong impression.

'Well, if you're sure. I don't want to put you to any trouble at this time of the evening, especially as you've had such a busy day.' She didn't know if she was doing the right thing; she was married, Rob wouldn't like it—or would he even care? *It's all innocent, anyway—no need to feel guilty. It'll be okay; you know you have to live a little. Why not?*

'It's a pleasure,' Sven said. 'I need some socialising outside of work anyway, I'd be delighted to make you a coffee, unless you would prefer something a bit stronger—but I've only got cider and beer.' He smiled.

'Okay, Sven, thanks. That sounds lovely, coffee will do.' His little cottage by the beach sounded so homely. She was curious to see how the locals lived; perhaps it was like her own seaside house on Henrietta Street?

On the way to Beachside Cottage, Sven opened the conversation. 'Do you get much time for yourself? My social life hasn't been too good of late, not much time for it. All that will soon change when my colleague returns.'

'I used to teach five-year-olds, but I gave that up for personal reasons.' She had to keep her bereavement out of the conversation. *Talk about something else.* 'You obviously love the life here?'

'Ya, sure, but it can be a bit insular at times. Everyone knows who you are and coming from a big city in Norway, I wasn't used to such a small community at first. But now I suppose I am part of the scenery and I don't mind, but it did take me some time to integrate, then slowly, it all began to fit into place.'

He took out the ignition key; Pippa got out of the van and closed the door. She heard the sea lapping on the shore and breathed in the odour of seaweed on the receding tide.

A row of white cottages stood at the bottom of the hill. The spread of pink Livingstone daisies on the wall of Sven's house had closed their blooms in the evening air. Sven opened the gate and gestured politely for Pippa to walk in front of him up the path. There was a conservatory like the one at Gilstone, and the overall picturesque design reminded Pippa of how she used to draw a house for Daniel. Sven opened the door and led the way inside. 'Take a seat. I'll make us a drink.'

The interior of the cottage seemed a mixture of the old and the new. Some antique-style furniture filled the walls—a glass cabinet and a chest of drawers, an old dining table—but there was a modern sofa, and a few pictures around the walls of birds, and paintings of Scilly. The washing up from the morning had been left out and Sven apologised for the mess. Considering it was a bachelor pad, Pippa thought it wasn't too bad. The views from the window of the bay were unrivalled. Her first impressions made her want to stay longer.

Sven filled the kettle. 'So, Pippa, have you found some "respite" today?' he said as he flicked the switch. 'Sorry it's only instant,' he remarked, pointing to the Nescafé. 'I couldn't help but think you looked a bit tired earlier on. All that walking, eh? I hope you don't mind me asking, but do you normally travel alone? It's not often I meet someone of our age who takes a holiday by herself. Sorry if I'm being nosey.'

Pippa didn't know what to say; was he being nosey or just kind? Instead, she nodded. 'Nescafé's fine.' It was all fine; she felt so very comfortable with him, to the point where it was a bit surreal. 'It's okay. I've had a rough few years,' she warned him. 'But you don't want to be bothered with my problems.'

'Try me if you like. Anything I can do to help? Milk? Sugar?' As he passed her the spoon to stir her coffee, she felt his brown hand brush against hers. There was something interesting about him; it was like wanting to touch a piece of fabric for its quality.

Sven sat facing her. 'I'm a good listener,' he said, encouraging her to say more.

'Right … well … I have to warn you, it's not a pretty story.' What was she doing, revealing her sadness to an almost complete stranger? But after all, he had offered to listen and she needed to unload. Would she be making a fool of herself? Nevertheless, it felt right. Something told her she was safe here; she didn't know why. Perhaps it was Sven: a happy-go-lucky, yet impulsive man who didn't seem to have a care in the world. He also had a great job. He seemed the best shoulder to lean on at this moment. But what if she told him about Daniel and then there were no more cups of coffee, no one to talk to during her holiday? Sven might even ignore her on the boat trips—but if he knew the guilt she had suffered, perhaps he would understand her better. Talk to her more.

'I don't mind, honestly,' he repeated, 'if it helps you talk things through. You know they say in my country "a problem shared is a problem halved". Isn't that the same in English?'

Pippa nodded again. His kindness seemed overwhelming and she felt her breath sucked from her lungs. She performed her calming and distancing routine in her head and thought about how to explain it all. *Slowly breathe in and out and focus on something interesting in the room.* She focussed on the photos she'd seen earlier. The older couple smiling out into the room were obviously his parents; Sven looked more like his mother. Pippa bit her lip and the whole story came rolling out systematically.

'Someone died … someone very close to me.' She cradled the mug in both hands, pursed her lips and blew the steam across the cup. 'Think of the worst thing that could happen in your life and that's what happened to me.' She took in another breath and slowly let it out again, blowing the heat away.

Sven sat still, his eyes fixed on her face, waiting for her to say more. There was a brief silence.

'You don't have to do this, Pippa. It's my fault for pushing the issue, sorry.'

'No, it's okay. Do you really want to hear the rest?' she sighed.

'Only if you want to. As I said, it might help,' he assured her.

'Well … I'm here for some peace and quiet as I mentioned yesterday. My son died three years ago.' She saw herself in the hospital, and Rob telling her Daniel had passed away. Then there was the funeral and all the dreadful things she'd had to endure.

Sven pushed himself against the chair-back for a moment. 'Oh God, I'm so sorry, I didn't realise… I thought… well, I'm not sure what I thought. Something told me there might be a story behind your coming here—only a guess.'

'Was it that obvious? I decided to have a holiday for three weeks to see if I could get some respite from all the grief and bickering which has been flying around my house for the last three years. It's been awful.'

She wasn't sure if her mind was operating as it should. For a brief moment she didn't want to be with Rob any more. She wished she could stay here with Sven, just talking, nothing more. The coffee tasted as good as any other. His cottage had a wood-burning stove, probably very warm and welcoming in winter. The situation called her to an outpouring of her grief. She sensed a welling-up of tears; she mustn't cry, *mustn't* cry…

Sven saw the tears and was about to speak when Pippa spoke first.

'I blamed myself for a long time, and in a way I still do, but it was my husband's reaction that made things worse. We tried to do this together, you know, heal the wounds as husband and wife, but his work kind of got in the way of his family life. He's a trainee counsellor and a nurse at the local hospital and I feel it's changed him; he's more detached from our son's death these days. I can see what he's trying to do but it isn't working.'

'It sounds awful,' Sven replied, now feeling quite shocked.

Pippa nodded. 'Yes. You see, Rob and I, and our friends Terry and Joan, we're like family. We all got married quite young and our lives have gone through dramatic changes since then. Anyway, I don't wish to bore you, but Rob, Daniel, and I took a day trip here once, so I decided to come back and see if I could heal some wounds and move on.'

'I'm glad you came. You would have missed out on Scilly and we wouldn't be sitting here talking. I feel very sad for you.' He gave a sympathetic smile. 'I'm sorry, I didn't mean to pry…'

Pippa interrupted. 'It's fine, talking helps me. I appreciate it very much.' She gave a tight reassuring smile and nodded a 'thanks'.

'So where is your husband? Sorry … being nosey again.' Sven stirred his coffee. Pippa thought that perhaps he wished he hadn't asked about her problems and she tried to smooth things over.

'Oh, it's okay; let's just say since the accident things haven't been the same between us. I'm not sure what'll happen. Rob's studying to be a psychiatric nurse at the local hospital. He couldn't come for the summer; his holiday rota doesn't start until August and he's more of a mountain man. I had to get away to not go crazy; I feel our relationship is somewhat …' She sighed and wrinkled her nose. 'Cracked? Hence the reason I came away on my own.' She had bent the story; her marriage was more than cracked, and, in truth, she might not have one when she got home. 'Rob and I, we seem to be going in different directions now—he's drowning his sorrows in his work and doesn't have a lot of time for me; I'm doing my best to get over the accident and trying not to blame myself. Rob didn't want to come to Scilly and so here I am—I thought it might do me some good.'

'Perhaps if you make a plan for the weeks ahead, that might take your mind off things. I can help you learn more about birds.'

'Aw, Sven, thanks, that's very kind of you. All I want is to be normal again and get my happiness back. I mean, I'll never forget Daniel, of course, but I'm far too young to allow my life to continue in eternal grief. I can't live like that anymore. My doctor told me to get out and go birdwatching; he said working with nature would be a good way of healing myself.'

'True. Doesn't Rob mind you coming here on your own?'

'Our relationship is very fragile at the moment. We argue a lot. I really don't know how he feels right now. He seems so … mixed up. He was adopted and only found out just before we got married. It seems like his life fell apart for the second time when we lost Daniel. He went into counselling to help himself and ended up doing it as a job. I think it's made him worse.'

'Oh, that's a shame. Have you tried to work things out?' Sven took a sip of his coffee.

Pippa sighed. 'I can't get through to him since we lost Daniel. My being away for three weeks, we can get some space and know how we really feel. Perhaps it's a trial separation, although we haven't spoken about it that way. He blames me for losing Dan. I was in the hospital for almost a week with concussion; I kept on having convulsions for about a month afterwards. It was my friend Joan who helped me back to normality. It's been so hard in the last three years. I could accept the loss of my dad to a small degree, but a child, you never forget.'

Sven nodded in absolute agreement. 'You're going to need support while you're here. I'm glad you told me.'

Tears almost fell into her coffee cup. 'I feel like such an idiot sometimes.' She wiped her face on one of the tissues she always kept in her pocket.

Without a word, he put his arm on her shoulder as if to shield her from all the harm out there on the mainland. A warm sensation came over her; he seemed like a gift from heaven.

Sven took a deep breath. He had never known anyone so sad and so enthusiastic to learn. 'Pippa, I agree you have to move on. You've had a bad time. I think it would be good to help you learn more about the birds. Nature is a good healer; your doctor was right about that.'

Pippa stopped crying as he slowly released her and she took out another tissue to blow her nose. It was time to feel better; she couldn't let Sven take all her grief.

'Ok, tell me about you,' she sniffed. 'I mean, we only met yesterday on the quay, for goodness sake. I feel rather stupid.' She realised their friendship might beome more than she expected. She concentrated on a spot on the wall, taking calculated breaths.

'It's fine, Pippa. I am very interested in what you've told me, it's a pleasure to meet with you. To think you've had all this; here's me enjoying myself, and you out there. I can't bear thinking about it. I'm so sorry to hear about your son. You are right about it being one of the worst things to happen to anyone. I'm glad you shared your sorrow with me, I feel very …' He sighed, trying to find the right English word. When he couldn't, Sven smiled and shook his head in sympathy. He sat closer to Pippa and patted her hand. It was nice sitting next to her without talking. He wondered what he should do next. He began to sense her vulnerability and felt he should say something.

'I'm glad you have good friends back home who support you.'

'Yeah, but I'm sorry it had to be you who got the blunt end of my grief. Perhaps now, when we go out on the boats, you will understand why I am here and why sometimes I may not look too happy.' She changed the subject. 'So tell me about Norway, and how you got to be here on Scilly?' She sipped her coffee.

Sven smiled at her, pleased he had helped her recover from her tears. 'Okay, I'll tell you … I'm not married, no kids, working my socks off for the tourists and generally a Norwegian bum having a great time.' He chuckled, attempting to lighten the mood. 'I studied in Trondheim before I applied for a job in Scotland working on the dolphin project, and then I travelled to England and got this job, so here I am. What you see is what you get!' He smiled the kind smile Pippa had become familiar with.

'I think I'm beginning to like what I see.' He rolled his eyes and drank up the last dregs of coffee when she said this. Pippa almost kicked herself; she hadn't meant to say it in that way. She only meant … Oh, what *did* she mean?

'I usually hang around with Martin, The Birdman, and his wife Andrea. She is a true friend and spends a lot of time on her own. I rather … look in on her, when the boss is away. Don't get the wrong idea, I mean she's good fun and a bit older than me; we tend to keep each other company in the winter months. Andrea is sort of family for me—a good friend. I also admire her ability to organise events and make the most of her time on the islands and … she makes good cakes.' Sven grinned at Pippa. 'She's an excellent cook. Martin is a great person, I wish you could meet him, he might not be back in time before you leave—not sure yet.'

'It sounds like you have a great life. I'm very impressed at your knowledge of birds, but that's your job. What a great job, eh?'

'Oh yes, it's good—and for me it's the best. But—and it's a big but—you could find yourself going off the rails if you aren't careful, because the islands are so small and we lead quite an insular lifestyle. Gossip spreads around the island population faster than I can make a phone call.' Sven chuckled. 'It's *that* kind of place—you accept it, but everyone has been so good to me. I love it; I'm totally at home here.'

Pippa gestured toward the mantelpiece. 'The photo—is that your parents?'

'Yes.'

Pippa looked at her watch, not wishing to outstay her welcome. Sven had been too kind. 'I'll have to go soon; I am tired after such a long and wonderful day. Thanks, Sven. It's been a while.'

As promised, much to her relief, Sven offered to walk her back to Gilstone. He tossed the van keys on the dining table and closed the door behind him. The moon had risen, providing enough light to shine on the sea. Further on and closer to town, Pippa heard faint music coming from the pub. 'It's so deserted,' she said. 'Almost spooky. It's like a ghost town with music.'

'Will you be okay at Gilstone on your own?' He wasn't sure why he had asked.

'Oh yes. Thanks again, Sven, you've been very kind. I didn't expect to be pampered so much on my first couple of days here.' Pippa chuckled. 'I'll be fine, honest.' She wondered for a moment why he was paying so much attention to her, but it felt good, and so what if he was?

They walked through the narrow street together and crossed the road toward the house.

'Here we are, Gilstone,' Sven announced on their arrival. 'Don't worry, you'll be fine. I hope to show you a lot more about the islands, maybe do some drawings for you and provide you with a kick-start into bird watching.'

Pippa's insides wanted to sing and dance at the opportunity. 'Are you busy tomorrow evening, or is that a daft question?'

Sven paused for thought. 'No … er … I don't have anything planned, why?'

'Well … it's probably my turn for coffee. There's a conservatory at the back of this house, we could sit in there around the dining table—great for drawing. By the way, I also like to draw—well, I did before … you know … but I gave all that up. I'll make us something to eat, too. Glass of red wine suit you?'

'Sure, sounds good to me. There you are, I got you smiling already. Okay, see you tomorrow, eh?' Sven patted her arm. 'Sleep well and try not to worry. You'll have a great time here, I know you will. Good night, Pippa, and thanks. I'm glad you came back to Scilly. I hope our chat helps you sleep tonight, eh?'

Astonished by his kindness, she took a deep breath. 'I'm grateful for the company. Yes, you helped a lot more than you realise. Thanks again.'

'Take care now—good night,' he said. 'Sweet dreams.'

She watched as he walked across the road, almost bumping into a cyclist without lights. She smiled. It had been a lovely evening, and very unexpected.

As she closed the door, she couldn't help wondering what Sven had in mind for her. She wished she could stay here longer than three weeks, but reminded herself that it was a holiday, nothing more, although Sven's friendship might make it harder to leave. She was still thinking about him as she got undressed for bed.

CHAPTER NINE

Terry picked up the phone as Rob made coffee.

'Hello, Joan, it's me. I tried to call you earlier.'

'Oh, Tel love,' Joan sighed. 'Where are you?'

Terry thought she sounded weary. 'I'm back in Whitby. What time did you get in?'

'You have a key, don't you?'

'Yeah, but … we need to talk.'

'Oh, at last, you've come to your senses, have you?' she said, half-joking.

'Can I come round now?'

'Terry, no need to ask, for God's sake—you live here. What's the matter with you?'

Rob was eavesdropping from the kitchen. *Poor Joan.* He knew her well, she could be fiery at times, and having heard Terry's confession, he was upset for her. He wondered if he should be in there, supporting the two of them—but no, this was something they had to do on their own.

'Where's Jordan?' Terry asked.

'In bed, of course, out like a light.'

'Good, I'll see you in half an hour then, bye.' He replaced the receiver. 'Well, that's it then,' he concluded.

Rob looked shocked at the short sharp conversation. Once, there had been warmth and love. *Is it like that with Pippa and me?*

'How are you going to break this to her?' Rob asked. 'I mean, you will tell her, won't you?' He watched Terry's face, knowing he could easily back out. Terry didn't reply.

Rob shook his head, not believing the events of the day. His best friend had just confessed he was gay. This must have been difficult for Terry. Rob realised he would have to get used to it; it was a stigma Terry would have to suffer for the rest of his life. Terry had made his choice to come out. *Can't believe it.*

'Anything I can do to help, Tel?' Rob asked. 'I mean, this is a shock for me as well, mate. I never realised …'

'No, Rob, thanks, I'll have to face her, and you know what she's like. She won't believe me. I've practised what to say for weeks. Frank's been very understanding. He's given me lots of support in the last few weeks.' Terry's throat faded to a cracked whisper. 'I suppose I'd better get over there.'

'Don't linger. Just do it, Tel. I can talk to her if you like, but let's see how things go, eh? Good luck mate! Call me if you need a further chat.' Rob patted Terry on the shoulder as he went through the front door. 'See ya. Good luck.'

As Terry left the house, Rob wished today hadn't happened.

Terry decided to walk home to clear his mind. He left the car in town. They had bought an ex-council house at a reasonable price. He recalled when he and Joan used to live a few doors down the same street from Rob and Pippa, but their rented house was too small and they needed an extra bedroom for Jordan. Things seemed different then, easier.

He put the key into the lock. Knowing the door always stuck on the weatherboard, he gave an extra push. He really ought to replace it with a new one since it had been this way for about two years, and he'd kept promising to take care of it.

Joan stood in the hall; she noticed something wasn't quite right as he walked through the door. He had changed, his hair was different, longer, and his eyes seemed to be searching around the room rather than giving her a welcoming look. He held her in his arms but didn't kiss her. 'Come on, love, let's go into the lounge and talk.'

'Tel, what's the matter, love?'

'Look Joanie, I have something to tell you …'

He only called her Joanie when he wanted her to be calm.

Joan's face fell and she jumped to conclusions. 'Are you ill?'

'No … no, nothing like that, let me finish. It's a long story, really, and I've been trying to explain for the last four years. I have a confession to make.' He hesitated for a moment. 'I'm not the man you married.'

'You have a twin then, do you?' Joan teased.

'Come on, Joanie, listen to me, love, this is serious. It's taken me a long time to reach this point and I'm not going to allow this moment to pass any longer. I need your understanding. God! This is hard for me. It's to do with my sexuality. You might find this hard to believe, but I'm …'

'Okay, Tel, I know what you're going to say—you can't, you know … do it. I knew that. You just need to get some help, don't be scared, love.'

Terry almost sobbed, letting out a loud sigh.

'No, Joan. I don't know how to say this more gently.' He gave another deep sigh; the words he had thought about so many times sounded dirty and betraying.

'Joanie, please listen to me, love, I want you to take this seriously. I'm … I'm a homosexual. You know, *gay*.'

'Terry, don't be stupid. We got Jordan, you can't be.' Joan stared at him with horror in her eyes. 'You're crazy; you just need some advice, that's all. You got it all wrong, pet, it's something you need to talk to the doctor about. You're not one of those, you just made a mistake.'

Terry took her by the hand and drew closer to her.

'Joanie, listen to me, love, this is serious, I've tried so many times to explain. I swear I never went with anyone else before I went on the rigs. All those times I tried to make love to you and I found it very difficult, all those excuses I made … So much has gone on in our lives, how could I tell you? You're a lovely person, Joanie; I found it hard to make love to you, but it's me who has a problem, not you. It's all *my* fault. When Daniel died, we were so involved in helping Pippa and Rob come to terms with it all.' He saw the look on Joan's face and began to hate himself. He shouldn't have allowed the situation to come this far. 'Then I got the job on the rigs—a deliberate move to give me time to think. I didn't come out until a few weeks ago. I didn't understand why I had these feelings. I've suffered with depression for too long and tried not to show how I felt. Everyone around us was getting married; it was the right thing to do. I thought I loved you in that way. Being gay was never talked about. I now realise this was something I was born with. It's only in the last few months I felt confident enough to get some help. You gotta believe me. Joan, I'm so sorry, pet.'

Joan sat there, her face white. 'Bloody hell—you mean I'm married to a queer and we have a child? Is that why you never came home?'

'Joan, you are so old-fashioned sometimes. Gay men are coming out more these days and, yes, they can have children, I proved that—why not? Don't be so bloody daft, this is the eighties, not the Victorian era. This is not about you. It's about *us* and Jordan—our future.'

Joan stared at him in dismay. 'Shit, how do you know you are queer, erm … gay? What will this mean?'

'I got very down this year; I tried not to let you see how I felt. This guy on the rigs, Frank, he's my … my … well, anyway, he helped me through it. We're partners now. I'm sorry. Anyway, Joan, it's not like you and I have been "at it" like rabbits since Jordan was born.'

'What d'ye mean, partners?' Joan asked, glaring at him.

Terry looked her straight in the eyes. 'What do you think I mean?' He sighed and turned his gaze away from her.

'You mean you and him did things together.'

'God, Joan, you are so naïve!'

Joan stared into the void. She did not speak, nor blink. She felt dirty and wanted to get a shower as soon as possible. What was it all going to mean? Her mother had drummed it into her not to go off with strange men; she often talked to her of 'those kind of men', and Joan didn't know how she was supposed to react. She wanted to say 'you should have told me earlier'. Instead, her anger rose and she burst out with her true feelings.

'Get out of this house, Terry Marshall—get out, you cheated on me. I hate you for this, I don't want Jordan to see you again, especially not now, I don't want him influenced with your lies.' Her heavy breathing became a sob.

'Joan, please listen, love, I can understand your anger.' Terry felt injured and wished he hadn't told her. 'Please, Joan, please understand, I am trying to be honest with you.'

'Don't call me *love!*'

'Joan, listen to me please, being gay is a condition of my thoughts and the way my body works, it's something I can't help. It's not an illness but sometimes I feel that way. I told you I was *born* like this; it's not my fault! There are people like me all over the world. You're not listening to me. I didn't mean to cheat on you, it just happened, being away from home helped me come out. I need to know what we're going to do considering Jordan. I came here tonight hoping we could work things out.'

Terry's face turned a deeper pink and beads of sweat ran down his cheeks. *Frank was right. 'Say it as it is, keep telling her the truth and show her you really do care.'*

Jordan heard voices and began to cry. 'Mummy, Mu-mmy.'

'I'll go and see him,' said Terry.

'No, you will *not*! I'll get him, he needs me, not you! You haven't been here all this time, you'll scare him, and anyway he doesn't know who you are anymore.'

Terry sat back, astounded, and a deep hole seemed to penetrate his heart.

Joan left the lounge, her mind numb, she crashed into the small chest of drawers on the landing and stubbed her toe. 'Ow, ouch, ow, ooya bugger.' She sat on the floor, while Jordan howled, 'Mummy!'

Terry ran to see what had caused the commotion. 'What the hell have ya done?' he yelled, halfway up the stairs.

'My toe, my fuckin' toe,' she cried. 'Fuckin' 'ell. Ow ow oucha!' Her face distorted with terrible pain.

Terry saw his son standing beside his mother. Jordan went quiet for a moment and then screamed when he saw Terry.

'It's okay, Jordan pet,' said Terry. 'Here's Daddy. My, haven't you grown?'

Joan groaned in pain.

'What do you bloody well expect, he's two now and you didn't even send him a present last month, You hurt us both Tel. How could you? Ow, ouch!'

'Joan, I don't live in a town; I can't go shopping like we used to. I phoned you, didn't I? Are you awright?'

Jordan began to scream again and huddled into his mother, refusing to look at Terry, then ran into the bedroom and hid under the covers.

'The kid's terrified of you. Ouch, bloody oucha, no I'm not awright,' she echoed, rubbing her fingers over her big toe, which began to swell.

Terry ran downstairs, brought a packet of frozen peas, and placed them with care on her foot.

'I'll do it! Jordan pet, stay in bed. Go to sleep. I'll be alright, sweetheart.'

'Should I kiss it better, Mummy?' Jordan called.

'No, sweetie, it's okay.' She looked at Terry. 'He's a really good kid,' she said, sniffing back her tears.

'Here, let me help you downstairs,' Terry offered.

'No, I'll manage, don't touch me!' She hobbled into Jordan's room and sat by his bed.

Terry watched and wanted to hold Jordan in his arms. 'Hello, Jordan, come to Daddy. I'm sure he'll be okay.'

'Leave him, Tel,' she screamed. 'I don't want you near him, influencing him in your ways; it feels dirty.'

'Joan! Don't! Please, for God's sake—not in front of the kid. I'm suffering enough, can't you see that?'

He went to pick up Jordan in his arms but she had been right.

'Mummy, Mummy!' Jordan screamed, twisting and flailing to escape from his dad.

'He's been ill,' Joan said, 'he's a lot better today, just tired. Best leave him.' She tried to be calm for Jordan' sake.

She hobbled to sit on the top stair, going down each one hanging on to the banister. 'Leave me alone, don't touch me.'

Terry realised Jordan had become Joan's child and not his own. He felt his role as a father snatched away. She had everything in order; the house looked clean and tidy, with all Jordan's toys neat and in their place. He caught a glimpse of himself in the mirror on the landing and stared deep into the image. He concentrated on his eyes, then his lips, and thought how warm Joan had been when they first met. What had he done to her? He hated himself. They'd enjoyed good times together. He couldn't—no, mustn't—hang onto her any longer; it wasn't fair on any of them. She was still young enough to start again, he must give her a chance; that was the least he could do. She would surely see it differently one day.

He crept into the room. 'It's okay, Jordan, Daddy's here. I'll tuck you in.' It was as if he had some contagious disease and couldn't give his son a goodnight kiss in case Joan shouted at him again.

Jordan hid under the covers with his thumb in his mouth.

'Goodnight, son, remember Daddy always loves you.'

Terry was leaving in a couple of days and he realised he might not see his son again for some time. The feeling in his chest became a heavy stone weighing him down. *Shit, what the hell have I done?*

He thought about Frank. For the first time, he knew what love meant. Frank was good-looking, rugged, and there was a sense of mutual trust and understanding between them. If it wasn't for Frank, Terry thought, he might have been living a lie for the rest of his life. 'You can't go on like this,' he'd said. 'Tel, you mean a lot to me and we're more than good mates now, you got to tell Joan.'

Terry went back down the stairs as Joan nursed her toe.

'Is it okay?' he asked her. 'Do you think you broke it?'

'No, it's not okay, thanks to you. God, Tel what have you done? Where do we go from here?' She was quieter now, her mind on her two kinds of pain. 'Who else knows about this?'

'My dad does, and today I went to see Rob while I waited for you.'

'You mean you told every bugger in Whitby about this before you told me?' she said in horror.

'No, no, it wasn't like that, honest. I needed Rob's support. I had no idea what to say and him being a nurse an' all that, I thought he might understand. Also with Uncle Ronnie being inclined that way, I thought *you* might understand. You've met him and he's a nice guy, you wouldn't know about his sexuality unless someone told you. Even Mam doesn't realise, it's all part of her upbringing. Anyway, I'm still Jordan's dad, for goodness sake; I need to see him when I come home. Even Rob spends more time with him these days than I do. I just can't … Oh, shit, I can't do this.'

'I think you're missing the point, Tel. Whether you like it or not, you've cheated on me. It's not a disease? Is it inherited? I mean … Jordan won't get it, will he? All that AIDS stuff you see on the telly, it sounds horrendous, you might die or something. Have you thought about that?'

'Yes,' was all he said with a sigh, thinking it might be too late. 'And no, it's not inherited, don't be silly.'

'And I expect Pippa knows about it?' Joan butted in sharply.

'No, she doesn't. I think she'll find out anyway, but she's left Rob, hasn't she?'

'No, she bloody well hasn't. Did Rob tell you that?'

'I kind of presumed … Oh hell, this is far too much for me to take in.'

'Well, don't presume. You seem to do a lot of that recently. Pippa is away on a break, which brings me back to our situation— what do we do about it? I thought I still loved you until today.' Her bottom lip trembled as she spoke until it gave way into a sob.

'I'm sorry, pet, I thought I loved you in that way too … It became a nightmare for me; I honestly didn't know what it meant, it was as though it was happening to someone else. I suppose I've been in denial about it since I was about fourteen. Joan, you have to listen to me, I'm so sorry it had to happen this way.'

He leaned forward to kiss her on the forehead.

'Get off me, Terry. Please, you don't seem to understand at all.'

Terry hesitated for a moment. He took a deep breath. 'We should talk about divorce. I don't think you'll want me to be your husband anymore. I'll still keep sending money for you and Jordan, but I think you'll be better off without me, both of you, and I'll stay in touch, I promise. I'll be staying at mam and dad's tonight, I'll tell them some excuse or another. Mam would freak out if she knew about me. She must never know; it would kill her. She doesn't understand these things, so please don't tell her.'

Joan looked at him and scoffed. 'It's about time she knew who her son really is.' She stepped back and sat on the stairs, still nursing her foot wrapped in frozen peas. She thought about the bigger picture and looked back at how it had been over the last few years. The news Terry had brought became clearer as she pondered on the their years together.

'When I look at Pippa and Rob, and then you and me, I suppose we were all pushed together by our own circumstances. I mean, all our teenage lives we seemed locked together as friends. We isolated ourselves from the real world, just the five of us, including Dan, doing everything together: weekends, holidays, everything. There was a time we couldn't do anything without each other, and you and Rob were more like brothers than good mates. Pippa didn't have a dad or a mum, Rob is adopted, and you have a gay uncle. No wonder we were all bloody mixed up about ourselves!'

Joan began to cry again, her bottom lip tucked tight under her front teeth. She sobbed.

'Yes, I'm sorry, pet, I find this really hard too. As I said, I only wanted to be honest with you, we can't go on like this—just think how it might be in ten years' time. I might have fallen ill with the stress and … well, living together would be awful.'

Joan said nothing and sniffed into the sleeve of her jumper.

'I'll be round at Mam's for a couple of days if you want to talk about it. I think it's best I leave now without prolonging the agony. Talk to Rob about it; he's good at these things. I'll tell Mam we had a disagreement. Dad understands, he'll smooth things over for her and for you and Jordan. I'm going to have a chat with Uncle Ronnie too.'

'So bloody soon? You mean you came to tell me all this and now you're buggering off to your mam and dad's? And stop calling me pet! I am *not* your pet anymore.'

'Oh, Joan, don't, please. Look, I'll come and see you before I go back to Aberdeen, okay?'

'Is that it? Is that all you can say to me?' she bawled.

Sadly, yes. I don't see any point in me hanging around, do you? I hope you'll see very soon I've done the right thing for you and Jordan. You won't have to live with the stigma of me living in the area. No one will have to know about this.'

He opened the front door. 'I'm sorry, Joan. I'm really, really sorry.'

Joan stood with anger in her heart as she tried to slam the door behind him. The door stuck and she had to push it. She now had a new status in life—single mother. She blew out her cheeks and stood in the hall with her back to the front door, then slid down to the floor. She broke down in a moment of anger and shame. It wasn't as if she hadn't expected Terry to come home one day, asking for a divorce; it had crossed her mind once or twice since his absence. She had even imagined what she would do if he left her. But this … being jilted … the end of her marriage as she knew it, the shock of it all …

CHAPTER TEN

The following day, Pippa took a boat to Tresco. She packed her bird book, a pencil, and her new pad for the bird records. With binoculars swinging as she walked, her mind and stature in 'authentic birdwatching mode', she stepped on board the *Black Swan* with another fifty or more passengers. The morning had been foggy; the calm sea now reflected the blue sky. Pippa closed her eyes and soaked in the warmth.

The boat slid through the water as the sun glistened in the wake. Pippa arrived on Tresco for a walk around the Abbey Gardens. Sven had mentioned the flowers were at their best this week. After leaving the boat at Carn Near, she followed the narrow path toward the entrance to the tropical gardens. With the heat of the morning sun on her shoulders, she listened to the sound of pheasants clucking.

The echoes of the island rang in her ears everywhere she turned. A black-backed gull called a rapid *ha-ha ha-ha* as it flew overhead and she wanted to laugh back at it.

She paused a while to listen to the 'shushing' sound of the lapping sea as though she were listening through a shell. The perfume and the buzzing of bees—it was all here. She had arrived in a special place at a time of her life when she needed inner peace. Her spirits lifted, as she walked toward the garden gate to pay her entrance fee. Simple peace and happiness overcame her on this perfect summer day.

Rhododendrons bloomed, and through the greenery poked the turrets of Tresco Abbey. Pippa stood and read a plaque screwed to the wall.

Awake my Muse, bring bell and book
To curse the hand that cuttings took

She walked the many paths, up and down steps and into small niches where she captured the perfume and the colours. She felt quite splendid sitting on a seat, gazing at the flush of tropical plants. *If only Rob had been interested in all this.* She thought hard about what she really wanted in her life. Perhaps she could make her marriage work. There had been days when Rob was kind and generous, but the chemistry between them seemed to have vanished. He could be so deep, but he never wanted to share his inner thoughts. She had needed him to ensure her survival, to understand their shared grief. But perhaps her need for Rob had waned; she had got this far almost without him.

Enjoy the moment, she thought with a sigh. What was the sense in spoiling this wonderful cloudless day?

Peeking inside the Valhalla Museum, she gazed at the ships' figureheads on display. She walked and kept on walking; with every corner she turned, her eyes fixed upon amazing plants. If only she could name them, as some of the women who had passed her on the path could, and as Sven had been able to do so easily with birds. The butterflies drew nectar from the flower heads and the hum of the bees calmed her. The heads of pink velvet proteas reached out toward the sky; the flame trees' colour made them live up to their name. There was a tang of pine, combined with the salt of the sea in the air. Pippa could hardly believe this was England.

Her thoughts and feelings were now calm, without her usual anxiety. It had been a long time. She enjoyed the sensation of fresh air and felt the muscles in her thighs working as she ascended the Neptune Steps. Palm trees and flowers lined the path to the highest point. Although somewhat breathless, she felt happy that she made it to the top and surveyed the scene: flowers everywhere—*oh, the gloriousness of it all!* Sven was right, she ought to learn more about nature conservation. A rush of inspiration welled up inside her; she had been blind all these years. Standing here had to be the most wonderful thing. She lingered at the top for a while and took in the view of the blue sea over the tops of the trees before moving on.

On arrival at the café, Pippa ordered a cheese salad with a bread roll, and dropped the occasional crumb for the thrushes, blackbirds, and starlings. She made notes about her walk and drew pictures of flowers.

She checked her watch. The boat would return soon; it was time to start making her way back. Sven would be visiting her, and she wanted to prepare. In the distance was the sound of a helicopter's rotor blades. Before leaving, she visited the garden shop and bought a straw sunhat to protect her face from advancing freckles. She tied her hair in a knot inside the brim of the hat, and strolled toward the boat for the return trip. The flimsy red scarf wrapped around the brim of the hat flowed down her back and she felt like a film star on holiday.

That morning, Sven guided a group of birdwatchers from his native country around the Higher Moors Nature Reserve. He'd advertised the tour in a magazine in Norway. He knew he was on his best form speaking his native language, although it had been a while. His mind turned to Pippa. Maybe he could encourage her to enjoy herself. He thought she needed a friend as much as he did. He knew he probably fancied her, but wasn't sure what he should do about it. She was married and the last thing he wanted was to be involved in the break-up of someone else's relationship.

He rode home on his bike and made a mental note of what he needed to take with him to Pippa's place that evening. At least she would go back to Yorkshire having discovered a new hobby. Yes, she would go home and forget him, just like the others had done. There was Marcia from Bristol who wanted to "eat him to bits", and Alice who was far too immature for her age. None of them were interested in wildlife. They'd been here for a couple of weeks with parents and friends, then gone forever. *Doesn't anyone want a nice guy with an adventurous job?* He chuckled to himself.

Pippa seemed different; she wanted to learn and he was keen to show her his life and the nature on his own doorstep. He felt she would not turn him down. He had three weeks to learn more about her, but she lived hundreds of miles away. Besides, she might be offended and then he would feel stupid. Anyway, she was married. Why did he keep doing this to himself? There was nothing wrong in having dinner with her; it might help to cheer her up a little. Her tragedy had been dreadful; he couldn't imagine what it must have been like. What she didn't need right now was him messing up her life even more. All he wanted was to show her the birds and the islands and take it easy, give it time. He knew himself too well; he must control his impulsive mind, but three weeks was not a lot of time.

After arriving at Gilstone, Pippa showered, changed, and made a chilli dish with salad.

At seven o'clock, Sven knocked on the door, looking more suntanned than the day before. Pippa smiled as she got the door for him.

'Come in and make yourself at home. Though I would think you know this place better than me!'

'Thanks! Actually, I've only been here once before to visit Peter Stowes, Janice's husband,' Sven informed her.

Pippa moved her straw hat from the settee to the coffee table.

'Nice hat,' he remarked.

'Yes, I bought it on Tresco today. Did you have a good day at work?' It was a question she'd often asked of Rob, almost every day of their marriage. She felt her question must be rather weird from someone Sven hardly knew. His work couldn't be too stressful, after all, it almost seemed like play. She scolded herself for asking.

'Ya, sure. I was speaking Norwegian, some mates of mine from home were there; I did a tour on dry land for a change. I prefer it—that is my real job.' He sighed.

She busied herself for a moment laying the table, putting out two coasters and wine glasses.

'Can I help?' Sven offered. 'This is great, thanks for the invitation. It makes a change not to have to cook for myself!'

'No, it's fine, I'll be back in a moment. I've got it all ready, so take a seat, it won't be long.' She made her way to the kitchen. 'Can't say it'll be any better than what you would cook, mind you,' she called. 'You've probably got your own favourite Norwegian dish, just as I have with Yorkshire Puddings.'

'Ya know something? I've never had Yorkshire Pudding—you have it with beef, right? I rarely go out for dinner, too busy these days. Martin's wife, Andrea is into stuff that is more exotic. She's a good cook.'

Pippa wondered about Sven as he sat in the lounge. His time in the sun and his tousled hair had already begun to do strange things to her feelings. She listened and his English pronunciation was interesting; it was lovely to hear him speak. It was all fantasy, pure fantasy, and why not? Fantasy was good for you.

'How did you get on today, Pippa, on Tresco?' Sven inquired.

'It's an amazing place; the gardens are so full of colour. Is it always like that?'

He poked his head around the kitchen door and smiled. 'Yes, most of the year. They plant for all seasons.' The aroma of food wafted his way. 'Mm, that smells really good.'

'It's so full of friendly faces here, isn't it? White beaches and the colours of the Livingstone daisies on the garden walls are like a dream.' Pippa stirred the chilli as she spoke.

Sven laughed. 'Well, now you know why I live here! Although the winter can be harsh, it never lasts very long. I'm used to the cold weather, of course. I hope they let me stay here a little longer. I don't know yet what'll happen. My contract may be up soon, although they extended it for Martin's time in Africa.'

'Tell me about Martin—that's the Birdman, right?'

'Yes, he's quite a character, part of the island structure, so to speak. He's a good bloke. I often go around to his place; he and Andrea are lovely people.'

'I got the impression you are part of the structure here too,' Pippa said with a smile.

'Oh, yes, me too I suppose. I will be sad if I have to leave. That reminds me … I have something for you after dinner.' He opened his rucksack, producing his cassette recorder. 'I brought some bird calls. You'll need these if we are birding.'

'That sounds interesting, should I put some music on for now? What do you like—*Dire Straits, 10cc, Elton John?* Probably stuff visitors left behind or maybe Janice has left it for the guests. I hope you're hungry.'

'Ya, for sure,' he said in answer to both questions, and he chose a Dire Straits tape he found among the pile of cassettes. 'I love the track *Telegraph Road*. It reminds me of our road here of the same name. I sometimes go whizzing down there on my bike,' he chuckled.

Pippa brought in the bowls of food, placed the salad tongs in the dish and put a serving spoon in the chilli-con-carne. She offered him the salad.

'I tried not to make the chilli too hot,' she said. 'Would you mind dealing with the wine?' She handed him the corkscrew, aware that he was gazing at her.

'Tell me more about where you live,' he requested as the bottle went *'pop'*.

She told him about the North Yorkshire moors and the steam railway through the Esk valley. 'I often pack a bag and some sandwiches and go walking on the moors. Rob used to go with me, but these days, he's stopped all that.'

'By the way, you'll notice I got a new rucksack,' he said with a grin. 'There's this place down the quay, they've got some really strong canvas bags.'

'Nice one. I like the colour; we almost match.' Pippa pointed to her own blue bag on the floor in the corner of the room.

They sat opposite each other making small talk and eating their chilli. Pippa felt odd entertaining him. It was as if she had taken a jump too soon. Maybe a coffee and biscuits would have been enough. *What would Rob say? Sod Rob, this is 'me time'.* She hadn't meant to feel so mean. It was all about letting go and getting away from it all; surely she didn't need to feel guilty about that?

She brought the fruit salad and Sven offered to serve her.

'More?' he said, smiling.

'No, that's fine. Thanks for coming, this is incredible, you, here, having dinner with me, I never thought … ' Pippa found it hard to find the words to finish her sentence. His eyes kept following her—and that comforting smile of his! How she wished Rob would do more of that.

'It's a real pleasure, Pippa. It's great food, thanks for inviting me.' He patted her arm. 'Let me help you clear the table, then we can listen to the tape I brought.' He helped her move the dishes to the kitchen.

'Okay, shall we then?' He moved his chair around the table and sat closer to her. Again, her odd feelings returned. Did he fancy her? *How stupid is that?* Sure as hell, she wished it could be true. Yes, fantasy was good for you, for sure. She giggled to herself. *How embarrassing.*

She watched as he drew a picture of a sparrow. *He's good, very good. His drawing is delightful.*

'I used to do a lot of drawing at Dan's school before the accident,' she said.

'Yes, I remember you saying about teaching. I can imagine you won't feel like going back to that, though.'

'Yeah, you're right, I gave it up. It's a pity because I'd just started, but maybe, who knows, I might have the confidence to do it again. I ought not to give up on all the hard work I put into it.'

Pippa wasn't used to drinking more than two glasses of wine and like the perfect gentleman, Sven kept topping up her wine glass. She leaned forward, nodding here and there as he spoke. She thought he was charming. Her eyes kept meeting his and it was hard to stop. Did he realise?

'It's probably best to start with the colour of the bird, its approximate size and shape. Try to check on the profile of its beak, especially if you have a good pair of binoculars. You might only have a few seconds to make a decision about what species you are looking at, but its tail shows you a lot during flight, so do a quick check if you can—long tail, short tail, forked tail, you know, that sort of thing. You can look it up in your field guide afterwards. When you are well practised at doing this, you can tell which bird you are looking at from a silhouette in the sky and the bird's call.' He pointed to the diagrams he had made about plumage, wings, under-parts and head, and the song of that species. He played the tapes and Pippa listened to the calls of the birds and the difference between the blackbird's song and the song thrush's repetitive notes. He demonstrated her how a blackcap sounded similar to a blackbird. She couldn't help but listen to the way he spoke and some of the time, she wasn't listening to what he said, only how he said it.

He showed her how to tell the sexes of each bird according to its plumage, which was often easy but not in the case of the robin. She raised her eyebrows, then remarked, 'I'm glad we can tell male from female, most of the time.' *Shit—did I really say that?*

She hadn't meant to sound so forward; it had just come out that way. Anxious she might have scared him away, she thought she'd have to spend the rest of the holiday avoiding him.

Sven laughed and said with his usual politeness, 'Yes, me too,' giving her a coy smile. 'Now I want to show you the difference between a willow warbler and a chiff-chaff.' He pointed at what Pippa thought were two identical species in the field guide. 'Can you tell the difference between these two?'

'They're the same, aren't they?' Pippa questioned as she traced the shape with her finger.

'Well, you have to listen to the call. One is a cascade of notes, that's the willow warbler, and the chiff-chaff has the same name as its call, like this…' He played the sounds.

'Oh yes, I can hear why they named it a chiff-chaff.' Pippa yawned. 'Oh, sorry, I think it's the wine. It's been so interesting to learn all these new things.' She hoped she wasn't sounding more interested in Sven than the birds; that would be doubly embarrassing. 'I've enjoyed the evening so much, I really did.'

'Oh, it's nothing, that's okay, I'll stick around in the next few days and maybe we can do a few trips together on the boats this week—but I am quite busy, it's the time of year, of course.'

'Thanks for all your understanding.' Pippa smiled.

'I can see you're tired, so I'll say, "god natt", as we say at home, and I've enjoyed myself too. That meal was delicious, thank you.'

'Come again,' Pippa said, and she meant it.

They stood up at the same time. He seemed glued into his sandals, shorts, and T-shirt. She had never seen him in anything else and it seemed wrong to imagine him in posh trousers and a shirt. Rob always wore jeans or smart trousers for work. He was quite the opposite from Sven. A thought struck her—she must stop comparing Sven with Rob.

Sven closed the bird book and tidied up the table. 'Can I help with the washing up?'

'No, thanks, don't worry; I'm happy for something to do when you're gone.'

He turned to her and spoke as an afterthought. 'I'm going to St. Agnes in the morning so I have to leave earlier. Would you like to come?' He picked up his rucksack and put all the teaching aids inside.

'Oh … well, that's kind of you, thanks, but I er … no, I need to do some shopping.' It was best to show restraint. He was obviously keen to help her, but a line had to be drawn. The respect he had for her predicament was what she needed. Perhaps she should accept the situation, relax and enjoy the moment. Isn't that what the holiday was all about? No, she would exercise self-control. After all, it was all safe; she was married, but having a friend to guide her around the islands was most refreshing.

He made his way toward the door. 'Good night, Pippa, see you soon. I'll probably call round in the next couple of days to see how you are getting on. Take care and thanks again.'

'Oh Sven—thanks so much, I've really enjoyed the company.'

He left the house and crossed the road into the darkness. He had wanted to kiss her goodnight, once on either cheek, as he would have done back home—but no, another time, when he'd got to know her a bit more. He broke into a smile; recently, he had become more English than Norwegian.

The next day, Pippa had promised to have coffee with Jan and Lisa. As she sat with them at the Porthcressa Restaurant, Jan seemed paler than the last time she had seen him. She held his skinny hand and told him to hang in there. Lisa encouraged him to eat some of the cod she had ordered. It seemed to Pippa that the pain of watching him fork the small flakes of fish into his mouth was more than she could bear. *Poor Jan.* It made her realise how lucky she was to be alive. 'Everything sad comes in threes,' her aunt had told her. 'Just live your life and enjoy it, you're too young to hide away like this.' She liked her mother's sister, who seemed to understand what she was going through; she had taken care of Pippa when she was a child.

Lisa interrupted her thoughts. 'Had a nice time so far?'

'Oh yes, I did some entertaining last night,' Pippa said proudly. 'Remember Sven from the boats, the nature warden, the one at the slide show? He was up at my cottage for dinner.'

'You didn't waste time then?' Lisa grinned. 'I mean it's really good you have found a lekker, I mean, er … a nice friend.'

'Well, he's not a close friend really, just a guy who is helping me to learn more about birdwatching. Although I agree with you, he is very nice, but I have to tell you, I have a husband at home.'

'Oh, I thought you were single, Pippa. I hadn't realised.'

'Well, things are a little awkward at the moment; we had a sad loss in the family.'

Lisa seemed to understand as Pippa changed the subject.

'Anyway, how are you feeling today, Jan?' Pippa asked.

'Oh, it goes well, thank you. I live by the hour and if I am lucky, I will live by the days.' He gave a weak smile.

Pippa looked at Lisa; she knew that look of despair. She understood and felt that Jan was being very brave, but what option did he have? None really.

They sat sipping their tea. If she didn't say goodbye to them soon, she feared she might fall back into grief mode. Perhaps it was a little selfish, but it made her think how lucky she was to be fit and healthy. Maybe there was a lesson here.

CHAPTER ELEVEN

Rob decided he needed a haircut. There was enough time to go down to the unisex salon in town; they would close in an hour. The phone rang. It was as if the person on the other end knew he was leaving.

'Hi, Rob, have you got a minute?'

Oh no. 'Oh, hi, Joan, I'm just on my way out, love. Can I phone you back later?'

'This won't take long,' Joan said. 'You spoke with Terry?'

'Er … yes, but if I can ring you back later we can talk longer.'

Joan ignored him. 'I think I sorted it out, I'm putting in for divorce tomorrow.'

'Hang on, Joan; don't you think that's a bit on the hasty side? I mean, you only just found out about Terry's predicament.' He thought she was trying to be brave by sweeping her situation under the carpet, *typical of Joan—always impulsive.*

'Well, I have to be practical about it. Being married to someone who is gay is hardly a marriage and he's got someone else, this Frank character—did he tell you? What's the point in hanging on when it's all cut and dried, don't you think?'

Rob ignored her question. 'Flippin' heck, Joan, don't you think you should wait a bit? I can understand your anger, you're very vulnerable right now, I know. But you can't treat Terry as if he never existed. Yes, we have to talk, I agree.'

'I don't want to hang around. I loved Terry as a husband, not as a one of them "nancy boys". That's not my style. He is the father of my child and that's it! I want to get on with my life. You sound angry with me, Rob?'

'Well, no, just shocked at your attitude. I know it's difficult at the moment. Look, love, I have to go out. I'm on days this week; perhaps we can meet up at the pub? Call me tomorrow and we'll set a time. Sorry I have to work but I do want to talk to you, honest, I do.'

'Okay, I'll do that. Thanks, Rob, you're an angel. I need to talk to you too. Bye then.'

He was about to leave when the phone rang again. There was no one there and the line went dead.

Bloody hell, leave me alone will yer?

It rang a third time.

'Hello, Rob Lambton speaking'

'Ah, Mr Lambton, this is John Grover from Grover and Pearson, solicitors in Kingston upon Hull, sorry to bother you. We would like to call and see you. It's a delicate matter concerning your family.'

'Why, has someone died?'

The voice on the other end didn't answer his question.

'Our Mr Carmichael is in your area this evening and we wondered if it were possible for him to visit you. The matter is a little urgent and we need to clarify we got the right person.'

'Who did you say you are?'

'John Grover, solicitors in Kingston upon Hull.'

'Oh, I see,' Rob said, puzzled.

'We hope our colleague can sort this out for you. I feel sure it will be to your benefit. As I said, it's a delicate family matter. Stephen Carmichael will bring his card and we are in the Yellow Pages. I can assure you the matter is genuine, apologies for being so cautious, I hope you understand.

Rob thought he sounded sincere enough, but these days you couldn't be certain.

'Are you sure you've got the right person?' Rob asked, anxiously hoping to get out of the door. 'I don't have any relatives that I know of.'

'I do apologise for sounding a little evasive, but in cases like this, we don't usually like to discuss with clients on the phone—we need to see you in person. Will seven o'clock be okay for you? Sorry this is such short notice.'

'Yeah, fine,' Rob replied. It was bound to be a sales representative for insurance. *Bloody hell, what was that all about?* He didn't know whether or not to ignore the call and hoped this Stephen Carmichael wouldn't be the bringer of more bad news in his life. *Solicitor, eh?*

He was sitting on the settee pondering the last call, when the phone rang again. He wasn't going to answer it, but what if it was Pippa? Did he care? Well, maybe she would shout at him for not being there, he'd better check.

'Hay-lo, Rob Lambton,' he said, sighing. 'Oh, is that you, Pippa? I thought it might be.

'You've been on the phone for ages, Rob.'

'So what if I have?' he said.

'I tried to get through. You sound annoyed, love.'

Rob sighed again and shook his head in frustration. 'I'm busy, that's all.'

'Too busy to talk with your wife, then?'

'No, too bloody busy with other people. I need to have some time to myself.'

'What's up?' Pippa tried to calm the situation.

'Oh, nothing really.' He wasn't going to tell her about the call or Terry. *She can find out when she gets back—if she gets back.*

'How's Scilly?'

'It's great. I've met some really nice people.'

'Lucky for you, eh?' Rob said.

Pippa's anger got the better of her. 'Rob, what is it with you? You're always sarcastic; it's more than I can stand. I phoned to see how you are, not to have a bloody row.'

'Look, Pippa, I'm sorry, but today hasn't been a good day. Joan just phoned me, I'm about to do my exams, I got time off in the week to do it and there's you and me and you know…'

'Rob, do you love me?' Pippa interrupted.

'Why would you ask me something like that right now? I could ask you the same question.'

Pippa thought it was the same old arguments going around, nothing had changed. She couldn't believe he was so stroppy.

'Phone me during the week,' said Rob, 'and I might feel different. I mean, where do you see us going with our lives?'

'Rob, I don't know. Can we talk about this when I get back? It's all gone wrong, hasn't it?'

'And where do you feel it's gone wrong?'

'Rob, you're counselling me, *don't* do that. You know perfectly well where our marriage has failed, that's a stupid question. I only want to know if you still love me, that's all.'

'I'll tell you what I feel at this moment, I think it's better we cool it for a while. We used to get on really well and I think we need to make some positive decisions without dragging the whole damned business into the gutter. We could have a trial separation, I suppose, as we're doing now, but longer.'

'What the hell is up with you today? What do you want me to do?' Pippa shouted in tears.

Rob sighed, then relented. He could hear she was genuinely upset. He replied to her question. 'You're probably right, look, I'm sorry, our lives have been turned upside down and I don't think it's fair to keep pretending like this. Where we should be finding mutual empathy, it has turned us both into, well … monsters. I don't want to do anything we might regret, but I can 't live like this anymore; it's interfering with my job and I can't have that, Pippa, I need to work to live.'

'I still care about you, Rob,' Pippa said. 'Maybe we should get some help, from your lot at the hospital, some counselling.'

'Don't be so bloody stupid, I couldn't let the guys at work get that close to my private life. It would ruin my job. Anyway, I'm already doing counselling, or have you forgotten?'

'Yes, but we could find a private counsellor, marriage guidance?'

'I know too much in that respect, I've learned too much, it wouldn't work for me. I'd be looking at myself coming backwards,' Rob said. 'As each day passes, we live with the guilt of Daniel. If we're to be sensible, I think we need to start afresh. Let me know how you feel when you come home. I can't see us continuing, can you?'

Pippa realised he was pushing her away. It all felt like abandonment and she didn't want to go there.

'Rob, how can you do this to me? I was hoping we could patch things up when I got back, and not do this on the bloody phone, for God's sake.'

'Okay, I know. Call me back in the week; I might feel better. Sorry, I didn't want to spoil your break, but I haven't had a very good day and I've tried three times to get out of the house this afternoon, so I'm going. Sorry, Pippa. Just have a good think about it and we can talk soon when I feel less stressed, it's been a helluva day. Okay?'

Yeah right! 'Bye then, I'll phone you again soon,' Pippa said, feeling forlorn and beaten up.

This time, Rob's determination prevailed; he had to get out of the house before the phone rang again, and if it did, he wouldn't answer it this time.

Sitting in the salon, Rob wondered where his life would take him next. He felt some sadness that he'd rowed with Pippa on the phone. The small talk with the girl who had just washed his hair seemed trivial. The man who was coming round to see him, this Carmichael bloke, he had no idea if it was real or just someone coming under false pretences to sell him insurance.

'You want all of this off?' the hairdresser said.

'Yeah, quite short please, but not skinhead.'

'You sure? I mean, you got nice hair.'

'Yeah, please. I'm trying to create a new image.' Rob smiled.

'How's your wife, Rob?'

'She's away at the moment.'

'Haven't seen your mate Terry Marshall in here in ages. He used to come in here—what happened to him? John used to cut his hair; it was only the other day we were saying we hadn't seen him.'

'Works on the rigs now,' Rob told her.

The hairdresser snipped away the strands of black locks. A young apprentice was sweeping up the hair that fell to the floor. The hairdresser had been in a year lower than Pippa at school. She was Joanne something or another, he couldn't remember it exactly. There seemed to be no escape from the past in Whitby.

'There you go, Rob, is that short enough?' she said.

Rob looked more closely in the mirror; he was glad she hadn't skinned him.

'I think that looks better, nice and tidy.' he said. 'The new me! Thanks.'

He paid, and then looked again at his new hairstyle. Clean and handsome again, he would go to the pub and then back home and perhaps have a think about his conversation with Pippa. He knew his mind felt distorted; he needed to be fair. Maybe she was right, he might be good at counselling his patients, but was he any good with sorting himself out? He reckoned the answer was no.

By the time he arrived home, Stephen Carmichael was already knocking on the door.

CHAPTER TWELVE

In three days, Pippa had seen Sven only once. It was on her return from an afternoon trip to the Eastern Isles where she saw him chatting with some tourists. She had missed seeing him around the quay and hoped she hadn't chased him away.

'I'll try and catch up with you very soon,' he said, sounding as if he should have done it earlier. 'I've been so busy working; perhaps we can meet up later when I have more time off.'

'Okay, Sven, don't worry, you know where I am.' Pippa smiled and gave a little wave.

'Sure do,' he replied as she walked past him.

She felt disappointed he hadn't been in touch; it was almost as if he should have told her he wasn't coming. She scolded herself for her feelings. She didn't own him, after all. He had warned her he was busy. In the light of her conversation with Rob, she needed company; he had provided her with a good reason for feeling resentful. Now that Sven was too busy, it was hard not to feel that way again.

Walking through town, she had visions of Daniel walking beside her. It had been quite a day and she wished she hadn't bothered to phone home; Rob had depressed her.

Later that afternoon, Pippa lay on Porthcressa Beach reading her *Secrets* book. She loved the Danielle Steele novels. How often she had lost herself within the stories. She had two weeks left but in another two days, she would be finished with the book.

The sea looked tempting. Despite the islands lying in the path of the Gulf Stream, the temperature of the water was not for the faint-hearted. Fronds of seaweed slipped in and out of her toes and she listened to the sounds of the herring gull as it mewed over the shore. The sound reminded her of home.

She thought maybe it was time to leave the beach, but something caught her eye. The spectacle of terns diving—she watched them, the way they dropped like stones out of the sky. But something else made her look harder up the shore.

She recognised the vehicle parked some distance away and wondered if Sven was home. Sitting on her towel on the sand, she squinted in the sun and turned her back to the town looking out to sea.

As she traced her finger in the damp sand, she wrote PIPPA & ROB; it wouldn't be long before the sea would nudge it away. She scribbled out ROB and almost wrote Sven's name to see what it looked like. She stopped herself. *What a daft idea.*

With the trials of life left behind, a delightful solitude seemed to take over. Leaving the islands would make her feel sad. Perhaps she and Rob would have yet another row and all her problems would start again. Why would she want to go home at all? What did he want from her? She couldn't bear to think about it a moment longer.

Sven finished his work and arrived home earlier than usual. He scanned the bay with his binoculars looking for birds and spotted Pippa instead. Smiling to himself when he saw her, he had an idea. He walked some distance along the path before using the back road to the beach. Perhaps she wouldn't turn around before he got to her. He removed his sandals and hid out of sight, creeping up behind her.

Pippa felt a pair of warm hands around her eyes. She jumped. 'Guess who?'

'Oh, hello!' she said, placing her hand on her chest. 'I wondered who the heck that was.'

'Fancy a swim then?' Sven said, looking down at his feet as he stood on the sand beside her, hopping on one leg. He stepped out of his cut-off jeans, revealing a pair of tight blue swim shorts. 'If you weren't here, I'd be swimming without these,' he joked as he gazed at her head to toe.

'What's stopping you?' Pippa said, laughing.

She had the urge to put out a finger and touch him. He made her feel overwhelmed by his brown body and good looks. She wasn't sure what to do about him, or how she was supposed to respond. As he bent down to sit on the sand, she saw how he was brown below the waistband of his shorts. *Maybe he really does go skinny-dipping.*

She knew he was getting too close to her. Something had changed. He was more relaxed and open. She didn't need the stress of a failed marriage, but her marriage was already on a rock somewhere out there in the bay, and after her conversation with Rob, it was hard to make any decisions about anything.

Without warning, he grabbed her hand, pulling her towards the sea, and teased her about being a wimp in the cold water. He was behaving as if he were a school kid let out of class to play football. It was a side of him she hadn't seen before. He seemed to have changed from being serious about birds to this other personality and he certainly wasn't acting his age. She smiled to herself, thinking she preferred him that way.

'Come on, girl, get in the water. It's wonderful. We sometimes swim even with the snow on the ground in Norway,' he said. 'You look nice in that outfit.' He pointed to her bikini. 'Green suits you. It goes well with your hair.'

'What?' Pippa laughed.

'Come on, let's go swimming together. The sea isn't that cold today. I've asked Charlie James to help; I deserve one day off at least.'

'Ahh! Don't! It's freezing.' She let out a squeal of delight as the cold sea shocked her. He pushed her into the salt water.

'My God, the girl is drowning. I have to save her,' he shouted.

Pippa was laughing so much she found tears dripping down her face. He picked her up in his strong arms and splashed her back into the water. Her heart was about to burst being with this man who was so impulsive.

He gazed into her eyes. He seemed to want more play. She had to be faithful to Rob. She knew Sven was only being kind to her in view of her problems, but she didn't want him to feel sorry for her.

He sat on the sand and dried his midriff with the blue towel he had brought to the beach.

Pippa watched as he stretched out to sunbathe.

'Have you got any plans for this weekend?' he asked.

'Not really, maybe go to one of the islands, and then I don't know. I don't like to make plans, I just let it happen. My life isn't into planning things anymore.'

'Pippa, my friend, would you like to spend it with me? I mean, we can take a picnic perhaps. Go on, it'll do you good. You know, I need the company too on my days off.'

The warm breeze blew gently across Porthcressa Beach and Pippa laid her towel on one of the rocks to dry in the sun. She couldn't help smiling to herself. Was this supposed to be a date? What was she doing? It was a bit sudden, but he seemed harmless enough.

'Okay, I'll come with you. Nice of you to ask. Being alone here is fine, but not all the time.'

Sven beamed at her. 'Great.'

'Anyway, where have you been the last couple of days?' Pippa asked, hoping she wasn't sounding possessive.

'Oh, I've spent a lot of time working on the boats and it's been a difficult week. I wish I knew the date Martin was due back; I could do with a longer break. When I work normal hours, I get more time off at the weekends, especially in the winter. Maybe when we go down to the nature reserve, I'll introduce you to the other volunteers before the end of your holiday.'

'Yep, that would be nice.' As Pippa listened, she built a collection of limpet shells and placed them in a circle on the sand. She wondered if Sven already had a pretty girl amongst the volunteers. Surely, such a good-looking chap must have a woman in his life. Then why was he always alone?

'I'll tell you what,' he said. 'We'll go to Old Town, do the picnic thing and then we could drive up to the bird hide at the nature reserve in the afternoon to listen to the coot and other wildfowl. It'll give you a different perspective on water birds.'

This was the serious side of Sven; he loved the outdoor life. 'You don't mind, do you? I only want to help you enjoy yourself.'

'Of course not. You're right; it'll be good for me. Thanks.'

She couldn't believe he'd come out of nowhere and now he was asking her out on a friendly date.

'Now you're really enjoying yourself,' he said, laughing. 'You need me for therapy!' It had felt good the other night comforting her. He saw a different side to her; she was a fun-loving girl who had lost her way and he wanted to bond with her. He knew very well what it felt like to be abandoned, left out to dry. He couldn't help himself—he was naturally pushy, but he thought she wouldn't mind. He kept telling himself she was married, that he couldn't have her, but another part of his mind told him he could at least find out more about her. He had to be sure; he certainly didn't want to be 'the other bloke' in a marriage break up.

The beach. The lapping of the waves. The moment. He felt himself being part of her. He wanted to hold her hand, to touch her again and take her back to Beachside Cottage. He couldn't explain his reasons; it felt right.

'I've been thinking about you,' he said, 'and the things you told me the other night. I mean, you cannot live your life as a … erm … what's the English word … erm … oh yes, *hermit?* You are a good person and I only want to help you improve your quality of life before you go home. Give you something positive to hold onto. To remember Scilly and the reasons you came here.' He hoped it would be more than that, but he would have to wait, and patience in these matters had never been one of his stronger virtues.

'Well,' said Pippa. 'You mustn't feel sorry for me, okay?'

'No,' he replied. 'I like you.' He looked at her with a raised brow, lips in a tight smile, worried in case he had stepped beyond her comfort zone.

'Well, I like you too, Sven,' Pippa said politely. 'You've been a kind of rock for me in the last few days and I want to say thanks for that. You're right; it is difficult for me. I am having a bad time with Rob, our marriage and so on. I appreciate your support.'

Sven liked being direct. He would dive right in and tell her.

'No, I don't think you get it, do you?' His air seemed to change to a more serious note. 'I *really* like you. I don't have time to mess about. You only have a short time here. Is there any chance we could get to know each other?' There was a short silence.

Pippa gave a nervous smile. 'Oh, that sort of *really* like? Oh, I wish it were that easy. I am still grieving—you realise that?'

Sven put the towel around her shoulders, his muscular arm lingering between her neck and ear lobe. She felt protected. She fancied him, but couldn't possibly step over the boundaries. Yet she needed love. *Oh hell, he's gorgeous, but I can't do this, it's not real. A holiday romance, they never work. I'll end up with more heartache, shit… what do I say?*

Most of the day trippers had deserted the beach. They were almost alone, hidden by the rocks. Sven laid the towel on the sand for Pippa to sit beside him. 'Hang on, you got thirty seconds to think about it while I get the sand off my feet, I want to put my sandals back on.' He was nervous and didn't want to sit in an embarrassing silence while she contemplated his question—and what if he had made a mistake? He'd made one big mistake five years ago, had his fingers burned by someone else's infidelity. What if he was doing it again? He must have more confidence this time.

Pippa didn't need to think too much. It must have showed. How could she have a relationship or even a quick fling with him before going home? She had thought the unthinkable. It was an absolute 'no', but going back to Rob? Sven was making it difficult. She gazed at the title of the book she had been reading; she could have secrets of her own and not a soul would know.

Alone, like this, she might be able to accomplish her search for happiness. If she allowed herself to be sucked into this illusion, did it matter? Rob would never know and probably wouldn't care. She wasn't sure anymore. Here, she could put her worries behind her, for a short while at least.

She slid her fingers across her lips, back and forth as she watched him washing his feet in the sea. She couldn't take her eyes off him. With his blonde hair falling over his ears, he was difficult to resist.

On his return, he sat with his legs stretched out, his hands patting the wet sand, and his back against the sun-warmed rock, a place he had sat before where his thoughts often turned into reality. He saw how she had written her name in the sand and scrubbed out another name—he retraced her writing and with his index finger he wrote *SVEN*, after *PIPPA &*.

Pippa realised what he had done and what might be coming next; she had to be prepared, but now was not the right time—and would it ever be?

'Look,' he said. 'No matter what happens, you need to become *you* again.' He looked at her questioningly. 'Yes? Am I right? It could be you and me together having a great time; all this sadness must have pulled you down like a drowning animal. Dreadful to have gone through all that stuff.' He took hold of her hand. 'You're a great person, Pippa. I know we have just met, but it feels right. It's you I care about, and I mean it! I wouldn't want to do anything you didn't want as well.' He thought about what he'd said and wondered if perhaps a 'here today—gone tomorrow relationship' would be enough to satisfy both their needs. No, he had told her the truth; he didn't want that, he wanted more. She was lovely, but would she take the risk?

She pulled away from him tactfully and played with the loose threads of the towel.

'You can go home and forget about me if you wish, but that's not what I want.' He dried her back with the towel. 'I've thought about you a lot,' he said as he touched her smooth skin. Her legs seemed to beckon him to reach all the way to the top. His libido was increasing and he couldn't help himself. The green bikini and the bare flesh in between turned him on. He kept telling himself to walk away for a moment, do something else. He wrapped the towel around his waist to hide his desires. He needed to hear the right words before he would kiss her. Sensing her feelings, he desperately wanted to be part of her. Yes, her life was still on hold, but he wanted to help her make the changes. It had to be her decision and he felt his heart beating faster, wondering how she would respond. Should he be doing this at all?

Pippa's yearning to be with him deepened, but she held back, refusing to allow herself to make a stupid mistake.

There was silence. Sven was everything Rob was not. She raised her head and looked into his eyes. She had only known him a few days and the whole idea seemed ludicrous. His face willed her to say 'yes' but now, suddenly, she could tell something bothered him.

'Look, first I need to explain something to you,' he said. 'Perhaps I understand what you are going through. You see, I also have a story to tell. It's part of the reason I live here. I have also escaped from a trauma. About five years ago, my relationship broke up. I didn't want to tell you the other night because it wasn't appropriate. I had this wonderful girlfriend, Astrid; we were due to get married in Norway. She was the best thing that ever happened to me. I couldn't stop thinking about her; I suppose I was … what's the word? Erm … head over heels in love with her. She was beautiful and kind and everything I ever wanted.'

Pippa raised her eyebrows. This wasn't what she had expected him to say. 'So what happened?'

'She slept with my best friend, that's what happened. We had the wedding planned, everything: the guests, where we would go for our honeymoon, all the usual things you do, and she was about to choose her wedding dress. I was the happiest man in all of Norway. About three months before the date, I had gone out to do some birding with a group from the local club. It was snowing and very cold and we all decided to stop for the day. I came back earlier than expected to my apartment in Trondheim to discover she was in bed with Mads, my best mate. Can you believe it?'

'Oh dear Sven, I am so sorry,' Pippa empathised. 'It must have been awful for you.' She saw how his eyes gazed upon the sand and his thoughts seemed far away in Norway.

'My God, I bet she had a problem talking her way out of that one. So what happened after that?'

'She married him! I have no idea why she changed her mind; I gave her everything she could ever want. Her excuse? She didn't know why she had done it. I was devastated. The trouble is, I never understood her reasoning either. Something just didn't seem to add up. I searched my soul for months asking what I had done to deserve it. I left Norway in a hurry; I didn't want to be there anymore. You can imagine what that did to me.'

'I bet,' Pippa said. 'So you came here, eh?'

Sven looked down, his eyes gazing upon the white sand. 'Well, like you, I also came to Scilly on a wing and prayer hoping to find happiness again, but I made a mistake. Scilly is not the place to find love. Oh sure, I love my job with all my heart and I've been out with a couple of local girls to date, but they leave for the mainland and that's it—gone! The truth is I'm a bit lonely here despite all the hundreds of people who visit each day. Many of them are over fifty … they might want a toy boy!' he said with a chuckle.

Pippa smiled. 'Oh Sven, I'm sorry. What a pair we are, eh?'

'Do you still love your husband, Pippa?' Sven needed to know.

'That's a hard question. I suppose I do in an odd way, but now it's like he's just a best friend and not someone I feel like going to bed with—sorry, I didn't mean to talk in that way.'

'It's okay.' Sven hesitated. 'Could you see yourself in another relationship? You see, the thing is, I feel I might be … you know … more than just liking you as my friend.' He smiled and looked into her eyes. 'I haven't stopped thinking about you since we first met.'

Pippa felt like crying. He was lonely, he was lovely, he was kind and gentle, he was handsome, interesting, and a dream of a guy, how could she refuse? She didn't want to tell him how she felt. It was all too soon.

'How can you say those things, Sven? You hardly know me.'

'Sometimes you don't have to know someone a long time, it just feels right. I didn't invite you for coffee the other evening without being curious about you. There was something that turned on a bright light for me.'

'Aw, Sven, I … I don't know what to say.' Pippa felt tears returning, but this time they were tears of joy.

'Say yes?'

He'd made her want to say 'I feel the same way too,' but because of Rob, she couldn't say it. She had to be sensible and it wasn't too late to refuse.

Sven leaned toward her to give her a hug. He pushed back the stray strands of auburn hair blowing in her face and gazed into her green-blue eyes. He'd got nearer to her than he'd expected when he felt her breathing and her lips became a temptation. He held her close as they lay on the beach, oblivious to the sound of the waves, and to the terns screaming along the shore. His lips pressed gently against hers, caressing her face.

After a few moments, Pippa pulled back. 'Oh God, sorry … I'm in such a muddle. I don't want you to be messed about.'

Sven was firm. 'Pippa, stop. We are in the here and now and I'm sorry … no, no, I'm not sorry. I feel so good about you. Please, don't stop now.' He begged her. 'Maybe I am going too fast for you. Forgive me. The trouble is, we don't have much time and it's tearing me up.'

'There we go, both apologising to each other,' she said. Again, she felt close to tears but she didn't want to cry. 'Let's see how it goes, shall we?' She knew it was crazy, and a huge mistake if she got it wrong. Yes, it was wrong, but oh … so tempting to be part of his life.

Sven put his arm around her. He was overwhelmed with joy, but also scared he might lose her through being impulsive, he became afraid of the consequences. She was so far away from home; her husband hadn't seemed to care about her coming to Scilly—at least that's how it seemed. Would he be breaking Rob's heart too? Somehow, he didn't think so, but what did he know about Pippa?

'You're gorgeous, you know that?' he said. 'Come on, let's go home and have something to drink. We can talk there and if you want a shower, you can have one. It's my fault you got soaking wet.' He chuckled. 'I didn't mean to upset you, Pippa, I only want to make you happier.' He stopped himself, thinking he had said too much already.

Taking her by the hand, he led the way to the cottage.

They plodded up the loose sand and he kissed her on the cheek, touching her nose with his index finger. 'I've thought about you a lot on the boat trips in the week. I couldn't wait to find you again. I saw you today and took the chance to ask you if you could see yourself being a part of me.'

Pippa thought she could listen to him for hours.

'Whoa there! I haven't said yes! One kiss doesn't make a romance.' She smiled at him. 'I have a husband back home to contend with and I have to think about this holiday romance thing. We have to be realistic. I feel as if I have opened yet another complication and I'm not sure how to deal with it. Although you're such a darling that you make it hard for me to resist you.' She hugged him as a thank you.

Sven stiffened for a moment. 'I hope this isn't a holiday romance, Pippa. I think, at this moment, you might break my heart! Look, erm … I know I'm racing on here, but to be honest it's been difficult for me as well. I don't want to lose you. I felt my luck was in when we met, and on our second meeting, it was great having dinner together. Each time I saw you, I wanted to be with you. And … you're a great kisser!' he laughed.

'Aw, Sven, that's so sweet of you.' Pippa melted. 'No one's ever spoken to me in that way.' *Not even Rob.* She couldn't blame Rob. She mustn't forget, he had lost his son too and Daniel had been his pride and joy. Saying what they meant to each other had become harder with each passing year. She admitted to herself Sven had swept her off her feet, but Rob had never spoken to her in that way. Sven was fun to be with and she needed fun—but at the same time, she mustn't forget her son.

'Maybe I shouldn't have pushed you. I hope it's going to be all right,' he said as they got nearer to the house.

'Too late, I crossed a line and I promised myself I wouldn't,' Pippa said as she stroked Sven's cheek. 'But thanks for giving me some hope.' She hugged him again.

They arrived at the door of the whitewashed cottage. The colours on the garden wall were amazing; Pippa appreciated them even more in the daylight. Wall-to-wall daisy jewels in varying shades of pink and yellow seemed to cascade down the wall of the small granite boulders. Tamarisk grew along the edge of the path. A large brown spider had built a web among the feathery vegetation.

If only she could live in a cottage like this. Looking out every morning to the blue ocean, instead of the cold grey North Sea. The whole of the afternoon with this wonderful man had changed her life. It didn't matter if it was only for today. Pippa had visions of herself waking up every morning to the pounding of the Atlantic and the call of the wild birds. If she had a relationship with Sven, she could be brewing the biggest storm of her life. Would she have the strength to survive all the stress with Rob?

Sven removed his arm from around her waist and escorted her into his home. He didn't want anyone to see them together; he was just not ready for the population of Scilly to broadcast his personal life.

'Here's a clean towel, Pippa, the shower is at the top of the stairs. Enjoy!'

He imagined how it would have been to step in there with her, but he mustn't chase her away. He knew he was going too fast but found it hard to stop himself.

'Oh, thanks, I shan't be long. I gather you got some shampoo in there.'

'Ya, try the lemon one,' Sven agreed, 'it's got conditioner in it.'

Pippa smiled at his reply and the feelings of happiness as she undressed for her shower. As the water sprinkled to her shoulders, she thought about the afternoon and the kissing. His gentle first-time kiss, with fingers down her spine and his other hand firmly on her shoulder … He had caressed her face and looked into her eyes and oh … he was so sweet, kind and everything she had longed for. She had responded to his kiss and was probably about to have an affair. Maybe she should have a good time and forget about it. If it were a holiday romance, it would be something good to remember through her life. She couldn't stop thinking about his rugged but boyish good looks; the muscles in his arms that could hold her so special. Never had a man allowed her to feel so much like a woman, so free, and spontaneous. She smiled to herself and sighed. *Life is so full of twists and turns.*

Since losing Daniel, Rob had become aggressive and impatient. At New Year, he'd become too close to Joan's sister Carole. It was only a kiss under the mistletoe, but it had been passionate. Pippa remembered feeling strange about it. Then there was the girl from Australia he'd met at the pub; they'd walked down the road together after closing time and he was home two hours late. She could smell a perfume on him; it certainly wasn't one of hers. She had put it all down to his aching mind, preferring to forget the incident. She'd had to trust him. She was sure he hadn't had sex with any of them, or had he? *How many more females did he like to snog under the mistletoe? He doesn't love me, I know he doesn't.* If *he* could kiss someone else, it sure made it easier to think that she didn't need to feel guilty about kissing Sven. Perhaps she was justifying her kiss. It was all very confusing.

Sven watched as Pippa came down the stairs smoothing down her T-shirt. He wanted to hold her in his arms and love her with all of his heart. Her freckled face, the green-blue eyes, and the hair that reminded him of sunset fascinated him.

Pippa met his gaze. It seemed to say, 'Well, what do you think about us?' She thought he'd waited too long for her reply.

'I like you a lot, Sven. I have to say it's all rather surreal; I'm only trying to be realistic. I hope you understand. I mean you're such a great guy, who could resist you?' She cupped her hands around the mug of tea he'd given her and looked into his face.

He came closer. 'I tell you, Pippa, you'll break my heart when you leave on the ferry.' He kissed her cheek. 'Mm, that shower gel smells really nice.'

'But Sven, listen to me, I've been thinking. I live five hundred miles from you; it's a journey over the sea and about ten hours on the train to Whitby. How can we have a relationship like that? And how can I go back to Rob and never think of you again? It can't possibly work, no matter how we try. I may have lost myself in the last few years, but I still have my sense of right and wrong.'

'Let's talk it through—what have we got to lose? How do you feel about me right now?'

'Well, I think you're adorable and kind and lots of good things.'

Sven smiled back at her with an air of 'thanks'.

'You told me your marriage is a mess. We both lost our way in life, so what better thing to do than be together? Make it right again, support each other. If you want to be with someone, you will go to the end of the earth to stay with them. Is Rob doing that for you?'

'Wow, Sven, that's a bit unfair. I mean, Rob has been my rock since my father died and then Daniel, I cannot … just leave him.' Pippa's eyes filled with tears.

'Sorry, I didn't mean to be harsh; it just came out that way. I suppose I've also had enough of hanging around waiting for something better to turn up and I sensed it with you as well.'

Pippa thought for a moment. He was right. Rob wasn't exactly running marathons to ensure she stayed with him, but he was Daniel's father. Decisions like this must be considered carefully. It was like an odd nightmare waiting to be unleashed.

'So what should we do?' she asked.

Sensing her fears, he reached over to the box of tissues and wiped her tears away.

'Come here,' he said and held her close, looking into her eyes while his hand stroked her face. He kissed her brow and worked his way down her face until he reached her lips. She responded as he cuddled her closer to him for reassurance.

'Look, what I suggest is that we discover all about each other during your stay here, see how it goes, enjoy every moment we have left and if by the end of that time we end up hating each other, then we can say we tried and we both made a big mistake.' He held her hand. 'I know, Pippa, I know I have made this difficult. I'm so, so sorry, but I can't help the way I feel about you. I just seemed to gel with you, that's all.'

'And what about Astrid? Is she still in your life?'

'Well, I do think about her because my mother told me she got divorced this year, but I doubt I will ever see her again—she lives in Norway. I have to start afresh. So … ?' He wondered what else there was to say.

Pippa looked at his face and smiled. 'You can be so persuasive, and something tells me you're right. With all these bad times, perhaps being with you for another two weeks will open new horizons for both of us.' She stroked his arm.

Sven hugged her. 'You are very beautiful, Pippa. Mmm … And loving,' he added. 'Welcome to Scilly, and let's enjoy every moment together. Let me show you about nature here. I want to give you a good holiday but I hope we can see each other afterwards. I want to make it clear; I don't want a holiday romance. I am looking for a girlfriend with a future. May I?'

She liked the plan and maybe she shouldn't worry about a relationship with Sven. But a girlfriend with a future? Had Sven made the biggest mistake of his life? She looked proudly at him. How lucky she was to have found him, but the guilt began seeping into her mind as she folded her towel in her rucksack.

'What time are you going to go out tomorrow?' She asked, trying to sound normal.

'I'll pick you up around 10.30, if that's okay?' he said.

'I'll make the sandwiches and I have another bottle of wine.'

'You're too good to me, Pippa,' Sven chuckled.

She was about to leave him, when his eyes met hers and he drew closer to her. He took her in his arms and kissed her until goose bumps tickled her spine, and she didn't want to let him go. His kisses were so gentle. She didn't ever want it to stop, but she thought she'd better leave before they both went too far.

'Sven, this is lovely, but…' She felt her heart racing. 'I have to go, sorry.'

'Why go? So soon?'

'Sorry, it's nothing you have done, it's *me*. I need to go home and think about all this. I have a lot more at stake than you do, Sven.' She wanted time to consider her feelings, a place by herself to think.

'Yes, I know. I understand, but tomorrow is another day and we can spend it together. You still want to, yes?' Sven asked, hoping he hadn't made a huge error.

'Of course I do. Although I'm feeling a little overwhelmed and need some time.'

'Sorry, Pippa, That's how I am. I'll try and slow down—promise.'

'There's no need to keep apologising. I don't mind, honest. And don't worry, I need to go home and relax and then I will dream about you,' she said, then kissed him. She squeezed his hand and made her way toward the door. 'I do like you, honest, I do. In fact, I think I could fall for you, too, in a big way, but I have to think about all this. Do you really want to take me on with all this grief hanging around me? I'm not sure you know what you're doing. Give me until tomorrow and we'll talk then.'

Sven hugged her again.

'See you at ten o'clock then. I'll be ready,' she said with a smile. 'Thanks again for a lovely afternoon.'

Sven held her hand as she walked out of the door, then let go and watched as she made her way to Gilstone.

Pippa shook with elation when she arrived home. 'Yes, yes and *yes*,' she said aloud with both fists banging the air. 'What the hell am I doing?' She sucked in her breath and let it out slowly, allowing the adrenaline to subside. She had a fantasy: Sven making love to her on a deserted beach with palm trees, and a beautiful affair where he whisked her off into the night under the moon on one of the deserted islands. 'What the hell!' Pippa sank to her knees in tears and sheer relief, remembering what he had written in the sand. 'Pippa and Sven,' she whispered to herself. *'Pippa and Sven, Pippa and Sven. Yes, yes, yes.'*

That evening, Pippa climbed into bed thinking of all the things that could go wrong. Would Rob ever find out? The relationship seemed impossible to repair; they knew each other too well. Yet how could she leave Rob without taking away his home, pulling the rug from under his feet? It was her house, she inherited it from her father. How could she leave her son in the graveyard, with no more flowers? Would she tell Joan about Sven? Two weeks of holiday romance, and she would go home renewed and perhaps never see Sven again: just a fond memory. Then she remembered he'd said he wanted a lasting relationship; perhaps only Sven could help repair her sorrows. She had to discuss it further with him to find out what he really wanted of her. It was all going too fast.

CHAPTER THIRTEEN

Pippa looked in the wardrobe to find her new jacket. Outside, the rain drizzled down her bedroom window. On hearing the engine of the van and the door closing, she ran down the stairs and opened the front door. He stood there with his welcoming smile, waiting for her.

'I should have looked at the forecast for today. Not to worry,' he said. 'Let's go on up to the bird hide, have our sandwiches, and see if any new birds have flown in. Anyway, good morning, my lovely,' he said as he kissed her on the cheek. 'How are you?'

'Fine thanks,' Pippa said, amused at the words "my lovely". 'I'm all packed, wine, sandwiches, coffee in the flask—okay, let's go.' She stepped outside.

Sven drove to the Higher Moors nature reserve through the rain, the windscreen wipers going back and forth. He liked her new jacket and saw she had her binoculars strung around her neck. He was smiling to himself.

He parked on the side of the road and didn't bother to lock the van. As he strode beside her, he helped pull the hood over her head as heavier rain began to fall. On reaching the bird hide, he took her hand and held her close, shielding her from the weather and they passed through the dripping doorframe. Inside it was very dark and Sven opened the hatch with a view onto the large pond and the reed beds on the other side. They sat on the high seat in the bird hide and made themselves comfortable.

Once inside, Pippa sensed the odour of the damp earth floor. They startled a mallard, so Sven spoke in whispers. The rain splattered on the water, splashing noises echoed over the pond. Coots gave a repetitive 'kowk' and a couple of great crested grebes slid along with the mallards. Pippa watched, thrilled by the tranquillity, and listened as Sven pointed out the birds.

'*Podiceps cristatus*,' he whispered. 'A smart looking bird, eh? Another one for your list … ' He pointed to the great-crested grebe gliding in the water. 'The female grebe carries her young on her back. Oh yes, see, there they are—small striped babies.'

'Oh, aren't they sweet?' Pippa said, with delight and softening her voice.

'And there's a gadwall, Latin name, *Anas Strepera*. Look, there it is—over there.' Again he pointed, this time to the left.

'Oh yes—I see it. To me, it's just a duck.' She admitted. 'And you said it's a what … ? Gad—wall? The grebe babies are lovely, aren't they? Look … aw look, they're getting closer to us!' She whispered with some excitement.

Sven nodded and smiled. 'Hm, ya.' He adored her enthusiasm. 'Great, eh?'

Pippa sensed an inner peace, one she had felt only a few times in her life. She was aware of Sven's breathing as he looked through his binoculars. Beside her was a caring beautiful man who could lead her into happiness but she knew it would only be living out her fantasy. She needed more convincing than just a kiss.

'Did you sleep okay last night, Pippa?'

'What do *you* think?' Pippa smiled coyly. 'It wasn't easy after yesterday—my brain was going around in circles. I had so many questions. And you?'

'I suppose I did sleep after a while, but I was also thinking about yesterday. I really shouldn't have pushed you that far, I'm sorry.'

'No, no, it's okay. I really enjoyed being with you, Sven, honest I did—and, well, what more can I say? I came with you today, so it must have been good.' She looked at him, hoping he wasn't about to back down on her.

'It's strange, you know; I feel I've known you all my life,' Sven explained, interrupted by mallards fighting on the water.

'We might end up like those ducks!' Pippa turned to him, 'so what do we do now, start building a nest?'

Sven laughed, but she was right, although 'nest building' might have to wait a while.

Sven lifted the strap of his binoculars over his head and placed them on the bench. He stood up. 'Come here,' he said. 'I want to give you a hug.'

He opened his jacket to wrap her inside. She was close to him, warm and comforted, and he kissed her; it was more of a passionate kiss than yesterday. Lips to lips, he caressed her face and in his passion, he spoke to her in Norwegian. His aftershave and the aroma of the dank earth floor seemed to enhance the atmosphere. She had never been kissed in that way. He pulled her closer and she turned her back to him to lay in his arms as he kissed her neck and ears. Yes, she could feel his emotions all right. She talked to him, ensuring he stayed focused.

The rain began to pour heavily on the roof of the hide. They couldn't hear each other speak.

'Perhaps we can go somewhere else after this,' Sven explained above the noise of the rain. He placed his nose into her hair and took in the perfume of her shampoo. 'I think you are a very brave woman, Pippa. Maybe during our time together, you can tell me more about yourself. I'm a good listener.'

'Yeah, I appreciate it; you are so nice to me, Sven. I can't …' Pippa stood up before a tear ran down her face. She turned around and gazed into his eyes, wiping away a stray drop of rain on his cheek. Then he kissed her again, deep and loving, his hands around her face, stroking her hair. 'Pippa, you're so lovely. I really want you to share the good things with me and we can go on the boat together, it will be great fun.'

Pippa put her finger to his lips. 'You don't know what you are saying, Sven, honest you don't. You have to get to know me better. I know I keep saying this but … do you really want to take on someone with all these dreadful problems?'

Again he kissed her, his hands now stroking her back. She wanted him to lay down with her on the earthen floor of the hide to share her emotions. But she mustn't, she had to take her time with this. Life would never be the same again and what if she got pregnant? Being on the pill was never a guarantee. After Daniel, she didn't want any more kids unless things changed for the better. Anyway, you had to be careful these days with all those warnings on the TV. She felt sure Sven was not jumping into bed with every woman he met, but how could she be so confident about him? They had only just met; it was all so bizarre.

'Mm, I hope you are enjoying this as much as I am,' he said. 'I think we both have to make the best of it. You are right. I think for now we should just go along as we please.'

'I agree, but it's going to be hard,' Pippa replied.

Sven gave her a derisive look and a kiss. 'I think it's already hard,' he chuckled, and then wished he hadn't said it.

'Come on, let's not go down that path,' Pippa giggled. 'There's a picnic to be eaten, and it's lunch-time already.'

'Aw, spoilsport,' he said, laughing at her comment.

Pippa opened the sandwich box and offered Sven a choice. She munched on her salmon and cucumber sandwich as Sven looked through the telescope at the paddling gadwall. Today, for the first time in years, she felt the happiness she once had as a child. Sven could be the man of her dreams forever and ever; he could end all her troubles, but nothing was that simple. Where would she live? Here on Scilly? Hell, no, that was way beyond her imagination. Leaving Daniel behind would be impossible.

'Sven, are we really doing the right thing?' Pippa asked. 'I mean, what exactly do you expect of me?'

'I told you, I need someone to share my life and I hope it's you. We can have a lot of fun together and I think we both need this. I'm just glad I found you, Pippa. Sorry, but I cannot explain it any better, it just feels right. I hope you feel the same way as I do.' Sven stood, looking into her eyes.

Pippa stood with her back to the hide door. 'I think I do, it's just I have a lot at stake and I hope you can understand,' she sighed.

'Yes, of course. Come here, my lovely red-haired lady. Let's hug and then we'll go back to Gilstone for the rest of the afternoon—is that okay with you?'

Pippa packed up the sandwiches as Sven downed the last wine in his beaker. They would finish the bottle back at Gilstone.

CHAPTER FOURTEEN

It was the weekend. Joan phoned as she always did on a Saturday morning.

'Just checking—are you okay, Rob?' she said.

'I think it should be me asking if *you* are okay.'

'Yes, I think I am. What am I supposed to feel? Any news to tell me then?'

'Pippa called the night she arrived, she seems fine. Trouble is though, I'm in a bit of a quandary about what happens when she gets home. We'll sort it all out, I'm sure.' Rob sighed. 'There's no reason to think we can't have a trial separation or even a "friendly" divorce under the circumstances.'

'What's all this talk about separation and divorce, Rob? What's it all about? This is news to me. You're not suggesting … surely? You've never mentioned it before. I don't want you and Pippa to split up as well! This is all going wrong, isn't it?' Joan sighed.

'Well, our problems have been going on since Daniel. In our case, I hope it'll be straightforward. Look, Joan, I'll tell you more about it when I see you. Have you seen Terry?' Rob asked.

'Nope, he's gone back to Aberdeen without even calling here to see me. He promised he would. His Mam phoned me. She said, "Now, Joan, you haven't had one of your tantrums again, have you? You'll push him away you know; he's a sensitive man, and I know all about it, believe me."' Joan mimicked her mother-in-law, then rolled her eyes. 'But then I heard his dad shout "Phyllis!" down the phone, you know how he does, and she shut up; tried to get out of it, she did. If only she knew, poor woman. He should try to explain it to her, get her used to the idea. After all, she thinks she knows her son best and it's obvious she doesn't! I'm wondering if I should tell her with time, break it to her gently—trouble is, she wouldn't believe me.'

'And you? Are *you* used to the idea?' Rob asked, feeling that Joan was being too cheery for the news she had received. *It's only natural she's in denial.*

'My toe still hurts a bit. It's broken, but it seems to be getting better now. It went black for a while, I think I might lose the toe-nail.'

'No, I mean, how are you in view of Terry leaving? Glad to hear it's improving. I shouldn't ask this but … did Terry hurt you? I wondered if it might be that he pushed you when you hurt your toe? That's all. I'm sorry to ask, but as a friend and health worker, I'd like to be sure it was an accident.'

'No, it was my fault, Rob, and I'm fine. I stubbed it during a row with him. He was actually quite caring about it. He would never hurt me, but thanks for asking. Well love, I'll come and see you soon, when Pippa comes home,' Joan said, trying to be cheerful. 'She'll be hellish shocked when I tell her about Terry, it's bloody awful, isn't it?'

'Listen, Joan, I think you have to understand how it's been for Terry as well. It's not something that's awful; it's actually quite natural. You must try to understand how he feels as well.' Rob knew he had to talk to her soon; she was being far too cheerful.

'Yeah, I suppose so. Thanks, Rob. This gay thing is all so new to me, I really don't understand it—I mean, after all these years we've been together.'

'Okay, love, I know how it was with your mam and dad, they were always rather stiff about things like that. I can understand how you might feel. Look, er … How about meeting up tomorrow night at the pub and we can have a long chat? I did promise I would spend some time with you, so let's talk there, eh?'

'Thanks, Rob, I'll do that. See you soon, love, bye.' Joan sighed as she put the phone down. It was always Rob who had been around since Terry had been away. The shower unit, the motorbike, and the occasional time with Jordan when she'd had to go out in a hurry. What was the matter with Pippa that she couldn't get on with him anymore?

It was Monday morning. Rob slumped into the settee. On the shelf above the wood-burning stove rested the letter from Grover and Pearson. He knew he could have opened it, but he hadn't considered it a priority; his mind was in so many places.

He sat staring at the envelope. What time was it? *Oh yes, I must go shopping.* He made a mental note of the food he needed to buy.

That was usually Pippa's job. He must vacuum the floor in the lounge where he'd spilt crumbs from a cake he'd eaten the night before, and then there was the washing up. Pippa would normally do those things. In a way, he began to miss her. He knew he shouldn't feel like this because of the housework but things were beginning to get on top of him. Stephen Carmichael's visit had been very strange. He hadn't stayed long, only long enough to ensure he had the right name and date of birth. 'I'm sorry, I can't tell you any more, except that there is this letter for you. It was left with us some years ago. Personally, I have no idea what's in the letter; I was just asked to give it to you. I work part-time up here, and my job is with probate; I'm contracted to Grover and Pearson. I happened to be passing through Whitby, so John asked me to call in and see you. I hope it's good news,' he'd said. 'I only had to ensure I was giving it to the right person.'

Rob sat staring at the shelf for a while, then stood up and opened the envelope with care, expecting to see an advert for a solicitor's office in Hull. *Solicitors don't do things like that though, do they?* Stephen Carmichael had seemed genuine enough; he wasn't selling double-glazing after all.

Inside were two letters. One in a blue manila envelope, slightly tattered, and the other a pristine official-looking letter from Grover and Pearson.

DEAR MR LAMBTON

THE ENCLOSED LETTER IS FOR YOUR ATTENTION. WE HAVE KEPT IT IN OUR FILES FOR A NUMBER OF YEARS FOR A CLIENT OF OURS. WHEN YOU HAVE READ THE LETTER AND IF YOU WISH TO TAKE THIS FURTHER, PLEASE CONTACT US AND WE WILL TAKE THE APPROPRIATE ACTION.

YOURS SINCERELY,

JOHN GROVER

Rob held the blue envelope in his hand. *There is no postmark.*

He was careful to slit across the sticky flap on the back of the envelope with a small kitchen knife. *Who has sent me this? It's written on airmail paper.* Pulling out the flimsy blue paper, he proceeded to read it.

Rob stopped reading for a moment in shock. *A letter from my real mother, my God, bloody hell. Oh no, this can't be real.* He sat on the sofa to read on, his mouth half open in anticipation of what came next.

Rob almost fainted; his mouth was open in awe of the letter and he couldn't believe what he had read. *Peter Haines? Oh my God, I've heard of him somewhere from work.* He wasn't sure whether to laugh, cry, phone someone or deal with it himself. He read on.

Rob's heart beat faster as he read the words 'mental health'.

strict, controlling, and old-fashioned in her ways and she didn't approve. I feel sure she never thought once about my feelings. It was all about her snobbery and my father's Rotary Club friends. All she could think of was protecting her image. She was well known in town. I was only just seventeen and Mum couldn't take the scandal. They sent me away to a life of hardship and much sorrow during the pregnancy. One little mistake and it cost me my happiness. If only I could have found you. Your real father is a good man and we are all proud of him. I have placed this letter with John Grover, he is not only a solicitor, but an old family friend. He was best man at our wedding. He has promised to help your father work with the adoption people to find you. It might take years, but I want you to know we have tried. I have given instructions that if anything should happen to me, you will receive this letter. I don't know if they will ever find you. My heart aches to think I may never see you. I am writing this because it makes me feel better to know that one day you might read it. If you do read this, please get in touch with the person who gave it to you. I want you to know I always loved you.
Your loving mum,
Fiona Haines

Rob sat with the letter on his knee. He stared at a spot on the wallpaper. The more he stared, the more he thought his life had crashed. He wasn't sure what to do, what to say, whether to stand up or sit down or call his parents. He sat there, staring into an imaginary void.

Right now, he needed Pippa—well, no, it couldn't be Pippa anymore—but maybe it should be. In his confusion, he dialled Joan; she was the one person who would understand in view of Pippa's absence.

'Hi, Joan, erm … sorry to bother you, it's me … erm, I've had a bit of a shock, a letter from a solicitor in Hull. They found my real mother.'

'What? Oh—my—God! Should I come round and see you?'

'If you want to. I'm not sure what to do about it, to be honest. I need someone to talk to. I'm feeling a bit strange about it all.'

'Okay, I'll be there in about fifteen minutes. I'll ask Carole to take Jordan; he's playing in the garden. Just need to wash his face and hands.'

On arrival, Rob handed Joan the letter. 'See this? I'm in total shock…'

Joan read it, her mouth opening and closing. 'Blu dee hell, Rob. Oh shit, I don't believe this. You got a real Mam! Wow, this is amazing, how wonderful.'

'Well, it's not quite like that,' said Rob. 'Read on.'

Joan kept reading. 'You got a sister called Penny and a brother called Bruce. Oh heck! Are you going to try and find them?'

'For goodness sake, Joan, I've only just read the letter,' Rob reminded her.

'Yes, sorry, I do tend to jump in with both feet, don't I?' she said, looking sheepish. 'This is really weird though—and you're sure it's real? This letter, I mean.'

'Oh yes, I feel sure it is now, though before—I didn't. I suppose I'll have to tell my real mam and—well, no, not my real ones, I mean *my* mam and dad. Oh hell, this is confusing.'

'I know what you mean, Rob. Yes, you ought to phone them and tell them. They brought you up and they are your real Mam and Dad in that respect. They're the ones you should tell first.'

Joan read part of the letter again. 'And this guy who is your father is a doctor? That's weird, you being a nurse at the hospital and all that.'

'I ought to tell Pippa before she comes back from Scilly, we have lots to discuss and … shit, there's too much going on. I don't have a phone number for her.'

'I'll support you for now,' Joan said. 'Don't worry, you can tell her at the right moment. It might make a difference to your lives, best not to spoil her holiday under the circumstances. It'll be a huge surprise for her when she comes home.'

Rob didn't hear her last comment. 'But I think my real mother is dead.'

'Oh, jees. Don't you just wish Pippa was here now?'

'Oh, don't, please. It's all too much.'

Joan began her usual advising. 'It's almost two weeks before she gets back, you must tell her when she phones. I think you ought to phone Benidorm and tell your parents and then phone the solicitor—that is, if you want to.'

'Yeah, you're right,' Rob said. 'I kind of knew in my heart one day this might happen. In my head I wanted it, but you know I've always been afraid of what I might find, like opening Pandora's Box, that sort of thing.'

'Chat with Ralph and Sally! They are the parents who brought you up. I'm sure they will help you understand what to do.'

'I'll phone them. It's a pity they're so far away. It's times like these when you need a family member,' said Rob.

'I'm surprised you didn't go and live in Spain with them when you had the opportunity.'

'If you remember, Joan, I was studying for my nursing career; I didn't want to give it up.' Rob shrugged. He suddenly realised that if he had gone to live in Spain, Daniel would more than likely still be alive. He tried to stop thinking about it.

'Okay, I know,' said Joan. 'Well … do that, and if you need to talk, call me, right? Gosh, this is quite a revelation, eh? Bit weird though, isn't it?'

He smiled to himself. *Joan, always there to help.* 'Yes I know, I'm sad now that I never knew my real mother.' *What the hell am I supposed to do?*

'Maybe you can find your real dad though?' Joan suggested.

'Possibly—I don't know. Anyway, we'll see. I don't want to upset my mam and dad, despite the fact I don't see them much these days. You and I seem to have gone through some bad times recently; it's comforting to know you are there for me at times like this.'

'It should be Pippa you need to thank—not me.'

'No, Joan, you're wrong there—it's more than that. Look at you and your circumstances, and me in mine … We have to try and find a way to get through this, don't we?'

'So what do we do, Rob, this *you and me,* where will our lives take us next, I wonder?'

'Honestly, Joan, I have no idea. I should make this phone call before I do anything else.'

'I'll have to think about me,' Joan said sadly. 'I don't want to be left behind. I have to make a new start soon for the sake of Jordan. One day, I'll have to tell him about his dad, and I dread it.'

'Joan, it's not so terrible, Terry still cares about you and Jordan, I know he does, he's just not … well, um … not that way anymore.'

'It's a real shit life for me now,' she said. 'I don't think he's ever coming back.'

Rob had never seen her in this mood; she had always been so positive, old-fashioned and mothering. He liked her for all those things. 'I'm sorry you feel like that, love.' He wanted to help, but he could not focus.

'Let's talk about it another day, shall we? I really do have to sort this matter of Fiona Haines.'

'Okay, Rob, sorry. I'll see you soon.'

Joan left the house. Hurrying home back to Carole and Jordan, her mind churned over. She always had to pass the place where Daniel was run over. She would avoid it today if she could. She knew she was losing both Rob and Pippa; she felt it. What would she do next? She had to think of how to solve her predicament, but, as she drove along the road in the pouring rain, she couldn't think; instead she cried all the way home.

CHAPTER FIFTEEN

Time seemed to be closing in fast. Sven had been working again and Pippa had explored the outer islands with him. She had enjoyed every moment and not only had she got to know him better, but she felt more comfortable as a birdwatcher and confident with the birds' names. He had taught her a lot.

'That was a great meal, Pippa, thanks. You can certainly cook. Shall we sit somewhere more comfortable?'

They moved away from the dining table at Gilstone; Pippa opened a window and closed the kitchen door to keep out the smell of fried food. Sven sat on the settee before sliding down to the floor to stretch out.

'Can of beer for you?' she asked, handing it to him before snuggling up beside him.

'Oh thanks, now this is really cosy.' The can fizzed open with a tug of the ring pull and Sven quickly supped the foam from the top of the can.

'So tell me more about your life in Norway,' Pippa said as she settled down and pushed a cushion at her back. She gave Sven a peck on the lips.

'There isn't much to tell really. My life is here now. My father is ill, and my mother takes care of him; he had a small stroke about a year ago and he seems to be improving now. My mother is a retired college teacher—she specialised in teaching English. That's about it, really, except, well, you know … I was going to get married and it's all in the past now.' Sven stroked her cheek. 'Gosh, Pippa, you've had it rough too, haven't you? Far worse than me for sure.'

'See what I mean? You don't really know me yet; all these things take time for us to learn about each other. Sorry to ask again but are you really over Astrid now?'

'I think so. I just get lonely here, that's all. I missed the company until you came along. You can have lots of people around you here but still be lonely at the same time.'

Sven stared at the cracks in the stone floor as he sat on the multi-coloured rag rug someone had spent hours making many years before. It had left an impression on his legs as he moved to get more comfortable. He put his arm around her and they sat side by side, his brown legs crossed in front of him. He wore a navy-blue Isles of Scilly T-shirt and his denim shorts; he'd kicked off his sandals under the coffee table.

Pippa moved closer to him, and their eyes met as he took another sip of beer. She enjoyed the warmth of his touch and the cosiness of being in his arms.

'I want to take you to St Agnes. I have a job there in the coming days and I'm expecting Martin back after next week. So we've got plenty to keep us busy.'

Pippa stroked his cheek. 'I can't believe I'm doing this.' She shivered at the thought of going home again.

'Yeah, I feel like that as well, it's all too good to be true.' He kissed her, sensing her soft cheeks with his lips.

Pippa knew she had to stop doubting herself. It might be wrong, but after all she had been through, it also felt very right. She hoped she wasn't hiding a subconscious plan to use him; she didn't want him to feel that way.

He kissed her on the lips, but this time, it was no ordinary kiss, it was a passionate and desiring kind of kiss and she felt the love welling up inside her. She knew he felt it too and she never wanted it to stop.

He smoothed his hand across her neck and traced a finger to her cleavage. He mustn't make love to her; he would surely lose her. He must show her he cared.

Pippa took hold of his hand and gazed into his eyes, her heart beating faster; she didn't want to think too much about it. 'What are you waiting for?' she whispered.

Sven stopped short for a moment. 'You mean …'

'Yes, I mean … yes.'

'You sure?' Sven's eyes widened.

'Never more sure,' she said, whispering in his ear.

'Pippa my love, I didn't prepare, er … I mean … I didn't think you would want to. It's too …'

'It doesn't matter. It's okay my darling, I understand if you don't want to,' she said softly. It was the way he looked at her, his innocent expression, the way he cupped her face with his hands and looked into her eyes, he really did know what she wanted. Oh, why hadn't she met him before this? *There's no such thing as love at first sight. Why do I feel this way?*

'Oh, I think I do want to, but …' he said with a smile and stroked her cheek. 'I'm not sure, maybe you don't know yourself, my love. You are so fragile at the moment.'

Pippa looked him in the eyes. 'I'm absolutely sure, Sven, honest I am. I want to sleep with you tonight. I need you to love me, issues and all—honest.'

His pause for thought kept her in suspense.

'What's the sudden change of heart?' he asked. 'This is a big jump.'

'I know it is, but it feels right.'

'Mm, I think I agree,' he said, kissing her.' I'm just thinking about you, that's all.'

'Let's stop being sensible and live a bit.' Pippa heard the words she had spoken but it was as if they were coming out of the book she had just read. One last moment of questioning: did she really know what she was doing? She decided that she did.

'It's not very comfortable on this stone floor and the sofa isn't much better. Should we go upstairs?' he said.

For the first time, he'd found it hard to speak as he climbed each step to the top. He'd wanted to tell her his feelings were the same. On the landing, he took her hand and pulled her gently toward him. He stroked her neck and licked her lips before kissing her full on, his tongue meeting hers.

Pippa shuddered with excitement; his warm hands stroking her face, his Norwegian words whispering in her ear had sent her to a new place in her life. The emotion spilling from her heart overwhelmed her.

He led her by the hand to her room, feeling he might not go all the way with her yet; he was very aware he could lose her. He knew she was vulnerable and wondered if he should treat her like a china doll. What was he doing to himself and to her?

They stood in front of the long mirror and she watched him, holding her in his arms, kissing her hair, caressing her face and telling her how much he wanted her. She wanted to cry and she closed her eyes as he undid the buttons on her blouse.

'You sure, Pippa? I don't want to do something we both might regret,' he whispered. It scared him, he hadn't had sex with a woman for some time and his body was eager to perform. He kissed her and she kept whispering 'yes' to him. He knew he wasn't using her for sex, he was making true love to her, but he questioned himself just in case.

By the time he could answer his own question, she was standing naked in front of the mirror and he was kissing her all the way down, her hair falling over her shoulders, his Norwegian words so full of meaning, only for her.

'Jeg elsker deg, Pippa, jeg elsker deg.' He breathed out slowly and his honeyed Norwegian words kept pouring from his lips. Pippa listened but didn't understand. She watched her reflection; he'd excited her more, seeing him fired with love for her.

'My God, Sven, you're amazing—you know that?' she whispered.

'I want to treasure every moment of today with you, my darling,' he said with a smile, 'and the next day and the next.'

He led her to the bed, then slipped off his shorts and T-shirt and came to her naked. Pippa saw how he really was brown all the way down. Seeing him without his clothes provided her with a blissful outpouring of emotion and for a brief moment, it made her nervous even when she wanted to cry with happiness. The only other man she had been to bed with was Rob. What would Sven expect of her? Would she disappoint him? It had been some time for both of them and with every kiss loomed excitement and passion. This Norwegian god of a man who kept telling her how much he cared, she wanted him to love her for the rest of her life. Running her fingers down his spine, she squeezed him closer to her, skin to skin. His hair felt soft and freshly showered and she brushed it out of his eyes. She had him for herself and wished it would be forever.

Sven stroked her nipples, exciting her. Once again he asked, 'You sure?'

Pippa's voice faded into a whisper. 'Yes, Sven, I need you, want you, yes, yes, yesss.'

He moved closer to her, responding to her words, feeling for her as he entered her.

Pippa's cheeks flushed with emotion and she closed her eyes while he rocked her into euphoria.

He wanted his lovemaking to be the experience she would never forget, in case he never saw her again and he could remember the moment all his life. He wanted to be like Sasha, his friendly seal, twisting beneath the sea, surfing the ocean. There had never been a rushed moment, every stroke of his hand, every kiss ensuring Pippa felt comfortable in his passion. He must prove to her he was genuine about his feelings. He knew he had fallen in love with her; he couldn't help himself. It was like his first time all over again—no, better. For some time, they lay together, turning back and forth in their passion, until he couldn't hold back any longer. It was now or never. 'Yes, now, oh yes … now.'

Pippa let out an emotional cry. 'Sven,' was all she could whisper. 'My lovely Sven.'

She lay there, her eyes watering, overwhelmed in lovemaking. Sven wiped away the tears for her. There was a silence, both looking into each other's eyes; what had she done? She wanted to speak but the words wouldn't come and she took a moment longer to recover. He was so handsome. Why had he chosen her of all people? She didn't think she was *that* pretty; Rob never told her anything like that.

'No regrets?' he asked, breathing heavily as she lay on top of him.

Pippa sniffed back her tears. 'Sven, I … I don't know what to say. Is this really happening to us?' She sighed and pulled the sheets over them. His hair was damp, beads of sweat ran down his forehead and she took a corner of the sheet and wiped his brow.

He smiled and kissed her. 'I absolutely adore you, you know that? But you're about to break my heart. Must you go back home—can't we elope?' he said with a cuteness that made her want to melt again.

'Yeah, I know what you mean,' she whispered, 'we're in deep trouble, aren't we? Looking back, I don't think I expected us to go this far so soon. I must be stupid, naïve or something. You are so lovely, Sven. I feel very lucky to have found you. I just wanted you, it felt right.' They kissed and she fell back to lie beside him.

'That was so good, mm … and stop worrying, everything will be fine,' he said as he hugged her and tickled her ribs. 'Oim sure we'll think of something, my lovely, oi need yew and yew need me,' he said with a laugh as he tried to mimic Don.

Pippa giggled and Sven laughed with her; he was glad he'd made her happy. He snuggled himself into her arms. At the end of her holiday, he wondered how he would ever manage to see her again. Leaving her would be a heart-wrenching moment as they said 'goodbye' on the quay. Why was his life always so complicated with women? She was right—they had created a whole new set of problems they might regret, but no longer did he want Pippa to be just his friend. He wanted her for himself, forever.

That night, Pippa closed her eyes in the darkness of the room. He would break her heart; that seemed certain. How could she go back to Rob and sleep with him after all this? Then there was the house on Henrietta Street, the place she grew up. She would have to leave it all behind, leave Daniel. What had she done? This self-inflicted situation made her wish it could have been different, but Sven was everything she ever wanted. But Daniel … how could she be so thoughtless and selfish?

CHAPTER SIXTEEN

'Hello, Robert love, how are you? Nice of you to phone,' Sally Lambton said, from the Finca Limoneros near Benidorm.

'Mum, I need your help, something weird has turned up. Is Dad there?'

'Yes he is, what's the matter, love?'

'Well, this concerns all of us, Mum. It's to do with my adoption,' Rob said.

Sally had dreaded those words all of Rob's life. She called for her husband to come and listen in on the extension phone. 'Ralph, it's Robert, he wants to talk to both of us.'

Rob heard the phone go 'click'.

'Well, Mum and Dad, what I'm about to read may be upsetting. Don't worry, I'm not going to do anything drastic. I only need your support and some advice.'

He began his story about the visit from the solicitor and then read the letter to them.

Sally's silence when he'd finished worried Rob and he could hear his father's asthmatic breath wheezing down the phone.

'Mum? Dad? Are you all right?'

At last Sally spoke, her voice low and faltering. 'I knew this might happen at some point, didn't you, Ralph?'

Rob knew that tone; it bordered on upset and tears.

'Yes, sure, but the thing is what are you going to do about it, son?' Ralph asked.

'Well, it's difficult really. I know how hard it was for you and Dad when you first married, not being able to have kids of your own. You are my mum and dad and always will be, but I've got a real brother and sister I've never met. Isn't that weird? I don't even know if my real father is still alive. If I ignore it, I might regret it and if I don't, I might still regret it—can't win.'

'Listen, Rob,' his father said. 'Under the circumstances, maybe you ought to go and see the solicitor and find out more and get back to us. I mean, we are your parents, but it was always a worry your maternal mother might turn up on our doorstep one day asking to take you back. I knew she couldn't, of course, but it was still a fear we had. I suppose it's the same with most adoptive parents; they don't really tell you to expect these things as you get older, but it does happen. Kids get curious about their real parents, life has moved on so fast since then.'

'It seems it wasn't my mother's fault that she had to give me away; I know she was forced to do it. Imagine that! I don't even know if she is still alive—I doubt it. She says she was ill when she wrote the letter. Perhaps she had cancer or something.'

Sally sighed, 'It makes me feel rather guilty, but we gave you a good life, good education and lots of love.'

Rob concurred and heard his father agree too. 'It's shocking. Now that you are older and mature, we have to leave the decision to you, but we don't have any argument if you want to do it. Just be careful you don't get your fingers burned, that's all. I think it would be great for you to find your brother and sister; I just hope they feel the same way. I would love to meet them. It all sounds very intriguing. Good luck, Robert—do what you think is right, and we'll support you.'

'Thanks, Dad. They didn't tell you about my real parents when you adopted me, did they?'

'Certainly not,' Sally replied. 'I had no idea and nothing as positive as you got now, love. I've always been very curious to know where you came from.'

Ralph continued. 'Have you thought about what to do?'

'Well, I'm going to have another think about it and then maybe I'll get in touch. I mean, I can hardly ignore it, could I?'

'Dreadful circumstances about this Fiona woman, eh?' said Ralph.

'Well, good luck, pet. It's very hot here today. Call us when you hear more, we'll be keen to know as well. How's Pippa? What does she say about it?' Sally said.

Rob didn't want to tell them; he told them she was fine and he would talk to them later.

An hour passed and Rob spent the time thinking about the conversation with his parents. He held the letter in his hand and read it one more time. *Bruce and Penny, wonder if they look like me.*

Rob dialled the number of the solicitors' office and asked to speak with John Grover.

He waited, listening in anticipation at the sound of busy typewriters and phones ringing in the background. He felt his right leg shaking up and down and tried to make it stop. John Grover's voice was saying goodbye to his client as he picked up the receiver on the phone.

'Oh good afternoon Rob, sorry about that. I was expecting you might call, or rather, I hoped you would.'

'I'd like to find out more about the Haines family,' Rob said.

'Of course. I now have more information on this case. I am sorry to tell you but your real father died a few weeks ago and left a will, and that letter was included within the will. I'm sorry I couldn't tell you this before, but I had to exercise discretion and I had to be sure you were the right person. Stephen updated me on the situation when he got back to the office. He only deals with the probate on the estate. It had to be for you to read that letter in your own time; it's a very private thing in these circumstances. We were only reconciling for the time being.'

'Yes, I understand. So it was my real father who died, eh? Oh dear, I thought I might meet him.' Rob felt he should be crying with emotion about his sad loss, but there was no emotion, just a pair of people he knew nothing about.

'I'm sorry. While your father was alive we did our best to try to find you, but it has taken a long time and lots of paperwork. He was in fact a good friend of mine. I will miss him. The point here is that you need to come into our office or meet me somewhere. Now that my colleague has been to see you, I can inform you that you have a third share in your real parents' will. They left a clause in case you were found. Your siblings, Penny and Bruce, are younger than you.'

'Oh hell, this is incredible. Is there any chance I could find them and talk with them?' Rob enquired.

'All in good time, Rob. Give me a few days and we will try to confirm a few things for you. I want to meet with you first. It must be very weird for you, eh? Although, sadly, I have to explain, your real father was involved in a car accident several months ago from which he never recovered. He was a prominent figure where he worked at Hull Infirmary.'

Rob suddenly realised something. 'Oh goodness me, I recall this guy. Wasn't it a hit and run?' He remembered he was talking about his father.

'That's right, how did you know that?' John asked.

'I work at the local hospital, heard about the incident. I knew he was a well-known doctor, but I had no idea he was my father, oh my God!' Rob put his fingers to his lips in shock. 'Look, John, I'm grateful for your help, but you're right—it *is* all very strange to me at the moment. I'm not sure which way to turn.'

'Yes, well … let's just take it one step at a time, shall we? Allow me to help you sort out a meeting with your family. Do you think you would like that?'

'I think so, but it's a big step. I mean, they might not want to meet *me*.'

'Leave it with me—I'll call you next week and let you know. You are due some of the inheritance. I have yet to read the will to your family. Your real mother had been looking for you a long time. She got very sick and depressed, I'm afraid, and then later on she was diagnosed with breast cancer. She was in Switzerland at a clinic.'

'Oh, I see. Dreadful. I thought I'd had enough traumas to last a lifetime when my son passed away.'

'Yes, I'm sorry, but you're right, things are going to change for you now, you have been left a substantial sum of money in the will.'

'Really?'

'I don't have the full details yet; I have to arrange things with your siblings.'

'Oh my goodness, the other members of the family aren't going to like me nudging in on their patch, are they?'

'I know them well; Fiona Haynes brought them up as good kids. They're not the troublemaking types; they're educated and they wanted to find you as well for the sake of their parents. And now their father has passed away, it has brought them closer together; they know about you and want to meet you.'

'Yes but this money—surely it will be a bit weird, some stranger coming into their lives.'

'Rob, you are *not* a total stranger, and you are entitled to the money; it's as simple as that. You are their son; this is what your parents wanted. Leave it with me and I'll get back to you and try not to worry, I understand how much of a shock this must have been for you. I must impress upon you, I don't want you to do anything you can't handle, okay?'

'Yes, I understand.'

'Look, erm … I'll leave you to consider all this a bit longer and I'll get back in touch with you as soon as I know more. It's all very sad about the Haines family; they've had it tough recently.'

'Yes, I understand. I lost my young son and it doesn't get any easier. Thanks a lot, John, I'll look forward to it.' Rob replaced the receiver. He'd never felt as alone as right now.

CHAPTER SEVENTEEN

'Hi, Rob. We need to talk.' Pippa had called him from Scilly.

'Hello, love, how are you? Having a nice time, eh? I miss you.'

Pippa's alarm bells rang loud and clear. His words were a memory from a long time ago. The Rob she used to know, the lovely man she married. At this moment, she didn't want him to be lovely.

'Pippa? You still there?' he said.

'Gosh, that's a change of heart from our last phone call. What do you mean, you miss me?' she asked.

'Well, I do, three weeks is a long to time be away. Anyway, it won't be long now until you get back.'

He became aware of how quiet she seemed and he thought he should apologise for the way he had behaved in the last few weeks. Perhaps he had better explain; after all, she would be home soon.

'Look, erm, I've behaved rather badly, I know, and now I can't wait for you to get back.'

'Rob, what's going on? Has something happened to make you have a change of heart?'

'Well, I've had some interesting information. I won't get a chance to tell you everything on the phone, but it looks like we might be due for an inheritance. Someone contacted me and, to cut a long story short, they found my real family.'

'What? Oh my God! That's incredible.'

Pippa's insides wrenched sideways. The phone box with its stench of stale cigarettes was hardly the place to take it all in. The last thing she wanted was to go home to Whitby before her holiday was up, but perhaps she should be with him.

'Where does that put us, I mean you and me?' she asked.

'What do you mean, Pippa? You got your inheritance from your Dad and now apparently I'm getting mine. All square, let's enjoy it together.'

Something in his tone of voice sounded like he was getting back at her for not sharing with him.

'Rob, I have shared everything with you. You know Dad gave me the house before we married; it was in his will. He didn't know we would get married. The money was in a trust fund for me until I was twenty-one. I just kept it in my account for us to spend. Remember it was your idea when we married to have separate bank accounts. You weren't working at the time. I just paid for everything; we never thought much about it.'

'Pippa, hush for a moment, let me tell you. I do miss you,' Rob said. 'I hope you are enjoying yourself down there.'

Pippa went quiet. She couldn't talk for a moment; her insides were mangled. Sven was waiting for her back at Gilstone, and hearing Rob saying those words sent severe anger through her. She was tired of being messed about. She tried to stay calm.

'I'm happy for you about the news, but I doubt this will change things between us. Perhaps you can tell me more when I get back.'

He kept trying to assure her it would be a change for the better and things were going to be fine. He explained about his brother and sister and the phone call with the solicitor. 'I do miss you, honest I do.'

Pippa wanted to scream. *No, you bloody well don't miss me. Just because you got money coming to you, you think that'll make a difference?*

'Anyway Joan is upset now, I think you ought to call her, she has something to tell you about Terry.'

Oh what now! What else can go wrong? Makes me wish I hadn't phoned. 'Can't you tell me?'

'Well, not really, I think it's better coming from Joan, you see.'

The pips sounded and before she got cut off she garbled the words down the phone. 'Okay, I'll give her a call, bye, call you later when I got more change.' She didn't feel like putting more money in the slot, and in any case she didn't have that much change in her purse.

She opened the door of the phone box, slipped into the fresh air, and walked a few steps into the park to sit on a bench. As she caressed her own cheeks in contemplation, she stared at the blue agapanthus towering above the shrubs, the sea air drifting into her nostrils. *Oh shit, shit and bloody shit.* She kicked a stone on the path. She needed to tell Sven. What she had with Rob was a husband who was just as mixed up about their relationship as ever. But there were still deep uncertainties about Sven; it could never work, although she wanted to be with him with all of her heart. And yes ... how could she love someone after only two weeks? The situation was out of control.

Back at Gilstone, Sven had made coffee.

'Hello my darling, how did it go?' he said.

'Awful!' She wailed. 'I feel as though he's scheming to make me feel guilty. He says he misses me, but only last week he was talking about separation and divorce. Hell, this is so hard.'

She told Sven about the phone conversation and Rob's new-found family. 'I don't think I should go back early. The reason I'm here in the first place is his lack of support; why should I support him now? It's always me who keeps the peace in our house; I've had enough of it. I can't live this hot and cold existence.'

'It's quite a story, isn't it?' Sven felt some fears of her returning to Rob creeping up. He sighed. 'What do you want to do, Pippa?'

'I don't want to go home; I want to stay with you.'

Sven smiled down on her and hugged her for the comment. 'Why don't you? No, I know you can't do that, you have responsibilities.' He remembered the three-week pact they had made and how he couldn't push it. It had to be up to Pippa. Perhaps this thing with Rob might turn the tables on him. He didn't want to think about it. He felt like collapsing in a heap on the floor with the thought that he might have lost yet another woman in his life. He waited for her to speak.

'I'm going to continue our agreed time here with you, Sven,' Pippa said with a smile. 'Then I'll go home, see what Rob says, and sort it out. It's *me* who doesn't want to live with *him.*

If he's got some money, he can find a place of his own now. He doesn't need me.' She lowered her eyes as she said it. She knew Sven had shown her new hope; why would she want to go back on herself?

'Pippa, I want to ask you something.' Sven turned to her, kissing her forehead. She had opened a path for him to say how he felt and his relief seemed to show.

'While you were out, I was thinking. We've had a short time together, but could you trust me enough to be my girlfriend for real? I mean for as long as we both want to be together? I think this pact of ours has gone further than we both intended.'

'What do you mean?' Pippa looked lost for a moment.

'Well, why don't you go home to Whitby as you said, then come back here and live with me at Beachside. I could help you do it when Martin gets back.'

'Jeeps, Sven! That's one heck of a proposition.' She put her arms around his waist and hugged him. 'You are so sweet; I love you to bits. You can be so impulsive at times, but surely that's not possible.' She chuckled at his puppy-dog expression.

'Well, yes, it is possible; I just want to make you happy, that's all. You've had a hell of a life and you aren't even as old as me yet. We are both kidding ourselves. I know I've fallen in love with you and it's tearing me up.' He gazed upon her sun-freckled face. 'Look, I don't want to steal you from Rob, but if, as you say, things have been unbearable for you, then doesn't it make sense to start afresh? Rob is unlikely to come 500 miles down here to smash my face in, is he?'

Pippa laughed, then cried at the same time.

'I love being with you Pippa; I just can't help it. You're the best thing to happen to me in a long time. I'm going to be devastated if you don't come back to me. Sorry, that's unfair of me, but I had to say it. I didn't want to put you under any pressure, honest I didn't, but things have taken a sudden change, haven't they?'

Pippa sniffed back her tears. 'I don't know what to do. You've blown me away! I'm so overwhelmed, I find myself wondering how I got into this mess.'

'Yes I know, I understand, my darling.' He began to feel sorry for causing her so much pain. He had got her to this point and now he had to try and help her fix it.

'What do I do now?' Pippa asked, feeling both despair and happiness at the same time. And what should she do about Rob? He needed her. No, he didn't, he was just saying that, but he was her husband and she should have a sense of duty. Duty or happiness, what was it to be?

Sven put on a serious face. 'First, I think, before we get too far down this track, you and I will continue as we are. This will give us a few more days to decide if this is real or not.'

'Yes, I agree.' Pippa smiled and kissed him on the cheek. 'What I have here is the chance to get a real life and travel and do all the things I have never been able to do. My only regret would be leaving Daniel in Whitby with no one to tend his grave. I couldn't go back very often if I lived here and Rob hardly ever goes to the cemetery. My life has been in Whitby, but Scilly has lots of similarities, and I could feel just as at home here. I have to live by the sea. It's a wonderful offer—give me until tomorrow to think about it again. I have to ask myself if I am chasing rainbows. I have a lot to consider back home.'

'That's my girl,' Sven said as he hugged her. 'Very sensible. Perhaps I have a rainbow to chase as well, so let's just enjoy chasing it together while we can. I'm having such a great time with you. I will always support you, my darling; you only have to ask.'

Pippa felt in awe of his proposition to live with him. How could she leave Henrietta Street? It had been her childhood playground. She had loved going to the beach outside her back door and down the steps. The cobbled street where, as children, she and Joan had played 'Jacky Five Stones' on the doorstep with a few other kids—Thomas, Geraldine and Ingrid whose father was a Danish fisherman. The aroma of the kippers, with their flattened and gutted bellies on racks in the blackened smokehouse, and old Mr. Fulton hanging them on tenterhooks ready for smoking. The local kids used to call it the 'black treacle house', as the blackened interior glistened in the sun. The number of times they had counted the hundred and ninety-nine steps to the Abbey; they always got it wrong. Pippa smiled to herself; Joan used to argue and say she had counted two hundred.

Now that Rob had changed his attitude, she couldn't quite fathom it. Had he been chatting to Joan? Had she told him to behave himself? She remembered the conversation from a few weeks ago. She and Joan had a heart-to-heart about Terry and Rob. Joan was worried she hadn't seen Terry or had any phone calls. Then she made that strange comment about how it was so easy to marry the wrong person. Perhaps Joan had news of Terry; she would phone her later.

Sven glanced at Pippa who was miles away in her thoughts.

'Come on, drink up my sweet,' he said. 'We'll work something out, I know we will.' He held up the coffee mug. 'Cheers! To our future happiness, no matter where that may be.'

CHAPTER EIGHTEEN

Rob waited in the 'Duke of York'. He had a date with Joan, the 'I'll meet you at the pub for a drink, see if I can help you sort yourself out' kind of date. They had known each other too long for the relationship to be anything else but friendly. It was how it had always been. Perhaps tonight, they could sort out each other's problems, but he wanted Joan to talk things through about Terry; after all, she had been there for Rob to talk about his new family. They needed each other right now.

'What can I get you?' Rob said as Joan walked into the pub.

'Orange juice, please.' She sat on the plush red velvet bench and placed her shoulder bag beside her. 'I got a call from Pippa. She told me you'd asked her to phone me. I didn't tell her everything about Terry. I didn't want to upset her on her holiday. It was difficult. I just said he was depressed and trying to sort himself out. I'll tell her when she comes home.' She tried to change the subject. 'What about you, Rob?'

'You should have told her, Joan. That was a bit daft of you,' Rob scolded.

'Yeah, well …' She shrugged her shoulders.

The conversation with Pippa on the phone made Joan think she wasn't talking with the same best friend who had left her the previous week; it was the Pippa she used to know before Daniel died. Joan realised Pippa was having more than a good time. She was laughing, happy, and full of information about birdwatching, visiting islands and going on the boat trips and the guide who had showed her all the new birds she'd never seen before. She seemed so happy; it had made Joan feel she couldn't tell her about Terry.

'How *is* it going with you?' Joan asked again.

Rob thought Joan looked tired.

'I'm fine, I suppose, although it's a bit strange not having Pippa around. There's so much to do at home. I absolutely hate doing housework, and with this family situation, I'm waiting for a phone call from the solicitor. It's all becoming a bit of a nightmare. I'm supposed to be meeting my new family when they can arrange it.' He sighed. 'Then there's all this business of Pippa and me. The other night, I was thinking maybe I should just give in and with this money due to me, we could start a new life, maybe try again.'

'Money, money, it's all about money, isn't it?' Joan said with some anger in her voice. 'I would say, first, you have to consider Pippa's feelings, Rob.'

'What d'ye mean?' he asked, puzzled.

'Well, there you are counselling your patients and the one thing you missed is the feelings of your own wife.'

'Joan, dear.' He lowered his voice in a patronising tone. 'I thought we came here to talk about you tonight, to see if I can help you with your future, not for you to help me with mine.'

'Sorry, Rob, but it had to be said. You're a great person, I've always appreciated the way you have been so caring with me and Jordan. Perhaps you need to talk to Pippa when she gets back. I wish things were like they used to be, but they're not, are they?'

'Okay, I know what you mean. I'll wait for her to get back, then we'll sit down and have a talk, I promise.' He knew Joan was like a scolding mother, but sometimes, he needed it and she was right. He scoffed at himself.

It was getting dark outside when they left the pub and Rob offered to walk Joan to the car park. They discussed Joan's future on her own with Jordan, and by the time they reached the car, Joan was in tears.

'I can't do this, Rob, a future on my own. I feel I'm losing you and Pippa—I only have Mam, and I couldn't tell her about Terry. Carole is moving to Leeds soon so I won't have a baby-sitter.'

Rob put his arm around her and gave her a hug. 'It's going to be all right! You and Jordan can have a wonderful life together and maybe in the future you will find someone else to love you.'

'No I won't. Terry was my life.' She was sobbing her heart out. 'Who wants a woman with a kid?'

'Look, I'll drive you back home and I'll walk back. It won't take me long and it'll do me good.'

He took the keys from her and got into the car. She was sniffing all the way up the hill with a wet handkerchief rolled in a tight ball in her fist.

On arrival, Rob got out of the car and escorted her back to the front door. 'Will you be okay?'

'Yeah, Jordan is with Phyllis tonight. All I need is a good sleep. Thanks, Rob,' she sniffed.

'Well, I think it did us both good to talk and thanks for the company.' He gave her a hug and kissed her cheek. 'G'night, Joanie, see yer, love, and don't worry.'

Joan went to bed even more depressed than the hour before and worked her mind into a frenzy about Terry leaving her in the lurch. She saw the pills on the dresser and wondered if she should take a couple to help her through the night.

CHAPTER NINETEEN

'I've made you a sandwich, Pippa. Awful weather, eh?' Sven was tidying up around him. 'I just got in about half an hour ago.'

'Did you hear the weather forecast, twelve-hour gales, eh? And at this time of year, too!' Pippa replied as she hung up her jacket on the peg. 'Can't stay long though.'

Outside, the wind gusted. With tourists grounded for the day and flights out of the islands cancelled, Pippa realised how easy it was to be isolated here, but it was still cosy. And with Sven by her side, what more could she want?

'I wondered if you might like to come to St Agnes with me. You haven't been over there yet, have you?' Sven asked.

'Thanks, Sven, I'd love to, but not in this weather,' Pippa replied with an anxious look on her face.

'No, no, silly,' he laughed and gave her a peck on the cheek. 'I thought tomorrow would be nice; the weather's going to be fine by afternoon. I got a job to do over there and maybe you can help me; we are checking the shoreline for oiled sea birds.'

Pippa's face lit up; she could do that. She decided she would tell him about her experiences with the RSPCA in Whitby. 'Oh, that's great,' she said.

'Elsker deg.'

'It means *love you*,' Sven said when he saw her puzzled look.

Now she understood what he had said at Gilstone. He was truly amazing. When he spoke his native language, it gave her goose-bumps. She gave him a hug and wanted to stay longer but couldn't. 'Love you too, but I must go and get some shopping. We've run out of milk and eggs. I'll meet you later, okay?' She picked up her shopping bags, kissed him on the lips, and left Beachside Cottage in the wind. She hung on to the shopping bags as she was blown around the next corner. St Agnes would be great and she looked forward to it; she hoped this awful weather would improve as Sven had predicted.

After lunch, Sven left home as his neighbour Nanette returned from town. She smiled at Sven over the granite wall. 'Looks like you're havin' a good time then, young man!'

Sven grimaced. 'And you too, Nan.' 'Sopskoilt,' he whispered to himself in Norwegian; she was such an annoying woman. She always wanted to know everything about him; she and Margaret at the office were friends. Nanette had to be the nosiest woman on the islands, peering through her windows each time he went out, as though she was spying on him. He supposed he didn't really care. He'd lived with it for long enough now.

The following morning, Pippa packed a lunch for both of them. As they stepped on board the *Lily*, she found a seat at the back thinking it might help Sven avoid the gossip.

'Hey man, who's the red head?' Don asked. He had seen them chatting on the quay.

Sven pretended to look around. 'Who? What red head?'

'Your new girlfriend, wasn't she on the boat last week? I think I've seen her around town—who is she?' Don put the engine into reverse and started out to St Agnes, the sun glistening on the water in St Mary's harbour.

Sven felt pushed into a corner. He wanted to protect Pippa, but this time, Don seemed insistent on meeting her.

'Pippa!' he shouted above the boat engine noise, and beckoned her with a smile. 'This is Don. Don, meet my friend Pippa.'

She moved forward in the boat to a seat closer to Sven.

'Pleased to meet you, young lady. Yes, I've seen you two chatting and I wondered if there was romance in the air,' Don teased. 'Where're ye from, m' dear?'

'Oh, I live in Yorkshire,' Pippa replied. 'I've come to Scilly for the birdwatching. Actually, I did meet you a few years ago, but I was a passer-by. You were telling me about the history of your boat—she's quite old, isn't she?'

Don nodded. 'Oh, oi never forget a face.' He grinned at Sven.

Pippa cringed; what if Don really did remember? Her hair always gave her away. She hoped that with all the visitors over the last five years, he would have forgotten. If he did remember her, he might discuss it with Sven. It was knowing he had met Rob and Daniel—well, it wasn't that important, just a bit embarrassing.

'Yeah, *Lily* is my pride and joy,' said Don. 'My dear departed wife used to say I love this boat more'n I loved 'er. She was wrong, of course, but the boat is all I gawt 'ere now, 'cept young Sven, he's like a son to me.'

Sven laughed and agreed.

'So, we're awf to Aggie this afe'rnoon. I likes Aggie best, they do a good pint at the pub. On the bowts though, I'm not supposed to drink and droive,' he drolled, 'so I'll 'avta 'av an apple juice or somethin'.'

Pippa beamed at him; no wonder Sven had picked up a Cornish accent, having spent so many hours with Don. She thought Sven looked amused, and wondered what he was thinking.

As usual, Sven's binoculars were poised against his eyes. St Agnes had no shelter from the lagoon and the sea swell made the crossing choppy. Pippa stood with him and Sven gave up trying to birdwatch. She was laughing and the crowd at the back of the boat were making 'Whoa' sounds as each wave tossed the boat toward the sky. Don adjusted his speed to give the passengers a less bumpy ride.

As the boat pulled into the quay at Kallimay Point, Sven had some jobs to do.

'We have to sort out this tragedy with the oil,' he said in a dismal tone. 'We got a shortage of sand eels for the common tern chicks and the puffins aren't bringing in as much food as we had hoped. It's all a bit of a disaster really. This morning, we have to collect the mortalities along the shore and later on, we'll take them to be examined by the vet. The volunteers are also collecting data on the oil spill,' Sven told her.

'So what can I do to help?' Pippa asked eagerly.

'I'll give you this plastic bag. Don't go picking up any birds without the gloves on. Walk along the beach and any dead ones you find, pop them into the bag. Discard the skeletons, only the recent mortalities,' he called to her as they walked in opposite directions.

She strolled along the beach alone, combing the shingle. She found a starfish and two dead crabs. Further along, she discovered a dead tern. As there was no sign of oil, she took off her oversized gloves. The bones were sticking out so she concluded the bird had probably died of starvation. As she smoothed her fingers over the soft white feathers, it made her sad to see the lifeless form in her hand. She caressed the bird as she had done with her son before his funeral. It had been a terrible thing to see him lying there. A senseless death, a waste of life. She would never forget. In a way, she wished that she hadn't seen him like that, but they had made him look so beautiful despite the injuries.

By the time they had been on the beach for an hour, they had found three dead terns, a dead puffin and one guillemot still alive and unable to fly. She knew a little about guillemots and called Sven to pick it up. He stalked the bird and then ran a short distance along the beach with the creature helplessly flapping its wings. He stooped down to pick it up. 'Gotcha,' he said.

Pippa ran toward him. 'I took care of a guillemot once. I washed it when Dan was small, and we looked after it for six weeks and then put it back in the estuary on the river Esk. Dan loved all animals; he was like my dad.'

'So you know how to feed them and so on—useful. I'm not surprised about the terns; it was a hard year for them, all this overfishing. I hope there's no disaster due soon; we found too many birds for the short time we've been on this beach.'

They wandered back to the pub, Sven with the gilly nestling under his arm and a hand around its beak. He asked the landlord for a cardboard box to place the bird in. They would take it back to St Mary's and give it a wash.

Leaving it outside at the back of the pub in the shade, they continued on their way until Don returned with the boat. As they walked the island, the pungent aroma of camomile filled the air and Sven pointed out the flora from the field guide.

'Oh my God, what the heck's that?' Pippa jumped back from the path as she said it.

Sven knelt down and picked up a large insect.

'Now here's an interesting thing. It's an oil beetle, a female.'

'Yuck, it's grotesque!' she exclaimed, gazing upon the black glistening form of a large insect in his hand.

'I think she's rather beautiful,' he said. 'You have to be careful not to upset them because they release an oily substance from their legs that can make your skin blister.'

He played with the oil beetle for some time, allowing it to wander over his hand before placing it with care on the grassy verge to avoid someone stepping on it.

'Come on, then, we ought to be getting back,' he said. 'You did great this afternoon, Pippa, maybe we can find you a job here.'

I wish. Pippa rolled her eyes in dismissal.

Before leaving the island, they collected the cardboard box from the pub and showed Don what they'd found. The return journey saw calmer weather as they steered closer to St Mary's. Pippa sat with her hand in the sea, looking down to the clear depths. She noticed Don looking at her from the wheelhouse—or was it her imagination? Perhaps Sven would explain her circumstances to him. She knew she shouldn't feel guilty, but she did. She had left home to get away from prying eyes and she was sure Don might wonder about her being with Sven.

Arriving on St Mary's, they took the bird through the office and outside to the old stone sink. Pippa watched as Sven washed the bird with a toothbrush and showerhead, using a mild detergent as shampoo—and it occurred to her that maybe she could help him with this kind of work in the future. *The future. Oh gosh!*

Could I really live on Scilly? Sven spoke and her train of thought became interrupted.

'Watch your fingers, Pippa. Here, give me that elastic band until he's dry again, and then we'll feed him some fish. I'll keep him inside, because he needs a chance to become waterproof again. It's a bridled gilly, you see the white stripe around the eye?'

Pippa stroked the bird, bedraggled and wrapped in a towel. 'Sven, do you think Don remembered me from the last time I was here?' she asked.

Sven laughed. 'I doubt it, he tells everyone that. He's a curious sod, always has been.'

'Yes, but he met Rob and Daniel, you see. I just wondered, that's all. The thing is, when we were here before, Daniel fell over and Don picked him up for me and we put a plaster on his knee. It might stand out in his mind.'

'Oh, I see. Well, try to not worry, it won't mean anything to him and if he does ask me, I'll explain. Are you worried about it?'

'Not really, it's just Don seems like such a nice guy. I wouldn't want him to think I was bad for you, that's all.'

'Oh Pippa, it's okay, honest. Don's a great person, he wouldn't do that anyway. I promise to tell him soon, he'll understand when he knows about your sad loss. Try not to worry about me, it's no big deal, honest.'

'I know, sometimes it's hard for me to put all the little things aside. I was just concerned for some silly reason I can't explain, it gets me like that. When I have more confidence in myself, then I hope all these doubts will go away.'

Sven stopped towelling the bird to give Pippa a hug and a kiss.

'Come on, let's get this job done and go home. I'll put this gilly under the infrared lamp to help it dry out.'

In the small storeroom outside next to the office, Pippa watched as he plugged in the lamp and stroked the head of the guillemot before placing it on a bed of straw. She sensed his caring and related to the bird's dilemma. It hadn't asked to be messed up in this way. Sven let the bird go free on the table top and it flapped its wings to shake away the excess water. Pippa realised she had also been given a second chance and perhaps she could learn a lot from the way Sven had provided her with love and care. He had rescued her as well.

CHAPTER TWENTY

Margaret entered the office and realised Sven was on the phone. She had a piece of paper in her hand with a message, so she left it on the desk.

SVEN. Just to let you know Martin will be back on Saturday lunchtime with the BBC film crew. He says to meet him off the helicopter at noon. Must dash – going into town for my lunch break. Back at the usual time. Mary

Sven glanced at the slip of paper and cringed. Martin's return was also the afternoon Pippa was going home. He'd wanted to spend those last moments with her.

'Oh, no,' he complained. He was pleased that his best mate was returning, but torn because Pippa was about to leave him and nothing mattered more than her.

He had taken the afternoon off; his call had been to Charlie James asking if he would step in for him to guide a party of birdwatchers around the headland. He left Margaret a note telling her he would see her in the morning.

Pippa made her way to Porthcressa to meet Sven. They walked up the garden path together toward Beachside Cottage.

'I must get changed,' Sven said, opening the front door. He went upstairs. 'Come on up, see the rest of the house, I have a super bird book up here you can borrow.'

The rooms were smaller than Gilstone where they had spent most of their time. Pippa looked out of the window. *Oh my, what a lovely view of the bay.*

He put on clean shorts in front of her. Rob never thought to undress in front of her; instead he took off his clothes in the bathroom. How he had distanced himself when he could have been helping the romance in a relationship! Yet she always undressed in his presence in the hope that it might inspire him to be more romantic. It didn't seem as if Rob understood true romance in his approach to their lovemaking. What Pippa had experienced with Sven had blown her mind; how could she go back to Rob now that she knew the true meaning of affection?

Pippa realised how much importance she had placed on Sven. It thrilled her to share his life. He pulled on his dark blue sweatshirt with the 'Isles of Scilly' logo on the front, and zipped up his khaki shorts, then kissed her cheek. 'We'll drive to the beach; I got a nice little spot where we can watch the world go by. Here's that book, by the way.'

Pippa took it from him and saw it contained real photos of birds and not drawings. She would take it home later and study it.

After packing a blanket in the rucksack, Sven opened the fridge door and raided the last of the beer before leaving.

'Beer, orange or cola?'

'Cola, please,' Pippa replied.

'Okay, ready? Shall we go, elskling?'

He saw her puzzled look and added, 'It means *darling*.'

Pippa picked up her rucksack smiling at his Norwegian endearment. *Mm, elskling, what a nice word.*

They closed the door behind them.

Driving to Pelistry beach, Sven said, 'It'll be sheltered up here and we can nestle in the dunes. No locals, only a few tourists.'

After a short walk, he laid down the plaid blanket in the Marram Grass and raised his binoculars.

'It's raining over there, probably heading our way. We'll get a chance to eat and if we're lucky, it'll miss us.' The shower headed toward Tresco from the Western Isles. 'Oh look, see the shag,' said Sven, pointing beyond Tolls Island. 'I love it when they pack together in rafts like that. They always look so … how do you say it in English?'

'Snooty?' Pippa offered.

'Snooty? What does that mean? I've never heard of that word, it's a funny one.'

'It means *snobbish* or *toffee-nosed*,' she said with a chuckle, and flicked her finger under her nostrils to show him what she meant.

'Oh, ya, I know what you mean, that's a new one for me. Mm, snoo-tee,' he said with a chortle. 'Am I snoo-tee?'

'Now you're being daft.'

'Daft?' he teased her. 'Your accent always amuses me. Do they all speak that way in Yorkshire?'

Pippa giggled. 'Honestly, you are funny.' She shoved him into the sand where he landed on the blanket with a thud, and then put out her tongue at him. She turned up her nose and laughed. Sven grabbed her and they rolled in the sand together. He was almost on top of her before he kissed her passionately.

Pippa looked into his blue eyes, unable to speak. Her heart spoke passion and adoration every time she looked at him.

Sven sat up, opened a beer, and then dropped the ring pull into his rucksack. Pippa opened the box of sandwiches.

'Always make sure you take these home,' he said, pointing to the ring pull. 'The gannets tend to make nests with all this stuff. Also those bloody plastic things, they get tangled up in birds' feet, you know, the ones they keep the beer cans packed together. The number of birds I've rescued with plastic around their necks too … it's dreadful to see them suffer in that way.'

He watched an older man cross to Tolls Island where, at high tide, the island became cut off from the beach. 'He's left too late to cross over there, though he should be okay for another hour.'

Pippa listened to the sounds of the sea, disturbed only by the lapping of the waves at low tide. The sun came out and the odour of beached kelp filled the air. Sand flies hopped in front of her as she watched a herring gull snatch a bite of a forlorn sandwich left behind by yesterday's tourists. She heard voices and the sound of footsteps from the path above her that seemed to vibrate a low thud underneath where they sat. Two more people came to the beach and they leaned their bikes on the grass.

'Dad, why do lobsters turn red when you cook them?' a child asked, and his father's answer faded on the breeze.

Peace prevailed. Three small boats rocked gently in the bay, and the Eastern Isles spanned the distant shore. The buzz of a light aircraft broke the peace, but was soon gone. The air was warm and filled with the scent of camomile and seaweed alternating on a summer breeze.

Sven waited; he felt Pippa's calmness, and the time was right to ask questions. 'What was he like, your Daniel? I'd like to know, if you feel you can talk about it.' He put his arm around her.

'Yes, sure, it helps me I suppose.' Pippa smiled as she reminisced. 'He was a cheeky little boy, but we had a lot of fun together. He would have been ten next birthday. He was a son of which any mother would have been proud. A bit impulsive, reminds me of you, he had blonde hair as well.'

'I would like to have children one day.'

Pippa smiled at him. 'That's nice,' she said, trying not to enlarge the subject. He smiled back at her and gave her a kiss.

Visitors to the beach continued to arrive and the father and son team returned. 'Are you sure this is the right way?' asked the young boy. 'And look, there are loads of limpet shells here.'

The man and boy jogged back along the footpath, stopping to do press-ups on the way. There was laughing and joking, the panting of breath as they ran, their voices melding into the dunes.

Nothing could have spoilt Pippa's and Sven's day together. The laughing of the black-backed gulls, the scream of the terns and the wonderful beach to which he had brought her all seemed unreal, and Pippa never wanted it to stop.

Sven searched again across the knoll of Tolls Island and could see the man returning. Had he left too late to cross the sand bar?

The man walked down the rocks with his camera swinging. Then he climbed down toward the shore, not realising that the tide had come in and the water had become deeper.

'Hey, Pippa, see that bloke over there? He's in trouble, I think; I might have to help him.'

'Oh, yeah … he's not going to try and cross, is he?' Pippa peered through her binoculars.

The man seemed surprised to discover how quickly the tide had come in. Nonetheless, he took his first steps into the strong current. 'Hey!' shouted Sven. 'Don't cross! It's dangerous.' But the man took no notice of the warning. Before Sven could get close to him, he was waist deep in the middle of the sand bar. The current had pushed him sideways; he fell in. He managed to stand up again and continued to wade the short distance to the shore. His pride seemed hurt and his camera ruined, but nothing more.

Sven called to him. 'You okay sir?'

The man smiled. 'Yeah, I forgot the time and didn't realise how deep it gets.'

'You were very lucky,' Sven said. 'You can so easily get swept away out here.'

The man thanked him and walked in the other direction, dripping with every step and looking most uncomfortable.

Sven returned to Pippa. He raised his eyebrows and smiled as the man went on his way. 'I suppose it could have been worse. I can never understand why they ignore the warnings.'

'His camera's probably ruined.' Pippa didn't mean to giggle, but it was really the man's own silly fault. 'Poor bloke. I hope he's got a towel and an understanding wife.'

Sven returned to his cosy spot on the sand and reminded himself what he had to tell Pippa. 'Oh yes, I forgot, I have to tell you something. Some news. It's a bit difficult really.'

Pippa's heart missed a beat. Was he about to say this was the end of their time together? No, it couldn't be.

'Don't look so worried,' he smiled. 'It's some good news. Martin is back from South Africa, and well ... I'm told today that he arrived in Bristol with Andrea. He's bringing the film crew back with him from the BBC. I have to meet him from the helicopter.'

'How lovely—will I be able to meet him?' Pippa's relief showed.

'Yes, sure, but there is a problem—he's coming home the day you leave. I didn't want to be disturbed, if you see what I mean. I want to be with you.'

'Oh yes, of course. Oh dear. So what will you do?'

'I thought about it and maybe we could all have lunch together. I mean, it's not an ideal goodbye. The timing is all wrong.' He had to find a way to bid farewell to Pippa while welcoming Martin and the film crew; it wasn't going to be easy. 'I think it would be good to meet up for lunch at the Old Town Café. You could meet the crew and we could slip away afterwards a couple of hours before the ship sails.'

Pippa agreed and sighed. She was thrilled about meeting The Birdman but it reminded her that time was not on their side. 'You know I met that nice couple from Holland? Did I tell you he's very ill and unlikely to live another few more months?'

'I ... don't recall, but I've seen them on the boat and I thought he looked a bit sick.'

'I keep meeting them on my travels around the island, and they're such a nice couple. Jan has a tumour—it's dreadful; made me consider that you never know what's coming at you in life. There was a really nice chap I met back home, walking with his wife in the cemetery. He told me I would find my direction around some corner where it's been waiting to meet me. He had lost a family member too. That's so true, you know.'

Sven tried to speak and Pippa stopped him. 'Let me go on. You see, I have a plan. You won't be able to contact me directly at home because of Rob, so I'll phone you when he's not around. It might take me a while to sort it all out, maybe six weeks. I'll just have to tell him about us. I honestly do feel very bad about what I've done to him, but I think it's time I moved on. I really can't imagine myself growing into old age with Rob the way he is.

'Yes I agree but … I'll never last out all that time.' Sven looked sad. 'Once you get home, you might change your mind about me.' He bit his lip, thinking he might get the wrong response.

Pippa sensed his uncertainty, and smiling reassuringly, reached over for his hand and kissed him. 'Don't worry, I'll come back.'

Sven lay on his back and looked up at her. 'Six weeks is a long time. I do understand, but I don't want us to be apart for that long.'

'Yeah, I know,' she said with empathy in her voice. Was she brave enough to tell Rob about Sven? Perhaps she should just leave Whitby and say nothing; she didn't want him to know she had cheated on him. Just leaving would be easier on them all. She would tell Joan. Her best friend would find it hard to understand, but this was a chance for a new life and she had to take it.

Sven began to look lost. 'I can't help the way I feel about you. It's a great feeling but I'm also aware all this could go wrong, and it scares me.'

Pippa, concerned that Sven was upset, tried to smooth things over. Looking in her rucksack, she took out a piece of card and a pen, and wrote down her phone number. 'I'll phone you first—I need to be sure Rob isn't around. Pity you don't have an answer phone at Beachside.'

'I don't like answering machines, they'd be phoning me all hours, day and night.'

Pippa laughed. 'You shouldn't be such a popular guy.'

The weather had closed in just off-shore and they dashed up the dunes back to where Sven had parked the van.

Within a few minutes, they had returned to Sven's cottage to spend more time together.

Sven realised the time for Pippa to leave was too near, a time he didn't ever want to come. He hugged her. 'God, I'm going to miss you! You've changed my life.'

The phone rang and he answered it.

'Hei Sven!' said the familiar voice.

'Hei mamma, hvordan står det til? Hvordan het med pappa?'

Pippa looked puzzled. She hadn't the faintest clue what he was saying. She realised after a few seconds perhaps it was his mother. She smiled, pleased for him that a member of his family had phoned from Norway.

But a few moments later, she felt strange. She thought she heard the word "Astrid". She'd never seen the angry side of Sven, and his furrowed brow seemed to say it all. He was shrugging his shoulders, making helpless gestures with his hands, and his voice rose to a higher pressing tone before falling to its normal self.

'Jeg håper hun ikke kommer hit,' he told his mother. He was hoping she hadn't been interfering again and that Astrid would stay out of his life forever.

Still chatting in Norwegian, Sven told his mother he would call her back because he had a visitor. Pippa wondered about his agitation. She would ask him when he finished the conversation.

Pippa appeared impassive, and since she couldn't understand a word, she pretended to read a magazine instead. Secretly, she was listening to the language; it sounded like singing and it was so interesting to hear. It would be good to learn to speak it.

After several minutes, Sven put the phone down with some deliberation and blew out his cheeks. In deep thought, he realised his world had just turned upside down. Hearing his mother talk about Astrid gave him a nasty taste in his mouth. He could see Mads on the bed apologising to him. He was reminded of the look on Astrid's face when he had walked in on them having sex and how he'd punched Mads in the face. He remembered how he had felt such deep pain and sorrow about what she had done. He had adored her, and the bitch had killed all his faith in human nature. How dare she think she could just waltz back into his life as though nothing had happened? His mother had been very upset at having to cancel the wedding plans, but she was a forgiving soul—that was the problem. She often met Astrid in the supermarket and this time they'd had coffee together.

Sven tried to smile, covering up his anger. It was too late. Pippa had seen it and he didn't know what to say to her. If this was the time to tell a lie, then he had to do it to prevent Pippa from worrying. Five years of freedom: he'd just about got over it when lo and behold, like some nasty bug, Astrid seemed to be lurking in his life again. He hoped not. What the hell was she doing?

He would bend the truth, he knew Pippa didn't need any more worry in her life. He would tell her how his mother sometimes interfered too much. Being an only child, there was no one except his father on whom to lavish her attentions.

'I gather that was your mother?' Pippa asked with a grin.

'Yes, she goes over the top sometimes even though I'm not in Norway anymore. She wants to come here next summer and for me to go back there before the winter.' He remembered a conversation he'd had with her only three weeks before. He hated himself for lying.

'Will you go?' Pippa asked, wondering how something like that could possibly cause him so much pain. Maybe it was their culture to talk in this way; perhaps she hadn't heard him say 'Astreed'. He spoke so fast, all the words seemed to meld together; maybe it was just a normal Norwegian word meaning something else. She knew she could be paranoid at times.

'I might do, it depends on how it goes,' he said. 'I can't go home just like that; she doesn't seem to understand. I have the "Twitchers" month coming up in October, but I might be able to go at Christmas instead—we shall see. Sometimes she just bugs me, always making plans for me instead of letting me do my own stuff. I'm a big boy now' he grinned.

'Aw, Sven, you're lucky to have a mother. She obviously cares about you. I wish I'd had a mother to care for me. Dad was great, but he couldn't teach me to knit or tell me about period pains and having babies and all that—I had to rely on hearsay and friends, and sometimes, it was difficult.'

'Well, we got a lot to plan, haven't we, in the next three days?' Sven tried to change the subject, but inside he was seething with his mother for interfering in his affairs.

'Let's just enjoy the rest of the day together,' Pippa said. 'The weather has changed and it looks nice out there now. Shall we take a walk?'

Sven began to smile again; he would deal with Astrid in his own way if she phoned him. He hoped there was no need to get upset about it or to worry Pippa. Living on Scilly sometimes made it harder for people to get in touch with him. So he had nothing to fear—but what did his mother mean when she said Astrid had something to tell him?

CHAPTER TWENTY-ONE

Rob arranged to meet John Grover in Harrogate. He had driven there, not knowing what to expect. His father had already spoken with John on the phone a few days before and he seemed fine with what his son was about to undertake, although his mother less so.

Across the room in the Hotel Royal York, Rob strode into reception and asked for John Grover. The lawyer was already waiting in the hall and introduced himself.

'I've arranged a private room,' he assured his client.

'Oh?' Rob queried nervously.

'First I have to ask you how you feel about getting in touch with your sister and brother, Penelope and Bruce Haines.'

Rob made a face of angst. 'It's rather daunting. I've spent the last week or so thinking about it. I'm not sure really, but I would love to, I suppose, though it's all a bit scary.'

'Okay, so what if I gave you the opportunity to meet with them this afternoon?'

'What, today?'

'Mm, yes, today.'

'Oh, bloody hell, I hadn't thought about it.' Rob panicked. He placed his hand on his chest. 'Oh, I don't know about today. I think I'll have to sit down; I need a drink.'

'Follow me.' John led the way to a room off the hallway. 'I'll bring you one.'

'Are they in there?' Rob asked with suspicion.

'No, but the reason you are here is that Bruce and Penny Haines are dying to meet you and I have the will from your parents. I thought we'd do this together but only if you feel you want to.'

Rob's anxiety was all too obvious. The words 'your parents' seemed surreal. The palms of his hands began to sweat and he hesitated for a moment, pursing his lips, and pausing for thought.

'You mean … I'll meet them today?'

'Isn't that what you wanted?'

'Er … yes, of course, but I didn't think … oh heck this is hard. But okay, let's do it,' he said.

John Grover left Rob by himself for a while; he wanted to check that his other two clients had made it to the hotel and give Rob time to take it all in.

Rob sat alone, wondering if he had entered into something he couldn't handle. What was he doing here? A will? Penny and Bruce? How would he get used to it all? *Too many issues going on all at the same time.* For a moment, he wished Pippa were back and he could run out of the hotel never to be seen again.

John discovered Bruce and Penny Haines huddled in a corner of the bar, their glasses almost empty. He held out his hand and they each shook it in turn.

'Hello, you two—glad could make it. Traffic okay? I may as well say I have pleasure in informing you that your brother wants to see you.' He gave a cheerful but nervous smile.

Penny stood facing her brother. 'Oh my gawd, I'm not ready for this.'

'Don't worry, Rob is as nervous as you,' John said with a smile.

He led them through the lounge and into the hallway before entering the room where Rob was sitting.

Startled, Rob turned around. He saw Penny standing there, a young girl with a nose like his, dark hair like his, and the same coloured eyes; her brother was a little older. Penny wore smart grey trousers and a red blouse with a blue and red striped scarf at the neck. She reminded him of one of those air hostesses he had seen in a British Airways advert.

She stepped forward with a look of apprehension as she strode in her high heels across the wooden floor. Immediately, her perfume wafted toward him. *Oh God, she's lovely. What do I say?*

His heart almost missed a beat. He searched her eyes and before either of them could speak, he knew she was his sister. *This is weird. Bruce looks so familiar too.*

Penny cried. 'I can't believe it, you look so much like my dad.'

'Oh my God, you two are so …' Rob was lost for words, tears about to flood his eyes. A powerful sense of déjà vu stabbed his feelings. Bruce wore a blue shirt, grey jacket and jeans. As a child, Rob used to dream about how his brother would look if he had one. He was almost exactly as he had imagined. He drew in a deep breath and felt a shiver down his spine.

Bruce blew out his cheeks, overwhelmed by Rob. He saw Penny crying and stood back to allow his sister to have her moment.

Rob sensed everything happening all at once. He had waited all these years with a fantasy that he would find his real family and here they were right in front of him. The sensation scared him for a moment until Penny put her arms around him.

'They found you. I'm so glad they found you.' She choked back her tears. She kissed Rob on both cheeks and hugged him tight. The resemblance to her father was almost like looking at the photo of him when he was the same age as Rob.

Rob knew now this was his real family. As a child, he had wanted a brother or sister, before discovering it wasn't possible. Now the emotion was too much to bear and he cried in Penny's arms. His feelings of his bad times with Daniel, his uncertainties about Pippa, and his loneliness about his adoption were spilling out of him. His life had been like the toys that Pippa had stuffed in the wardrobe waiting for someone to pick them up and love them again. At last, he was relieved of the uncertainties surrounding his childhood.

When the tears and introductions had died down, Rob saw how Penny couldn't keep her eyes off him. Rob couldn't keep his eyes off Bruce; it was like looking at a mirror image of himself. They all kept sighing and laughing, then crying again, finding their feelings and calming their emotions.

'Maybe when we get this over, you will come and stay with us and we can show you lots of photos of our parents,' Penny said. 'Later on, I'll show you a few I brought with me.'

She put her arms around Rob. He seemed to adore all the attention and had to keep reminding himself she was his sister.

'Where's your wife?' Bruce asked.

For the last few hours Rob had put Pippa behind him.

'She's away for three weeks. Unfortunately, we've both been through difficult times like you, but I think we'd better chat about us first. I am so thrilled to meet you both, it's been … well, I don't think I need to tell you, do I?'

John Grover allowed the trauma to settle down. He left the room and a short while later returned, holding a cup of coffee. 'Now, let's talk business. Take a seat all of you,' he said. 'My colleague Stephen Carmichael has already discussed the situation with Rob. It is so sad to think neither your mother nor father will ever know their son. My condolences to you both, and of course to Rob, whom I'm sure feels sad about this too. Your father died only six weeks ago. This is also very sad for me because I knew him as a fine doctor and client. It was only *three* weeks ago that I managed to confirm the information about Rob, hence some delays in the reading of this will. It seems that it was your parents' wish for you all to find each other and share in the family inheritance. It wasn't Rob's fault that he was adopted nor was it your mother's fault. We all know the story now, so I won't go into that.'

John Grover cleared his throat, took out the paperwork from his briefcase and opened *The Last Will and Testament of Peter Haines.* 'The will states that, in the event of your father's death, the estate is to be split three ways. We would always have kept Rob's share and placed it into a trust fund. Your father states that, if before your fiftieth birthday,' he turned to Rob, 'we hadn't managed to find you, the money would be split again between Penny and Bruce.'

Rob looked down at his hands. What right did he have to take away part of their inheritance? He was sure Bruce was thinking the same things.

'It was what your parents wanted,' John assured him.

'I miss my Mum,' Penny said. 'I'll tell you about her and Dad. We haven't had an easy time in the last few weeks.'

'I can relate to that,' Rob said with a tight smile.

'Okay, shall we continue?' John said, after realising their sadness and bewilderment.

He pushed his spectacles further on to his nose. 'I have some documents for you all to sign and then we can arrange for capital to be placed in your respective bank accounts. There could be some tax to pay, but I'll explain all that soon. Bruce, Penny, your father wanted me to handle the sale of your house and as you are both at university, we can arrange all the necessary details. You are all over twenty-one so there shouldn't be any problems. The house is split three ways and there is the capital in the bank—a substantial sum. Once we get all the probate sorted, you should all be comfortable for the rest of your lives. There's something in the region of three hundred thousand pounds each, plus the sale of the house.'

Rob gulped, his father was a millionaire? He was going to be rich, but it was all too much to take in. He realised he had stepped into a family he hardly knew and they were going to give him part ownership of a house and a share of the proceeds. It was like winning the football pools. For a moment, he thought he was going to be sick. What would he do with all that money? He could hardly believe what he was hearing and naïvely thought he'd better say something.

'Can't Bruce and Penny still live in their own house? Isn't there a way round this? I mean …'

'Well, they could, but it's a big house and will take a lot of upkeep,' John explained.

'I don't really want to sell the house,' said Bruce. 'It *is* my home.

Rob thought about it. 'Can I help?' he said, thinking it might be possible to leave Henrietta Street and start afresh.

'It's a *very* large house, Rob; your father had a good job,' said John, smiling faintly.

'How large?' Rob asked.

'It's got ten bedrooms,' Penny said. 'Dad used some of it for his private work.'

'Oh, heck, that is big.' Rob had an idea. 'Bruce, what are you studying at uni?'

'Medicine.'

Rob light-heartedly asked, 'Did John tell you I'm a Charge Nurse at a local hospital?'

Bruce smiled. 'Really? That's weird—I mean, you, kind of following in Dad's footsteps without knowing it.'

'Look, I know this is too soon—I wouldn't want to jump in as a total stranger and take all this away from you—but as I'm here, maybe I can help. Perhaps this is something we could discuss in the coming weeks. I fear it might tear us apart, all this money; we have to do something sensible and agreeable to all of us.' Rob realised he had become the older brother already.

Penny hugged Rob. 'Welcome to the family, big brother.'

Rob saw the look on Bruce's face reminding him that Penny was still quite young and over-enthusiastic.

'It's a big relief, Rob,' said Bruce. 'Your absence in our family has caused us a lot of pain over the years. If only Mum could have found you before it was too late—it's so sad.'

John Grover agreed with Rob: it was something they could discuss between themselves. 'Let me know what you decide,' he said. 'I will get back to you within a week or so. In the meantime, I must go now. I have another client to see back at the office. Probate on these matters takes a few months, so don't expect anything to happen immediately. I'll stay in touch so I can explain it all to you. If there's anything you need to ask me in the next few days, call me. Otherwise, have a wonderful day together, all of you. There's lot of catching up to do, eh?'

They chorused their thanks to John for his help and he left the hotel lobby.

Trying to pull himself together, Rob sat with Penny on the leather sofa in the bar. The hotel was quiet except for a few locals having a drink.

'Isn't this amazing? I'm so sorry to hear about your parents.' Rob realised he meant his parents, too. 'It's going to take me some time to get used to this and you guys as well, eh?'

'Do you want to see a photo, Rob?' Penny asked.

She took out a picture of the family taken when she was about sixteen years old. 'That's me and Bruce with Mum and Dad.'

Rob held the photo and his heart sank. His mother Fiona had been a beautiful woman. Her eyes seemed to reach out to him. His father, dark-haired and handsome, stood proudly with his children. Rob should have been in this photo; it was as if he had died or never existed. He wanted to rage but couldn't do it; instead he opted to tell them his feelings.

'It makes me feel sad to look at this. Cheated perhaps—lost for words.' He wiped the tears from his eyes and Penny put her arm around him.

'I know. It must have been awful for you. We've all been through so much in the last few years. Mum never gave up looking for you and it affected the relationship I had with her; we used to argue about it. I could never believe this day would actually happen.' Penny linked her arm with Rob's and couldn't stop gazing at him.

'Oh my God! Where do we go from here?' Rob asked, wiping away his tears. He was glad to be in a corner of the room where the other customers couldn't see him.

'Tell us about you, Rob,' said Bruce. 'We don't know anything except John said you'd had a dreadful tragedy too.'

'Well, I'm not sure it's appropriate to tell you in view of all your own recent problems.' Rob wasn't sure he'd have the strength to walk that path again.

'It's okay,' Bruce consoled. 'We're trying to get used to it, but you never do, I suppose.'

Rob told them briefly about Daniel and then tried to change the subject.

'Oh, Rob, I'm so sorry,' said Bruce. 'Maybe we can start afresh, all three of us.'

'So, your wife?' Penny asked.

'We are kind of lost souls at the moment. It's a long story. Meeting you now couldn't have come at a better time really. I rather suspect we might all need each other now. Perhaps you will meet her very soon. She's on a break, getting some respite from our sorrows. I've told her but she is in Cornwall and hasn't really had a chance to take it all in.'

'I hope she will soon,' Penny said. 'I just wish Mum could have seen you.'

Rob nodded in agreement. 'John told me your dad died three months after having been in an accident, eh? It was strange because I heard about it and never thought he was my *dad*. He was so near to me and yet so far away, I can hardly bear to think about it.'

'Yeah, hit and run,' said Penny. 'He lived in a lot of pain for a while and they did everything to save him, but he went downhill and never recovered. We tried to get him a liver transplant, but he passed away before one became available.' She gave a knowing look at Bruce. 'The police are still looking for the person who did this to him.'

Rob sighed. 'This is so dreadful for us all, but we must get together very soon and discuss our future. I'll give you my phone number and I'll come down and see you in the next couple of weeks. I'm so thrilled to have met you! My adoptive parents are keen to hear how I got on today; I'll phone them tonight. They are Ralph and Sally Lambton, which of course is why Lambton is my second name. They would love to have met you but they live in Spain now, perhaps they'll come back for a reunion party.'

Penny went to visit the powder room before they left and Bruce waited with Rob to say goodbye.

'I'm sorry about all this, Rob, it's so difficult for me to think I have an older brother, but it seems you're an okay kind of guy,' said Bruce. 'Let's agree to get to know each other better, eh?'

'That's fine with me, honest it is. I fully appreciate you might need time to accept me into the family. I rather suspect we will be meeting up quite a bit in the coming weeks and months. I promise to help you as much as I can.' Rob patted Bruce on the back and gave him a brotherly hug. 'Thanks. You're an okay guy as well. I'm just so overwhelmed today.'

'Yeah, me too. It's all bizarre stuff, isn't it? The things life throws at us. When you think you've made it through, something like this happens,' Bruce said with a smile. Rob shook hands with his brother and smiled at him as Penny returned.

'Bye Penny, it was lovely to meet you both. I'll call you soon when my wife gets back from Cornwall.' He gave her a hug, not sure how he should treat her.

As he left the hotel and crossed the road to the car, he took out a cigarette and placed it to his lips, then paused. He removed it and put it back in the packet. He passed a litter bin and popped the packet inside. Today would be the day he gave up smoking.

CHAPTER TWENTY-TWO

Joan sat in her kitchen, her chin resting on cupped hands. She'd phoned Rob but he was at work. She wanted to die but remembered she had Jordan. She cried into the tea towel she was holding, never feeling as low as she felt today. The situation with Terry had finally hit her with a stab.

Terry had been home again from the rig. She only knew that because his mother had phoned to ask when she was coming round with Jordan. She thought that she could match make her son back with his wife. Joan thought she had wanted Terry back, but questioned her feelings. Perhaps she should phone him and get him to leave on better terms. She needed him to stay in touch with Jordan despite what she had told him. She wanted company, someone to talk with; she had been left holding the baby.

'Tel, it's me,' Joan cried down the phone. 'Why don't you come round here this afternoon and we can talk?'

'Okay, I will,' he said, relenting. 'See ya, love.'

She found it hard to accept that he still called her 'love'.

During the afternoon, Terry arrived and hugged her. Touching her was nice, but it wasn't anything close to what he felt when he was with Frank.

'Hello you.' he said to Jordan. 'What a big boy you are for Daddy, eh?'

Jordan put out a pet lip. Terry thought he should better take things slowly.

'I still care for you, Tel,' Joan said, wanting to kiss him. She would try one more time, but somehow what she felt didn't seem right any more.

'Don't, Joan. I'm with Frank now; we are partners.'

'But can't we stay married and be together?' she said, not fully appreciating the partnership thing.

'No pet, we can't, sorry. I told you I would still care for you and Jordan, and to be honest with you, I feel very sorry for you at this moment. Anyway, Rob always seems to be round here these days.' Terry gave Joan a sideways glance.

Joan's anger got the better of her. 'Don't be so fuckin' stupid, Tel. He's Pippa's husband, and your best friend! He's fixing your bike. I know we get on well and Pippa hasn't left him, you know. She's coming back home soon; I think now you're just being really stupid.'

'If there was anyone in this world I would have to keep an eye on you and Jordan, it would be Rob,' Terry said.

'What d'ye mean? You're his dad, for God's sake; *you* should be looking after us. This is ludicrous.'

Terry shrugged his shoulders. 'I suppose Rob told you about his windfall? He got three hundred thousand quid from his real parents and a big house in the country. He has to share it with his brother and sister. He's a rich guy now. He has a new family. He'll take the money and run and we'll never see him again, and by all accounts, we might not see Pippa either.'

Joan slumped into the sofa. 'I don't know about that.'

'I'm sorry, Joan—about us, I mean. It isn't fair, is it? Are we going to go ahead with this divorce?'

'No! I don't want a divorce, Tel. I want things as they were.'

'Joan, pet, you can't do that. I'm gay and that's all there is to it, you have to let me go. We don't have a marriage and never really did. Start by being honest with yourself, it has to be this way.'

Joan cried, and Jordan, not understanding the situation, thought he had to cry as well. Terry comforted them both and encouraged Jordan to sit on his knee. 'We have to do this, Joanie, really we do. It makes sense.'

'What about our Jordan, *our* son?' she said sniffing.

'I'll stay in touch, I promise.' It was all he could say; he had never been very good in a crisis.

He spent another hour with Jordan and left the house as he had done on his last visit. It was then that Joan realised he might never return.

Carole had taken Jordan for an overnight visit at her house and Joan tried to busy herself. A bottle of painkillers stood on the coffee table. She had meant to take a couple. She had a headache, a very bad headache. Feeling at her lowest ebb, she wondered if life was worth living without Terry. What if Rob and Pippa left her too? Would Rob really take the money and run as Terry had said? She sat and cried herself ill. Her mind wasn't working properly. With every second, she felt progressively sicker and the longer she lay there, the more she wanted to die. She knew she loved Jordan and wished she could rescue herself and the terrible desertion that had happened to her. Pippa's marriage was on the rocks, Terry had left, and now she was going to be alone in her misery. She had always been the brave one holding the flag for everyone else and now, no one was there to hold her flag when she needed it.

She thought she could hear Jordan crying, but he wasn't at home. His tears and screaming became louder with every second she lay there; she knew it couldn't be real. She tried in desperation to reach out to him, being sure she could hear his cries. She wanted to go to her son and in a moment of insanity and following the realisation that she was alone, she opened the bottle of pain killers, hoping if she took one, the pain would go away. Without a further thought, she didn't take one tablet, she swallowed as many pills as she could, forcing them into her mouth and gulping them down with a glass of water. In her frenzy, she wanted to end it all. Half an hour later, nothing happened; her headache was still there, the sickness got worse, and gradually Jordan's imaginary cries lessened. She knew she wasn't dead yet.

Realising what she had done, she tried to retch and stuck her fingers down her throat. 'Oh shit, what did I do? Jordan, I'm sorry, Mummy loves you. I wanna die, no—I don't want to die … oh … ' Her voice was heard by no one. She lay on the settee and awaited her fate, wondering if she should call an ambulance. She knew she had made a dreadful mistake. She stared up at the ceiling and watched a huge spider crawl along the border on the wallpaper. The creature just got bigger and bigger and she shut her eyes, hiding her face in the cushion, in case it landed on her. The pain in her head became unbearable and she blacked out.

Half an hour later, the phone rang on the coffee table. The ringing noise made her stir and she reached out a floppy arm and managed to pick up the receiver but said nothing.

'Hi, Joan—it's me, Rob. Just thought I would call you and see if I can come round to finish the bike. Did Terry come round to see you?' There was a silence on the phone. He could hear sobbing. 'Joan? Joan? It's Rob. Are you there?'

'I'm not going to be here much longer,' Joan sobbed, wishing she hadn't done it because she felt dreadful. The pain was still bad and sleep seemed to dominate her head.

'What the hell have you done?' he said.

'I've taken something, lots of something.' Her voice cracked.

'Where's Jordan?' Rob asked.

'With … oh,' Joan breathed heavily, ' … feel terrible … ' Her voice went quiet.

'God, Joan, stay awake, I'll get some help.'

Rob dialled 999, attempting to stay calm while speaking with the emergency services. Knowing Terry was home, he called him, but discovered he had left for Aberdeen. 'Buggeration!' he scolded. He told Terry's father nothing; it was too early to alarm his parents.

He called the ward sister to say he would be late, then raced round to Joan's on his way to work. Much to his distress, he found Joan lying there and the ambulance paramedics trying to revive her.

He escorted the ambulance to the women's ward and assisted the doctor with her treatment. Joan looked very white and sick. He held her hand and talked to her to make her stay awake.

'Joan? Joan, love, it's me, Rob.' He was almost in tears seeing her close to death.

He tried for another two hours to keep her conscious. 'Don't leave us, Joanie, it's going to be okay. I'm here, it's Rob, Joanie, come on gal, it's going to be all right.'

She came around for a few moments, sniffed, and tears ran down her face. 'I've got nothing left now, my life is ruined,' she groaned. 'Everything I ever wanted has been taken away. I wanted to die. I hate you for that.' Her voice faded to a croak and then she was sick.

'No, you didn't want to die! And you don't hate me! You have Jordan. You were feeling very sorry for yourself and you can't say it was your fault; you've been through so much in the last few days. Come on, Joan, stay with me, love.' He rattled her hand. 'Let's talk about something nice.'

'There isn't anything left that's nice; I've got nothing now. I lost Terry to some bloke or another and I feel I'm losing …' She fell asleep again.

'Joan, come on, don't give up. Jordan needs his Mum. I care about you. I always will.' He patted her hand. There was no response.

He waited by her side for another hour and monitored her blood pressure and heart. He did his best to try to keep her awake. He thought she looked pathetic lying there, pale and tear-stained. It was not the Joan he knew, the woman who was always neat and a bit old-fashioned. He had lost his own son and now Joan had tried to take her life. *What if she had … ?* No, he didn't want to think about it. He wasn't going to let his old school friend die. In his own way, he had special feelings for her. Besides, perhaps he needed something like this to shake him up to patch up his own life. 'Come on Joan, stay with me. I can't live with myself knowing I might lose you as well.'

CHAPTER TWENTY-THREE

It was some time after five o'clock when Pippa returned from seeing Jan and Lisa leave on the boat. She had embraced them, knowing that she might never see Jan again. It was a poignant goodbye moment. Lisa whispered in her ear. 'Follow your heart and your heart will tell you what to do.' Pippa smiled, and Lisa promised to return to Scilly in the future. 'Where can I find you?' she asked.

'Oh, just send a letter to Beachside Cottage, I will be waiting for you there.' Pippa wondered if she could really be that confident about her return to Scilly. She hugged Jan and wished with all her heart he wouldn't die. She knew there were people with worse problems than hers. Losing a child was bad enough but when you knew you were going to die soon, surely that must be the ultimate heartache, waiting around for it to happen, becoming thinner and thinner with each day, starving to death. Jan had taught her to be strong. She waved them into the distance, thinking that soon she would be on the same heart-breaking journey. She turned away and walked briskly into town trying not to cry.

Sven pulled up in the van at Beachside Cottage. He showered, pulled on a clean, wrinkled T-shirt, and opened a beer. Sitting in the garden on a green plastic chair, he closed his eyes in the sun and sighed to himself. He was thinking about Pippa. It was her last week on Scilly and he wanted to show her the rest of the islands and do some more birding. How would he fit all this in with the boat tours? He hoped and prayed Astrid wouldn't phone him. He tried to put it to the back of his mind.

Just then, he thought of an idea to help pull him out of his negativity. An evening trip down the Telegraph Road on bikes would be great; he could include a walk to see the Loaded Camel rock formation on Porthellick Beach. There was so much to see, and so little time. He seemed to have spent it all in bed. He smiled to himself. *She's lovely.*

He wondered how the plan would work when she returned to Whitby. He would wait for her to call him as she had explained; he hoped she would. He could trust her, but maybe Pippa was right—a holiday romance? She might return to her husband after all. The phone rang, disturbing his thoughts.

'It's me, Sven. God, this phone box stinks of cigs,' Pippa said as she opened the door to let in the fresh air.

'Oh, hello you. Why didn't you just come round here?'

'Just checking you're back, that's all—save walking up the road for nothing.'

'I'll make you sausage, egg and chips.'

'Now there's an offer a woman can't refuse! Sounds to me like good Norwegian bachelor-pad food. Okay, that's nice, love to.' Pippa chuckled at her own humour.

'I gather you can ride a bike?' Sven asked.

'A bike? Yes, sure, but it's been a very long time,' she said, wondering what he was going to come up with next.

'When you get here, I'll tell you why and I've also got some news for you.'

'Oh, okay—half an hour?'

'Half a minute! I miss you,' he laughed, knowing she was only five minutes away.

'Okay, I'll be as quick as I can. See you at your place.'

'Love you.' He replaced the receiver.

Pippa dashed home to get changed and, on her way out, locked the door behind her. On arrival at Beachside, Sven pulled her briskly through the door in case Nanette Bell saw her. Once Nanette knew about Pippa, there would be no stopping her. Perhaps it was too late anyway.

'Hello, my love.' Sven kissed her. Then he kissed her again and yet again. 'Mm … you look gorgeous.'

'Who ironed your T-shirt?' Pippa asked with a grin.

'Oh, I came in and threw it on myself.'

'You need a good woman around here.' She put her arms around his waist and kissed him again.

'I suppose I really do.' He hugged her.

'Now, tell me about this bike thing,' demanded Pippa.

'Our meal is ready; we'll talk about it when we sit down, eh?'

Pippa set the table; Sven brought in the meal: two sausages each, two fried eggs, baked beans and what seemed like a mountain of chips. They sat down. Sven patted the bottle of tomato ketchup with his hand and the sauce splurged over the chips.

'I got another call today to confirm the time Martin is coming.'

'Isn't he the guy from that wildlife programme on the TV?' Pippa was curious having read a recent local article about him.

'Ya, you guessed it, eh?'

'Wow, he's gorgeous,' she teased. 'How exciting.'

Sven gave a nonchalant reply. 'No, it's me that's gorgeous—or so you keep telling me.'

She giggled at his comment. 'Sounds wonderful.'

'So let's talk about this evening. I thought we'd do a bike ride around the island, go to some places you've never been yet.' He ripped a paper tissue out of the Kleenex box and wiped a blob of tomato sauce from Pippa's lip. 'Looks like you're wounded.'

'Oh! Right. Yes … that would be nice, let's do it! Although I'll have to ask you to ride slowly, because I'm not used to it.' Pippa rolled her eyes at him.

'There is so much to see here, I don't want you to miss it all. We seem to have been so wrapped up in each other, I almost forgot about showing you the rest of the place.'

He put the last chip on his fork and fed it to her. 'For you.'

Pippa put down her knife and fork. She knew how much Sven loved the islands. 'I'll have to go back and pick up some things though, let the dinner settle down first,' she explained.

'I'll come round with the bikes and we'll set off at what … say, er … seven?' Sven looked at his watch. 'I gotta go and see someone first about a bike for you.'

'Okay, that's fine.' Pippa stood up from the table. 'I'll get ready now, and let you get on with it. Great sausages, thanks.'

She was glad for the walk, as it gave her a chance to think. Whatever Sven had in mind, she had the feeling, judging by his enthusiasm, that it would be fun. Smiling to herself all the way home, she couldn't wait to find out what he'd planned. *Riding a bike, me on a bike! Who would have thought it? It's a pity I don't do more of this at home—too hilly.*

It was seven o'clock. Sven waited outside Gilstone with two bikes. 'I borrowed this one; I think it will be the right size. It has six gears. Are you ready?'

Pippa smiled at him. His sea-blown hair probably hadn't been combed since he got up this morning, and it didn't seem to matter. *I think it makes him look even more desirable,* she thought as he straddled the frame of the bike.

She set off and wobbled her first few yards. She felt Sven's steady hand against her back. 'I'm getting the hang of it now. Gosh, it's been ages. You never really forget, do you?'

She rode up the hill toward the church, puffing and panting with Sven behind her.

'I'll have to get you fit. Don't stop pedalling, and put it in a lower gear, Pippa.' He turned left near the top of the hill and they rode together past the school and along the narrow roads toward Telegraph Road.

'We'll come back down that road eventually,' Sven pointed out to her as they passed the junction. 'First, I want to take you to see the Loaded Camel. You can only see it properly from the side and we didn't get the chance last week.'

'I have actually seen it during my last visit, on the island bus trip, but it would be lovely to see it again.'

Pippa puffed her way along the lanes until they made it, cycling past the flower farm at Lunnon. Up and down the hills they rode, until she got off the bike feeling breathless. Sven stopped at the top and waited for her.

'We'll take a walk.' He pointed and leaned his bike on the grass.

Pippa parked her bike up against a stone wall and followed him down the path toward Porth Hellick Beach.

'There it is Pippa—look.'

'Oh yes, I see, it does look like a camel with a pack on its back. Oh that's brilliant,' she said, enthralled. She stood feeling comforted with Sven's arm around her waist, breathless and slightly muscle-torn after cycling. Together they stared out beyond the bay and then Sven kissed her. 'Mm, you are lovely,' he said. 'Come on, let's walk a little further.'

They made their way past a yellow burst of gorse bushes. The soles of Pippa's sandals were getting muddy and Sven assisted her over a puddle. 'Best we continue on our way now before it gets dark,' he said. 'It's not so hilly now, the worst is over.'

They rode on passing Pelistry, a place Pippa already knew from her ride in the van, and then cycled through the lanes and hedgerows where the honeysuckle and fuchsia bloomed, entwined between the stone walls. They turned the bend toward Holy Vale, a tropical paradise nestling in a small niche in the island's geography. The palm trees and flowers were in full bloom; the blue agapanthus, the smell of rosemary and camomile filled the air on a summer evening.

'Wow! Smell that!' said Pippa as she took in the fragrance of the honeysuckle. 'And look at the clematis on the wall of that lovely old house, it's delightful.' She began to feel her muscles had stretched to their limit. 'I'd like to walk a little now.'

'Okay, let's do that—get a chance to talk a bit too,' Sven replied, hoping to discover more how she felt about leaving the islands. He got off his bike and walked alongside her.

'Let's sit on this seat for a moment.' Pippa parked her bike against a tree. 'What do you want to talk about?'

They sat together on a bench in a shady spot away from the road and held hands. The bees buzzed in the clover on the grass verge. A helicopter pounded the air as it passed over them. They looked up and watched it disappear over the treetops.

She turned toward him and he cupped her face with his hands and kissed her. 'Pippa, I love you, I really do!'

Pippa's chest pounded with joy; he had told her so many times—how could she turn her back on him now?

'I know I'll come back to you, I promise. It might take a bit of time but I don't want this life with Rob any more.'

'Oh Pippa, you are so lovely and you seem to have made my life complete.' Sven lingered in her arms; he laid his head on her lap as he stretched out on the bench, looking up at her.

'You're crying,' he said as she turned her head away from him.

It was a cry she had longed for. At last, someone truly loved her and had told her so. She had to return here; he was the most wonderful person she had ever met. He really did love her, she knew it. Nothing must stop her coming back to Scilly.

'Sorry,' she sniffed, 'you make me very happy.'

Sitting there, it dawned on her that the man at the cemetery in Whitby had been her guardian angel. She recalled his words. 'Maybe you'll find direction around the corner where it's been waiting to meet you.' She wiped away her tears of joy. *This is it!* She smiled down on Sven and looked into his eyes, thinking how lucky she was.

'Let's move on,' Sven suggested, 'before we lose the light. There are even more surprises at the end of this lane.'

He made her laugh as he cycled 'no hands', his arms and fists waving in the air in triumph like someone winning the Tour de France. They were in love; she knew it. They cycled on past the pond on Pungies Lane and took a quick look at the hybrid mallards showing off to their females, flapping their wings and making happy duck calls.

Sven waited for her at the top of Telegraph Road. 'I'll race you to the bottom,' he said. 'No, better still, change of plan, we'll ride it together. There are a few potholes in the road and I don't want you to fall over.'

Pippa's smile told him more than he could have hoped.

He started the ride from the junction and they rode hand in hand for a while until the road became steeper. He saw how relaxed she seemed as they freewheeled down the hill with the wind in their faces and the sound of gulls overhead.

He kept looking back at her and mouthing 'love you.' Her pink shorts and white T-shirt, the curve of her breasts and her windblown hair: she seemed ecstatically happy. The fact she had bought a pair of open toe sandals much like his own made his heart speak. *You belong to me, Pippa. One day I will make you Pippa Jørgensen, and we can go birding together for the rest of our lives.*

The pace picked up, faster and faster; his hair pressed back against his skull, as he willed his feelings to last forever. He wasn't sure if he was dreaming and wondered if pinching himself might bring him back to reality; he hoped not.

They arrived in town feeling renewed. 'That was brilliant,' Pippa said with a grin on her face. 'When I come back, we'll do it again.'

CHAPTER TWENTY-FOUR

Sven had to be up again for work; he looked at Pippa lying there in bed, her eyes closed. It was Friday and they had spent the night at Gilstone. In less than a day, she would be gone. His desperation gnawed at the knot in his stomach. She had taken so many risks for him, and now he felt like a man about to lose his sense of normality. He wanted her to stay on Scilly. Should he ask her not to go back to Whitby? It was a pity to wake her. He had to be down at the boat for ten o'clock.

'Come on my love, time to get up, we have to go to Bryher.'

He prepared breakfast, and put flowers on the table, setting it neatly to impress her.

'Toast?' he asked as he placed the rack of slices on the table.

'Yes please, thanks.'

She seemed miles away, he thought. Well, soon she would be. 'Coming with me today?' he asked, as if it was just a trip down the road in the car.

'Yes of course' she said sleepily.

Within the hour, they left and were back on the ocean with Don. She finally got her trip to Bryher.

Sven worked through the morning on the island discussing business with the islanders while Pippa walked the footpaths and had coffee with the tourists. Later, they met to sit on the white sand at Rushy Bay. He had left his wet suit in a wooden hut along the shore and changed into it, stripping down to his waist. He looked very handsome and Pippa felt an urge for him to make love to her on the deserted beach, but soon realised the beach wasn't all that deserted that afternoon.

Sven scanned offshore with his binoculars. 'I want you to see Sasha. I hope I can find her.'

It was too cold for Pippa to swim without a suit of her own, so she watched as Sven entered the water and sank beneath it.

Moments later, she heard him calling some distance from the shore and looked through her binoculars. A seal had surfaced and then disappeared under the water again. Sven signalled to Pippa that he had found her. Sasha swam around him several times before coming close. As Sven came toward Pippa, the seal followed curiously and made splashing noises with her flippers before disappearing under the water, as if playing hide and seek. As Sven swam closer to shore, he almost persuaded Sasha to leave the sea. Pippa realised the incentive; he was holding a fish in his hand. She laughed. Was there anything he couldn't do? Sasha swam off and Pippa had a sudden sad thought she might never see her again.

Don arrived and placed a plank between the boat and the beach. Pippa waded into the water and climbed onto the plank to board the boat. There were other passengers on board for the gig racing.

'There ya go, young lady, hope you and Sven had a lovely day together,' Don said, assisting her. Sven pulled the plank on board and they continued on their way.

As the *Lily of Laguna* chugged across the sea, they spotted fulmar resting on the surface and kittiwake dipping their wing tips in the glassy curves. Their calls 'kittiwake, kittiwake' echoed across the lagoon as they fluttered down to fish in the calmer Atlantic swell. Bishop Rock Lighthouse, the real 'first and last 'outpost', stood on a craggy outcrop, ghostly and proud on the horizon, and Pippa felt exhilarated as she drew in the tang of salt-ridden air.

Sven pointed to shearwater, puffins and a peregrine falcon nesting close by, and Pippa, swept along by the thrill of it all, watched the sun going down on the horizon. Don manoeuvred the boat around the island of Samson and spotted the rowers from the Gig Club. Friday night was always Gig Night. In the distance, he heard the visitors cheering on their favourite team. 'Come on Golden Eagle, come on Bonnet, pull harder!' He steered toward them to enable Pippa to cheer the gigs as well.

As the last glow of orange was about to leave the sky, they returned to St Mary's. Climbing out of the boat and up the steps, Sven held Pippa's hand. They walked together to the end of the stone pier. Sven helped her to sit on the wall, then climbed up next to her.

'Look,' he said, pointing over the sea. 'The sun, between the two hills of Samson. Isn't that a sight?'

Pippa laid her head on his shoulder. 'Wow, this is so romantic. You make it very hard for me to leave tomorrow. I feel like running away with you, chasing that sunset.'

'Do you have to go, Pippa? Can't you just phone up and say you aren't coming back?'

'Oh, Sven darling, don't tempt me. You see, it's Rob and the house and all my personal stuff, which is awkward. I have to settle everything first. I might have to sell the house and I can't just throw him out of it. These things take time. I'll have to try and be delicate and tactful about it; I want to do it that way because of Daniel—it's the right thing to do.'

'Oh, okay,' Sven said. 'I didn't fully understand that.' He looked puzzled for a moment.

'You see, the thing is, Rob never questioned that my dad left it to me in his will, it was all a matter of trust, and right now trust is not the most favourable word. I can't chuck him out. I have to make it as fair as possible.'

'Yes, I agree,' Sven said, nodding and appreciating her words.

She didn't want to tell him how she felt when she had cheated on Rob; she wasn't proud of what she'd done to him. She had never thought her relationship with Sven would go this far and she wondered how she would deal with it all when she returned home. *I can just see it now; Rob storming around the house screaming at me for what I've done to him.* He had often made her feel stupid and a number of times she had backed down, just to keep the peace. Joan had once said, 'It's a wise woman who keeps her mouth shut.' This time, no matter what, she would be brave, tell him, and let the consequences take care of themselves. Of course Rob would be angry, but he would get used to it, and he'd get over it, surely? After all, he was the one who wanted the divorce in the first place. He couldn't have it both ways—he'd pushed her in this direction. It was all quite sad. Was she doing the right thing by leaving him? How could she live like that for the rest of her life?

The sun had left the sky, only the orange glow remained. They lingered on the wall as Don passed by. He'd taken the boat out in the bay to anchor in deeper water for the receding tide and returned in the dinghy.

'Hello, you two love birds. So you're leaving tomorrow?' he said as he looked at Pippa.

'Oh hi, Don,' Pippa said. 'It was a great boat trip tonight, thanks. I feel honoured that you did that for us.'

'I'll miss her, but she's coming back soon,' Sven told Don as he put his arm around Pippa's waist and gave her a hug as if to be certain she would return.

'I 'ope you enjoyed yer time 'ere, young lady.'

'Oh I did—it was more than I could possibly explain.'

Sven assisted Pippa in climbing down from the wall and the three of them walked off together. As Pippa strode along the quay hand in hand with Sven, she wondered if her life would ever be the same again.

'Birdman's coming back tomorrow, Sven,' said Don.

'Yeah, thank God, it's been too long. I'm picking him up in the morning before lunch.'

'Gawd, that man's got a good job, eh? Flying 'ere and thur.' Don looked at Pippa again and laughed. 'No doubt you and Sven will be gallivantin' awf hither and thither soon—'n me? I'm a Scillonian; I don't think I'll ever leave this place. I got everythin' I want 'ere. I 'aven't bin awf this island for the last five years.'

As they walked toward *The Mermaid*, Don offered to take them out for a drink.

'Sorry, Don, we can't, but thanks anyway. It's our last night and Pippa is packing.' Sven knew Don would understand.

Pippa agreed; she didn't want to be with anyone other than Sven, but it was kind of Don to ask.

As they walked up Hugh Street together, Sven didn't feel like hiding the woman in his life and blatantly walked arm in arm with Pippa along the road. No one noticed. They were only a couple in love, walking along the street. Pippa smiled at him as he pulled her closer to him; she felt like waltzing up the road so everyone could see them, but in her head she was very aware of how she had cheated on Rob and the dread of what might happen next filled her thoughts. How would Rob take it, his wife leaving him for another man? It sounded dreadful when she thought about it that way and Pippa wondered if she really had been stupid.

As they walked along the road, Sven smiled at Pippa. He was glad he had made her happy and his life would be complete when she returned to Scilly. In the meantime, he would miss her so much. His heart was breaking and he wanted to plead with her not to go home, but with the house and everything, she had to sort it out to win her freedom. He understood. He would keep in touch with her every day.

That night, they stayed at Gilstone. Pippa folded her clothes into the rucksack. She needed to talk. 'I really don't know what I'm going to tell Rob, maybe I'll start by saying ... '

Sven interrupted her and put his finger to her lips. 'Elskling, I don't wish to interfere but I suggest you let *him* open the conversation, stay quiet and see what his other news brings, it might open a new dialogue for you to do something positive.' He slowed his words, speaking more softly and looking into her eyes. 'See how it goes, don't sit there worrying or practising your opening lines, just go with the flow—that's what I would do, let him lead the way. It's not easy for me either. I don't want to steal someone away from their marriage, but I love you and that's the way it is. It's also a huge risk to my morale that you might not make it back here.' He kissed her on the cheek.

'I suppose you're right, but what if he makes a huge fuss? Oh God, there's so much to sort out, I need to find a way to tell him about us—how can I do that without a row? I can't give him the house—that was the agreement in the will. Dad wanted to give me a good start in life. That house might take ages to sell and do I really want to sell it? My roots are there. But …'

'Try not to worry, my love. Surely Rob can stay there until he needs to move? Maybe give him a deadline or something. I mean, if he has all this money now, he can survive on his own, surely. How do you really feel about him, anyway?' Sven asked, looking for some reassurance.

'Well, he hasn't always been this bad. We've had a few ups and downs; he is unpredictable, always has been. I don't know the full story on his adoption thing; I feel very sorry for him in that respect. His parents didn't tell him until just before we married. His insecurities seem to have rubbed off on me in recent years. The only regret I have is leaving Daniel and my parents at the cemetery.'

Sven hugged her. 'I understand, but some time, we can go there together and you can show me around Whitby, visit your son …'

'I don't know, darling, maybe it's time I moved on from Rob. All this has come at the right time. I wish I could let go of Daniel and allow him to become a fond memory for the rest of my life.'

'Give it time. Time is a good healer.' Sven held her hand and led her to bed. It was a warm sticky night; the temperature had risen and the house was slow to cool down. Sven wrapped the white sheet over them and, like the proverbial peas in a pod, they became one as they slept.

CHAPTER TWENTY-FIVE

The following morning, Sven rose early and made Pippa a cup of Yorkshire Tea, her favourite brand. With The Birdman arriving later that morning, Sven had to leave soon to meet him at the helicopter.

Pippa watched as Sven put his arms into a T-shirt and pulled it over his head. With his hair tousled, he looked quite unkempt; it made her want to drag him back to bed and cosset him. He pulled on a pair of frayed denim shorts and zipped up the fly. He borrowed Pippa's hairbrush to smooth his hair.

'I'm going now. Sorry this is such a rush, but I have to be at the office and discuss things with Margaret before I go to the airport. Don't forget, twelve o'clock.'

'Okay, I won't.' Pippa yawned and then blew him a kiss.

'Come up the hill on the bike and down the other side and you're' at the Old Town Café. You can't miss it.'

'Thanks, I know where it is,' she assured him.

'You look gorgeous this morning.' He paused for a moment to slip into his sandals. 'I wish this wasn't happening, but I must go. Bye, Pips.' He kissed her and then dashed down the stairs without breakfast, rushing out the front door to the van. Pippa heard the engine start and then silence as the van disappeared up the street.

Lying in bed, she thought about everything that had happened to her. It seemed as if Sven had swept her off her feet, literally.

She felt nervous about going back to Whitby; could she stay here forever and not return? Perhaps she could miss the boat and go back a few days later than planned. No, that would be putting it off cowardly. In the old days, Rob had been good to her most of the time, but this 'old friends thing' seemed to have got in the way of the meaning of true love. It occurred to her she might have been too young when they married.

Aware of what Joan would say to her when she got back, she wanted her to understand that she hadn't deliberately set out to do this; it wasn't like that. She would make sure her best friend understood the reasons for her departure. Maybe Rob had already told her about their conversation on the phone. Joan liked to spend time with him, they'd always had a good relationship, and since Pippa knew that Rob would always remain friends with Joan, she would be a good ally. Perhaps he had married the wrong person! Joan would probably never move on in her life, she wasn't made that way. She was a local lass and always seemed happy in her own world of Terry and looking after Jordan. Pippa had often wished that Rob had paid less attention to the Marshall family and more to her. He'd often said he owed it to Joan for all the kindness she'd provided during the months after Daniel had died. Pippa had to agree, but sometimes, she felt uncomfortable about it, especially lately. She decided she had to be fair with

Rob and do this properly. She fiddled with her wedding ring and wasn't sure what to do with it, reminding herself she was still wearing it. She would give it back to Rob or maybe she should keep it in memory of the old days. She pushed it into her make-up bag and closed the zipper.

It was eleven thirty. Pippa got on the bike Sven had left outside the front door. She was early. They had promised to have lunch with Martin and his entourage. As she reached the top of the hill, she stopped to look at the view. If she had been able to write a poem, this would have been her chosen moment. *Wow! This is stunning.* As she looked back, masses of pink, purple, orange, and cream Livingstone daisies covered the walls, their colours flowing to the ground. She cycled further down the lane and there it was, in front of her, Old Town Bay in full blue tide with the church on the foreshore. With a sense of completeness and absolute love for the islands, there was no doubt in her mind that she had to come back. She thought perhaps she had fallen in love twice during her stay. Life here seemed so unspoiled and she hoped it would remain so forever. Sven had shown her how vulnerable these islands were with the oil spill and how important it was to protect them from the ravages of the outside world. 'These islands are the height of vulnerability itself,' he'd told her. 'Take what you have and cherish it all your life.' She had to support his quest. He'd told her how he wished everyone could make a difference to the world by doing one thing in their lives to save the environment. It was as if he, by himself, was attempting to take on the battle of the elements and the human race.

Pippa freewheeled down the hill and arrived at the café. She parked her bike, ordered a coffee, and watched the people passing by her table. She caught a whiff of coffee and cake from the next table and it reminded her of the first time she had met Sven. She closed her eyes in the sun and waited for the arrival of The Birdman.

Martin, looking well-tanned from the African sun, arrived with his wife Andrea. He was taller than Sven, and not unlike his colleague, he wore shorts, open-toe sandals and a Greenpeace

T-shirt. The film crew followed behind him carrying bags, tripods and camera equipment.

'Hi, mate!' Martin embraced Sven. He introduced him to the crew. 'Pete, Larry, meet my colleague Sven Jørgensen, the only Viking on Scilly!'

Sven shook hands with the camera crew.

'Hi Sven, great to see you.' Andrea waved at Sven, then welcomed him with a kiss on the cheek. 'Come on over for a meal tonight, I'll make us something special.' She turned to Martin before she left. 'Darling, I'll get home now.' She had ordered a taxi. She kissed her husband. 'Bye, love, don't be long, will you?'

Martin explained to Sven, 'She's gone back home to sort things out. You know she doesn't like travelling in the van.' He chuckled. 'Where did you say you were going, Sven—the Old Town Café? I'm starving. We can all take a break there. Good idea.'

'Ya, Martin, erm … there's someone I would like you to meet.'

'Who's that?'

'Oh, you'll see, bit of a surprise.' Sven gave a big smile as he walked beside his friend.

'Oh yeah?' said Martin.

'Come on, let's go.' Sven was anxious to see Pippa again.

As she left the airport, Andrea waved goodbye to everyone and Sven responded with a thumbs-up. Her blue denim mini-skirt and sea-green blouse showed off her suntan. Sven watched her go. It was good to have her back from her trip to Bristol to meet Martin. He wondered if she would befriend Pippa; he hoped so. He'd worried about Andrea last winter, being on her own while Martin was in the Antarctic. Nevertheless, she always seemed to manage. He admired her enthusiasm and humour.

'How are things?' Martin asked. 'You look great, Sven. Glad we're back, it's been a long tour.' He patted Sven on the shoulder as they left the small airport terminal.

Sven took the wheel of the van and drove into Old Town with the entire luggage and the film crew in the back. He filled Martin in about Scilly in his absence, feeling some relief he had more support now.

Pippa sat at her table admiring the view and drinking her coffee. She could hear the familiar sound of the van coming around the bend. She peered through the windscreen. *Yes, it's Sven!* In a moment, Pippa saw all the new faces invading her space. She waited, wondering how it would be now The Birdman was back.

The group almost rolled out of the doors and Sven smiled at her. He decided to be brave about the introductions.

'Erm, Martin … this is my girlfriend, Pippa Lambton.'

Martin looked astounded. 'Girlfriend?' He smiled warmly at Pippa, then grinned at Sven.

'Yes, I know who you are. I've seen you on the telly.' She began to think how different he looked, taller and even better than on TV. She shook hands with him. He seemed so friendly and outgoing. He waved at the café proprietor and then at someone in a car who passed by with a toot of the horn.

His sense of humour mingled with his manners; he seemed the perfect gentleman. Holding onto Pippa's hand, he grinned at her. '*Enchanté*, Madam.'

Sven laughed. 'Hey, man! She's *mine.*' Then he reminded himself that she wasn't his yet.

Pippa decided to match Martin's charm. 'My God, are all your friends this handsome, Sven?' They laughed at her comment and Sven jokingly whispered in her ear. 'Only the ones on Scilly!'

'I've been trying to get Sven fixed up with a girl for the last five years, then I go away and I can't trust him five minutes—sneaky bugger goes behind my back!' Martin pushed Sven's arm in play.

'This has to be a moment for a photo, eh?' said Pete.

Photos could mean trouble; they might end up in the press, Pippa thought.

With quick thinking, Sven replied, 'Oh, no photos *please*, let's have some lunch. Pippa is returning north this afternoon and we don't have much time together.'

'Thanks,' she whispered to Sven, from the corner of her mouth.

'Anyway, I hope to come back in the next few weeks.'

'Pippa won't have met Andrea yet, of course?' asked Martin.

'No, but I'm sure she will soon. We've been beating the Scilly Grapevine, so we didn't tell anyone about us,' Sven explained.

'Ha! Sure. Well, Pippa, when you come back, go and see her. She needs a new friend—well, I think she does,' Martin grinned.

'I will. Sven has told me a lot about her and what a great team you are.'

Pippa saw Martin give Sven a knowing look and wondered if she had met with his approval. After all, Sven and Martin had been friends for a long time—would she fit in?

Having completed his winter filming, Martin seemed very happy to return to his beloved islands. The five of them sat together, ordered fish, salad, a bowl of chips, and wine. Sven bought a huge Dame Blanche ice cream for Pippa and the holiday atmosphere prevailed.

Pippa listened, fascinated and in awe of Martin's stories about his trip to Africa. It helped to take her mind off the afternoon, the ferry back to Penzance and the train ride north. She held Sven's hand and put her foot on his under the table. Sven sat forward as she played footsie with him and gave her a discreet smile across the table. Sven noticed how Martin had tried to cheer them up; it seemed he had also felt the tension of her departure.

'Hey up, lass, 'ave a glass of wine, stop yer from bein' sea sick on't ferry.' He over-mimicked Pippa's Yorkshire accent. Pippa giggled. She already liked him. Sven stood up from the table. It was time to leave. He saw Pippa's bike propped against the side of the café and decided to leave it there; he would collect it later.

They all squeezed into the van. There were no seats in the back and they sat on a blanket and some cushions. Martin picked up the van keys where Sven had left them on the table. 'I'll drive,' he said. Sven looked at Pippa and made a grimacing face when he thought Martin wasn't looking. He whispered to her, 'I hope you're ready for this.'

'I see they still haven't fixed that big hole in the road,' Martin said as he drove toward Hugh Town.

'Oh, yes, it's been fixed twice, but the bad weather we had this winter didn't help,' Sven informed him.

Pippa was laughing with Pete and Larry as they sat in the back. Martin's driving habits were unpredictable and she soon began to understand Sven's comment.

Larry shouted from the rear. 'If I wanted a ride on a roller coaster, I'd have bloody well paid for it,' he called above the sound of the engine. 'Ouch, my arse!'

'Sorree,' yelled Martin. 'Forgot we're not on the African plains!'

Pippa couldn't stop laughing and Sven turned round to see what was going on. Pippa was hanging onto Pete in the back as they kept sliding forward on the downhill route. She laughed so much that tears ran down her cheeks. Pete offered her a sheet from the roll of kitchen paper that Sven had hung on a wire behind the seat. She took it, still laughing and crying, as they went over another bump in the road.

The group arrived in town passing Porthmellon and the view across the bay with the boats in the harbour. Pippa could see the *Scillonian* at dock; it reminded her it was almost time to leave. Martin and the crew got out of the van. They offered to meet later at Martin's house for a drink.

'See you later Sven,' he called. 'Bye, Pippa, come back soon and have a good journey up north.'

Pippa was still grinning at Sven as he drove home. Her cheeks ached from laughing so much.

'I didn't realise his driving would be that bad,' she said, stroking her face and trying to bring her cheeks back to normal.

'Oh, that's Martin, he arses around and shows off sometimes. What you see on telly isn't the same as when he's at home. He can be a bit of an idiot at times, but he's a fun guy.'

'I like him. You really are a team, aren't you, and … there's Don, of course.' All Pippa could see in her head was Sven and Don riding the waves on the *Lily*. She smiled to herself, thinking how wonderful it would be to belong to the team and come home on bikes each day down the well-remembered lanes.

There was one last thing Pippa had wanted to do. 'Sven darling, will you walk up the hill to The Garrison with me?' she asked.

'Of course,' he said, holding her hand.

Arriving at Gilstone, they picked up Pippa's rucksack from the porch. She looked around to ensure she hadn't left anything behind. The last thing she recalled was Sven sitting at the table on his first visit to the house.

'So long, house. It's been amazing—I'll be back soon.' She left the door key in an envelope as Janice had requested and with a heavy sadness closed the front door behind her.

Sven drove toward the quay; the ferry would leave in an hour. The ship's whistle would soon call the passengers.

'Will you walk with me to the seat at the top?' Pippa asked. 'It's the place I had the happiest memories of Dan during our last visit, and then maybe I can leave here knowing I'll have done what I set out to do.' She turned her eyes away from his face.

'Ya, sure Pippa, I understand.'

They walked up the hill together, Sven with binoculars swinging on his chest and Pippa feeling proud by his side.

Sitting on Pippa's favourite bench, they admired the view of the islands in the lagoon. A gull mewed loudly below the cliff as Sven began to talk. He waited until the bird passed over him.

'Promise me you'll call the minute you get back?'

'Yes,' replied Pippa, reassuring him. 'Of course I will. We're a couple now and nothing will stop me from coming back to you.' She prayed that her words would be true.

'I love you so much,' Sven whispered. 'You know, Pippa, you're amazing, and especially the way you have changed since we first met—I'm so proud of you.'

'Well, it's true, if it weren't for you I wouldn't have got this far—I mean, I feel quite different now.'

Sven held her hand and kissed her. 'Pippa, I'm scared it'll all go wrong and you won't be able come back. I want us to be together, nothing else matters.'

'Of course I will, I *absolutely promise* I will. I love you so very much. It's hard to leave, but I have to do the right thing.'

In the distance, Pippa imagined she could see the figure of the small boy, the one she had seen before, looking out to sea and pointing. It was as though he was trying to tell her something. It would always be a special place, somewhere to sit when things were not quite right in your life and you could contemplate how to repair your sorrows. Pippa knew Jan and Lisa had discovered that too. She kissed Sven. 'This one is for the view,' she said. 'Darling, you are so kind to me. There have been days when I wondered how I'll survive, but I know I will now, because of what we share, you and me, sitting here looking out to sea. I wonder when we're old and grey if one day, we will be sitting here again on this very spot, remembering our time and us together. It's been amazing. When I get back, I'll have to try to be brave. This has to be the hardest decision for me, leaving you and having to sort out the sadness at home.'

'I know you are a good person, Pippa.' He kissed her again. 'If things haven't been right for a while, then you have to do what's best, I suppose. I'm just a bit scared, that's all, because you'll be so far away from me.' He sighed. 'Can't you … *accidentally* miss the boat this afternoon?'

Pippa chuckled. 'Yeah, I thought about that one too. You know … ' She paused. 'I think I will always feel I belong here. I love Telegraph Road, the bike rides, the islands, everything! There are no words to describe it. I'm going all that way back to Whitby. I never want to stop thinking about you and all of this. I'll come back, I promise. I want to watch the birds, help conserve nature and do all those things we both enjoy so much.' She hesitated for a moment. 'Do you know what *tot ziens* means in Dutch? Lisa said that to me when she left. She told me that it doesn't mean goodbye forever. It means until I see you again.'

'Yes, I know. It's like *Auf Wiedersehen* in German,' Sven said. He squeezed her tight and kissed her. 'Come on, darling, let's go and do the goodbyes, shall we? Time is getting on.'

As they strolled down the hill, he thought she looked lovely walking along the track, her wispy auburn hair blowing in the warm breeze. He wouldn't let her down, he was sure. Would she have the strength to end it all with Rob? He must trust her; it would be awful if anything went wrong. He didn't want to think about it.

Martin was on the quay. He flicked his hand in a casual wave as he chatted to Don.

'Nice girl he got,' said Don.

'Yeah, amazing isn't it, I had no idea he had a girlfriend. I hope she comes back. Great legs!' Martin said with a grin.

Don laughed. 'You've been leaving that good wife of yours for too long.'

Sven took Pippa to a secluded corner of the quay and kissed her before walking to the ferry. He fussed over her. 'Now, do you have everything with you? Your train ticket, my phone number? You're at the youth hostel tonight, aren't you?'

Pippa whispered in his ear, 'I love you Sven,' and he wiped away his tears, wishing he could blame them on the wind and salt spray. Helping her with the rucksack up the gangway, he stopped at the top, holding her in his arms and gazing into her eyes.

'You know, Pippa, when you fall in love, it's a kind of madness. I'm sure we can sort it all out; we were meant for each other.'

Pippa's heart thumped; he had given her hope to return to Scilly, the place she had dreamed about since school. She felt sure there was a wonderful life ahead for both of them and the plan to live with Sven would be possible. Despite being scared at having to tell Rob, her confidence had grown and she now knew what she wanted. Once she had told Rob about her plans, it would be just a case of how and when she would leave. She dreaded the telling him bit most.

'Come back to me, Pippa,' Sven almost pleaded. 'I love you so very much.'

Pippa jumped as the ship's whistle sounded. They laughed together, and she flung her arms around him. 'I love you too. I will come back, I promise. Thanks for everything. I think you know how much this has meant to me—sharing your life, the birds, the islands, just everything, you've been fantastic. I will call you as soon as I can.' She sniffed into her handkerchief as the crew raised the gangway, then waved to Sven.

Sven blew a kiss, caught her eyes and mouthed the words, 'I'll never stop loving you.'

Tourists stood on the quay with Sven as he watched the ship reverse from the quay to sail around the bay toward St Agnes and out to sea. He waved as long as he could and made his way home with a heavy heart.

As the ship left the lea of St Mary's, Pippa stayed outside on deck. She had waved until she couldn't see him any more, standing there with tears in her eyes. Her heart screamed, 'Go back, go back!' Why had she done this to herself? Too late: she had already left St Mary's with such deep sorrow.

Hiding in a corner of the upper deck, she watched the islands disappear over the horizon. The sea crossing was lumpy and she began to feel queasy, cursing herself for not taking her travel-sickness pills. She had been fine on the little boats but the movement of the ferry felt different. She wished she hadn't had the glass of wine with her meal.

After a few minutes she threw up and felt ill most of the way. An hour later, the Cornish coast came into view and she threw up the contents of her meal into the sea for the third time and concluded that she wanted to die rather than suffer seasickness. She wished she hadn't had the ice cream along with the wine.

Pippa arrived in Penzance, took a taxi to the youth hostel, and met with Mike at reception. She had made conversation with him on her outward journey.

'It's good to see a familiar face,' she said, feeling she might vomit again.

'Hello, Pippa! Are you all right? You look all in—was it the ferry?' Mike guessed. 'I was expecting you around now, I have your booking down here.' He pointed to the diary.

'Yeah, I feel terrible, I was seasick.'

'Oh dear, it often happens, but how was Scilly?'

'Awesome—no, it was more than awesome, it was incredible.'

'Glad you enjoyed it. Can I make you a cup of tea?'

'Oh, Mike, I would love to say yes, but … I feel awful.' She wanted to talk about her time with Sven, the birds, the boats, Don, Martin, the islands, everything. 'I'm so shattered, I want to sleep and I think a cup of tea might not be a good idea right now. But thanks for the offer.'

'Despite the seasickness it sounds as if you did have a good time,' he remarked with a smile. 'You'll be fine in a few hours. Call me if you need help, okay?'

'Maybe we'll chat later.' Pippa let out a deep sigh.

Mike carried her rucksack to the top of the stairs and found her a room where no one was sharing. She thanked him and closed the door behind her, almost falling on the bed. She felt as if she was about to keel over. What had she done? Was it all real? Would she make it back?

As she lay on the bed, the room seemed to be going up and down from her boat trip. It was getting late; she felt hungry but couldn't eat any food in case she was sick again. She slept, then woke again an hour later, still feeling the motion of the ship. She would drag herself downstairs to the phone; it was nine thirty in the evening.

There was a tall mirror in the room and as she raised herself from the bed to wash her face; she looked at her reflection, tanned, wearing shorts, open-toe sandals, her eyes red with tears. *God, this is unreal. Dad, I need you.*

She dialled Sven's number. It rang for a long time. She tried twice more; she assumed he was at *The Mermaid* drowning his sorrows with Martin.

Again, she felt desperately sick and decided she would try again in the morning.

She set her travel alarm for six o'clock to catch the train at 7.30. Perhaps a shower would be the answer to her nausea. An hour later, she had cried herself to sleep.

Now that Martin was home, Sven deliberately busied himself. Andrea had invited him for an evening meal and prepared a cheese fondue with baked potatoes and salad. She produced a bottle of her homemade mulled wine and proceeded to pour a glass for each of them.

Sven tried to drown his sorrows, explaining to Martin and Andrea how it had all happened.

'Oh, you haf no idea how she has shanged my life,' he said after drinking his third glass of wine, plus three cans of beer. 'I've felt so different while you guys haf been away.'

Andrea realised his intoxication and smiled to herself. 'I said you needed a woman in your life,' she chuckled.

Martin joined in the conversation. 'Well, when Andrea and I got together, we were the same. I met her on holiday too, but we had a *normal* relationship. Nothing as whirlwind as you and Pippa, so … ' He paused. 'Do you think it'll work, being so far away and all that?'

Sven looked right at him and sighed. 'You know, you know … ' Sven paused in his thoughts, the drink wasn't helping him to think straight. 'I'f never been sho sure in all my life. I'd be devastated if I was wrong. I miss her already. You know … she is married but things are not going well.'

'God, Sven! Is she?'

Andrea's remark didn't seem to discourage him.

'Well, it's a bit complicated, but she's had a dreadful time and when she came over here, I could feel something was wrong and you know me, I asked her about it.'

Martin slumped further in his chair. 'Don't be so hard on yourself, Sven mate. You go for it, but watch you aren't cited in a divorce case. Pippa could lose a lot and you'll end up in trouble.'

'What do *you* know about divorces, Martin?' Andrea 'tut-tutted' at him.

'I know … well … nothing really, I only want Sven to take care.'

'I'll be careful. You know, she lost her son in a dreadful accident; he was only six.'

'Oh my God, is that right?' Martin said.

'Ya, it is. She might tell you about it herself,' he yawned, 'when she comes back here.'

Sven recognised Andrea's expression. He knew that 'sisterly' look too well. She seemed shocked that he'd become involved in someone else's tragedy and was meddling in their marriage.

Andrea had to keep reminding herself Sven wasn't the young twenty-something that first came to Scilly some years before. He was a good friend and she didn't want him to be the laughing stock of the island gossip.

'I donthink yaneeda worry about me,' slurred Sven. 'Even if it was a holiday romance, 'twas the best time for years. I know how I feel, but I'm trying to be realistic, despite whatyamight think.'

'Another beer, Sven?' Martin asked.

Andrea glared at Martin, then gave up trying to stop them from getting drunk. Martin always snored when he'd had one too many. She needed her sleep.

'Ya, go on, we may as well drown my sorrows.' Sven laughed. 'Well, I mean, she is such a beautiful woman, dontya think?' He seemed in his own world of love and leaned on the sadness Pippa had left behind.

'I've left the washing up to drain in the sink. I'm not going to dry it tonight, I'm too tired,' Andrea sighed. 'One of these days you might buy me a dishwasher.'

'Oh yes, bugger the washing up love, come and join us, have another glass of wine.' Martin clumsily grabbed hold of his wife and hugged her. She kissed him with a peck on the lips.

'I'm thinking of going on a trip myself soon,' Andrea announced as she sat on Martin's knee, fiddling with the bleached hairs on his legs and stroking his knee. 'The girls from the darts club are considering a long weekend trip to Amsterdam. Would you mind if I went too, darling? We can fly from Exeter or Bristol, if it just gets me off the island now and again. I love it here, but *you* know how it is, Sven. When did you last leave St Mary's?'

'Oh, ages ago,' Sven replied. 'But maybe that will change soon.'

'Nice idea,' Martin said. 'No going down the Red Light District though, do you hear me?' He chuckled.

'Don't be dull, of course we will!' She laughed and changed the subject. 'I don't think I can stand kissing you any more with that on your face.' She tugged at his facial hair and shook her head.

Turning toward Sven, she asked. 'Do you think Pippa really will come back here?'

'Don't put doubts in his head, love,' said Martin. 'She's a nice girl, you'll have to meet her.'

'I hope so 'cos I love her to bits.' Sven slunk down into his chair and stretched his long suntanned legs in front of him.

Andrea loved Sven's quirky personality. It was endearing, and she would flirt with him and tease him about his "Nor-ways" if only to cheer him up. The age gap between them was not too wide but she had felt from day one that Sven needed guidance. She hoped Pippa would do the right thing by him; he didn't deserve to be hurt. He was a good man and knew his job well; he had always been a valuable asset to Martin and the islands.

Martin fell asleep on the settee; he was still feeling the effects of travel. Andrea seemed to have enjoyed her time in Bristol with him. She loved Martin's ruggedness and his ability to succeed in life although now that he was a TV personality, her own life had changed. They had no children yet but she hoped they would start a family soon. She hadn't been ready, and now she was almost thirty-five she began to think perhaps it was time, before it was too late. Maybe she should talk it over with him again soon; she hoped he would spend more time at home.

Slightly worse for his beer, Sven chatted with Andrea. 'I should get a call from Pippa tomurro; I can't wait t'zee how shees doing.' His mouth wasn't working with his brain and his Norwegian accent was more pronounced than usual.

'Well, I hope you do,' said Andrea. 'It would be a shame if she got back and had second thoughts. Maybe you should be at home now waiting for her call.'

Sven wasn't listening. 'We had sushagrea'timetoge'er—you know we did that thing I told you about, you know, you know, the bikes. It was awesome, you gottatry it.'

'Actually,' she said, 'I did try it, in April this year. Margaret and I freewheeled down Telegraph. It was fun. Martin thought I was bonkers when I told him; he thought we were like two kids.'

She pointed to Martin who had his eyes shut and let out a loud snore in the back of his throat. She and Sven rolled their eyes and smiled at each other.

Sven poured another glass of wine for Andrea, almost spilling it on the carpet, and while Martin was breathing even louder, Sven was on the brink of sleep as well. As he stood up to go home, he was in no fit state to walk alone up the road. Andrea suggested he go upstairs and sleep over on the spare bed. She helped him climb the stairs and managed to push him down on the single bed, still wearing his shorts and T-shirt. She took off his sandals and Sven told her, 'Don't bother taking 'nything else off—I'm really shy when I'm drunk.'

Sven laughed and giggled. 'Sshhh, you'll wake Martin!' Andrea whispered. Sven hummed a tune and in low voices they sang, *show me the way to go home.'* Andrea giggled as she tucked him up in bed. She put out the light and closed the door.

'Whew, men!' she exclaimed aloud as she went down the stairs.

A voice from the bedroom said, 'I heard that, Mrs. Birdman, go fook yerself!'

Andrea heard him and couldn't help laughing. Sven always swore when he was drunk, but it sounded quite comical. She knew it was another side of him she'd seen many times on those days when they'd all had too much to drink. She hoped the evening had helped him to overcome his parting from Pippa. He really was in love, she could tell. Andrea thought that she knew more about Sven than he knew about himself. The Birdman and The Viking were a team and she was proud of them both.

Pippa was about to leave the youth hostel that morning and passed the time with Mike until the taxi arrived to take her to the station.

'I really had a wonderful time on Scilly,' she said.

'I hope you are feeling better this morning—you didn't look at all well last night. I hope to see you again, Pippa; you're one of those people I could not forget when you left here. We had such a lovely chat on your last visit. I suppose I remembered the colour of your hair. I bet everyone says that though.'

'Oh yes, Mike, I'm used to it now, but thanks. Look, I might be coming back this way soon. I hope you are still going to be working here; it would be nice to chat with you again. I could be *living* on Scilly soon.'

'You got a job over there?'

Pippa beamed. 'Nope, I got a new man in my life.'

'Oh, that's a shame, I was hoping to ask you out. I missed my chance, didn't I?' he laughed.

'Oh, Mike, that's so sweet of you, yes, we did have a nice evening chatting and eating our fish and chips last time. I appreciated the company.'

'Never mind, you know where I am if you need a friend.'

'Sure do. Don't forget to come and see me on Scilly, but I will call in and see you soon. Thanks again for being so nice to me. It's hard when you're on your own, but I hope all that will change soon. See ya. Bye.'

Pippa picked up her rucksack, as the taxi was waiting. She knew there was no point in trying to contact Sven just yet; he would be fast asleep in bed; it was too early to call. She imagined him lying there, his hair tangled in the pillow, breathing quietly to himself. She would try calling him later before the train arrived.

The next morning, after Andrea had insisted he ate a good breakfast, Sven made his way home. On arrival, Nanette told him that his phone had been ringing. He tried to appear calm. 'It's rung twice fer ages. I 'eard it when I was in the garden,' Nanette said with the usual curiosity in her voice.

Oh God! I hope I haven't let her down. Yet it might not have been Pippa who had called; he still lived with the fear that Astrid might phone. What if that was *her* on the phone, and not Pippa? He told himself not to be so stupid. What did he have to be afraid of? He'd done nothing wrong, but his head was full of self-scolding.

He knew he couldn't contact Pippa just yet. The waiting was agony; he missed her a lot and wished in a way it could have been different. He had the phone number, but was unable to contact her becuase she'd asked him to hold back until she had spoken with Rob. Sven sighed impatiently. Wild thoughts went around his head that he might have lost her forever. What if she didn't phone to give him permission to use the number, what if he really had been just a bit of fun on her holiday? He tried not to think about it.

CHAPTER TWENTY-SIX

Rob stood waiting at Darlington for Pippa. It was his day off and he felt good but not confident about his plans for the future. He was anxious to tell Pippa about Joan and Terry and especially about his new-found family. He wondered how she had managed with her holiday. Would she be more relaxed around him now?

Poor Joan, he thought. He was glad she was in recovery now. He would visit her and try to arrange some care for her and Jordan. Perhaps seeing Pippa again would make her feel better.

Pippa was tired and hungry after her long journey. In the late afternoon sun, she arrived in Darlington and made her way to the front of the train looking for Rob. Her heart was aching, her eyes swollen with tears—what would she tell him?

She searched the platform but couldn't see him. Then, as the train pulled out of the echoing station, she caught a glimpse of him. At first, she couldn't believe her eyes; he'd been to the hairdresser and he looked smart. It was a feeling of surprise more than anything, but it was still Rob. The moment she saw him, she wanted to turn around and go back the way she had come.

As she dropped her luggage on the platform, he came to her and flung his arms around her. Her body went limp.

'Hey, how was it? I missed you,' he said, giving her a surprising peck on the lips.

Pippa said nothing. Why was he being so affectionate? She gave a weak smile. 'I'm very, *very* tired,' she said, closing her eyes and shaking her head. 'The journey from Penzance was very long. I've been travelling since yesterday when I left Scilly.'

'Yes, you look tired; your eyes are very swollen. Are you ok?'

'Yes, I suppose so. I was very seasick.'

He tried to kiss her again but she bent down and pretended to fasten the shoelace on her trainers. He never kissed her when she left three weeks ago from this very station. What was he doing?

On the way home, she tried to think of anything and everything that could possibly stop her from crying. She just kept nodding and agreeing with everything he said.

A couple of hours later they reached Whitby. Rob put Pippa's silence down to the long journey she'd endured.

Travelling along the moor road, Pippa fell asleep, perhaps subconsciously doing anything to help her avoid entering into conversation with Rob.

The next thing she knew, Rob was patting her knee. 'Come on, Pip, home-time. We're almost there, love.' He sounded like her father, and for a moment she was a child in the warm back seat of the car, being woken by a parent and lifted up to a cold bed in the house.

'Huh? Oh yes, Whitby,' she said, remembering where she was. Being home made her realise how much she wished she wasn't.

They passed over the swing bridge and Rob parked his car in the side street, then carried Pippa's rucksack. He tried to hold her hand, but she darted into a shop for some chewing gum; if she was chewing, he might not want to kiss her. He waited for her and then they walked on together down the cobbled street. She folded her arms close to her as she walked.

As she entered the house on Henrietta Street, the odour of fried bacon hit her nostrils. On the table rested a photo of Daniel and one of her father. A wedding photo of her and Rob back in 1976 stood on the dresser, along with another photo of Terry, Joan, herself, Rob, and Daniel taken by a local photographer on the day of the Whitby Regatta. She wanted to scream: what was the point?

'I'll put the kettle on, love, and then you can tell me all about Scilly,' Rob said, trying to lighten the mood.

Pippa sat quietly. She had nothing to tell him; everything was about Sven. Her heart was five hundred miles away, and with Sven's face in her head, how could she tell Rob anything?

'I was very ill yesterday. It might take me some time to recover,' she said, as she put the chewed gum in the bin. 'I had a wonderful time. It was fantastic.' She started to open up to Rob but wished he would leave the house so she could phone Sven.

Rob sat down with her. 'Look, er … I've some good news and some bad news. Joan is in the hospital. We didn't want to tell you because I knew you were coming back, anyway—it only happened a few days ago.' He proceeded to explain all about Joan and Terry.

Pippa looked away, sighing, and allowed herself to cry. 'Oh my God, I didn't expect this. How is she? Something told me Terry was depressed. I've talked to him a few times about it, but he kept clamping up. He's a bit of an oddball, but now it all makes sense.'

'Well it's a bit more than that, but let's take one thing at a time.'

Rob explained Joan's progress and said they could visit this evening if Pippa felt well enough.

She dabbed her eyes, her eyelids drooping; she couldn't take any more.

Rob tried to comfort her, but each time he came near, she made an excuse not to be close to him. Avoiding his affections, she wondered how long she could go on in this way.

'I also have a wonderful bit of news.' Rob had thought he would save it until last. 'We came into some money, but a whole lot more than I expected.' The whole story began to tumble out in big chunks.

Pippa seemed to go into a trance. She stopped listening. 'Rob, sorry, I have to go to bed, I feel quite ill.'

'Oh, I thought you might be happy for me. And I've given up smoking; I thought you'd be pleased.'

'Oh, good for you. Of course I'm pleased, but I only just got back and things are rather fuzzy. We'll talk later about it if you don't mind. Why don't you let me sleep, and perhaps you go and have a beer or something. Then I'll be able to take it all in afterwards.' She paused a moment. 'We need to talk as well. Things might change for us.'

'What d'ye mean?'

'Just with your situation and how it was before I left for Scilly.'

'Oh, I see,' said Rob sharply. 'Look, I think you're right, I will go to the pub. You have your sleep. I'll see you in a couple of hours, okay?'

Pippa looked into his eyes; it had all been too much. She liked his new hairstyle, but it didn't seem like the Rob she had left behind three weeks before: the husband who talked divorce, who made excuses not to tell her he loved her. What was he trying to do to her feelings? He wasn't going to make her feel guilty right now; it was too late. He'd come into some money and if he thought that would change things, then he was wrong. She decided she didn't love him; she had learned what love meant and it wasn't with Rob. The tables had most definitely turned.

Rob left the house and Pippa sat brushing her hair, wondering what she should do. She put the brush on the dressing table. She noticed the blonde hairs tangled in the brush and smiled to herself, then almost cried again. This could be the only evidence she had of Sven. She had to phone him now. *Yes, now.*

She dialled the number. The phone rang several times but there was no answer. She felt like a tormented cat. An hour later, she tried again, but again there was no reply. Where was he? Her heart cried out for Sven to pick up the phone. Perhaps the goodbye had been forever.

CHAPTER TWENTY-SEVEN

'Afternoon, guys and gals,' Sven said as he walked through the door into the yard to greet the volunteers.

'Hi Sven, how's it going?' said Jacqui.

'Fine, I think we're winning now, but it's been a huge job, eh? I want to thank you all for your help.' Inside him, he wanted to say all was *not* fine, he was in love and couldn't do a darned thing about it. Why hadn't Pippa phoned?

'What is it with Charlie these days? Sometimes he can be dead nice and other times he's dead grumpy.' Beth gave a sigh. 'I can't get on with him.'

'He always tells me he canna understand a werrd I'm sayin',' Linda explained with a grin.

'I do.' Sven grinned. 'We used to be neighbours once, up there in Shetland. Isn't that where you used to live, Linda?'

Linda nodded. She knew what Sven meant.

Martin was listening. 'Still, we mustn't complain; he does a good job, which brings me to consider our tasks today. I think we might be lucky this time with these birds, but if you guys could collect the ones we found this morning, maybe give them a wash and then we'll collect the rest for the helicopter, they can go to the RSPCA on the mainland. We just don't have the room here. I got three gannets yesterday, vicious little buggers. Watch your eyes, Beth.'

The volunteers stood around the sink and each filled a washing-up bowl with water. Bottles of mild detergent stood on the work surface and Linda took one of the razorbills out of the cardboard pet carrier and held it over the sink. 'God, yuck! This one is so emaciated. Alan, look, I can feel its breastbone sticking out.'

'Give it a scrub, it'll be all right. We'll feed it later,' Alan replied.

Sven joined in. 'The good news is that the oil spill seems to be dispersing. Some foreign tanker has apparently leaked into the Irish Sea. Bloody idiots! We've been lucky though. Scilly might have lost all its tourism and God knows what else.' He picked up a gannet from the box. 'Aren't they good-looking birds? Look at this one—despite the oil, I think it's going to be fine. I love their eyes.' He took the bird outside to wash it.

Beth whispered to Jacqui, knowing Sven wouldn't hear. '*He's* a good looking bloke too, isn't he?' She nudged Jacqui.

Jacqui smiled. 'Do they really call him The Viking?'

'Oh yes, he's always been called that from the first day he arrived here,' said Beth. 'The Birdman and The Viking, ha! It sounds like a film title.'

'What're you two whispering about?' said Alan.

'Men!' Beth grinned.

'Oh, don't even go there,' Alan replied. He took the shower out of the basin and pointed it at Beth. 'Alan! I'm soaked, you Aussie git! Ahh, don't,' Beth squealed.

'I'm not an Aussie, I keep telling you that. I'm a Kiwi. You only say it to annoy me.'

'You remember Mrs Arginson had some kittens to give away?' Linda announced. 'Well, I found a home for two of them and I took one back to the mainland for my niece.' As she spoke, she tied an elastic band around the beak of a guillemot to stop it ingesting the oil. She looked as if she was miles away.

Beth was laughing at Alan; neither of them listened to Linda.

When Sven returned, he smiled when he saw how they flirted with each other. Scilly stirred all kinds of feelings for romance. He dangled a sand eel in front of the guillemot he had finished drying. It tried to open its beak, and at the right moment, he pushed the food down its throat. Success! Once it had the idea, he continued the feeding process. Clever little devils, he thought. *The gannets will be more of a challenge.*

'The sooner we get these big buggers back to sea, the better!' he exclaimed. 'They don't feed easily, as they're plunge divers, and it can be rather dangerous trying to get food down *their* throats. They love to take a stab at you.'

An hour later, the *Scillonian* arrived with yet another boatful of tourists. Sven finished his bird cleaning job and went down the quay to see Don. As he leaned against the rails, all he could see was himself kissing Pippa as she left on the ferry. The whole place seemed empty now without her.

'Bet yer missin' er then, eh Sven?' Don called from the boat.

'Ya, it's like someone stole a part of me,' he said with a sigh.

'Heard anuthin' then—phone call?' Don was wiping the seats on the *Lily*.

'No, not yet but I've hardly been home and I was round at Martin's last night. I'm just so busy with this bloody oil spill; I'm knackered. I know she'll phone me, no problem.'

The crew tied up the ship and they stacked the luggage on the back of the lorry ready for delivery.

Don had to take the *Lily of Laguna* out to anchor in the bay. Sven made a decision to go with him. He needed the company. He would go home after this and wait for Pippa to phone. Now realising the importance of having an answer phone, he promised himself he would order one soon.

As they started the outboard motor for the return journey, something made him turn around and look toward the quay. Two girls were standing on the pier. He thought he was mistaken and checked through his binoculars. As he got closer, he swung the outboard around the other side of the quay and Don almost fell in the water.

'What the ... *fuck* is she doing here?' Sven declared.

'Sven mate, what the hellya doin'?' Don asked, looking shocked.

'Bloody Astrid!'

'Huh?' Don had no idea what Sven was talking about.

'She's the reason I came to Scilly. I suppose that's the only thing I have to thank her for. It's my mother's fault; she shouldn't have told her where I live. Astrid is touring the UK apparently, with her friend.'

'Who is she, mate?'

'Only the woman I almost married!'

Don turned down the corners of his mouth in sheer surprise at Sven's announcement; he'd no idea, and Sven had never mentioned her before.

'Why the hell can't she leave me alone?' muttered Sven.

He wasn't able to see the girls any more as they turned the corner of the pier. He would approach from the other side; thank God she hadn't seen him.

He hoped she had come on the day trip and she would be gone by five o'clock. He could avoid her and she might get the message.

If he did it right, he could moor the dingy some distance away from where she was standing and walk along the pier from behind her. Perhaps if he was lucky she might be gone soon. He couldn't believe she had actually come to Scilly; this was the second time she had tried to contact him over the last few years. If all she wanted was to apologise and free herself from her own guilt, then he didn't wish to be part of it.

Don found it rather amusing but kept his amusement to himself. 'I'll drop you here, mate. I'll go round and approach from the other side, if that's okay?'

Sven climbed the steps and looked around. *Phew! She's gone.* Perhaps it wasn't her—no, it had to be, it was too much of a coincidence.

He reached *The Mermaid* and then he saw her in front of him, some distance up Hugh Street. *Oh shit, it is Astrid, and Kjerstin.* He would hang back and go home another way. He walked over The Garrison to avoid her.

On arrival home, he plonked himself on the sofa. He shut his eyes, puffing out his cheeks. *What have I done to deserve this? What if she comes knocking at Beachside Cottage?* He hoped no one would tell her where he lived.

Seeing Astrid standing on the quay was as if she had never been away from him. They'd had good times together, but he could never forgive her. Why did she have to come here all the way from Norway? Was she stalking him? He would scold his mother for doing this to him. He should have told her about Pippa.

The phone rang. He didn't know if he should answer it.

'Sven's phone,' he said.

'Darling, it's me. I got back safely but I won't have much time to talk. Rob has gone out and I'm waiting to speak with him.'

'Oh. Pippa, thank goodness you phoned, I've been so worried about you. Are you okay, elskling?' He wanted to jump for joy on hearing her voice, but something in her tone made him realise all was not quite right.

'I'm very tired, but there's been some difficult things happening here. I don't have time to tell you everything except Joan is ill, Terry has left her and Rob's got himself a few hundred thousand pounds more than he had when I went on holiday.'

'God, that's amazing—will it change anything? I miss you,' Sven said softly. 'Come back soon.' He quickly realised he might not have time to say everything.

'I miss you too, but it's going to be hard to talk at the moment, just wanted you to know I'm doing my best, nothing's changed. I still love you.'

Sven gave a sigh of relief.

'I'll phone you later, okay?' she said in a hurry, trying to be caring at the same time. She heard Rob coming through the front door. 'Must go, sorry, back soon, bye,' she whispered.

She put the phone down and feelings of abandonment crept into Sven's skin. He knew she would phone him back, but it was all so frustrating not being able to be with her, knowing she was back home with Rob. *I wonder if she's told him.*

It was five o'clock and Sven wanted his self-imposed internment to end. It might be safe now to go out on the street. He was glad he had missed Astrid's visit; he was sure it was her, but by now she would be gone on the ferry back to the mainland. Was his mind playing tricks with him? He was thrilled Pippa had phoned and after he'd thought about it, he understood her sharp phone call. Maybe she would change her mind about them being together if Rob had all this money. Somehow, he didn't think money mattered to Pippa. He was pretty sure she only wanted to find happiness, but what if he was wrong? *Maybe it's always going to be like this.* How long would he need to wait for her to return to Scilly? He missed her so much he thought his heart might break. They were meant for each other, he told himself repeatedly.

His thoughts turned to Astrid. What did she want to have come all this way? Three years before, he had gone home to Norway and discovered she frequented the same bar as he used to go to. It seemed more than coincidence, as she never used to go there. He'd had to avoid her, even then. He could never forgive her. Did she still care about him? Well, too bad, Pippa was part of his life now—or was she? The stress overwhelmed his thoughts.

He needed a drink. Being on his own again wasn't what he wanted. It was almost as if Pippa hadn't been there at all. As if she had been a figment of his imagination in the last three weeks. He walked down Hugh Street and called in at *The Mermaid*.

The guys from the gig club were drinking together. The barman said 'Hi Sven,' and Sven ordered a beer. He sat on the stool in the bar with one foot on the floor and another resting on the stretcher, a pint in his hand, lonely again. His mind was mostly on Pippa and the things that might have been.

Someone put money into the pool table and the balls came clattering down the ramp; the noise was too much. Sven gulped down the last dregs of beer and left the pub to take a walk along the beach. It wasn't going to get dark until late.

He walked a long way. Up and over the headland, the prints on the soles of his sandals making patterns as he walked along the sandy footpaths with the occasional look through his binoculars at a passing bird. With the call of the wild around him, and the voice of the sea, a lump came to his throat. Why did he have to do this to himself each time he found someone he loved? Every time—snatched away. The sound of the waves comforted him but his legs dragged and his heart felt as if it would stop. He needed to go home to wrap himself in the duvet and hide for a day.

On returning to Beachside Cottage, exhaustion overtook him. From his room he looked across Porthcressa Beach at the incoming tide. He was about to go to sleep when the phone rang. Should he answer it? What if it was *her?* It wouldn't be Pippa or Martin at this time of night, he was sure. He would let the phone ring and put his head under the pillows. He was too tired to be bothered to go all the way downstairs.

What if it really was Astrid calling him? She'd often phoned late at night when he was in Norway. The duration of the ringing phone got the better of him. What if it was his mother calling about his dad? He decided to answer it. Before he could pick it up, it stopped. He knew he was being stupid but he couldn't go through all that again. They would call back if it was urgent. He returned to his bed. Pippa was his soul mate and he needed to talk to her—now. If only he could phone her.

The following morning, Sven met with Martin at the office. He needed to catch up on the events of the last three months. Margaret had left him a message on his desk.

Hi Sven,
A young lady came in here yesterday, she said she was from Norway and was asking about you. She left the attached envelope for you. Apparently, she was a friend of yours from some time back. Mary

Sven banged his fist on his desk. *What does she want from me?* It occurred to him that perhaps he was making a big thing out of it and he should just relax. He had loved Astrid but how could he go back in time and forgive her? Pippa was his love and all he wanted was to take care of her. They needed each other, he realised that now.

Each time the phone rang, he wondered if he should answer it. He thought he would talk to Margaret.

'Hey, Marg, erm … can you vet all my calls before you put them through? I'm a bit busier than usual. I'd rather filter who I want to talk to and those I don't—and don't let anyone in my office, please. I want everyone to make appointments to see me; I'm too busy.'

'Oh, okay,' Margaret seemed taken aback. 'I didn't think you were *that* busy, now that Martin's home, but okay, I'll do it.'

Sven wondered if he should open the letter immediately. Perhaps it could wait, but, as an afterthought, he reckoned it might provide some insight into why Astrid was here. If he opened it now, he could clear up the matter and get on with his life. He decided to be brave about it.

He slit open the envelope and immediately recognised the writing in his own language. It really was from Astrid! What was she doing here?

Dear Sven,
Hope you don't mind me getting in touch like this. I had coffee with your mother a couple of weeks ago; she looks well. Anyway, she told me you are working here on the Scilly Islands. Kjerstin, my best friend, you might remember her, is with me on a tour of the south of England. We love Cornwall. We were in Devon a couple of days ago and caught the train to Penzance. We found a nice little bed and breakfast on St Mary's and took a risk that maybe after all this time, we could put our past behind us. Perhaps we could meet up for a coffee. There are things I would like to tell you. I will understand if you don't want to see me. I know last time wasn't exactly under the best of terms but I just wanted to put it all to rest. I will be on The Garrison tomorrow lunchtime and I will ask Kjerstin if she wouldn't mind doing her own thing so we can talk. If you can make it, I will see you at 12.30 pm.
Love, Astrid

Sven held his breath. The love at the end of the letter didn't seem right. He didn't really want to see her. What could she possibly have to tell him that he did not already know and yes, to dig up his feelings like this, after all this time was typical for Astrid. She had chosen a place so dear to Pippa's heart to meet— she really knew how to annoy him, all right! He realised she couldn't have known this, but it just made him angry. Astrid must have realised how it had affected him all those years ago when he found her with Mads. His head was in turmoil with all this waiting for Pippa.

CHAPTER TWENTY-EIGHT

'Pippa, come to bed, love,' Rob shouted from the upstairs bedroom. 'It's getting late. We can talk.'

Pippa sat in the lounge wondering what she should do. He might want to 'do it' and she knew she couldn't, and he would ask why, and she would have to tell him. It would certainly be a long night and she knew a dreadful row was brewing. She couldn't take it after her long journey. How was she going to get out of this one? Tonight was not the right time to discuss their future.

She undressed in the bathroom, put on her least sexy pyjamas, and liberally applied cream to her face in the hope she could turn him off. Perhaps she should spend time talking and boring him to sleep. Maybe she could sleep in the other room; all she wanted was some breathing space from her journey and a chance to think about the best way to explain everything.

Instead, he opened his arms to her and lowered his head as if he were about to kiss her on the lips. Pippa pulled away. 'I can't do this, Rob, I don't feel like it, sorry.'

'What do you mean—*sorry*? You've been asleep most of the day, you've been away from me for the last three weeks—how am I supposed to behave?'

'I know I have, but ...' She turned away from him. She was about to tell him she was leaving him when he pulled her playfully down on the bed and put his hand up her pyjama top.

'Come on, Pippa, it's been a long time. Let me hold you.'

Pippa stiffened in terror. Her thoughts were screaming *'no, no I don't—want—to—do—it, don't make me do it.'*

'What's the matter with you? Why don't you want to?' He noted the white ring around her suntanned finger. She wasn't wearing her wedding ring. Yet she had been wearing it; perhaps she'd left it in the bathroom.

'I can't,' she said, thinking she was being unfaithful to Sven and not the other way around. She pulled away from him. 'Rob, for God's sake, you have to give me time.'

'How much *more* fuckin' time do you need? Come on, give us a bit,' he said in a last desperate attempt. 'I need you, you're my wife and we're supposed to love each other.'

Pippa lay there in sheer torment. She didn't know what to do; she felt pinned to the bed. 'Rob, let me go, *please*.'

He released his grip. 'For fuck's sake, Pippa, what're you trying to do to me? We haven't done this in months, you go away and now you won't let me near you—what the hell is going on?'

'Let go of me, Rob. Don't do this—I don't want sex with you!' she screamed.

'Look, Pippa we can't carry on like this.'

'You bet we can't! I'm not sleeping in here tonight. I don't want to be with you any more.' She stormed into Daniel's room and Rob followed her.

'But ... Pippa love, things have changed since you went away. We got money now and you have to let me explain, things will be different. I've changed; I have a brother and sister now and well ... you have to let me ... Oh shit! Why do I bother?'

'Bloody money—is that all you care about?' She growled, turning away from him. 'Go away, we'll talk in the morning.'

'I think I still love you. We have to sort this out, I'm sorry.'

'You *think* you still love me? You didn't love me two weeks ago when you said you wanted a divorce, and last month, and the month before that. I don't want to talk about it, just go away. You're such a mixed up person, I don't want to be with you any more. All this counselling and stuff hasn't changed you one bit.'

'I'm not mixed up; it's *you* who is mixed up. Things have changed; I keep trying to tell you.' Rob cajoled as best he could.

She pulled the duvet over her head and closed her eyes, denying herself the thoughts of what life might be like if she stayed with Rob in Whitby.

'Come on, Pippa, just let me show you, I want you back.' He put his arm around her.

'You're lying, Rob. Don't think I haven't noticed *things* over the last few years.' Her voice was muffled from under the bed covers.

'What things?'

'The mistletoe with Carole. The way you look at Joan. How could you? I mean, how could you, Rob! Don't talk to me about wanting me back now you got some money.

'What do you mean Pippa?'

'Hm! Look, just leave it, will you? Give me time to think about all this stuff with you, that's all. I'm not in the mood.'

'You're never in the mood. This has to stop,' he said firmly. He grabbed her again. 'I still don't understand what you mean.'

'I always knew you married the wrong person!' Pippa blurted out. 'Fuck off, Rob! When I say no, I mean *NO!* This is typical of you; you don't know how to love someone, it's all grab grab, and wham bam. I hate it. You'll never change; I know that now.'

The following morning after Rob left the house, Pippa tried to phone Sven again but couldn't reach him.

Feeling as if she had lost Daniel all over again, she wrote to Rob and told him she didn't want to stay with him. She couldn't face him. Then she threw the letter in the bin. When she couldn't reach Sven at home, she rang his office; it was all too much.

'Sven is out at sea at the moment,' said Margaret. 'Just gone over to St Agnes. He'll be back soon, though.'

Pippa left a message to say she would phone later at home.

Oh, shit what's happening to me? Was Sven a man of his word? Was he avoiding her now she had left the islands? How could she tell Rob her intentions with Sven so far away, and with no news?

CHAPTER TWENTY-NINE

Sven decided the best course of action was to go and see Astrid. Then, he could put it all behind him and get on with his life. He felt increasingly concerned about her reason for visiting him. There had been a five-year gap since he last saw her; she would have changed, and he had no feelings for her anymore, so perhaps it couldn't do any harm.

He raced up The Garrison in his lunch hour, forgetting to take his sandwiches with him. His mind was in too many places trying to put everything back into perspective. When would Pippa phone and how had she got on with telling Rob about leaving him?

As he walked up the hill, Astrid hadn't yet arrived; he was a few minutes early. He sat with his arm across the back of the bench and waited with anger still in his thoughts.

Then he saw her, and his heart raced. Old memories began to stir: his time in bed with her, the way she used to tickle his toes, the time they made love in the snow on the forest floor on Christmas Day and how he'd almost had frost bite on his buttocks. Astrid herself had taken all his fun away. It wasn't his fault.

As she came toward him, her dark blonde hair blew on The Garrison breeze. She wore black leather clogs and a long flimsy blue-green wraparound skirt, which flapped in the wind like a loose sail on a yacht. Sven stood up to kiss her on both cheeks, to show politeness. She put out her arms to give him a hug.

'Hoi, Svennie, it's good to see you again. How are you? Glad you came. I wasn't sure you would. You look different; you never used to have long hair, and you were always … ' she hesitated.

'Smarter?' he offered with some sarcasm in his voice.

Astrid didn't reply; instead she sighed.

Sven tried to restrain his thoughts. 'How do you like my islands?' He said, looking out to sea wishing to be somewhere else.

'Shall we sit down?' Astrid suggested. 'I wanted to see you because I am very sorry about what I did. I've never forgotten you, and the reason Mads and I got divorced is purely because I made some dreadful mistakes. I think I still love you, Sven.'

'Oh, Astrid, here we go. This is just emotional blackmail.'

'No, Svennie, you've got to listen, please. The thing with Mads was a spur of the moment thing, and we didn't want to hurt you. It was a one-off and didn't mean anything. A final fling, you might say, before our wedding day—a kind of juvenile silly joke that went wrong. I'll regret it for the rest of my life, honest I will. I would never have told you about it, because it was just stupidity. I never meant to hurt you so bad. You left Norway before I could explain. It all seems such a long time ago now.'

Sven turned to her. 'I can't imagine what brought you this far thinking I might come back to you just like that. There has to be another reason.'

'Kjerstin and I decided to take a holiday in the south of England. I felt I should take the opportunity to come and tell you this, as your mother told me you grieved about me a long time. She thought you were still upset, as you hadn't found anyone else in the last five years. We had a long chat and we both thought you might like to talk about it. I'm on my own now and I still think about you, Svennie.'

Sven waited a few seconds before replying. 'I think you came here on a mission which has failed, Astrid,' he said coldly, annoyed she had got his mother involved in this.

Not being sure about his relationship with Pippa, he took a risk. Seeing Astrid made him realise he still had *some* feelings for her, but not the same feelings as he'd once had; she had broken his heart. He had to be blunt with her.

'I already have a girlfriend and we are very close.' *Close* was not the word; distance was the biggest bugbear and he might be throwing away something he would regret for the rest of his life. Astrid or Pippa? He mustn't even think about it. He had no choice and anyway, Pippa was his love now. He must have faith that she would make it back to the islands.

Then the inevitable question flew from Astrid's lips. Her eyes gazed upon his sandal-clad feet. 'Oh I see. How long have you been going out together?'

'Not long,' he said, avoiding the truth. It was none of her business anyway.

Astrid came closer. He could almost feel her breath upon his face. 'Sven, I miss you so much,' she said as she linked her arm with his.

'You should have thought about that when you got into bed with Mads. You hurt me, Astrid, hurt me real bad, and I can never forgive you.' Sven turned away from her. 'Did you really think by coming to Scilly you could persuade me to come back to you after all this time? You must be crazy.'

'Sven, listen, I travelled all the way from Norway to tell you I'm sorry.'

'What! After five fuckin' years, you come to tell me you married the wrong guy. You had me, me who loved you—and you blew it.'

'Please don't swear at me, Svennie. I miss you.' Astrid's tears fell down her face.

Sven stood up. 'Don't do this to me, not now,' he said, knowing he had to get back to work soon.

She sobbed, the queen of sobs. He thought she sounded genuine and he put his arm around her to comfort her. She looked up at him and then she kissed him full on the lips.

For a few seconds he felt confused. It was the kiss he remembered when he proposed to her. He pulled away from her. 'Astrid, stop, don't do that. You and I, we ...'

'Don't tell me you don't love me any more.'

'The truth is, after I left, I lost all faith in love, women, and sex, everything after I lost you. I came to Scilly to start a new life. The last thing I expected was for you to follow me here five years later to apologise to me. You're sick, you know that?' He stood up and moved away from her. 'I'm sorry, Astrid, but I can't do this.'

She looked distraught and Sven's natural kindness seemed to flow within him. He sighed as he began to feel sorry for her. He felt some remorse about what he'd just said.

In a quiet moment, Astrid spoke. 'I lost our baby, Sven. I mean *our* baby.' She looked into his eyes.

'What!? Now I know you really are crazy.' Sven almost felt sick with anger. He stood up from the bench and looked again at the view of the other islands.

'I was pregnant when Mads and I were ... well, you know. I never told you because I didn't know. I got to seven months and she died within me. I know she was yours. I had morning sickness for a few weeks before Mads and I got together for that one time. I had no idea it was a pregnancy; I assumed I was a bit ill.'

'Astrid, are you stupid or something?' Sven turned to her.

'I didn't know about how it would be to have a baby then, or how I was supposed to feel. I was only twenty-two at the time; we were young and knew nothing. The baby had to be yours, they told me at the hospital, and they reckoned she was longer term than I had told them. I worked out the dates. I saw her, Sven, she lay in my arms so small and sweet, then they took her away and we had a small funeral. Mads never knew the baby wasn't his until I had to tell him. I made some terrible mistakes and I'm sorry. You have no idea what it did to me—and Mads, too. I'm just a stupid person. Sven, I only came to tell you I'm sorry. You had to know about it, that's all, I had to tell you the truth.'

'Astrid, if this is true, why did you tell me after all this time? I mean, are you saying it was my child? How could you do that?'

His insides thumped with anger. His child was stillborn and his ex had married his best friend instead. How was he supposed to feel? He wanted to hide from her, wishing he had ignored her. With this new revelation, his day, his whole life had turned upside down.

Astrid sobbed. 'I'm sorry, Sven. I'm so, so sorry.'

He held her in his arms to comfort her again. What was he supposed to do about it? He wanted to believe it wasn't true. He had to meet Don in twenty minutes and fifty passengers were going to St. Martin's; how could he go on the trip with his mind on this? He felt sick at her revelation and time wasn't on his side. How could he let his birdwatching group go on a walk without him? Martin was busy catching up on his work, he couldn't possibly ask him to help. He took a deep breath.

'Astrid, look, I'm sorry and at this moment, I know it seems a bit thoughtless, but I have to go back to work. I only get an hour for lunch and then I have a tour on the boats. How long are you staying on the islands?'

'Two more nights.' Astrid sniffed into her handkerchief.

'Oh, I see. Maybe I'll find time for a drink before you go back. Please don't ask me to commit to you. I have Pippa now and we have a wonderful relationship. I can't be part of your life anymore, sorry. A child makes no difference. I don't feel anything. It's like you're talking about someone else.' He wasn't sure if he had told the truth.

He looked into her swollen eyes, with the tears still rolling down her face. The thought that he might have been a father confused him. He would always remember how unfaithful she was. Her revelations didn't mean a lot to him; he felt numb and rather unconvinced, not sure what to say to her. He would never have come to Scilly, led a wonderful life and met all these lovely people if she hadn't gone with Mads. Perhaps in her own way, Astrid had given him a chance he would never have had if they hadn't parted.

'I'll meet up with you before you leave, I'll buy you and Kjerstin a drink and we'll have a chat together. I don't want to leave you on bad terms, but I have Pippa and I could never let her down or upset her in any way. I love her very much.'

'Oh … I see … Where is she today?' Astrid sniffed into her paper handkerchief.

'Er … she's away in the north of England for a week, gone to sort out some family business.' Sven realised he shouldn't have told her. He knew he was just an honest bloke and not very good at telling lies.

'Well, maybe she would understand how it's been for me, too.'

'Look, Astrid, I'm sorry. Life goes on. It makes no difference. Sorry, but I have to get back to work, I'm afraid. Come on back into town with me and we'll meet with Kjerstin. I think I remember her from college—is that the same person?'

Astrid sniffed back her tears. 'Yes.'

Sven was shocked, but didn't think this would change anything. He thought of his wonderful life on Scilly and how he really didn't want to go back to Norway.

His hatred for Astrid began to subside. If only Pippa would come back, if only he had an assurance that she would leave Rob. *I love Pippa*, he kept telling himself. Going back to Astrid would never be an option; he knew now she couldn't be trusted.

CHAPTER THIRTY

'I'm going to go and see Joan at the hospital, do you want to come?' Rob tried to smile but couldn't. 'If you were there too, you might cheer her up.'

'No, I'll see Joan in my own time, thanks.' Pippa replied. I'm not sure if I want to.'

'Look, when I get back, we have to talk. We can't go on like this anymore.'

She looked into his eyes, battered. 'Rob, I'm leaving you.'

'Come on, don't be silly. Try to pull yourself together, Pippa. What's the matter?' He tried to treat her like his wife and not one of his patients. He moved to get closer to her, thinking he'd make it up to her.

'Get away from me!' she cried. 'You almost raped me last night.'

'Oh Pippa, come on. No, I did not! I was so frustrated and I was trying to cheer you up. Look, I'm truly sorry for what I did. It's not like me to behave in that way, but I needed you and you weren't there for me.'

The tears leaked down her cheeks like small streams. All she could see was Sven holding out his arms to her.

Rob held her hand and she let him. 'Come on, Pippa, we can have a wonderful life together now. We can go on those holidays we could never afford, and have a new family life with Bruce and Penny, my brother and sister. It will be amazing. Come here, let me hold you.'

Pippa's tears burst forth into wailing. Sven had said the last same words in the bird hide. Rob held her in his arms, but it was not Rob, it was Sven who had kissed her.

'Come on, love, it's going to be all right,' said Rob.

'No! It isn't.' She pulled away from him with a determined air in her voice. ' Rob, I'm leaving you. I've found someone else in my life and I can't go on like this any more. You have money now, a new life. I have the house and no ties.'

'What! You got another bloke?' shouted Rob. 'Pippa, how could you do this to me? Who is he?'

'Someone I met on the Isles of Scilly,' she sobbed loudly.

'Ha! A holiday romance. I knew it! I thought I could trust you. That's what all that palaver was about last night—now I understand. How stupid can you be? No, how stupid am I? Did you have sex with him? I bet you did. You are so naïve, aren't you? He only wanted you because you're on your own—men do that, Pippa, it's the same old story women fall for every time. A bit of cheap fun on holiday, no wonder you didn't want to open up to me last night. I get it now; I see.'

'No, it wasn't like that,' Pippa pleaded.

'Now come on for God's sake.' He stood glaring into her face. 'You need help to understand your inner self, I mean it. Your mind is still not clear, is it? I know you find it hard to think straight since … Oh, why should I bother—I've had enough of this!'

Pippa thought about his words. Was she losing her mind? No, she bloody well wasn't.

'Rob!' she shouted. 'I do *not* need counselling, all I want is to have some freedom away from all this dreadful life we have together. This is the only way. I don't want to be with you anymore. If this is all about money, then forget it. You and I can live independently; we don't need each other anymore.'

'You can't leave me, Pippa, where will I live?' All Rob could think about was the timing of the situation. He needed a cigarette and realised he'd given it up.

'I've already thought about it, you can stay here until the house is sold. You'll have plenty of time and your own money will be through by then.' Pippa saw the forlorn look on his face and decided she needed to say more. 'Rob, this is our chance to start afresh, don't you see? We had a great time together, but with Daniel gone—it's all gone—every single bit we ever had—vanished. I lost my mother, then my dad and then our son and now I'm choosing to leave. I've had enough. This is our chance to move on in our lives. We've spent too long with Joan and Terry and as much as I adore Joan, I think she realises it too. Anyway, you spend too much time with Joan and not me, don't think I haven't noticed.' She wondered how she would tell Joan about Sven, was it necessary? Joan seemed too sick and she was putting off visiting her for another day or so.

Rob stood up in anger and walked out of the lounge. Pippa heard the front door slam behind him. For a moment, she felt a silence she'd only heard once before, the day he'd told her Daniel had died. She sat down and fixed her eyes on the empty grate in the stove. She had done the same thing when she returned from the hospital, staring at the glowing embers and wishing she had died with her son.

'Sven's phone.'

'Hi Sven, it's me.'

'Oh, thank goodness. Hello my love—are you all right? My stomach is in such a knot, I've been so worried about you.'

His Norwegian accent sang down the phone line. For one moment, she was back on the islands with him, sitting on the white sand, with her back against the rocks on Porthcressa Beach.

'Sven, I'm so confused. I told Rob; well, I didn't tell him who you were. He's gone out to see Joan, she's out of the hospital, I have to go and see her later. You gotta help me here, what do I do? Should I just pack up and travel back to Scilly?'

With those words, Sven's heart jumped. Astrid was still lurking on the islands. He had to make sure she got back on that ferry.

Pippa started to cry again and Sven longed to be with her—to hold her in his arms.

'Do you still want me?' she cried. 'I don't know what to do.'

'Elskling, of course I want you. He's bound to make it difficult, but the decision has to be yours.' Sven wanted to assure her he would take care of her for the rest of his life. 'I love you, Pippa, with all my heart—come back to me.'

Pippa sobbed down the phone. 'I don't know how to do this and then there's Daniel in the graveyard, how can I leave him?'

'Pippa, my love, sometimes you have to find that direction—remember what you told me? Perhaps this is your one and only chance, but you have to make this choice yourself. Believe me, no one understands more than me about making choices. I came to Scilly after a broken love affair, remember? I thought we were made for each other, but it's you I love now, Pips, honest I do. I just wish you were back here, loving me. We're both feeling very lonely at the moment and very insecure.'

Pippa thought she knew what he meant. She was feeling more than insecure, but time wasn't on her side to think too long.

'Yes, me too. Can I phone you back? Rob will be home soon. I love you too, Sven. There has to be a way. I'll call you this afternoon when he's gone to work.'

Sven made kissing noises. 'I'll be at home around three, call me then, okay? I'm coming home early today. Bye, elskling, and good luck—hope to see you soon, as I have an idea that might please you. I'll explain when you phone back. Love you lots, bye.'

Pippa slowly replaced the receiver, his lovely voice echoing in her ear.

Sven knew he had to talk with Martin. He'd never been to Yorkshire; perhaps a holiday would do him good. He could get away from the insular lifestyle of Scilly for a week.

He wanted to tell Pippa about Astrid, but if he told her now, she might change her mind. The revelation about her having his baby all those years ago, losing it after such a long term, and never having told him. Would Pippa understand? Perhaps he wouldn't bother to tell her at all; it might spoil her feelings toward him. Well, maybe he should, but not now. He would choose the right moment when she came back. She would surely understand.

'Yoo hoo Sven, it's me-ee,' Andrea shouted through the porch.

Sven stepped into the lounge from the kitchen. 'Hi Andrea, how lovely. This is a surprise.'

'I brought you your favourite—chocolate brownies,' she said. 'I thought it might cheer you up.'

'You're too good to me, you know that.' Sven chuckled as he took the Tupperware box from her hand.

'Everything going well, then? Martin's gone over to Tresco today so I thought I'd call in. We missed you while we were away. It was lovely to see you again the other night.'

'I have to thank you for letting me sleep over. I was rather pissed, wasn't I?'

'Nooo, of course you weren't! Just happy, that's all,' she said, laughing. 'Have you heard from Pippa? She sounds lovely, I am dying to meet her. Is she coming back to St Mary's soon?'

'Well, yes, I've had some good news and some bad.' Sven sighed. He proceeded to tell Andrea the whole story about Astrid. He needed her help to off-load his feelings and was relieved that Andrea had paid him a visit.

'Is there anything I can do?' she asked.

'Just be there for me, Andrea, please—as a woman I'm sure you understand how other women think. I don't have anyone else I can talk to, except Don and he belongs in the last generation. He's a bloke—so I need to talk to you right now.' Sven sighed.

'Of course, I'm always here for you, Sven, you know that. So … Pippa is coming back soon, eh? May I ask you if you really love her? I mean, enough to spend the rest of your life with her? You hardly know each other, I suppose,' Andrea said, playing the role of a parent.

'I know what you mean and yes— it's been hard not to see Astrid as we used to be. We had such great times together. I absolutely idolised her. She was my soul mate, and that's why I asked her to marry me. She kissed me yesterday. Of course, I spurned her. It stirred up all kinds of things in me. I hated what she did to me, the whole incident gave me such an odd feeling, but when I got home, I realised she could destroy me again and again.' He shook his head and turned down the corner of his mouth. 'With Pippa … yes, she has some grief and stressful baggage to overcome, I know, but when she does come back here, it'll be just a matter of her getting a divorce from her husband. I love Pippa very much. Besides, despite the fact we have only been together a short time, she loves the things I love. She and I have something far more special now and I don't think I could ever love Astrid again.' He decided not to mention the baby thing: best not to complicate it further. He must tell Pippa first.

'When is Pippa coming back? I mean a three-week relationship has to be something extraordinarily special.' Andrea gave a sympathetic smile.

'It is special. I don't know yet when she's coming, I want to speak with Martin. I have an idea. Astrid is going home soon. I hope she's not here when Pippa comes back, that'd be the end for me, my worst nightmare. I don't think Pippa would understand, it would destroy her.'

'The way I see it, Pippa seems right for you. By the way you described her the other night, you seemed completely bowled over by her.'

'I know—you're right.' Sven smiled at her comment. 'But all this is confusing me.'

'I like Pippa already,' Andrea told him, trying to sound positive. 'She sounds like one of us, but you are really going to have to be very careful, Sven—you're treading on dangerous ground. I'm worried that you will end up being hurt again.'

'Mm, I know,' Sven said pensively. 'It's just there's something about her which tells me she is genuine and understands me. It's not the same as when Astrid and I were together, it's more … more grown up, if you see what I mean.'

'Don't worry, everything will turn out fine. You only need to see Pippa again and Astrid is another problem you have to try and sort out pretty soon. Look, sweetie, I must be on my way now—sorry to cut this short. You will come round and see us soon, won't you? Let me know how it's going. The only advice I can give you right now is to follow your heart.'

Andrea wished Sven good luck and left him with the chocolate brownies.

'Call me if there's anything I can do, you know I'm a good listener. And why don't you have a chat with Don as well? You know he thinks a lot about you.'

'Thanks, Andrea, I just needed to talk, that's all. You know what it's like here.'

Sven watched her as he waved goodbye. 'Thanks for the brownies,' he called with a smile as she walked down the garden path. *Good old Andrea. Martin is so lucky to have her.* He knew that was how he wanted his relationship to be. Travelling the world with the woman he loved: genuine support for each other and a perfect partnership. There was no doubt Pippa had the same interests. He wasn't going to leave Scilly and go back to Norway; it was all so long ago. Anyway, if Astrid could lie to him once, she could do it again. Besides, she had also lied to Mads. No, it was best this way. Fate had certainly taken a hand.

CHAPTER THIRTY-ONE

'Your blood pressure is a little higher today, Joan,' Rob said as he tugged the band away from her arm. He pulled down her lower eyelids. 'Mm, nice and pink. I would think in the next few days you'll be fine. You look a lot better than the other day when I saw you in the hospital. I'll tell Dr Kumar I called in to see you.'

'Carol had Jordan today for me and she did my hair, do you like it?' Joan turned her head from side to side. 'Yes, I know I made a stupid mistake the other day. I was so down about Terry and the thought of being left on my own. I'm still feeling lonely. How are things with you?' Joan asked, wondering why Pippa hadn't been to see her.

Rob realised she wasn't ready to talk about her suicidal frenzy and he didn't want to talk about Pippa either.

'Okay, I suppose. Perhaps now isn't a good time to discuss it.'

'What's the matter, Rob? Is it Pippa?' Joan asked, looking into his eyes.

Rob nodded. He hadn't come to see Joan to discuss Pippa, but he supposed it was inevitable; the two women were friends, but for how much longer he didn't like to guess.

Joan patted Rob's arm. 'You know the way I see it, both of you need your heads banging together and the same goes for me. I suppose none of us likes change. It's unsettling, especially when you are left alone to cope with it.'

'Joan, I have something to tell you. I'm sorry but it's not very good news at this difficult time. Pippa told me this morning she has found someone else.'

'What? Another bloke, you mean?'

Rob nodded grimly.

'My God, when did this happen? Rob, I'm so sorry.' Joan wondered what Pippa had been doing since she'd been to Scilly. Everyone was leaving her and what was she supposed to do? She began to feel abandoned again.

Rob gazed at the floor: he had failed. His son was dead, his wife had betrayed him, and now he knew how Joan must have felt when she took the pills.

Joan put her arm on his shoulder. 'Rob, how do you feel?' She had meant to say, how do you really feel, but something stopped her just in time.

'A bit of a failure at the moment,' he said, turning down a corner of his mouth. 'But my training keeps me positive. I have to believe this is not happening but somehow it's like … I don't have any feelings at all. I was hoping with all this extra cash from my real parents, we could do something different. At the moment, my world's been turned upside down.'

'Money doesn't buy happiness, Rob. We all know that. I'll talk to Pippa later and see how she is. I don't want to be left on my own. I'll miss you both and then what am I supposed to do with my life?'

'You and me, Joan, it seems we have been through such troubled times in recent months,' Rob said. Joan was sweet and kind to him and he needed it right now. She had always known how to talk to him, she had been stronger than Pippa in many ways, but she hadn't had a tragedy in her life until Terry had left. She'd had Jordan and he was her pride and joy. *She'd obviously blocked the kid out of her mind when she took those pills.* He adored little Jordan, and he'd often looked after him when Joan had gone shopping. He thought about how much they needed each other right now.

He kissed her on the cheek. 'Must go, Joan, I'm off to work this afternoon, pet. I'm feeling a bit lost for words.'

'It's understandable,' Joan empathised. 'I mean, you have both been through such a lot of pain over the last few years.'

'Let me try and sort this out, Joanie. I'll come and see you later. I have the feeling Pippa might not be around much longer, and I can't stand living like this any more. I need love and understanding, not a daily boxing match where I get knocked out in every bloody round.'

Joan smiled at him, feeling a bit piggy in the middle. 'You're right; it's awkward, isn't it? Let me know if Pippa is really going. I'm upset about it too. Who's this bloke she's got?'

'Some bastard from the Isles of Scilly—no idea. I'm worried in case it's all a stupid phase, a holiday romance. She won't go back there surely, and it's too far. I daren't ask her about it; she just clams up. I'm on nights again tomorrow, in bed all day. God!'

He wanted to kiss Joan again, for her caring, but at the last moment, he got cold feet and gave her a hug instead.

Joan smiled a quick flirtatious smile. 'Promise to come back soon, please?'

'I will. Now you go and get some rest; I'll be late for work.'

She looked at him and he caught her glance. 'I wish … ' Before he stood up to leave, she held onto him in a lingering way.

'Rob?'

He smiled at her, conscious of her gaze

'I know,' he said squeezing her hand. 'Give me a bit more time.'

CHAPTER THIRTY-TWO

'I suppose I can do without you for a few days,' Martin agreed. 'I think you deserve some time out. Anyway, Sven, let's talk about it later this afternoon at the office.'

Sven had waited patiently for Martin to say those words. He didn't mean to inconvenience his colleague by asking for time off when he had just got back from his tour, but knew his friend might understand.

After a brisk walk into town, he took his sandwiches and sat on a step at the top of the quay, his mind a million miles away. He dangled his feet over the edge. There were tiny fish in mini shoals and he watched a small crab claw its way along the bottom of the sea. He took a bite of his chicken and lettuce sandwich and some of the crumbs fell in the water; the small fry came to the surface to nibble.

He pondered if he should take a car or catch the train. Then he realised the worst of his problems would be when he got there. It might be awkward. What if he met Rob and there was a slanging match? He didn't want to think about it. He knew the train journey would be arduous; he would ask Andrea if he could borrow a map of Great Britain if he took a car.

How he missed Pippa. Each time he thought about her, he wanted to make her happy again and take her away from the misery of her life with Rob. He had visions of her living in a quaint cottage like his, and her husband ignoring her all day. How could she possibly have an amicable divorce? Perhaps Rob needed a fresh start as well. Anyway, going north would get him away from Astrid—she might decide to stay, and it would get him off the hook if he left the islands. He was about to take a risk, but would he regret it?

Behind him, someone tapped his shoulder. 'I'm leaving today; I'm so glad we talked.'

'Oh, er, hi Astrid, erm … yes I see.' Sven shook himself out of his world.

'I shall never stop loving you, but I realise I can't have you.'

'Let's just say you could have had me, Astrid, but it was not to be and we'll leave it at that, shall we? I'm only here in Scilly because of you and I suppose I have to thank you for that. I'm very happy living here and I don't want to come back to Norway. You do understand that, don't you?' He looked into her eyes to make her understand he definitely wasn't going to change his mind.

'You are lucky, you know. Your life here looks great. It really is very beautiful around these islands. I've enjoyed myself despite everything. I'm sorry, Sven. I hope you'll forgive me.'

Sven became aware of the look on her face. It was a look of 'you must feel sorry for me'. He'd seen it all before.

'I named our baby Petja; I wanted to let you know she had a name. I think maybe she looked like you, but she was so small, it was hard to tell. I lost her in January the year we were supposed to … you know … get married. Perhaps your girlfriend understands how I feel, will you tell her about me?'

'She knows,' he replied coldly. 'I'm glad you see things in a different light now, Astrid, thank you. I'm so sorry about the baby.' He realised what he'd just said; it was as if the baby was in his imagination and not his child—and perhaps it wasn't. Maybe Astrid wanted sympathy for her wrongdoings; it was hard to tell. He ought to give her the benefit of the doubt. He made his apologies, telling her he had to get back to the office. He hugged her and she kissed him one last time and then burst into tears.

'I can't do this, Sven, please let me stay with you, please darling, let me!'

Kjerstin called to her in English. 'Come on, Astrid, the boat is leaving any moment.'

'I'm not going, Kjerstin, I can't do this, I want to stay here with Sven,' she replied.

'Astrid, you *can't* stay here—you have to go home,' Kjerstin pleaded. 'Please don't mess up our holiday!'

Sven realised he had to be strong. 'Kjerstin's right—you have to go now. These islands are not the place for you, Astrid. I'm sorry but I don't love you anymore. Please just go home, it's too late for all this, far too late.' He ushered her, almost pushed her, toward the *Scillonian.*

Kjerstin held onto her arm and drew her toward the ship. The crew were taking up the gangway. She urged Astrid to get a move on.

Astrid sobbed as she made up her mind whether or not to leave. Sven couldn't take it anymore. He and Kjerstin walked along holding one each of Astrid's arms, escorting her to the gangway. 'Go home to Norway, Astrid; I really don't want you here, okay? Sorry, Kjerstin, can you calm her down when you get on the ship, and make her see sense?'

Astrid broke down in floods of tears as Sven looked away from her. Kjerstin nodded. 'Come on Astrid. We have to go. Say goodbye to Sven and let's get on this boat.'

'I'm sorry, Astrid, but I love Pippa now and, well … I'm not changing my mind. Goodbye, and maybe one day I'll see you in Norway. Who knows where our lives will go in the future? Good luck.' He didn't kiss her goodbye and knew he'd pushed her on the boat. He smiled at Kjerstin apologetically. He hated the way he'd treated her, but he really didn't want her anymore; he knew that now. *I have to go and find Pippa.*

Some of the local boatmen stood and watched, unable to understand what was going on. Astrid had no right to make a fool out of him in front of the islanders.

He made certain the gangway was up and walked away as they set sail. He caught a glimpse of her sobbing. *A baby? I never thought ...* He shook his head in disbelief. She was obviously very insecure, but it could be true and secretly he wanted to believe he could father a child.

'Hi Sven, let's go into my office and then we can talk in some peace and quiet. God, I've had a busy morning and everyone wanted to ask me about my trip.'

Sven sat down, his mind perplexed after his farewell to Astrid. No one he knew had ever carried on in that way.

'Tea?' Martin asked, starting to fill the kettle.

'*Please,*' he said, feeling grateful.

'So Pippa is coming back after all, eh?' Martin sat down on the swivel chair at his desk and stretched with his hands clasped behind his head.

'I hope so.' Sven was quiet. He hoped Martin could spare him some time off.

'Well, I've been thinking about this since I got back. I hear you've done a great job, I'm very grateful for all the work you put in. Anyway, I have some good news for you. Head Office has given me the chance to renew your contract with the Environmental Trust on a more permanent basis.'

Sven's chest pounded. He thought he had come to discuss Pippa and his time off. He stirred his tea and preferred not to have the milk that Martin was pouring into his cup; it looked a bit suspect anyway.

'Oh hell, I haven't really had time to think about it, but yes, it is something I would like to do very much, I mean, to stay on here. I couldn't imagine leaving Scilly now,' he confessed.

'From all accounts, you made a name for yourself while I've been away. I see *The Viking* has become an icon,' grinned Martin. 'I think if they were to end the contract, I would be in deep trouble with the folks on these islands. As long as there is funding for you, we can keep going.'

Sven smiled. 'Hm … I've only just been doing my job, but that's great news.' His mind was still feeling the negativity about Astrid and the look on her face as she left on the boat. He wasn't proud about what he had done.

Martin continued. 'Now because of this, and with the situation between you and Pippa, I had an idea. In view of what you told me about her teaching skills and her enthusiasm about wildlife, I feel she would be a valuable asset to these islands. I was told this morning they are going to fund an education officer for us.'

'My God, that's fantastic! You think … ?' Sven stopped before he jumped too far ahead.

'Margaret retires next year and I think we could consider Pippa as her replacement—but in the meantime we need someone to go into the schools and help with our wildlife projects and so on. Having a qualified teacher as part of the team would be great. What do you think? I could interview her when she gets back.'

Sven smiled, feeling grateful, but his mind jarred for a moment—what about following local protocol? 'Well, I think that's great but it's rather premature—and shouldn't we be giving this job to an islander?'

'I know what you mean, but I have been asking around. There's Sue Carruthers on Tresco who seemed interested, but then she gave up on the idea. One of the local teachers said she would like to do it and promptly changed her mind because of the extra commitment, and then I thought about Margaret helping us part time, but she wants her retirement. I shall put up an advert in the library and on the door of our office and I might put one in the local magazine, too, to be fair.'

'Okay, I'll see what Pippa says when we get together. Thanks, Martin, that's a very interesting offer.'

'You say you wanted to go north and bring her back? Won't she be able to come here on her own again?'

'She needs me right now. You see, it's not that easy for her at the moment. We've made this, erm … arrangement?'

'Sven, you idiot, you don't have to ask, of course you can go.' Martin laughed at Sven's expression. 'When are you leaving?'

'In an hour?' Sven joked.

'I saw you both on the quay; I don't think I've ever seen anyone more in love than you two. She seems a lovely girl. Congratulations. I hope it works out. I would like to meet with her again when she gets back, get to know her better, and generally find out what she can do for us.'

Sven's life began to blossom. His time with Pippa had been wonderful and this offer had exceeded his expectations.

'How about if I pack my gear later this afternoon and fly out tomorrow? I can drive up to the airport and see if they can take me in the morning. I might have to stop over at the youth hostel and then go up north the next day. The YHA is handy; it's cheap and pleasant enough. Pippa stayed there too.'

'That's fine, Sven. Do it.'

'I think I'll go by train and then take a car; it's a long way to drive on my own. I fancy a nice relaxing journey; I'll have to borrow a map. Does Andrea have one I could use? She does a lot of driving on the mainland, doesn't she?'

Martin laughed at Sven. 'I can tell you already had this planned in your head, mate, eh?'

'Is it that obvious?'

He finished his coffee and couldn't wait to burst out of the office. The phone rang. Martin answered it, chatting to someone Sven couldn't hear.

'You got an injured gannet? Where is it? Oh, I see—on the airfield? Yes, sure, have you caught it? Right, okay. Well, Linda is still with us, I'll ask her to drive up there and fetch it. If necessary she'll take it round to the vet … and while you're on the phone, Colin, Sven might want to ask you something. Hold on.' He handed the phone to Sven who raised his eyebrows, realising who it was.

'Oh, hi Colin. Have you any flights for tomorrow morning? It's only for me.'

Colin checked the list. 'No, sorry, none in the morning, but in the afternoon …' He checked down his list again. 'Yeah plenty, we got four seats free. D'ye wanna book it?'

Sven left the office not believing his luck. He would phone the youth hostel next and then make enquiries for the train and a car in Darlington. His nerves were holding up. Where did he really stand in this love knot? Pippa might be annoyed at him for coming up north and Rob was still lurking around. He could end up with more than a broken nose. He waited at home and as promised, at three o'clock the phone rang.

'Hi Sven, it's me.'

'Hi Pippa. How are things?' He thought she sounded tired.

'Awful. I'm worried in case this isn't going to work. I mean, how can I get to you? I've never walked out on anyone before.'

When Rob came home for lunch, she had been equally confused at the way he suddenly didn't seem that bothered about her situation, as if he had given up on her.

'Well, listen to me, elskling,' Sven continued. 'First I have some good news. How about if I come to Whitby? Martin has given me a week off work, and my contract has been renewed. Do you love me enough to be with me for the rest of your life, Pippa?'

'Oh Sven, you're so wonderful. Congratulations on the contract. Yes, yes, yes, please come to me. I need you right now, except we'll have to be careful Rob doesn't see us together. I don't want you to be meeting him in a pub. It's a bit like Scilly here, everyone knows everyone else. Word might get around. I'm feeling so lonely. Joan is telling me not to do it but then she kept asking me, "Did I really mean it?" They say I am stupid and it's a holiday romance. It's as if they have all turned against me. Rob thinks I need grief counselling. I know I love you. I want to live my life with you, the birds, the wildlife, the freedom. Who could blame me for wanting all that?'

'Then let's do it.' Sven smiled at the phone. 'I'll call you as soon as I'm on my way. Stay with it, Pippa, rescue is at hand. I know we're both mad, but that's what our relationship is all about—this crazy madness. I didn't want to break up someone's marriage but I have and I feel … bad enough. Listen, you and I were meant to be together, it's that simple. The hard part is leaving, but don't worry, we'll sort it.'

Pippa giggled with tears in her eyes. He still loved her. *What a relief.* Could she hold out until he made it to Whitby?

CHAPTER THIRTY-THREE

Sven almost ran around Beachside Cottage with joy. He was going to the mainland! It had been fifteen months since he last left the islands.

His time with Astrid had sealed his finality over his relationship with her.

He now had no regrets; he knew he could father a child and understood how it must have been for Pippa when she lost Daniel. Astrid had shown her own grief and perhaps he should have spent more time with her. But no, there was nothing more he could have done. He was destined to be with Pippa. Perhaps one day, they would have children of their own. He would tell her soon about Astrid and the baby. All he wanted was to go north and be with her. Perhaps he was making the biggest mistake of his life if it all went wrong—and would she change her mind? He tried not to think too much about it—now or never.

The following afternoon he landed with the helicopter at Penzance, then called in at the youth hostel and met with Mike.

'Can you spell your name for me, please?' Mike asked as he leaned over the reception desk.

Sven commenced the spelling. 'Jør-gen-sen.'

'I gather you've come from Scandinavia.'

'Yes and no. Actually, I live on the Isles of Scilly, but I'm originally from Norway.'

'Oh, right. I met a girl going to Scilly the other week; her name was Pippa.

Smashing girl she was, we spent a short time together on her first trip and then a quick chat when she went back up north. She got herself a boyfriend over there now.'

'Ha! That's funny, she's my girlfriend.'

Mike smiled to himself. 'Lucky you, it seems I missed the boat there. She's really nice although she seemed a bit lonely when I first met her. Anyway, you're in room twelve on the next floor. If you need help, just ask.' He hoped he would see them both again; Pippa had mentioned the local artists on the islands. 'Good luck, anyway. Please send my regards. Here's your key. Okay, see you later.' He watched Sven climb the stairs with his rucksack slung over his shoulder.

It was early morning as Sven boarded the train to Bristol with a change of train for Darlington. He expected to arrive in Whitby that evening and would collect the car and go to the Abbey Hotel where he had made a reservation.

On the phone, Pippa had told him where she lived, but he couldn't possibly go there. What if he bumped into Rob? Not that he knew what Rob looked like. Chasing after a woman he'd only known for three weeks had never been his way of doing things and Sven knew his own Scandinavian looks and the way he spoke made him stand out in the crowd.

The following morning, he awoke to the familiar sound of herring gulls mewing on the rooftops. His attention turned toward the white cottages and buildings on the narrow streets and alleyways of Whitby. The scenery looked all too familiar but the ring and bustle of a mainland seaside town felt different from the unique sounds of island life. He could hear traffic—lots of it, the squeal of brakes and doors slamming below his window. After breakfast, he took a walk into town and pretended he was window-shopping. He didn't dare walk past the house, yet it was so tempting to turn up and say, 'Hi, I'm here.'

As he stood at the end of the street, he scanned the view of the harbour, which gave him a feeling of being home again. He wandered down to the sea, and stood on the beach in case Pippa looked out of the bedroom window above him. He smiled to himself, deciding he loved the place, and hoped he might return in the future.

He longed for Pippa to walk out of the door and lingered for a while at the end of Henrietta Street. It was a tight feeling in his chest being so near to her and yet so far away. He must phone her, as soon as he got back to the hotel; it was the only way.

'Rob Lambton.'

Sven froze and the gap between the "pips" and the voice was enough for him to put the receiver down. Rob was at home. What had gone wrong? Didn't he work nights? Perhaps he'd got the shift wrong. No, he'd just phoned a bit too early. He had to tell Pippa he had arrived. Or had she changed her mind?

An hour later, he tried again and gave a sigh of relief.

'Hello,' Pippa said in a whisper.

'Hi Pippa, I've arrived in Whitby.'

Rob was still marauding around the house.

'Oh hello, er… Joyce,' said Pippa as Rob passed by in the hall. 'Haven't seen you in ages, where are you? Nice to hear from you.'

'Abbey Hotel,' Sven whispered down the phone.

'Oh! Er … yeah … erm … Okay, I'll come, be round there soon. I'm just seeing Rob off to work. We can have coffee together and catch up, eh? I've just got back from holiday, so can't be long. I need some fresh air.'

Hearing him and knowing he was around the corner up the hill made her heart jump with joy. She would have to act as if Joyce had turned up wanting a coffee, until Rob had gone to work. She waited for him to leave and the wait seemed tortuous.

She busied herself in the kitchen, making plans inside her head about what she was going to do. How could she possibly leave Whitby and go to Scilly with Sven? What did he have in mind? He really was crazy, but oh, so full of love and caring.

Rob was about to leave the house and he muttered 'Bye' to her as he wandered through the open front door onto the street. Pippa hoped she wouldn't bump into him on her way to see Sven. She would give it five more minutes.

Instead of going to work immediately, Rob went to see Joan. 'Just thought I'd call in and check on you,' he said.

'You didn't tell Terry's Mam about me, did you Rob?'

'No, did you?'

'I haven't told her about Terry yet, I didn't want her to worry. It scares me, and she'll find a way to blame me, you know. She's going to ask me why I haven't been round with Jordan. I'll have to go and see her. His dad is very sympathetic about it all, he rang me when Phyllis had gone out shopping. And oh yes—I spoke with Pippa on the phone but she told me very little about this guy she's met. I'm afraid nothing is going to change her mind. Rob; you're going to have to consider your future, too.'

Rob shook his head. 'Life's not fair, is it?'

'I don't know, I mean you seem to have done okay with your inheritance. I'm not sure what to say about it—I mean, Pippa's completely changed. She was so full of her time on Scilly, I hardly got a word in edgeways. I tried to get her to see sense.'

Rob was sitting on the edge of the sofa and Joan had the blanket strewn over her knees.

'Here, let me wrap you up a bit more,' he said. He pushed the blanket toward her and in doing so, touched her leg. Her smile caught his feelings.

'It's summer, Rob! No need. Look pet, I've been thinking,' she said. 'I mean I feel very alone at this moment and I know you do too, perhaps. I mean, while Pippa is still with you, it doesn't feel right, does it, especially with Tel being your best mate and all that? Maybe we should just continue being friends.'

Rob stiffened for a moment, not sure what to say. He loved Joan as his friend, but recently, they seemed to have been pushed together. When he thought he might have lost her, he realised they needed each other more than ever. He tried to move the conversation on. 'I think we both lost Terry, you know, I suspect we might only see him when he visits Jordan.'

'It wouldn't surprise me if we never saw him again,' Joan admitted. 'It's awkward.' She paused for a moment. 'So what are your plans for the future?'

'I'm waiting on Bruce and Penny contacting me. I have to go and see them at the house. It's all very sad, the way they lost their parents and my real mother going through all that stress and illness. They might lose the big mansion they live in, it's too big for them and we thought we might have a meeting to see if we can do something about it. Not sure what we can do, but it's worth talking to them. I want to be certain I fit in. I feel strange because it's their house and it doesn't feel as if I belong, but with time and lots of meeting up I am sure I can come to some arrangement with them. They're such nice people and Bruce looks like me—it's dead weird! Maybe...' He looked at Joan and then stopped.

She gave him a kiss on the cheek. 'You are so good to me. Thanks, Rob.'

He turned toward her and stroked her face. 'You're a bonny lass, Joan.'

He didn't know what he wanted anymore; he wanted to hug her, but it was too soon. Perhaps when this was all over ... he thought about the holiday he'd always wanted in Italy. What if he'd married the wrong person?

CHAPTER THIRTY-FOUR

Pippa closed the front door behind her. With her car keys in her hand, she walked to the car park to find her red Vauxhall Nova. She started the engine and drove up to the Abbey Hotel on the cliff top.

Confidant that no one would know her up there, she went to reception and asked to speak to Mr Jørgensen. It felt strange asking for him by that name; she had always used 'Sven'.

The receptionist called him. Pippa waited, fidgeting with her hair and earrings. 'Just go up to room five, it's on the landing through that door.'

Was it really Sven staying at this hotel? She couldn't believe it.

She knocked and he opened the door, slowly at first, then his head appeared. Wearing his usual summer gear, he looked tanned and welcoming. Pippa almost fell through the door as he spoke. He opened his arms and she sank into them as if nothing else mattered.

'Is it really you?' he said, pulling her inside and closing the door.

Pippa cupped his face in her hands. 'How on earth did you manage to come all this way just for me?' Her voice gave a cracked whisper and she gazed into his eyes.

Sven ran his fingers through her hair and kissed her tenderly. 'Cos I love you, Pippa. I missed you.'

'I feel I've been to hell and back. It's been torture. What a wonderful surprise. I never thought you would actually come up here.'

Sven kissed her again, his hands smoothing down her back and kissing her neck. 'Mm, love you.'

'I can't believe you're here, you know. It's kind of weird—no one has ever gone to such lengths for me before.'

'You deserve it my lovely, my elskling. We are going to be together at last.'

Pippa prayed he was right and that nothing else would go wrong. All she wanted was to find out what Sven had planned.

'How quickly can you pack up your stuff?' Sven asked. 'I want to take you back to Scilly before the end of the week.'

'What? Oh heck, it's all so sudden. I need some help but I can't just leave in two days, I have the house to sort out.'

'I thought the house was yours. Surely you can just leave it for a few weeks and come back when you need to and discuss with Rob about what he wants to do.'

'I don't know.' Pippa looked lost in thought, unsure of what she was supposed to do. The thought of leaving Henrietta Street made her sad and yet she knew Sven was right. Living on Scilly with Sven was by far the best thing she could do with her life and a chance to make wonderful changes. She didn't have to worry about the house anymore; she could sell it in a few months and give Rob time to sort himself out.

'Yes, you're right, it's a good plan,' she said. 'Rob's on nights for the rest of the week, we can spend more time together in the evenings, but we'll have to be careful.'

For the next two days, Pippa moved her clothes out of the house when Rob wasn't around. She packed the essentials in a suitcase and prepared to leave Whitby.

Taking a risk, she stayed overnight at the Abbey Hotel, an old mansion above the town and slept long in Sven's arms. By now, she knew he loved her and would always do the right thing.

While she was still sleeping at five in the morning, Sven got out of bed and left her a note. He laid it on the table next to the electric kettle. When Pippa saw it, she panicked. Scared to look, she read the words.

Hi Pips, love you, gone birding but will be back soon. Hope you don't mind, can't be here in Whitby without a quick twitch! Thought you might like to sleep a bit longer before we leave. Back in time for breakfast. Sven

P.S Did you know that on the day I came back to you, it was my birthday! Too much going on then, but maybe we can celebrate it together now?

Pippa laughed; she needn't have worried and now she knew everything would work out. She smiled to herself, then blew out her cheeks—*don't give me any more shocks like that.* She must learn to trust him more. Rob would wonder where she was at this time of the morning, but she often took an early morning walk, so she didn't have to be concerned. All she needed to do was act as normally as possible, but the nerves were beginning to set in and she wished Sven would hurry back.

Armed with binoculars, which he rarely left behind, Sven walked along the harbour. He stood on the sea wall looking down the river, staring at the rolling grey waves of the cold North Sea at the river mouth. There were cormorant and herring gulls as he knew them back home, which made him feel more desperate to leave. It was warmer on Scilly and he felt a shiver on his bare legs. He had become used to living without cars, traffic lights and traffic jams; he wanted to get on with his journey to Cornwall and go home to Scilly where it was more peaceful. He hated the confusion of the mainland. Looking across the river at Pippa's house, he had mixed feelings about taking her away from this lovely old harbour; it was a unique, ancient seaside town with monuments and dramatic scenery. He trained the binoculars on the house in Henrietta Street but couldn't see anyone inside.

He must tell Pippa about Astrid at some point. It was going to be difficult; he couldn't tell her now, as she might change her mind—and anyway it wasn't his fault Astrid had come to Scilly. Yes, he would wait a little longer. The weather had clouded over and with a brisk pace he returned to the hotel.

As he walked over the old iron swing bridge and up the hill, he reminded himself it was time to leave Whitby. Pippa would be waiting for him. On arrival at the hotel, he paid the bill and went up to the room.

Pippa kissed him. 'Glad you enjoyed yourself. Look, erm … I just got a couple more things to do. Give me half an hour and then we'll go south.'

She walked down the main street toward her house. She had the key but decided not to go back inside. She stood at the bottom of the hundred and ninety-nine steps, then turned around and looked down the cobbled street.

'Goodbye, Henrietta Street; bye, everyone.' She left a note for Rob and popped it quietly through the letterbox; he would be in bed and a letter was best.

Bye Rob, sorry it turned out this way, I think we made a mistake and I know you and Joan are loyal to each other. I haven't had my eyes closed all this time, you know. Please tell her I won't be angry. I know that look on Joan's face every time you walk in the room too well! You two have always supported each other. Tell her she has been loyal to all of us and I bear no malice. I still love you all in a very special way. I was drowning in my own sorrows and I couldn't see any of us changing; one of us had to see sense-one of us had to go. Poor Terry has suffered too, I suppose. Maybe now I understand how difficult it has been for him too. I always loved you as Daniel's dad, but we have changed, grown up, seen the worst kind of grief and it's time to leave it all behind. You can live a new life and so can I. Today I am slipping away from you so you can just get on with it-I hate goodbyes.
Good luck to all of us in the future, I will call you about your plans. I will always remember our time together as a family. Now that it's all broken up, what is the point in staying together? Enjoy your new life. We came into this relationship, all four of us, as friends and now I want to walk away as friends. I hope that's possible. Again sorry. Please visit Daniel.
Pippa

Sven took his left hand off the steering wheel and patted her knee while watching the road. She remembered he had done that some weeks ago on Scilly. It was comforting.

'I'm sorry you lost Daniel; you've suffered so much!'

'Wait! Stop! Turn left here up the hill,' Pippa ordered.

Sven looked at her. 'But the Moor Road is that way, isn't it?'

'The cemetery is that way. I have to say goodbye to Dan.'

Sven didn't say a word, simply carried out her instructions.

'I have to do it, sorry,' she said.

'That's okay. May I come too or would you rather be alone?'

Pippa hesitated for a moment. 'Yes, of course, come on. We'll say goodbye together.'

'I wasn't sure if you would want me there, that's all. I seem to have got to know Daniel through your memories.'

They stopped the car at the gate and walked up the path.

Sven stood back from the graveside as Pippa adjusted the candleholder and threw away the dead flowers in the vase. She put her hand in her pocket and placed her wedding ring inside the vase.

'Are you sure you want to do that?' Sven asked.

'Who else would want this?'

'Okay, but only if you're sure.'

They stood together as Sven read the words *In loving memory of Daniel Lambton.* When he saw the date of birth, he stopped.

'What is it, Sven?' Pippa caught him in a moment of sorrow.

He turned away from her—*such a young child, a tragic loss.* 'Sorry, I just felt rather sad, that's all. It has been almost as if Daniel was my son; we've talked so much about him.' He would have to tell her soon about Astrid. It just seemed every time he tried to tell Pippa, the moment wasn't right.

Pippa sat on the grass beside her son's grave. 'Bye Dan, I'll love you forever.'

She looked up at Sven's sympathetic face. 'He was a lovely kid, so full of mischief and clever for his age.'

Sven kissed her. 'We'll come back here some day, I'm sure.'

Pippa walked away leaning on Sven's arm. She had cried so much in the past, but now saying goodbye to her son … she told herself he was just a body without a person inside it. His soul would become the memories of their time together and as she walked away, she knew what she had to do. Daniel had been a wonderful memory. She must move on—but never, never forget. Sven was so kind, and to think he had come all this way to find her. She hoped that somewhere, although she didn't believe in those things, Dan would forgive her.

'Stratford on Avon, here we come,' said Sven. 'Now we really are eloping.'

There was silence in the first hour of the journey; Pippa needed time to calm her feelings, and Sven understood.

'Any regrets?' Sven asked as they reached the A1 motorway.

'Of course I do, it's only natural, but I love you. I've felt like a different person since we met.'

He signalled right to join the motorway on the slip lane, then switched on the radio; the DJ played Carly Simon's *You're So Vain*. Pippa mouthed the words and they sang it together as Sven drove on.

'I could live in Yorkshire—it was so wild on the coast, and I saw the whalebone this morning. I'm not exactly a supporter of killing whales; I have to keep my lips sealed when I go back home. You seem to have the best of both worlds, the moors and the sea, but starting tomorrow, you're an island girl,' he chuckled.

In Stratford, they stayed in a bed and breakfast. Over dinner that evening, Sven discussed with Pippa about living in Beachside Cottage and having Nanette as her neighbour. They both laughed before a brief silence fell. Should he tell her now?

'I'll have to phone my parents in Norway this weekend, they'll wonder what happened to me in recent weeks. They don't know about you yet.'

Pippa smiled. 'You know I hadn't thought of your parents, you only mentioned them briefly. I saw their picture at Beachside, and then there was the phone call from your mother. Does she still want you to come for Christmas?'

Sven hesitated and opened his mouth. For a moment, he couldn't speak and decided the moment again wasn't right. 'I don't know, I er … haven't spoken with her yet.'

The candle on the dinner table flickered and glinted through Pippa's hair. She smiled at him; he could hardly spoil the moment.

'Well, they're great folks and I hope you will meet them one day. We could go there. They live in Vormstad; it's a small town, and our house is outside the city. I miss my own culture, but Scilly holds so much more for me since I left.'

'I know it does, though I bet Norway is lovely too?'

Sven paused for a moment, remembering he also had something else to tell her. Perhaps this news would make it easier and would prove he meant everything he said. 'Now I've got a surprise for you. Martin wants to see you when you get back home. He has a job for you.'

'What sort of job?'

'Teaching at the school.'

'Bloody hell, you two didn't waste time, did you?' she laughed.

'Well, my wages aren't fantastic and it's best you have something to do during the day.'

Pippa continued reassuringly, 'And you say Martin is keen to help me? I'd better go see him about it. I don't mind living on Scilly with less money, there aren't many shops to spend it in and I do have some savings. We only need food and lots of love. Anyway, I'm with you and that's what counts the most.'

'Still, I think we have some serious planning to do.'

'Wow! I never thought I would have the confidence to go back to work. Martin is such a nice person; I shall have to thank him. Oh Sven, I forgot something—happy birthday, darling,' she said smiling. 'I wanted to buy you a present, but we didn't have time.'

'It's okay, *you* are my birthday present.' He blew her a kiss.

They left Stratford the following morning and drove the long journey to Penzance. Sven had phoned ahead to see if they could stay at the youth hostel.

Mike answered the phone. 'Of course! I'll try and find you a family room so you and Pippa can be together, is that all right?'

Arriving at the youth hostel, Sven shook hands with Mike, and Pippa smiled at how he always walked around the youth hostel barefoot. There was carpet on the floors and she assumed he was more comfortable without trainers.

'I've finished for tonight,' Mike said. 'Great to see you two again, now I can match you up. You make a great couple.' He chuckled. 'Fish and chips again tonight, Pippa?' He winked and grinned at her. He remembered how he'd given her a lift up the hill back to the youth hostel and they'd eaten their fish and chips together in the communal kitchen.

Sven looked at him, puzzled.

'Come on Sven—you like fish and chips surely?' Pippa said.

'Ya, sure.'

'You must come over to Scilly soon, Mike. Please come and see us and visit the galleries there. With you being an art student, the scenery is fantastic for your paintings,' she suggested.

'I will; expect me next year.'

'Come on, let's go and get some food,' Pippa said. 'Best fish and chips in town.'

They crossed the road and stood in the queue at the chippie.

'We'll walk down and sit by the harbour for a while, the ferry should be back now,' Sven said, opening up his meal. The aroma of salt and vinegar steaming through the paper made him hungry.

The following morning, the *Scillonian* was tied up in the harbour, but Pippa told Sven she couldn't stand another journey on the ferry.

'Perhaps we can go on the chopper?' she suggested. 'It will be fun, I've never been on a helicopter before.'

'It's quite expensive compared to the ferry, Pips; I don't think I can afford to pay for the two of us. I get paid at the end of next week.' Sven hoped to do some birdwatching at sea.

'Don't worry, I'll treat us. I have some money. I'll have to go to the bank before we leave, though. Please say yes—we'll get there a lot quicker. Consider it a birthday present from me.'

Sven kissed her as a thank you. 'If you're sure?'

'What about the luggage?' asked Pippa. 'It's a bit heavy.'

'Don't worry, let's go over to the ferry, I've got an idea. We can unload the car there before we return it.'

Sven went to see his mate George Taylor, a member of the crew. George greeted them. 'Hi, Sven how are you? I 'eard you were on the mainland. Yeah, I'll take yer stuff on the ship and you can meet us later on when we dock on the other side, ok?'

Sven laughed to himself. He hadn't been away long—now everyone would know about Pippa, he was sure.

He made the final arrangements and booked their tickets at the heliport. Within three hours, they managed to book a flight. The sun shone on a perfect morning. He phoned the office and Charlie answered the phone.

'Martin isn't here. Can I take a message for you Sven?'

'Just tell him Pippa and I are coming back on the next chopper flight,' Sven replied.

Charlie seemed to be in one of his light-hearted moods and wished Sven a pleasant trip.

'Thanks, Charlie, for the support—much appreciated.'

'Okay mate, see ya then,' Charlie said as he closed the call.

'This is like coming home,' Pippa remarked.

'I'm so glad you see it like that.' Sven kissed her again.

CHAPTER THIRTY-FIVE

Later that afternoon, they boarded the helicopter in Penzance and within a few minutes took off from the heliport, surging forward over Land's End and the Atlantic. Pippa smiled at Sven and they held hands most of the way. After a twenty-five minute flight, she could see the islands below: the blue sea and white beaches, the shapes of St. Martin's, Tresco, Bryher and St Mary's. 'That's an awesome sight, eh?' she said. 'I can see right to the bottom of the sea. It's wonderful.' A tear welled in her eye; now she really was coming home.

The helicopter circled around the airport at St Mary's before landing on a windswept grassy airport. Pippa looked out of the window. There seemed to be a lot of people milling around the terminal as she stepped down with her bag on her shoulder. Everyone was waving. She looked around to see whom they were waving at, and as she got closer she recognised Charlie, Martin, Linda, Alan and a dark-haired woman standing with Martin whom she presumed was Andrea. They held out a long banner.

'WELCOME BACK PIPPA. WHO'S THE BLONDE GUY?'

Pippa stopped for a moment with tears in her eyes.

'You're crying?' Martin said as he gave Pippa a friendly embrace. 'I'm glad you came back.'

'I'm happy, very happy.' She sniffed back her tears. 'Those guys out there sure know how to welcome you back.' She took in a breath of sea air as the wind blew a gust over the runway and her hair tangled around her face.

Martin smiled. 'Come on then, you wanted to learn more about birds? Well, you got the right blokes to teach you. Welcome back, Pippa. Hi Sven. Hope we can all work together soon, eh? I'll tell you what, we were all willing you to make it back here. Everyone, I mean round town, is waiting to meet you. It's been quite an adventure for us too; you've been keeping us all guessing.' He turned to the dark-haired woman behind him. 'Pippa, this is my wife Andrea.'

Andrea gave her a hug. 'Welcome back. I hope you'll come round to see us soon.'

'Welcome back, Pippa. He found you, eh?' Linda said with a welcoming kiss on the cheek. 'We had to do this today because we are all so happy for Sven. Martin suggested it, but we didn't need to be asked twice. We all love The Viking, you know.'

Pippa laughed. 'My goodness, I didn't expect all this for me. Hi Charlie, great to see you. I feel like a celebrity.'

'Hi Pippa,' Charlie said. 'Glad you got back, now you can come and help me with some work on the reserve.'

'I think I have to get fit first,' Pippa confessed

Andrea chipped in with a grin, 'And don't you let these guys boss you around, Pippa.'

They squeezed into the green van and Martin drove them to Beachside Cottage. His driving seemed to have calmed down since Pippa's last visit. Linda followed in her old pale blue Ford Escort, with Charlie, Andrea, and the others.

'I don't need you for the weekend,' Martin told Sven. 'Take the time off to relax and get yourselves sorted. I think it would be nice if we can start with a clean sheet on Monday morning.'

'Thanks mate, appreciated. I agree, we have a lot to talk about.'

Sven put the kettle on to make coffee. Pippa knew the routine by heart. She looked around the room at Sven's few possessions and decided she would make it more homely for them both. She would ask him later what he thought about it.

'I suppose I'll have to get a new double bed now,' Sven joked. 'We can't go back to Gilstone, Janice is fully booked for the summer. I'll have to order one from the mainland. It might take a couple of weeks, so it'll be cosy!'

Pippa turned around and kissed him. She could taste the salt from the sea air on the lips of this man who had made her feel wonderful and loved.

'I still can't believe I'm here, darling,' she said.

'Didn't we do well?' said Sven. 'Mm, I hope I don't wake up tomorrow morning to find it wasn't real.'

Later that afternoon, Sven drove down to the quay and collected Pippa's luggage from the ship. When he returned, they sat down to an early dinner.

'Happy birthday, my darling.' She raised her glass. 'To us!'

'I don't think I have ever been this pampered,' Sven told her.

'Well, you'd better get used to it,' Pippa chuckled.

It seemed the right time; he must tell her about Astrid. He held her hand and kissed it. In a quiet moment, he began to speak.

'Pippa, I have something to explain. I didn't want to spoil things when we drove down here, but I have to do the decent thing and tell you about something that wasn't my fault. It's not something I find easy to explain. Andrea knows a bit about it and my love for you hasn't changed. Okay?' He looked into her eyes and tried to smile.

Pippa looked at him with suspicion. 'What?'

'It's okay, it's just I tried to explain it while we were in Whitby but we got so wrapped up in each other. I know I ought to have told you sooner but it's like this, see. While you were away, my mother made a silly error. My fault, I should have told her about you. Remember that phone call I had from Norway? Well … she gave my ex-girlfriend Astrid my phone number, and one day last week Astrid actually came to the islands to visit me. She was on holiday. I couldn't possibly tell you, because I didn't think she would do it, but there was a reason.'

Pippa's jaw dropped. 'Here on St Mary's? What, all the way from Norway?' She sat there stiffening, wondering what terrible bombshell he was going to drop on her.

Sven nodded. 'She was on holiday and decided to visit the islands. My mother told her where I was. God, I was so angry.'

'So what did you say to her?'

'I was very straight with her. She wanted me to come back to her, and it got a bit complicated. Look, elskling, to put your mind at rest before I go on with the rest of the story, I want you to understand nothing happened and everything is fine with you and me. It was quite odd really, she made a bit of a fool out of me. Her friend Kjerstin and I, we had to almost carry her back on the ferry. It was unbelievable—and somewhat comical to prying eyes, I suppose.'

'She's gone back to Norway then?' Pippa's relief was obvious.

'Yes, but she told me something and I hope you can be understanding about it. To be honest, I'm not sure whether to believe her or not. I promise you I knew nothing about it until a few days ago. I'm afraid Astrid lives in a world of her own and this is why I didn't want to get involved with her ever again. I don't feel there will ever be a right time to explain all this.'

Pippa puffed out her cheeks in more horror, looking as if she'd made a terrible mistake.

'She told me she had been pregnant, but at seven months the baby was stillborn and I never knew about any of this. She claims it was mine. She came here to relieve her guilt. She actually married Mads and I think she made out it was his child, can you believe that?'

'A baby? Oh my God, Sven! Do you believe her?' She had to keep reminding herself he had come all the way to Whitby to bring her back to Scilly.

'Honestly, Pippa, I didn't know anything about it. I don't even know if it was true. Please believe me. She's very immature. I told her about you and that nothing could or would change my mind. After all this time, I don't know how she could possibly think I could go back to her. I needed to tell you the truth; I never wanted you to find out all this from someone else. It wasn't something I ever suspected.'

Pippa sat with her hands cupped around her face, looking around the room. There was that silence again, the one she knew only too well. She realised he had never tried to tell her any lies and the look on his face showed how upset he was. She calmed herself. 'I suppose I understand her motives, losing a child no matter what stage of pregnancy or age of the child. Perhaps she felt close to you because of the baby. How do you feel? I mean, you might have been a father.'

Sven sniffed. 'Mm, it's hard to believe.' He shook his head.

'What do you want me to say?' Pippa sighed, seeing how upset he seemed.

'I really don't know. I'm sorry, Pippa; I only wanted you to come back to me. You should have seen me trying to avoid her. I think you would have laughed. I mean, everywhere I went, she was there and I got phone calls late at night and didn't dare answer them. She used to do that to me in Norway before I left for Scilly.

I hoped it wasn't you—well, I wanted it to be you, if you see what I mean. That's why you might not have been able to contact me. Will you forgive me, darling?' Sven kissed her hand again.

'I'm glad I wasn't here. I don't think there is anything to forgive. You've told me the truth and I trust you. I remember the look on your face when your mother phoned and I wondered what might be wrong. You should have said.'

'How could I? You were so happy, I didn't want to spoil our precious moments together—and if I'd told you, we wouldn't be here now, surely? So nothing's changed.' He looked at her for reassurance. 'Sorry I had to tell you after your arrival here, but I couldn't find the right time to explain it all.'

'We ought to move on and be happy,' she said. 'Some things are best left behind.' How could this Astrid woman think she could just waltz back into his life? He was right, she must be crazy. Still, it was something she could understand, especially all the guilt and sorrow.

'Can you really forget her, Sven?'

'Yes of course I can! It just shocked me, that's all.' Sven widened his eyes and sighed.

'You shocked me too. I thought for a minute I'd come all this way for nothing.'

'Sorry darling.'

Pippa hugged him. 'You're amazing, you know that?'

Sven raised his glass. 'To our future, elskling. Thanks for being so understanding.'

'Well, let's say I hope you've seen the last of her. I love your honesty.' She smiled and kissed him on the cheek. At least he could father a child. Perhaps one day, they might have children of their own. She hoped Astrid would go away never to return.

A few days later, Pippa arrived at Martin's office.

'Sven tell you about the job, Pippa?'

'Yeah, brilliant. I would like to help if I can.'

'How about the end of September after the school holidays? We're anxious to get the project off the ground now we have the funds. You can liaise with Margaret, she'll explain about the general run of things. In the coming weeks, if you work with Sven each day, you can get to know the routine a little better.'

Pippa thanked him. There was nothing she would like more than to be with Sven discussing the job. At the end of the interview, which was more like a friendly chat, she made her way back to Beachside. It seemed her life was complete. As she walked along the shore, she stopped and looked beyond the bay out to sea, thinking about what had happened to her, the journey to Scilly—and back! The job would be perfect; it would get her out of the house, stop her moping, and she could start afresh.

At the cottage, she saw Sven in the garden. She thought he looked so much at home in his own environment. Everyone knew him and he knew everyone. He was hoeing around some lettuce. She had startled him. 'Oh … hello, darling.' He kissed her.

Nanette came out of her front door with a broom in her hand. 'Mornin' Sven.'

'This is Pippa, Nan.' Sven had dreaded this moment.

'Oh, I 'eard abowt you,' she said. 'Welcome to St Mary's.'

'Thanks Nanette, it's good to meet you.' Pippa smiled at Sven.

Nanette seemed to linger on her doorstep as the postman drew up in his red van. At the garden gate, Pippa took the mail.

'Morning Pippa,' said the postman. 'Enjoying your time here?'

'Very much! It's great.' She thanked him for the letters and gave them to Sven.

She realised that the grapevine had finally grown, regarding her living with Sven. She didn't mind; this was her home now. Soon, she would have to see a solicitor and speak with Rob, but she didn't want to think about it yet.

'Oh look,' said Sven, 'there's one here for you from Holland. It must be from your friend Lisa. How on earth did she know you were going to be living here?'

'Let's go inside.' Pippa opened the front door and carried on talking. 'Yes, I told her to send it here.'

Sven gave her a questioning look. 'But you … ?'

'Well, I hoped I would come back. I prayed it would happen. I knew you were right for me all along. I just hoped I could keep my promise to you.'

Sven chuckled. 'Love you.'

Pippa slit the flap on the white envelope. She feared bad news.

Pippa sat on the settee. She wanted to cry alone but Sven was with her.

'Elskling, you look a little sad, what is it?'

'Well, Jan is in his final days.' She held the letter close to her. 'I'm so glad we did this, you know.'

Sven sat by her and put his arm around her waist. 'I love you so much. This is all yours to share with me, this wonderful scenery on our own doorstep. Isn't it great?'

'I know. You see, Lisa and Jan provided me with the confidence to make the right decision.' She sighed, hoping Jan's final days would be peaceful. She would write to Lisa soon and she would never forget them.

She turned to Sven and kissed him. 'Love you.'

'Let's try and cheer ourselves up, shall we? I have an idea. Let's go swimming again. You know, I'll never forget our first kiss.'

Pippa smiled. 'Great, good idea, I'll go get changed.'

She wore her green bikini and picked up her bag pushing her hairbrush inside. As she walked to the cottage gate, she looked behind to see if Sven was following.

On Porthcressa Beach across the path, Sven put his arm around her as they leaned against a sun-warmed rock.

'Mm, this is lovely.' Pippa said, closing her eyes to the sun.

He pressed his lips to the back of her ring finger where the white mark from her wedding ring had begun to fade. 'When all this is over, I would like to make you Mrs Pippa Jørgensen.'

Pippa lowered her eyes. 'I wouldn't change this for the world.'

With a smile on her face she wrote 'Pippa & Sven' in the sand.

END